THERE ARE THOUSANDS of worlds, all different from ours. Chrestomanci's world is the one next door to us, and the difference here is that magic is as common as music is with us. It is full of people working magic—warlocks, witches, thaumaturges, sorcerers, fakirs, conjurors, hexers, magicians, mages, shamans, diviners and many more—from the lowest Certified witch right up to the most powerful of enchanters. Enchanters are strange as well as powerful. Their magic is different and stronger and many of them have more than one life.

Now, if someone did not control all these busy magic users, ordinary people would have a horrible time and probably end up as slaves. So the government appoints the very strongest enchanter there is to make sure no one misuses magic. This enchanter has nine lives and is known as "the Chrestomanci." You pronounce it KREST-OH-MAN-SEE. He has to have a strong personality as well as strong magic.

DIANA WYNNE JONES

The Chronicles of
CHRESTOMANCI

✦ VOLUME III ✦

Books by
DIANA WYNNE JONES

Archer's Goon

Aunt Maria

Believing Is Seeing: Seven Stories

Cart and Cwidder

Castle in the Air

Conrad's Fate

The Crown of Dalemark

Dark Lord of Derkholm

Dogsbody

Drowned Ammet

Eight Days of Luke

Fire and Hemlock

Hexwood

The Homeward Bounders

Howl's Moving Castle

The Merlin Conspiracy

The Ogre Downstairs

The Pinhoe Egg

Power of Three

The Spellcoats

Stopping for a Spell

A Tale of Time City

The Time of the Ghost

Unexpected Magic: Collected Stories

Wild Robert

Witch's Business

Year of the Griffin

Diana Wynne Jones

The Chronicles of
CHRESTOMANCI

✦ VOLUME III ✦

CONRAD'S FATE

THE PINHOE EGG

A GREENWILLOW BOOK

An Imprint of HarperCollinsPublishers

Eos is an imprint of HarperCollins Publishers.

This book is a work of fiction. References to real people, events, establishments, organizations, or locales are intended only to provide a sense of authenticity, and are used to advance the fictional narrative. All other characters, and all incidents and dialogue, are drawn from the author's imagination and are not to be construed as real.

The Chronicles of Chrestomanci, Volume III
Copyright © 2001 by Diana Wynne Jones
Conrad's Fate copyright © 2005 by Diana Wynne Jones
The Pinhoe Egg copyright © 2006 by Diana Wynne Jones

All rights reserved. Printed in the United States of America. No part of this book may be used or reproduced in any manner whatsoever without written permission except in the case of brief quotations embodied in critical articles and reviews. For information address HarperCollins Children's Books, a division of HarperCollins Publishers, 1350 Avenue of the Americas, New York, NY 10019.
www.harpercollinschildrens.com

Library of Congress Cataloging-in-Publication Data
Jones, Diana Wynne.
Chronicles of Chrestomanci / Diana Wynne Jones
   p.   cm.
"Greenwillow Books"
   Contents: v. 1. Charmed life. The lives of Christopher Chant—v. 2. Witch Week. The magicians of Caprona—v. 3, Conrad's Fate. The Pinhoe Egg.
   Summary: Adventures of the Chrestomanci, an enchanter with nine lives, whose job is to control the practice of magic in the infinite parallel universes of the Twelve Related Worlds.
   ISBN 978-0-06-447268-5 (v.1 : pbk.)
   ISBN 978-0-06-447269-2 (v.2 : pbk.)
   ISBN 978-0-06-114832-3 (v.3 : pbk.)
   [1. Fantasy. 2. Magic—Fiction. 3. Witchcraft—Fiction.] I. Title.
PZ7.J684 Cj   2001
00-39614
[Fic]—dc21

First Eos paperback edition, 2008

16 17 18 QGM 10 9 8 7

CONRAD'S FATE

✦

AUTHOR'S NOTE

The World of Chrestomanci is not the same as this one. It is a world parallel to ours, where magic is as normal as mathematics, and things are generally more old-fashioned. In Chrestomanci's world, Italy is still divided into numbers of small States, each with its Duke and capital city. In our world, Italy became one united country long ago.

Though the two worlds are not connected in any way, this story somehow got through. But it came with some gaps, and I had to get help filling them. Clare Davis, Gaynor Harvey, Elizabeth Carter and Graham Belsten discovered for me what happened in the magicians' single combat. And my husband, J. A. Burrow, with some advice from Basil Cottle, actually found the true words of the *Angel of Caprona*. I would like to thank them all very much indeed.

For Stella

1

❖

WHEN I WAS small, I always thought Stallery Mansion was some kind of fairy-tale castle. I could see it from my bedroom window, high in the mountains above Stallchester, flashing with glass and gold when the sun struck it. When I got to the place at last, it wasn't exactly like a fairy tale.

Stallchester, where we had our shop, is quite high in the mountains, too. There are a lot of mountains here in Series Seven, and Stallchester is in the English Alps. Most people thought this was the reason why you could only receive television at one end of the town, but my uncle told me it was Stallery doing it.

"It's the protections they put round the place to stop anyone investigating them," he said. "The magic blanks out the signal."

My Uncle Alfred was a magician in his spare time, so he knew this sort of thing. Most of the time he made a living for us all by keeping the bookshop at the cathedral end of town. He was a skinny, worrity little man with a bald patch under his curls, and he was my mother's half brother. It always seemed a great burden to him, having to look after me and my mother and my sister, Anthea. He rushed about muttering, "And how do I find the *money*, Conrad, with the book trade so slow!"

The bookshop was in our name, too—it said GRANT AND TESDINIC in faded gold letters over the bow windows and the dark green door—but Uncle Alfred explained that it belonged to him now. He and my father had started the shop together. Then, just after I was born and a little before he died, my father had needed a lot of money suddenly, Uncle Alfred told me, and he sold his half of the bookshop to Uncle Alfred. Then my father died, and Uncle Alfred had to support us.

"And so he should do," my mother said in her vague way. "We're the only family he's got."

My sister, Anthea, said she wanted to know what my father had needed the money for, but she never could find out. Uncle Alfred said he didn't know. "And you never get any sense out of Mother," Anthea said to me. "She just says things like 'Life is always a lottery' and 'Your father was usually hard up'—so all I can think is that it must have been gambling debts. The casino's only just up the road, after all."

I rather liked the idea of my father gambling half a bookshop away. I used to like taking risks myself. When I was eight, I borrowed some skis and went down all the steepest and iciest ski runs, and in the summer I went rock climbing. I felt I was really following in my father's footsteps. Unfortunately, someone saw me halfway up Stall Crag and told my uncle.

"Ah, no, Conrad," he said, wagging a worried, wrinkled finger at me. "I can't have you taking these risks."

"My dad did," I said, "betting all that money."

"He *lost* it," said my uncle, "and that's a different matter. I never knew much about his affairs, but I have an idea—a very shrewd idea—that he was robbed by those crooked aristocrats up at Stallery."

"What?" I said. "You mean Count Rudolf came with a gun and held him up?"

My uncle laughed and rubbed my head. "Nothing so dramatic, Con. They do things quietly and mannerly up at Stallery. They pull the possibilities like gentlemen."

"How do you mean?" I said.

"I'll explain when you're old enough to understand the magic of high finance," my uncle replied. "Meanwhile . . ." His face went all withered and serious. "Meanwhile, you can't afford to go risking your neck on Stall Crag, you really can't, Con, not with the bad karma you carry."

"What's karma?" I asked.

"That's another thing I'll explain when you're older," my uncle said. "Just don't let me catch you going rock climbing again, that's all."

I sighed. Karma was obviously something very heavy, I thought, if it stopped you climbing rocks. I went to ask my sister, Anthea, about it. Anthea is nearly ten years older than me, and she was very learned even then. She was sitting over a line of open books on the kitchen table, with her long black hair trailing over the page she was writing notes on. "Don't bother me now, Con," she said without looking up.

She's growing up just like Mum! I thought. "But I need to know what karma is."

"Karma?" Anthea looked up. She has huge dark eyes. She opened them wide to stare at me, wonderingly. "Karma's sort of like Fate, except it's to do with what you did in a former life. Suppose that in a life you had before this one you did something bad, or *didn't* do something good, then Fate is supposed to catch up with you in *this* life, unless you put it right by being extra good, of course. Understand?"

"Yes," I said, though I didn't really. "*Do* people live more than once, then?"

"The magicians say you do," Anthea answered. "I'm not sure I believe it myself. I mean, how can you *check* that you had a life before this one? Where did you hear about karma?"

Not wanting to tell her about Stall Crag, I said vaguely, "Oh, I read it somewhere. And what's pulling the possibilities? That's another thing I read."

"It's something that would take *ages* to explain, and I haven't time," Anthea said, bending over her notes again. "You don't seem to understand that I'm working for an exam that could change my entire life!"

"When are you going to get lunch, then?" I asked.

"Isn't that just my life in a *nutshell*!" Anthea burst out. "I do all the work round here *and* help in the shop twice a week, and nobody even *considers* that I might want to do something different! Go away!"

You didn't mess with Anthea when she got this fierce. I went away and tried to ask Mum instead. I might have known that would be no good.

Mum has this little bare room with creaking floorboards half a floor down from my bedroom, with nothing in it much except dust and stacks of paper. She sits there at a wobbly table, hammering away at her old typewriter, writing books and magazine articles about women's rights. Uncle Alfred had all sorts of smooth new computers down in the back room where Miss Silex works, and he was always on at Mum to change to one as well. But nothing will persuade Mum to change. She says her old machine is much more reliable. This is true. The shop computers went down at least once a week—this, Uncle Alfred said, was because of the activities up at Stallery—but the sound of Mum's typewriter is a constant hammering, through all four floors of the house.

She looked up as I came in and pushed back a swatch of dark gray hair. Old photos show her looking rather like Anthea, except that her eyes are a light yellow-brown, like mine, but you would never think her anything like Anthea now. She is sort of faded, and she always wears what Anthea calls "that horrible mustard-colored suit" and forgets to do her hair. I like that. She's always the same, like the cathedral, and she always looks over her glasses at me the same way. "Is lunch ready?" she asked me.

"No," I said. "Anthea's not even started it."

"Then come back when it's ready," she said, bending to look at the paper sticking up from her typewriter.

"I'll go when you tell me what pulling the possibilities means," I said.

"Don't bother me with things like that," she said, winding the paper up so that she could read her latest line. "Ask your uncle. It's only some sort of magicians' stuff. What do you think of 'disempowered broodmares' as a description? Good, eh?"

"Great," I said. Mum's books are full of things like that. I'm never sure what they mean. That time I thought a disempowered broodmare was some sort of weak nightmare, and I went away thinking of all her other books, called things like *Exploited for Dreams* and *Disabled Eunuchs*. Uncle Alfred had a whole table of them down in the shop. One of my jobs was to dust them, but he almost never sold any, no matter how enticingly I piled them up.

I did lots of jobs in the shop, unpacking books, arranging them, dusting them, and cleaning the floor on the days Mrs. Potts's nerves wouldn't let her come. Mrs. Potts's nerves were always bad on the days after she had tried to tidy Uncle Alfred's workroom. The shop, and the whole house, used to echo then with shouts of "I told you just the *floor*, woman! You've *ruined* that experiment! *And* you're lucky not to be a goldfish! Touch it again and you'll *be* a goldfish!"

But Mrs. Potts, at least once a month, just could not resist stacking everything in neat piles and dusting the chalk marks off the workbench. Then Uncle Alfred would rush up the stairs shouting and the next day Mrs. Potts's nerves kept her at home and I would have to clean the shop floor. As a reward for this, I was allowed to read any books I wanted from the children's shelves.

To be brutally frank with you—which is Uncle Alfred's favorite phrase—this reward meant nothing to me until about the time I heard about karma and Fate and started wondering what pulling the possibilities meant. Up to then I preferred doing risky things. Or I mostly wanted to go and see friends in the part of town where televisions worked. Reading was even harder work than cleaning the floor. But suddenly one day I discovered the Peter Jenkins books. You must know them: *Peter Jenkins and the Thin Teacher*, *Peter Jenkins and the Headmaster's Secret*, and all the others. They're great. Our shop had a whole row of them, at least twenty, and I set out to read them all.

Well, I had already read about six, and those all kept harking back to another one called *Peter Jenkins and the Football Formula* that sounded really exciting. So that was the one I wanted to read next.

I finished the floor as quickly as I could. Then, on my way to dust Mum's books, I stopped by the children's shelves and looked urgently along the row of shiny red and brown Peter Jenkins books for *Peter Jenkins and the Football Formula*. The trouble is, all those books look the same. I ran my finger along the row, thinking I'd find the book about seventh along. I knew I'd seen it there. But it wasn't. The one in about the right place was called *Peter Jenkins and the Magic Golfer*. I ran my finger right along to the end, and it still wasn't there, and *The Headmaster's Secret* didn't seem to be there either. Instead, there were three copies of one called *Peter Jenkins and the Hidden Horror*, which I'd never seen before. I took one of those out and flipped through it, and it was almost the same as *The Headmaster's Secret*, but not *quite*—vampire bats instead of a zombie in the cupboard, things like that—and I put it back feeling puzzled and really frustrated.

In the end I took one at random before I went on to dust Mum's books. And Mum's books were different—just slightly—too. They *looked* the same, with FRANCONIA GRANT in big yellow letters on them, but some of the titles were different. The fat one that used to be called *Women in Crisis* was still fat, but it was now called *The Case for Females*, and the thin, floppy one was called *Mother Wit*, instead of *Do We Use Intuition?* like I remembered.

Just then I heard Uncle Alfred galloping downstairs, whistling, on his way to open the shop. "Hey, Uncle Alfred!" I called out. "Have you sold all the *Peter Jenkins and the Football Formulas*?"

"I don't think so," he said, rushing into the

shop with his worried look. He hurried along to the children's shelves, muttering about having to reorder as he changed his glasses over. He peered through them at the row of Peter Jenkins books. He bent to look at the books below and stood on tiptoe to look at the shelves above. Then he backed away looking so angry that I thought Mrs. Potts must have tidied the books, too. "Would you look at that!" he said disgustedly. "That's a third of them different! It's criminal. They went for a big working without even *considering* the side effects! Go outside and see if the street's still the same, Conrad."

I went to the shop door, but as far as I could see, nothing . . . Oh! The postbox down the road was now bright blue.

"You *see*!" said my uncle when I told him. "You see what they're like! All sorts of details will be different now—*valuable* details—but what do *they* care? All *they* think of is money!"

"Who?" I asked. I couldn't see how anyone could make money by changing books.

He pointed up and sideways with his thumb. "Them. Those bent aristocrats up at Stallery, to be brutally frank with you, Con. They make their money by pulling the possibilities about. They look, and if they see they could get a bigger profit from one of their companies if just one or two things were a *little* different, then they twist and twitch and *pull* those one or two things. It doesn't matter to them that *other* things change as well. Oh no.

13

And this time they've overdone it. Greedy. Wicked. People are going to notice and object if they go on doing this." He took his glasses off and cleaned them. Beads of angry sweat stood on his forehead. "There'll be trouble," he said. "Or so I hope."

So this was what pulling the possibilities meant. "*How* do they change things?" I asked.

"By very powerful magic," said my uncle. "More powerful than you or I can imagine, Conrad. Make no mistake, Count Rudolf and his family are very dangerous people."

When I finally went up to my room to read my Peter Jenkins book, I looked out of my window first. Because I was at the very top of our house, I could see Stallery as just a glint and a flashing in the place where green hills folded into rocky mountain. I found it hard to believe that anyone in that high, twinkling place could have the power to change a lot of books and the color of the postboxes down here in Stallchester. I still didn't understand why anyone should want to.

"It's because if you change to a new set of things that might be going to happen," Anthea explained, looking up from her books, "you change *everything* just a little. This time," she added, ruefully turning the pages of her notes, "they seem to have done a big jump and made a big difference. I've got notes here on two books that don't seem to exist anymore. No wonder Uncle Alfred's annoyed."

We got used to the changes by next day. Sometimes it was hard to remember that postboxes used to be red. Uncle Alfred said that we only remembered anyway because we lived in that part of Stallchester. "To be brutally frank with you," he said, "half Stallchester thinks postboxes were always blue. So does the rest of the country. The King probably calls them royal blue. Mind games, that's what it is. Diabolical greed."

This happened in the glad old days when Anthea was at home. I think Mum and Uncle Alfred thought Anthea would always be at home. That summer Mum said as usual, "Anthea, don't forget that Conrad needs new school clothes for next term," and Uncle Alfred was full of plans for expanding the shop once Anthea had left school and could work there full time.

"If I clear out the boxroom opposite my work-room," he would say, "we can put the office in there. Then we can put books where the office is—maybe build out into the yard."

Anthea never said much in reply to these plans. She was very quiet and tense for the next month or so. Then she seemed to cheer up. She worked in the shop quite happily all the rest of the summer, and in the early autumn she took me to buy new clothes just as she had done last year, except that she bought things for herself at the same time. Then, after I had been back at school a month, she left.

She came down to breakfast carrying a small suitcase. "I'm off," she said. "I start at university tomorrow. I'm catching the nine-twenty to

Ludwich, so I'll say good-bye now and get something to eat on the train."

"University!" Mum exclaimed. "But you're not clever enough!"

"You can't," said Uncle Alfred. "There's the shop—and you don't have any money."

"I took an exam," Anthea said, "and I won a scholarship. That gives me enough money if I'm careful."

"But you *can't!*" they both said together. Mum added, "Who's going to look after Conrad?" and Uncle Alfred said, "Look here, my girl, I was *relying* on you for the shop."

"Working for nothing. I know," Anthea said. "Well, I'm sorry to spoil your plans for me, but I do have a life of my own, you know, and I've made arrangements for myself because I knew you'd both stop me if I told you. I've looked after all three of you for years. But now Conrad's old enough to look after himself, I'm going to go and get a life."

And she went, leaving us all staring. She didn't come back. She knew Uncle Alfred, you see. Uncle Alfred spent a lot of time in his workroom setting up spells to make sure that when Anthea came home at the end of the university semester she would find herself having to stay with us for good. Anthea guessed he would. She simply sent a postcard to say she was staying with friends and never came near us. She sent me cards and presents for my birthdays, but she never came back to Stallchester for years.

2

ANTHEA'S GOING MADE a dreadful difference, far
worse than any change made by Count Rudolf up at
Stallery. Mum was in a bad mood for weeks. I'm not
sure she ever forgave Anthea.

"So sly!" she kept saying. "So mean and secretive.
Don't you ever be like that, Conrad, and it's no use
expecting me to run after you. I have my work to do."

Uncle Alfred was tetchy and grumpy for a long
time, too, but he cheered up after he had set the spells
that were supposed to fix Anthea at home once she
came back. He took to patting me on the shoulder
and saying, "*You're* not going to let me down like
that, are you, Con?"

Sometimes I answered, "No fear!" but mostly I
wriggled a bit and didn't answer. I missed Anthea
horribly for ages. She had been the person I could go
to when I had a question to ask or to get cheered up.
If I fell down or cut myself, she had been the one
with sticking plaster and soothing words. She used
to suggest things for me to do if I was bored. I felt
quite lost now she was gone.

I hadn't realized how many things Anthea did in the house. Luckily I knew how to work the washing machine, but I was always forgetting to run it and finding I'd no clothes to go to school in. I got into trouble for wearing dirty clothes until I got used to remembering. Mum just went on piling her clothes into the laundry basket as she always had, but Uncle Alfred was particular about his shirts. He had to pay Mrs. Potts to iron them for him, and he grumbled a lot about how much she charged.

"The ingredients for my experiments cost the earth these days," he kept saying. "Where do I find the *money*?"

Anthea had done all the shopping and cooking, too, and this was where we all suffered most. For the week after she left we lived on cornflakes, until they ran out. Then Mum tried to solve the problem by ordering two hundred frozen quiches and cramming these into the freezer. You can't believe how quickly you get tired of eating quiche. And none of us remembered to fetch the next quiche out to thaw. Uncle Alfred was always having to unfreeze them by magic, and this made them soggy and seemed to affect the taste.

"Is there anything else we can eat that might be less squishy and more satisfying?" he asked pathetically. "Think, Fran. You used to cook once."

"That was when I was being exploited as a female," Mum retorted. "The quiche people do frozen pizzas, too, but you have to order them by the thousand."

Uncle Alfred shuddered. "I'd rather eat bacon and eggs," he said sadly.

"Then go out and buy some," said my mother.

In the end we settled that Uncle Alfred did the shopping and I tried to cook what he bought. I fetched books called *Simple Cookery* and *Easy Eating* up out of the shop and did my best to do what they told me. I was never very good at it. The food always seemed to turn black and stick to the bottom of the pan, but I usually had enough on top to get by with. We ate a lot of bread, though only Mum got noticeably fatter. Uncle Alfred was naturally skinny, and I kept growing. Mum had to take me shopping for new clothes several times a year from then on. It always seemed to happen when she was very busy finishing a book, and this made her so unhappy that I tried to make my clothes last as long as I could. I got into trouble at school once or twice for looking like a scarecrow.

We got used to coping by next summer. I suppose that was when it finally became obvious that Anthea was not coming back. I had worked out by Christmas that she had left for good, but it took Mum and Uncle Alfred most of a year.

"She'll *have* to come home this summer," Mum was still saying hopefully in May. "All the universities shut for months over the summer."

"Not she," said Uncle Alfred. "She's shaken the dust of Stallchester off her feet. And to be brutally frank with you, Fran, I'm not sure I *want* her back now. Someone that ungrateful would only be a disturbing factor."

He sighed, dismantled his spell to keep Anthea at home, and hired a girl called Daisy Bolger to help in the shop. After that, he was always worrying about how much he had to pay Daisy in order to stop her going to work at the china shop by the cathedral instead. Daisy knew how to get money out of Uncle Alfred much better than I did. Talk about sly! And Daisy always seemed to think I was going to mess up the books when I was in the shop. Once or twice Count Rudolf up at Stallery worked another big change, and each time Daisy was sure it was me messing the books about. Luckily Uncle Alfred never believed her.

Uncle Alfred was sorry for me. He would look at me over his glasses in his most worried way and shake his head sadly. "I reckon Anthea's going has hit you hardest of all, Con," he took to saying sadly. "To be brutally frank, I suspect it was your bad karma that caused her to leave."

"What did I *do* in my past life?" I asked anxiously.

Uncle Alfred always shook his head at that. "I don't know *what* you did, Con. The Lords of Karma alone know that. You could have been a crooked policeman, or a judge that took bribes, or a soldier that ran away, or maybe a traitor to the country—anything! All I know is that you either *didn't* do something you *should* have done, or you did something you *shouldn't*. And because of that, a bad Fate is going to keep dogging you." Then he would hurry away, muttering, "Unless we find a way you could expiate your misdeed, I suppose."

I always felt horrible after these conversations. Something bad almost always happened to me just afterward. Once I slipped when I was quite high up climbing Stall Crag and scraped the whole front of me raw. Another time I fell downstairs and twisted my ankle, and one other time I cut myself quite badly in the kitchen—blood all over the onions— but the truly nasty part was that each time I thought, I *deserve* this! This is because of my crime in my past life. And I felt horribly guilty and sinful until the scrapes or the ankle or the cut had healed. Then I remembered Anthea saying she didn't believe people had more than one life, and after that I would feel better.

"Can't you find out who I was and what I did?" I asked Uncle Alfred, one time after I had been told off by the headmistress because my clothes were too small. She sent a note home with me about it, but I threw it away because Mum had just started a new book, and anyway, I knew I *deserved* to be in trouble. "If I knew, I could do something about it."

"To be brutally frank," said my uncle, "I fancy you have to be a grown man before you could change your Fate. But I'll try to find out. I'll try, Con."

He did experiments in his workroom to find out, but he never seemed to make much headway.

About a year after Anthea left, I got really annoyed with Daisy Bolger when she tried to stop me looking at the newest Peter Jenkins book. I told her my uncle had said I could, but she just kept saying, "Put it *back*! You'll crease it, and then I'll be blamed."

"Oh, why don't you go away and work in that china shop!" I said in the end.

She tossed her head angrily. "Fat lot *you* know! I wouldn't *dream* of it. It's *boring*. I only say I will to get a decent wage out of your uncle—and he doesn't pay me half what he could afford, even now."

"He does," I said. "He's always worrying how much you cost."

"That," said Daisy, "is because he's stingy, not because he hasn't got it. He must be rich as the Count up at Stallery almost. This bookshop's coining money."

"*Is* it?" I said.

"I keep the till. I know," Daisy said. "We're at the picturesque end of town, and we get *all* the tourists, winter *and* summer. Ask Miss Silex if you don't believe me. She does the accounts."

I was so astonished to hear this that I forgot to be angry and forgot the Peter Jenkins book, too. That was no doubt what Daisy intended. She was a very cunning person. But I couldn't believe she was right, not when Uncle Alfred was always so worried. I began counting the people who came into the shop.

And Daisy was right. Stallchester is a famous beauty spot, full of historic buildings and surrounded in mountains. In summer, we got people to look at the town and play the casino and hikers who walked in the mountains. In winter, people came to ski. But because we are so high up, we get rain and mist in summer, and in winter there are always times when the snow is not deep enough, or too soft, or coming down in a blizzard, and those are the days when tourists come into the shop by their hundreds. They buy everything, from dictionaries to help with crosswords to deep books of philosophy, detective stories, biographies, adventure stories, and cookery books for self-catering. Some even buy Mum's books. It only took a few months for me to realize that Uncle Alfred was indeed coining money.

"What does he spend it all on?" I asked Daisy.

"Goodness knows," she said. "That workroom of his is pretty expensive. And he always buys best vintage port for his Magicians' Circle. All his clothes are handmade, too, you know."

I almost didn't believe that either. But when I thought about it, one of the magicians who came to Uncle Alfred's Magicians' Circle every Wednesday was Mr. Hawkins, the tailor, and he often came early with a package of clothes. And I'd helped carry dusty old bottles of port wine upstairs for the meeting, often and often. I just hadn't realized the stuff was expensive. I was annoyed with Daisy for noticing so much more than I did. But then, she was a really cunning person.

You would not believe how artfully Daisy went to work when she wanted more money. She often took as much as two weeks on it—ten days of sighing and grumbling and saying how over-worked and hard up she was, followed by another day of saying how the nice woman in the china shop had told her she could come and work there anytime. Finally she would flare up with "That's *it*! I'm *leaving*!" And it worked every time.

Uncle Alfred hates people to leave, I thought. That's why he let Anthea go to Cathedral School, so she could stay at home and be useful here.

I couldn't threaten to leave, not yet. You have to stay at school until you are twelve in this country. But I could pretend I was not going to do any more cooking. It didn't take much pretending, really.

That first time I went even slower than Daisy. I spent over a fortnight sighing and saying I was sick to my back teeth of cooking. Finally, it was Mum who said, "Really, Conrad, to listen to you, anyone would think we exploited you."

It was wonderful. I went from simmering to boiling in one breath, and I shouted with real feeling, "You *are* exploiting me! That's *it*! I'm not doing any more cooking ever again!"

Then it was even more wonderful. Uncle Alfred hurried me away to his workroom and pleaded with me. "You know—let's be brutally frank, Con—your mother's hopeless with food, and I'm worse. But we've all got to eat, haven't we? Be a good boy and reconsider now."

I looked around at the strange-shaped glass things and shining machinery in the workroom and wondered how much it all cost. "No," I said sulkily. "Pay someone else to do it."

He winced. He almost shuddered at the idea.

"Suppose I was to offer you a little something to take up as our chef again," he said cajolingly. "What could I offer you?"

I let him cajole for a while. Then I sighed and asked for a bicycle. He agreed like a shot. The bicycle was not so wonderful when it came, because Uncle Alfred only produced one that was second-hand, but it made a start. I knew how to do it now.

When winter came, I went into my act again. I refused to cook twice. First I got regular pocket money out of my uncle, and then I got skis of my own. In the spring I did it again and got modeling kits. That summer I got most things I needed. The next autumn I actually made Uncle Alfred give me a good camera. I know this was calculated cunning and quite as bad as Daisy—though I couldn't help noticing that my friends at school got skis and pocket money as if they had a right to them, and that none of them had to cook for these things either—but I told myself that my Fate had made me bad and I might as well make use of it.

I stopped the year I was going to be twelve. This was not because I was reformed. It was part of a plan. You can leave school at twelve, you see, and I knew Uncle Alfred would have thought of that. The rule is that you *can* go on to an Upper School, but only if your family pays for you. Otherwise you go and find a job. All my friends were going to Upper Schools, most of them to Cathedral like Anthea, but my best friends were going to Stall High. I thought of it as like the school in the Peter

Jenkins books. Stall High cost more, but it was supposed to be a terrific place, and best of all, it taught magic. I had set my heart on learning magic with my friends. Living as I did in a house where Uncle Alfred filled the stairway with peculiar smells and the strange buzz of working spells at least once a week, I couldn't wait to do it, too. Besides, Daisy Bolger told me that Uncle Alfred had been to Stall High himself as a boy. How that girl found out these things was something I never knew.

Knowing Uncle Alfred, I knew he would try to keep me at home somehow. He might even be going to sack Daisy and make me work in the shop for nothing. So my plan was to threaten to stop cooking just near the end of my last term and get him to bribe me with Stall High. If that didn't work, I thought I would threaten to go and get a job in the lowlands and then say that I'd stay if I could go to Cathedral School instead.

I worked all this out sitting in my room staring upward at Stallery, glimmering among the mountains. Stallery always made me wish for all the strange and exciting things that I didn't seem to have. It made me think that Anthea must have sat in *her* room making plans in much the same way— except that you couldn't see Stallery from Anthea's old room. Mum used it as a paper store now.

Stallery was in the news around then anyway. Count Rudolf died suddenly. People gossiping in the bookshop said he was quite young, really, but some diseases took no account of age, did they? "Driven to an early grave," Mrs. Potts said to me. "Mark my words. And the new Count is only twenty-one, they say. His sister's even younger. They'll be having to marry soon to preserve the family name. She'll insist on it."

Daisy was very interested in weddings. She hunted everywhere for a magazine that might have pictures of the new Count, Robert, and his sister, Lady Felice. All she found was a newspaper with the announcement of Count Robert's engagement to Lady Mary Ogworth in it. "Just plain print," she complained. "No photos."

"Daisy won't find pictures," Mrs. Potts told me. "Stallery likes its privacy, it does. They know how to keep the media out of their lives up there. I've heard there's electrical fences all round those grounds, and savage dogs patrolling inside. *She* won't want people prying, not she."

"Who's *she*?" I asked.

Mrs. Potts paused, kneeling with her back to me on the stairs. "Pass the polish," she said. "Thanks. *She*," she went on, rubbing in polish in a slow, enjoying sort of way, "is the old Countess. She's got rid of her husband—bothered and nagged him to death, I've heard—and now she won't want anyone to see while she works on the new Count. They say he's *well* under her thumb already and bound to be more so, poor boy. *She* likes all the power, all the money. *He'll* marry that girl *she's* chosen, and then she'll run the pair of them, you'll see."

"She sounds horrible," I said, fishing for more.

"Oh, she is," said Mrs. Potts. "Used to be on the stage. Caught the old Count by kicking up her legs in a chorus line, I heard. And—"

Unfortunately, Uncle Alfred came rushing upstairs at this point and upset Mrs. Potts's cleaning bucket and Mrs. Potts's nerves along with it. I never got Mrs. Potts to gossip about Stallery again. That was my Fate at work there, I thought. But I got a few more hints from Uncle Alfred himself. With his face almost withered with worry, he said to me, "What happens up in Stallery now, eh? It could be even worse. I mention no names, but someone's very power-hungry up there. I dread the next set of changes, Con."

He was so worried that he telephoned his Magicians' Circle and they actually met on a Tuesday, which was almost unheard of. After that, they met on Tuesdays *and* Wednesdays, and I helped carry up twice the number of dusty wine bottles every week.

And those weeks slowly passed, until the dread day arrived when the Headmistress came and gave everyone in the top class a School Leaver's Form. "Take this home to your parent or guardian," she said. "Tell them that if they want you to leave school at the end of this term, they must sign Section A. If they want you to go on to an Upper School, then they sign Section B. Get them to sign tonight. I want all these forms back tomorrow without fail."

I took my form home to the shop, prepared for

battle and cunning. I went in through the backyard and straight upstairs to Mum. My plan was to get her to sign Section B before Uncle Alfred even knew I'd got the form.

"What's this?" Mum said vaguely as I pushed the yellow paper in front of her typewriter.

"School Leaver's Form," I explained. "If you want me to go on at school, you have to sign Section B."

She pushed her hair back distractedly. "I can't do that, Conrad, not when you've got a job already. And at Stallery of all places. I must say I'm really disappointed in you."

I felt as if the whole world had been pulled out from under me like a carpet. "*Stallery!*" I said.

"If that's what you told your uncle, yes," my mother said. And she took the form and signed Section A with her married name. F. Tesdinic. "There," she said. "I wash my hands of you, Conrad."

3

✦➤◄

I STOOD THERE, feeling utterly let down. I
didn't know what to do or what to think. Then,
when I next caught up with myself, I was racing
downstairs, waving the School Leaver's Form. I
rushed into the shop, where Uncle Alfred was
standing behind the pay desk, and I wagged the
form furiously in his face.

"What the *hell* do you mean by *this*?" I pretty
well shrieked at him.

A lot of customers whirled around from the
shelves and stared at me. Uncle Alfred looked at
them, blinked at me, and said to Daisy, "Do you
mind taking over here for a moment?" He dodged
out from behind the desk and seized my elbow.
"Come up to my workroom and let me explain."

He more or less dragged me from the shop. I
was still flapping the form with my free hand, and I
think I was shouting, too. "What do you mean —
explain?" I screamed as we went upstairs. "You can't
do this to me! You've no *right*!"

When we reached the workroom, Uncle Alfred

shoved me inside into a strong smell of recent magic and shut the door behind both of us with a clap. He straightened his glasses, which I had knocked crooked. He was panting, and he looked more worried than I had ever seen him, but I didn't care. I opened my mouth to shout at him again.

"No, don't, Con," Uncle Alfred said earnestly. "Please. I'm doing the best I can for you. Honestly. It's your Fate—this wretched bad karma of yours—that's the problem, see."

"What's that got to do with anything?" I demanded.

"Everything," he said. "I've been doing a lot of divining about you, and it's even worse than I realized. Unless you put right what you did wrong in your previous life—and put it right *now*—you are going to be horribly and painfully *dead* before the year's out."

"*What?*" I said. "I don't believe you!"

"It's true," he assured me. "Lords of Karma will just scrap you and let you try again when you next get reborn. They're quite ruthless, you know. But I don't ask you to believe me just like that. I'd like you to come to the Magicians' Circle this evening and see what *they* say. They don't know you, I haven't told them about you, but I'm willing to bet they'll spot this karma of yours straight off. To be brutally frank with you, it's round you in a black cloud these days, Con."

I felt terrible. My mouth went dry, and my stomach shook, in wobbly waves. "But," I said, and found my voice had gone down to a whisper, "but what's it got to do with *this*?" I tried to flourish the leaver's form at him again, but I could only manage a feeble flap. My arm had gone weak.

"Ah, I wish you'd come to me first," said my uncle. "I'd have explained. You see, I've discovered what you did wrong. There was someone in your last life Lords of Karma required you to put an end to. And you didn't. You lost your nerve and let them go free. And this person got reborn and continued his evil ways in this present life, too. . . ."

"But I still don't see—" I began.

He held up a hand to stop me. It was shaking. He seemed to be shaking with worry all over. "Let me finish, Con. Let me go on. Since I discovered what caused your Fate, I've done every kind of divination to find out who this person *is* that you didn't put an end to. It's been really difficult—I don't have to tell you how the magics up at Stallery interfere with spells down here—but it was pretty definite even so. It's someone up at Stallery, Con."

"You mean it's the new Count?" I said.

"I don't know," said my uncle. "It's *one* of them up there. *Someone* up at Stallery has a lot of power and is doing something really bad, and they've got the exact pattern of this person you should have done away with last time. That's all I can find out, Con. Look on the bright side. We know where to find him or her. That's why I arranged for you to get a job up at Stallery."

"What kind of a job?" I asked.

"Domestic," said Uncle Alfred. "The kind of

thing you're used to, really. The steward up there—butler, whatever—is a Mr. Amos, and he's reckoning to take on some school leavers shortly, to train up as servants to the new Count. Day after the end of term he'll be interviewing a whole bunch of you. And he'll take you, Con, never fear. I'll put a really good spell on you, so he'll have no choice. You don't need to worry about getting the job. And you'll be right in the middle of things then, cleaning boots and running errands, and you'll have *ample* opportunity to seek out the person responsible for this terrible karma you carry. . . ."

I thought, *Cleaning boots!* And nearly burst into tears. My uncle went on talking, nervously, persuasively, but I just couldn't attend anymore. It wasn't simply that my careful plan had been no use at all. It was more that I suddenly saw where the plan had been leading me. I hadn't admitted it to myself before, but I knew now—I knew very fiercely—that what I wanted was to be like Anthea, to leave the bookshop, leave Stallchester, go somewhere quite different and make a career of some kind. I hadn't actually thought *what* career, until then, but now I thought of flying an aircraft, becoming a great surgeon, being a famous scientist, or perhaps, best of all, learning to be the strongest magician in the world.

It was like peeping past a door that was just slamming in my face. I could have done so many interesting things if I had the right education. Instead, I was going to spend my life *cleaning boots*.

"I don't want to!" I blurted out. "I want to go to Stall High!"

"You haven't listened to what I've been telling you," Uncle Alfred said. "You've got to get this evil Fate of yours cleared away *first*, Con. If you don't, you die in agony before the year's out. Once you've gone up to Stallery, found out who this person is, and done away with him or her, then you can do anything you want. I'll arrange for you to go to Stall High then like a shot. Of *course* I will."

"Really?" I said.

"Really," he said.

It was like that door softly swinging open again. True, there was an ugly doorstep in the way labeled "Bad Karma, Evil Fate," but I could step over that. I found myself letting out a long, long sigh. "All right," I said.

Uncle Alfred patted my shoulder. "Good lad. I knew you'd see reason. But I don't ask you to take my word alone. Come to the Magicians' Circle tonight, and see what they have to say. All right now?" I supposed I was. I nodded. "Then *could* I get back to the shop?" he said. "Daisy hasn't the experience yet."

I nodded again. But as he pushed me out onto the stairs, I had a thought. "Who's going to do the cooking with me gone?" I asked. I was surprised not to have thought of this before.

"Don't worry about that," my uncle said. "We'll hire Daisy's mother. Daisy's always telling me what a good cook her mum is."

I stumbled away up to my room and stared up at Stallery, twinkling out of its fold in the mountains. My mind felt like someone in the dark, stumbling about among huge pieces of furniture with sharp corners on them. I kept barking myself on the corners. No Stall High unless I went and cleaned boots in Stallery—that was one corner. The Lords of Karma scrapped you if you were no good—that was another. A person up there among those glinting windows was so wicked he had to be done away with—that was another—and I had to deal with the person now because I'd been too feeble to do it in my last life— that was yet another. Then I barked my mind on the most important corner of the lot. If I didn't do this, I'd die. It was this person or me, him or me.

Him or me, I kept saying to myself. Him or me.

Those words were going through my head while I helped Uncle Alfred carry the bottles of port up to his workroom that evening. I had to back into the room because I had two bottles in each hand.

"Dear me," someone said behind me. "What appalling karma!"

Before I could turn around, someone else said, "My dear Alfred, did you realize that your nephew carries some of the blackest Fate I've ever seen?"

All the magicians of the Circle were there, though I hadn't heard them arrive. Two of them were smoking cigars, filling the workroom with strong blue smoke, which made the place look a different shape and size somehow. Instead of the

35

usual workbench and glass tubes and machinery, there was a circle of comfortable armchairs, each with a little table beside it. There was another table in the middle loaded with bottles, wineglasses, and several decanters.

I knew most of the people sitting in the arm-chairs at least by sight. The one pouring himself a glass of rich red wine was Mr. Seuly, the Mayor of Stallchester, who owned the ironworks at the other end of town. He passed the decanter along to Mr. Johnson, who owned the ski runs and the hotels. Mr. Priddy, beside him, ran the casino. One of those smoking a cigar was Mr. Hawkins, the tailor, and the other was Mr. Fellish, who owned the *Stallchester News*. Mr. Goodwin, beyond those, owned a big chain of shops in Stallchester. I wasn't quite sure what the others were called, but I knew the tall one owned all the land around here and that the fat one ran the trams and buses. And there was Mr. Loder, the butcher, helping Uncle Alfred uncork bottles and carefully pour wine into decanters. The thick nutty smell of port cut across the smell of cigars.

All these men had shrewd respectable faces and expensive clothes, which made it worse that they were all staring at me with concern. Mayor Seuly sipped at his wine and shook his head a lit-tle. "Not long for this life unless something's done soon," he said. "What's causing it? Does anyone know?"

"Something—no, *someone* he should have put down in his last life, by the looks of it," Mr. Hawkins, the tailor, said.

The tall landowning one nodded. "And the chance to cure it now, only he's not done it," he said, deep and gloomy. "Why hasn't he?"

Uncle Alfred beckoned me to stop standing staring and put the bottles on the table. "Because," he said, "to be brutally frank with you, I've only just found out who he should be dealing with. It's someone up at Stallery."

There was a general groan at this.

"Then *send* him there," said Mr. Fellish.

"I am. He's going next week," my uncle said. "It couldn't be contrived any sooner."

"Good. Better late than never," Mayor Seuly said.

"You know," observed Mr. Priddy, "it doesn't surprise me at all that it's someone up at Stallery. That's such a strong Fate on the boy. It looks equal to the power up there, and that's so strong that it interferes with communications and stops this town thriving as it should."

"It's not just this town Stallery interferes with," Mayor Seuly said. "Their financial grip is down over the whole world, like a net. I come up against it almost every day. They have magical stoppages occurring all the time, so that they can make money and I can't. If I try to get round what they do—*bang*. I lose half my profits."

"Oh, we've all had that," agreed Mr. Goodwin. "Odd to think it's in this lad's hands to save us as well as himself."

I stood by the table, turning from one to the other as they spoke. My mouth went drier with each thing that was said. By this time I was so horrified I could hardly swallow. I tried to ask a question, but I couldn't.

My uncle seemed to realize what I wanted to know. He turned around. He was holding his glass up to the light, so that a red blob of light from it wavered on his forehead as he said, "This is all very true and tragic, but how is my nephew to know who this person *is* when he sees him? That's what you wanted to ask, wasn't it, Con?" It was, but I couldn't even nod by then.

"Simple," said Mayor Seuly. "There'll come a moment when he'll *know*. There's always a moment of recognition in cases of karma. The person he needs will say something or do something, and it will be like clicking a switch. Light will come on in the boy's head, and he'll *know*."

The rest of them nodded and made growling murmurs that they agreed, it *was* like that, and Uncle Alfred said, "Got that, Con?"

I managed to nod this time. Then Mayor Seuly said, "But he'll want to know how to deal with the person when he does know. That's quite as important. How about he uses Granek's Equation?"

"Too complicated," said Mr. Goodwin. "Try him with Beaulieu's Spell."

"I'd prefer a straight Whitewick," Mr. Loder, the butcher, said.

After that they all began suggesting things, all of which meant nothing to me, and each of them got quite heated in favor of his own suggestion. Before long, the tall landowning one was banging his wineglass on the little table beside his chair and shouting, "You've *got* to have him eliminate this person for good, quickly and simply! The only answer is a Persholt!"

"Please remember," my uncle said anxiously, "that Con's only a boy and he doesn't know any magic at all."

This caused a silence. "Ah," Mayor Seuly said at length. "Yes. Of course. Well then, I think the best plan is to enable him to summon a Walker." At this, all the others broke into rumbles of "Exactly! Of *course*! A Walker. Why didn't we think of that before?" Mayor Seuly looked around the circle of them and said, "Agreed? Good. Now what can we give him to use? It ought to be something quite plain and ordinary that no one will suspect. . . . Ah. Yes. A cork from one of those bottles will do nicely."

He held out his hand with a handsome gold ring shining on it, and Mr. Loder passed him the purple-stained cork from the bottle he had just emptied into a decanter. Mr. Seuly took it and clasped it in both hands for a moment. Then he nodded and passed it on to Mr. Johnson, who did the same. The cork slowly traveled around the entire circle, including

Uncle Alfred and Mr. Loder, standing by the table, who passed it back to the Mayor.

Mayor Seuly held the cork up in his finger and thumb and beckoned me over to him. I still couldn't speak. I stood there, looking down on his wealthily clipped hair, which almost hid the thin place on top, and wondering at how rounded and rich he looked. I breathed in smells of nutty, fruity wine, smooth good cloth, and a tang of aftershave and nodded at everything he said.

"All you have to do," he said, "is first to have your moment of recognition and then to fetch out this cork. You hold it up like I'm doing, and you say, 'I summon a Walker to bring me what I need.' Have you got that?" I nodded. It sounded quite easy to remember. "You may have to wait awhile for the Walker," Mayor Seuly went on, "and you mustn't be frightened when you see the Walker coming. It may turn out bigger than you expect. When it reaches you, the Walker will give you something. I don't know what. Walkers are designed to give you exactly the tool for the job. But take my word for it, the object you get will do just what you need it to do. And you *must* give the Walker this cork in exchange. Walkers never give something for nothing. Have you got all that?" he asked. I nodded again. "Then take this cork and keep it with you all the time," he said, "but don't let anyone else see it. And I hope that when we next meet, you'll carry no karma at all."

As I took the cork, which felt like an ordinary cork to me, Mr. Johnson said, "Right. That's done.

Send him off, Alfred, and let's start the meeting."

I didn't really need Uncle Alfred to jerk his head at me to go. I got out as quickly as I could and rushed upstairs to the kitchen for a drink of water. But by the time I got there, my mouth was hardly dry at all. That was odd, but it was such a relief that I hardly wondered about it at all. I wasn't even very scared anymore, and that was odd, too, but I didn't think of it at the time.

4

❧

I GOT MUCH more nervous as the week marched on. The worst part was the end-of-term assembly, when I had to sit on the left side with the school leavers, while all my friends sat across the gangway because they were going to Upper Schools. I felt really left out. And while I sat there, I realized that even when I'd found the karma person and got rid of him, I'd still be a year behind my friends at Stall High. And on my side of the gangway, the boy next to me had got a job at Mayor Seuly's ironworks and the girl on the other side was going to train as a maid in Mr. Goodwin's house. I still had to get my job.

Then it suddenly hit me that I was going off on my own to a strange place where I wouldn't know what to do or how to behave, and that was bad enough, without having to find the person causing my Evil Fate as well. I tried saying, "It's him or me," to myself, but that was no help at all. When I got home, I looked out of my window, up at Stallery, and that was terrifying. I realized that I didn't know the first thing about the place, except that it was full of powerful wizardry and that someone up there was thoroughly wicked. When Uncle Alfred came and took me to his workroom to put the spell on me that would make this Mr. Amos give me the job at Stallery, I went very slowly. My legs shook.

The workroom was back to its usual state. There was no sign of the comfortable chairs or the port wine. Uncle Alfred chalked a circle on the floor and had me stand inside it. Otherwise, the magics were just like ordinary life. I didn't feel anything particularly or notice much except a very small buzzing, right at the end. But Uncle Alfred was beaming when he had finished.

"There!" he said. "I defy anyone to refuse to employ you now, Con! It's tight as a diving suit."

I went away, shaking with nerves. I was so full of doubts and ignorance that I went and interrupted Mum. She was sitting at her creaky table, reading great long sheets of paper, making marks in the margins of them as she read. "Say whatever it is quickly," she said, "or I'll lose my place in these blessed galleys."

Out of all the things I wanted to know, all I could think of was, "Do I need to take any clothes with me to Stallery tomorrow?"

"Ask your uncle," Mum said. "You arranged the whole caper with him. And remember to have a bath and wash your hair tonight."

So I went downstairs, where Uncle Alfred was now unpacking guidebooks out in the back, and I asked him the same question. "And can I take my camera?" I said.

He pulled his lip and thought about it. "To be

frank with you, by rights you shouldn't take anything," he said. "It's only supposed to be an interview tomorrow. But of course, if the spell works and you do get the job, you'll probably start work there straightaway. I know they provide the uniforms. But I don't know about underclothes. Yes, perhaps you ought to take underclothes along. Only don't make it obvious you expect to be staying. They won't like that."

This made me more nervous than ever. I thought the spell had *fixed* it. After that, I had a short, blissful moment when I thought that if I was dreadfully rude to them in Stallery, they'd throw me out and not give me the job. Then I could go to Stall High next term. But of course that wouldn't work, because of my Evil Fate. I sighed and went to pack.

The tram that went up past Stallery left from the market square at midday. Uncle Alfred walked down there with me. I was in my best clothes and carrying a plastic bag that looked like my lunch. I'd arranged a packet of sandwiches and a bottle of juice artfully on top. Underneath were all my socks and pants wrapped around my camera and the latest Peter Jenkins book—I thought Uncle Alfred could spare me *one* book from the shop.

The tram was there and filling with people when we got to the square.

"You'd better get on or you won't have a seat," my uncle said. "Good luck, Con, and I'll love you and leave you. Oh, and Con," he said as I started to climb the metal steps into the tram. He beckoned and I came back down. "Something I forgot," he said. He led me a little way off across the pavement. "You're to tell Mr. Amos that your name is Grant," he said, "like mine. If you tell them a posh name like Tesdinic, they'll think you're too grand for the job. So from now on your name is Conrad Grant. Don't forget, will you?"

"All right," I said. "Grant." Somehow this made me feel a whole lot better. It was like having an alias, the way people did in the Peter Jenkins books when they lived adventurous double lives. I began to think of myself as a sort of secret agent. Grant. I grinned and waved quite cheerfully at Uncle Alfred as I climbed back on the tram and bought my ticket. He waved and went bustling off.

About half the people on the tram were girls and boys my own age. Most of them had plastic bags like mine, with lunch in. I thought it was probably an end-of-term outing to Stallstead, from one of the other schools in town. The Stallery tram was a single-line loop that went up into the mountains as far as Stallstead and then down into Stallchester again by the ironworks. Stallstead is a really pretty village right up among the green Alps. People go there all summer for cream teas and outings.

Then the tram gave out a *clang* and started off with a lurch. My heart and stomach gave a lurch, too, in the opposite direction, and I stopped thinking about anything except how nervous I was. This is *it*, I thought. I'm really on my way now. I don't remember seeing the shops, or the houses, or the suburbs we went past. I only began to notice things when we reached the first of the foothills, among the woods, and the cogs underneath the tram engaged with the cogs in the roadway, *clunk*, and we went steeply up in jerks, *croink, croink, croink*.

This woke me up a bit. I stared out at the sunlight splashing on rocks and green trees and thought, in a distracted way, that it was probably quite beautiful. Then it dawned on me that there was none of the chattering and laughing and fooling about on the tram that there usually is on a school outing. All the other kids sat staring quietly out at the woods, just as I was doing.

They *can't* all be going to Stallery to be interviewed! I thought. They *can't*! But there didn't seem to be any teachers with them. I clutched at the slightly sticky cork in my pocket and wondered if I would ever get to use it to call a Walker, whatever that was. But I *had* to call one, or I would be dead. And I realized that if any of these kids got the job instead of me, it would be like a death sentence.

I was really scared. I kept thinking of the way Uncle Alfred had told me not to be too obvious about taking clothes and then to call myself Grant, as if he wasn't too sure that his spell on me would work, and I was more frightened than I had ever been before. When the tram came out on the next level part, I stared down at the view of Stallchester nestled below, and the blue peaks where the glacier was, and at Stall Crag, and the whole lot went fuzzy with my terror.

It takes the tram well over an hour to get as high as Stallery, cogging up the steep bits, rumbling through rocky cuttings, and stopping at lonely inns and solitary pairs of houses on the heights. One or two people got on or off at every stop, but they were all adults. The other children just sat there, like me. *Let* them all be going to Stallstead! I thought. But I noticed that none of the ones with bags of lunch tried to eat any of it, as if they might be too nervous for food, just as I was. Though they *could* be saving it to eat in Stallstead, I thought. I hoped they were.

At last we were running on an almost level part, where there were clumps of trees and meadowlands and even a farm on one side. It looked almost like a lowland valley here. But on the other side of the road there was a high dark wall with spikes on top. I knew this was the wall around Stallery and that we were now really high up. I could even feel the magics here, like a very faint fizzing. My heart began banging so hard it almost hurt.

That wall seemed to run for *miles*, with the road curving alongside it. There was no kind of break in its dark surface, until the tram swung around an even bigger curve and began slowing down. There was a high turreted gateway ahead in the wall, which seemed to be some kind of a house as well—anyway, I saw windows in it—and across the road from this gateway, along the verge by the hedge, I was surprised to see some gypsies camping. I noticed a couple of tumbledown-looking caravans, an old gray horse trying to eat the hedge, and a white dog running up and down the verge. I wondered vaguely why they hadn't been moved on. It seemed unlike Stallery to allow gypsies outside their gates. But I was too nervous to wonder much.

Clang, clang, went the tram, announcing it was stopping.

A man in a brown uniform came to the gate and stood waiting. He was carrying two weird-shaped brown paper parcels. Barometers? I wondered. Clocks? He came over as the tram stopped and handed the parcels to the driver.

"For the clock mender in Stallstead," he said. Then, as the driver unfolded the doors, the man came right up into the tram. "This is Stallery South Gate," he said loudly. "Any young persons applying for employment should alight here, please."

I jumped up. So, to my dismay, did all the other kids. We all crowded toward the door and clattered down the steps into the road, every one of us, and the gatehouse seemed to soar above us. The tram clanged again and whined away along its tracks, leaving us to our fate.

"Follow me," the man in the brown uniform said, and he turned toward the gate. It was a gateway big enough to have taken the tram, like a huge arched mouth in the towering face of the gatehouse, and it was slowly swinging open to let us through.

Everyone clustered forward then, and I was somehow at the back. My feet lagged. I couldn't help myself. Behind me, across on the other side of the road, someone called out in a strong, cheerful voice, "Bye then. Thanks for the lift."

I looked around to see a tall boy swing himself down from the middle caravan—I hadn't noticed there were three before—and come striding across the road to join the rest of us.

Anyone less likely to climb out of a shabby, broken-down caravan was hard to imagine. He was beautifully dressed in a silk shirt, a blue linen jacket, and impeccably creased fawn trousers, and his black hair was crisply cut in a way that I could see was expensive. He seemed older than the rest of us—I thought, fifteen at least—and the only gypsy things about him were the dark, dark eyes in his confident, good-looking face.

My heart sank at the sight of him. If anyone was going to get the job at Stallery, it would be this boy.

The gatekeeper came pushing past the boy and shook his fist at the gypsy encampment. "I warned you!" he shouted. "Clear off!"

Someone on the driving seat of the front caravan shouted back. "Sorry, guvnor! Just going now!"

"Then *get* going!" yelled the gatekeeper. "Go on. Hop it. Or else!"

Rather to my surprise, all five caravans moved off at once. I hadn't realized there were so many, and for another thing, I had thought the gray horse was eating the hedge and not hitched up to any of them. I dimly remembered there was a cooking fire, too, with an iron pot hanging over it. But I thought I must have been wrong about that when all six carts

49

bumped down into the road, leaving empty grass behind, and set off, clattering away in the direction of Stallstead. The white dog, which had been sniffing at the hedge some way down the road, came pelting after them and leaped up and down behind the last caravan. A thin brown arm came out of the back of this caravan, and the dog was hauled inside with enormous scramblings. It looked as if the dog had been taken by surprise as much as I had.

The gatekeeper grunted and pushed back among us to the open gate. "Come on through," he said.

We obediently shuffled forward between the walls of the gatehouse. At the exact moment that I was level with the gate, I felt the magical defenses of Stallery cut through me like a buzz saw. It was only a thin line, luckily, but while I crossed it, it was like having my body taken over by a swarm of electric bees. I squeaked. The tall boy, walking beside me, made a small noise like "Oof!" I didn't notice if any of the others felt it because almost at once we came through under the gatehouse into a huge vista of perfect parkland. We all made little murmurs of pleasure.

There was perfect green rolling lawn wherever you looked, with a ribbon of beautifully kept driveway looping through it among clumps of graceful trees. The greenness rose into hills here and there, and the hills were either crowned with trees or they had little white-pillared summerhouses on them. And it all went on and on, into the blue distance.

"Where's the house?" one of the girls asked.

The gatekeeper laughed. "Couple of miles away. Start walking. When you come to the path that goes off to the right, take that and keep walking. When you can see the mansion, take the right-hand path again. Someone will meet you there and show you the rest of the way."

"Aren't you coming, too, then?" the girl asked.

"No," said the man. "I stay with the gate. Off you go."

We set off, trudging in a dubious little huddle along the drive, like a lost herd of sheep. We walked until the wall and the gate were out of sight behind two of the green hills, but there was still no sign of the mansion. A certain amount of sighing and shuffling began, particularly among the girls. They were all wearing the kind of shoes that hurt your feet just to look at them, and most of them had the latest fashion in dresses on, too, which held their knees together and forced them to take little tripping steps. Some of the boys had come in good suits made of thick cloth. They were far too hot, and one boy who was wearing hand-stitched boots was hobbling worse than the girls.

"I've got a blister already," one of the girls announced. "How much farther *is* it?"

"Do you think it's some kind of a test?" wondered the boy with the boots.

"Oh, it's bound to be," said the tall boy from the gypsy camp. "This drive is designed to lead us round in circles until only the fittest survive. That was a joke," he added as almost everyone let out a moan. "Why don't we all take a rest?" His bright dark eyes

51

traveled over our various plastic bags. "Why don't we sit on this nice smooth grass and have a picnic?"

This suggestion caused instant dismay. "We *can't*!" half of them cried out. "They're expecting us!" And most of the rest said, "I can't mess up my good clothes!"

The tall boy stood with his hands in his pockets, surveying everyone's hot, anxious faces. "If they want us that badly," he said, in a testing kind of way, "they might have had the decency to send a car."

"Ooh, they wouldn't do that, not for *domestic*," one of the girls said.

The tall boy nodded. "I suppose not." I had the feeling that up until then, this boy had not the least notion why we were all here. I could see him digesting the idea. "Still," he said, "domestic or not, there's nothing to stop people taking their shoes off and walking on this nice smooth grass, is there? There's no one who could see." Faces turned to him with longing. "Go on," he said. "You can always put them on again when we sight the house."

More than half of them took his advice. Girls plucked off shoes; boys unlaced tight boots. The tall boy sauntered behind with a pleased but slightly superior smile, watching them scamper barefoot along the smooth verge. Some of the girls hauled their tight skirts up. Boys took off hot jackets.

"That's better," he said. He turned to me. "Aren't you going to?"

"Old shoes," I said, pointing down at them. "They don't hurt." His shoes looked to be handmade. I could see they fitted him like gloves. I felt very suspicious of him. "If you really thought it was a test," I said, "you've made them all fail it."

He shrugged. "It depends if Stallery wants barefoot parlormaids and footmen with big hairy toes," he said, and I could have sworn he looked at me closely then, to see if I thought this was what we all intended to be. His piercing dark eyes traveled on down to my carrier bag. "You couldn't spare a sandwich, could you? I'm starving. The Travelers only eat when they happen to have some food, and that didn't seem to happen most of the time I was with them."

I fished him out one of my sandwiches and another for myself. "You couldn't have been with the gypsies *that* long," I said, "or your clothes would have got creased."

"You'd be surprised," he said. "It was nearly a month, actually. Thanks."

We marched along munching egg and cress, while the driveway unreeled ahead of us and more hills with trees and lacy white buildings came into view, and the other kids ran along ahead of us in a bunch. Most of them were trying to eat sandwiches, too, and hang on to coats and shoes and bags while they ate.

"What's your name?" I said at length.

"Call me Christopher," he said. "And you?"

"Conrad Te—Grant," I said, remembering my alias just in time.

"Conrad T. Grant?" he said.

"No," I said. "Just Grant."

53

"Very well," he said. "Grant you shall be. And you aim to be a footman and strut in Stallery in velvet hose, do you, Grant?"

Hose? I thought. I had visions of myself in a reel of rubber pipe. "I don't know what they dress you in," I said. "But I do know they can't be going to take more than one or two."

"That seems obvious," Christopher replied. "I regard you as my chief rival, Grant."

This was so exactly what I thought about him that I was rather shaken. I didn't answer, and we swung up another loop of drive to find there were now banks of flowers under some of the trees, as if we might be getting near the gardens around the house. Here a dog of some kind came lolloping from the nearest trees and put on speed toward us. It was quite a big dog. The kids on the verge instantly began milling about, yelling out that it was one of the ferocious guard dogs on the loose. A girl screamed. The boy with the hand-stitched boots swung them, ready to throw at the dog.

"Don't do that, you fool!" Christopher bellowed at him. "Do you *want* it to go for you?" He set off in great strides up the grass toward the dog. It put on speed and came sort of snaking at him, long and low.

I'm sure the kids were right about that dog. It was snarling as if it wanted to tear Christopher's throat out, and when it got near, it bunched itself, ready to spring. A girl screamed again.

"Stop that, you fool of a dog," Christopher said. "Stop it at once."

And the dog did stop. Not only did it stop, but it

wagged its tail and wagged its bunched-up hind parts and came crawling and groveling toward Christopher, where it tried to lick his beautiful shoes.

"No slobber," Christopher commanded, and the dog stopped and just groveled instead. "You've made a mistake," he told it. "No one here's a trespasser. Go away. Go back where you came from." He pointed sternly up at the trees. The dog got up and walked slowly back the way it had come, turning around hopefully every so often as it went, in case Christopher was going to let it come and grovel again. Christopher came down the hill saying, "I think it's trained to go for anyone who isn't on the path. Shoes on again, everyone, I'm afraid."

Everyone now regarded him as a sort of hero, savior, and commander. Several girls gave him passionate looks while they put their shoes back on, and we all limped and straggled on around another curve of drive. Here there were hedges, with glimpses of flowers blazing beyond and, beyond that, a twinkle of many windows from behind the trees. A path branched off to the right. Christopher said, "This way, troops," and led everyone along it.

We went through more parkland, but it was just as well everyone had put their shoes on again, because this path was quite short and soon branched into another, among tall, shiny shrubs, where it ended in a flight of stone steps.

The boys hastily put their jackets back on. A youngish man was waiting for us at the top of these steps. He was quite skinny and only an inch or so taller than Christopher. He had a nice, snubby face.

But all of us, even Christopher, stared up at him with awe because he was dressed in black velvet knee breeches, with yellow-and-brown-striped stockings below those and black buckled shoes below the stockings. He wore a matching brown-and-yellow-striped waistcoat over a white shirt above the breeches, and his fairish hair was long, tied at the back of his neck by a smooth black bow. It was enough to make anyone stare.

Christopher dropped back beside me. "Ah," he said. "I see a footman or a lackey. But it's the breeches that seem to be velvet. The hose are striped silk."

"My name's Hugo," the young man said. He smiled at us, very pleasantly. "If you'll just follow me, I'll show you where to go. Mr. Amos is waiting to interview you in the undercroft."

5

❧❧

EVERYONE WENT QUIET and nervous. Even Christopher said nothing more. We all trooped up the steps, and with the young man's buckled shoes and striped stockings flashing ahead, we followed him through confusing shrubbery paths. By now we were quite near the mansion. We kept getting glimpses of high walls and windows above the bushes, but we only got a real sight of the house when Hugo led us cornerwise to a door in a yard. Just for a moment there was a space where you could look along the front of the mansion. We all craned sideways.

The place was enormous. There were windows in rows. It seemed to have its main front door halfway up the front wall, with two big stone stairways curving up to it, and all sorts of curlicues and golden things above that, on a heavy piece of roof that hung over the door. There was a fountain jetting, down between the two stairways, and a massive circle of drive beyond that.

This was all I had time to see. Hugo led us at a

brisk pace, into the yard, across it, and in through a large square doorway in the lower part of the house. In no time at all we were crowding into a big wood-lined room, where Mr. Amos was standing, waiting for us.

No one had any doubt who he was. You could tell he was a Stallery servant because he wore a striped waistcoat like Hugo's, but the rest of his clothes were black, like someone going to a funeral. He had surprisingly small feet in very shiny black shoes. He stood with his hands clasped behind his back, like something blocky that might be going to take root in the floor, his small, shiny shoes astride, his blunt, pear-shaped face forward, and he made you feel almost religious awe. The Bishop down in Stallchester was much less awe-inspiring than Mr. Amos was, although it was hard to see why. He was the most pear-shaped man I had ever seen. His striped waistcoat rounded in front, his black coat spread at the sides, and his hands had to reach a long way back in order to clasp behind him. His face was rather purple as well as pear-shaped. His lips were quite thick below his wide, flat nose. He was not much taller than me. But you felt that if Mr. Amos were to get angry and uproot his small, shiny shoes from the floor, the floor would shake and the world with it.

"Thank you, Mr. Hugo," he said. He had a deep, resounding voice. "Now I want you all standing in a line, hands by your sides, and let me look at you."

We all hastily shuffled into a row. Those of us with plastic bags tried to lean them up against the backs of our legs, out of sight. Mr. Amos uprooted himself then, and the floor did shake slightly as he paced along in front of us, looking each of us intently in the face. His eyes were quite as awesome as the rest of him, like stones in his purple face. When he came to me, I tried to stare woodenly above his smooth gray head. This seemed the right way to behave. He smelled a little like Mayor Seuly, only more strongly, of good cloth, fine wine, and cigar. When he came to Christopher at the end of the line, he seemed to stare harder at him than at anyone, which worried me quite a lot. Then he turned massively sideways and snapped his fingers.

Instantly two more youngish men dressed like Hugo came into the room and stood looking polite and willing.

"Gregor," Mr. Amos said to one, "take these two boys and this girl to be interviewed by Chef. Andrew, these boys are to see Mr. Avenloch. Take them to the conservatory, please. Mr. Hugo, all the rest of the girls will see Mrs. Baldock in the Housekeeper's Room."

All three young men nodded, murmured, "Yes, Mr. Amos," and led their batch of people away. I think most of them had to catch the next tram down into Stallchester. I never saw more than two of them again. In a matter of seconds the room was empty except for Mr. Amos, Christopher, and me. My heart began to bang again, horribly.

Mr. Amos planted himself in front of us. "You

two look the most likely ones," he said. His voice boomed in the empty room. "Can I have your names, please?"

"Er," I said. "Conrad Grant."

Christopher said, with great smartness, "I'm Christopher Smith, Mr. Amos." I bet that's a lie, I thought. He's got an alias, just like me.

Mr. Amos's stonelike eyes turned to me. "And where are you from?"

"The bookshop," I said, "down in Stallchester."

The stone eyes rolled up and down to examine me. "Then," Mr. Amos said, "I take it you'll have had no experience of domestic work."

"I clean the shop quite often," I said.

"*Not* what I had in mind," Mr. Amos said coldly. "No experience of waiting on your betters, I meant. Being polite. Guessing what they need before they ask. Being invisible until they need you. Have you?"

"No," I said.

"And you?" Mr. Amos asked, moving his stony eyes to Christopher. "You're older. You must have earned your keep, or you wouldn't have had the money for those fancy clothes."

Christopher bowed his neatly clipped dark head. "Yes, Mr. Amos. I confess I have been three years in a household of some size, though not as big as this one, of course. But, in case you get the wrong impression, I was there more as a hanger-on than precisely as part of the work force."

Mr. Amos stared intently at Christopher. "You mean, as a poor relation?" he said.

"That sort of thing, yes," Christopher agreed. I thought he sounded a little uncomfortable about it.

"So neither of you have the sort of experience I mentioned," Mr. Amos said. "Good. I like my trainees ignorant. It means they don't come to Stallery with all the wrong habits. Next big question. How do you both feel about serving as a valet, a gentleman's gentleman? This means dressing your gentleman, caring for his clothes, looking to his comfort, running errands if he asks it, even cooking for him in certain cases, and generally knowing the gentleman's secrets—but never, *ever* breathing a word of those secrets to another soul. Can you do all that?"

Christopher looked a little stunned by this. I remembered how Christopher, so oddly, had not seemed to know why he was here, and I realized that this was my best chance *ever* of making sure I got this job. "I'd like doing that a lot," I said.

"Me, too," Christopher said promptly. "Looking after clothes and keeping secrets are the two things I do best, Mr. Amos." I began to think I hated him.

"Good, good," Mr. Amos said. "I'm glad to see you both so ambitious. Because of course it will take some years of training before either of you are up to a position of such trust. But both of you seem quite promising material." He rocked back and forth on his small, shiny feet. "Let me explain," he commanded. "In a few years I shall probably be retiring. When this happens, my son, Mr. Hugo, will naturally take over my position in charge of Stallery, as I took over from *my* father here. This will leave untenanted Mr. Hugo's current post as valet to Count Robert. My aim is to train up more than one candidate for this position, so that when the time comes, Count Robert will have a choice. With this in mind, I propose to appoint the pair of you to the position of Improvers, and I expect you to regard yourselves as rivals for the honor of becoming, in time, a proper valet. I shall naturally recommend to the Count whichever of you most meets with my approval."

This was wonderful luck! I could feel my face spreading into a relieved grin. "*Thank* you!" I said, and then added, "Mr. Amos, sir," in order to start by being respectful.

Christopher seemed equally relieved but also slightly bewildered. "Er, won't you need to see any of my references, sir?" he asked. "One of them is quite glowing."

"Keep them," Mr. Amos said, "for your own encouragement. The only reference I need is my own powers of observation, honed through many years of scrutinizing young applicants. You no doubt saw the ease with which I distinguished who, among your companions, was likely to make a kitchen apprentice, who were potential maidservants, and who could only become a gardener's boy. I can do this in seconds, and I am almost never wrong. Am I, Mr. Hugo?"

"Very seldom," Hugo agreed, from the other side of the room.

Neither of us had seen him come in. We both jumped.

"Take Christopher and Conrad to their quarters, Mr. Hugo, show them the establishment, and acquaint them with their hours," Mr. Amos said. "We have our two Improvers, I am glad to say."

"Yes, sir. Where do they eat?" Hugo asked.

We could see this was an important question. Mr. Amos looked gravely at us, looked at the ceiling, and rocked on his feet. "Quite," he said. "The Middle Hall will be their station once it is in use, but since it is not . . . *Not* the Lower Hall, I fear. Young men are too prone to horseplay with the maidservants. I think we must reluctantly do as we temporarily did with the footmen and allow them to eat in the Upper Hall until the period of mourning for the late Count is past and we have Stallery full of guests again. Show them, will you. I want them present and properly dressed when I Serve Tea."

Hugo held open the door beside him and said, in his pleasant way, "If you'd come with me, then."

As I picked up my plastic bag and followed Christopher through that door, I was nervous all over again, in quite a new way. I felt as if I had accidentally entered the priesthood and wasn't cut out for it. I expected Christopher to be feeling the same, but as Hugo showed us into a slow brown lift—"Strictly for Staff," he said. "*Never* show Family or their friends to a Staff lift"—and pressed button A, for the attics, I could see Christopher was wholly delighted, bubbling over with delight, as if he had just won a game. He looked the way I felt whenever Uncle Alfred pleaded with me to go on doing the cooking.

Christopher seemed quite unable to contain his

joy while the lift climbed sluggishly upward. "Tell me," he burst out at Hugo, "will Conrad and I learn your trick of entering a room through a crack in the floorboards? I once read a book where a manservant was always oozing in like some soundless liquid, but with you it was more like soundless *gas*! You were just *there*! Was it magic?"

Hugo grinned at this. Now I knew he was Mr. Amos's son, I could see the likeness. He had the big lips and the snubby nose, but in Hugo it was rather nice-looking. Otherwise, he was such a different size and shape, and seemed such a different sort of person, that it was hard to see him stepping into his father's place when Mr. Amos retired. "You'll learn how to enter a room," he said, leaning against the wall of the lift. "My father had me doing it for hours before he let me go into a room where the Family were. But the main thing you'll learn—I'm warning you—is how to be on your feet for fourteen hours at a stretch. Staff never sit down. Any more questions?"

"Hundreds," Christopher said. "So many I can't think what to ask first." This was evidently true. He had to stop and stare at the wall, trying to decide.

I seized the space to ask, "Should we call you *Mr.* Hugo?"

"Only in front of my father," Hugo said with another grin. "He's very strict about it."

"Because you're the heir to the butlership?" Christopher asked irrepressibly.

"That's right," said Hugo.

"Rather you than me!" Christopher said.

"Quite," Hugo answered, rather sadly.

Christopher looked at him shrewdly, but he said nothing else until the lift finally made it up to the attics. Then he said, "My God! A rat maze!"

Hugo and I both laughed, because it *was* like that up there. The roof was quite low, with skylights in it, so you could see narrow wooden corridors lined with doors running in all directions. It was warm and smelled of wood. I'm going to get lost up here, I thought.

"You'll be sharing a room along here," Hugo said, leading the way along a corridor that looked just like any of the rest. All the doors were painted the same dull red-brown. He opened a door like all the others. "You'll have to be careful not to make too much noise up here," he remarked. "You'll be among quite senior Staff."

Beyond the door was a fresh white room with a sloping ceiling and two narrow white beds. The little low window looked out at blue mountains, and sun streamed in. It smelled of warm whitewash. There was a carpet, a chest of drawers, and a curtained corner for hanging things in. It was rather nicer than my room at home. I looked at Christopher, expecting him to be used to much fancier bedrooms. But I'd forgotten he'd just spent a month in a gypsy caravan. He looked around with pleasure.

"Nice," he said. "Companionable. Twice as big as a caravan. Er—bathroom?"

"The end of the corridor," Hugo said. "The

corner room on every passage is always a bathroom. Now come and get your uniforms. This way."

I hurriedly dumped my plastic bag on a bed, wondering if I would ever find it again, and we followed Hugo back out into the corridor.

Here Christopher said, "Just a second." He took off his narrow silk tie and wrapped it around the doorknob on the outside of the door. "Now we can find ourselves again," he said. "Or isn't it allowed?" he asked Hugo.

"I've no idea," Hugo said. "I don't think anyone's thought of doing it before."

"Then you must all have the most wonderful sense of direction," Christopher said. "Is this the bathroom?"

Hugo nodded. We both stuck our heads around the door, and Christopher nodded approvingly. "All the essentials," he said. "Far better than a tin tub or a hedge. Towels?"

"In the linen store next to the uniforms," Hugo told him. "This way."

He led us in zigzags through the narrow corridors to a place with a bigger skylight than usual. Here the doors were slatted, although they were the same red-brown as all the others. He opened the first slatted door. "Better take a towel each," he said.

We gazed at a room twice the size of the one we had been given, filled with shelves piled with folded towels, sheets, and blankets. Enough for an army, it seemed to me.

"How many Staff *are* there?" Christopher asked as we each took a big red-brown towel.

"We're down to just fifty indoors at the moment," Hugo said. "When we start entertaining again, we'll go up to nearly a hundred. But the mourning period for Count Rudolf isn't over for another fortnight, so we're very quiet until then. Plenty of time for you to find your feet. Uniforms are this way."

He led us to the next slatted door. Beyond it was an even bigger room. It had shelves like a public library, and all the shelves were stacked with clothes. There was pile after pile of pure white shirts, a wall of velvet breeches, neat towers of folded waistcoats, stack upon stack of striped stockings, rails hung with starched white neckcloths, and more shelves devoted to yellow-striped aprons. Underneath the shelves were cardboard boxes of buckled shoes. A strong spell against moths made my eyes water. Christopher's eyes went wide, but I only dimly saw Hugo going around, checking labels, looking at us measuringly, and then taking down garments from the shelves.

We each got two shirts, two aprons, four pairs of underpants, four pairs of stockings, one waistcoat, and one pair of velvet breeches. Hugo followed those with neckcloths, carefully laid over the growing heaps in our arms, and then a striped nightshirt apiece. "Do you know your shoe sizes?" he asked.

Neither of us did. Hugo whipped up a sliding measure from among the cardboard boxes and swiftly found out. Then he fetched buckled shoes from the boxes and made us try them on, efficiently checking where our toes came to and how the heels fitted. "It's important your shoes don't hurt," he said. "You're on your feet so much." I could see he made a very good valet.

"Right," he said, dumping a gleaming pair of shoes each on top of the nightshirts. "Go and get into the uniforms and put the rest away and meet me by the lift in ten minutes." He fetched a slender gold watch out of his waistcoat pocket and looked at the time. "Make that seven minutes," he said. "Or I won't have time to show you the house. I have to start for Ludwich with Count Robert at four."

I put my chin on the shoes to hold them steady and tried to remember the way we had come here. So did Christopher. I went one way with my pile of clothes. Christopher, with a vague but purposeful look, marched off in exactly the opposite direction.

Hugo went racing after Christopher, shouting, "*Stop!* Not *there!*" He sounded so horrified that Christopher swung around in alarm.

"What's wrong?" he asked.

Hugo pointed to a wide red-brown stripe painted on the wall beside Christopher. "You mustn't *ever* go past this line," he said. "It's the women's end of the attics beyond that. You'd be sacked on the spot if you were found on the wrong side of it."

"Oh," said Christopher. "Is that *all*? From the way you yelled, I thought there must be a hundred-foot drop along there. Which is the right way back to our room, then?"

Hugo pointed. It was in a direction that neither of us had thought of taking. We hurried off that way, feeling rather foolish, and after a while, more by luck than anything, arrived in the corridor where Christopher's tie hung on the doorknob.

"What foresight on my part!" Christopher said as we each dumped our armloads of clothing on a bed. "I don't know about you, Grant, but I know I'm going to look and feel a perfect idiot in these clothes, though not as silly as I'm going to feel in this night-shirt tonight."

"We'll get used to it," I said grumpily as I scrambled out of my own clothes. By this time Christopher's confident way of going on was annoying me.

"Do I detect," Christopher asked, climbing out of his trousers and hanging them carefully on the rail of his bed, "a certain hostility in you, Grant? Have you, by any chance, let Mr. Amos's ideas get to you? *Are* you regarding me as a rival?"

"I suppose I'm bound to," I said. I turned the black knee-length trousers around to see which was front and which was back. It wasn't easy to tell.

"Then let me set your mind at rest, Grant," Christopher said, puzzling over the breeches, too. "And hang on. I think we need to put the stockings on first. These things buckle over the stripy socks and—I hope—help to keep the wretched things up. I sincerely hope so. I hate wrinkles round my ankles. Anyway, forget Mr. Amos. I shall only be here for a short time."

"Why?" I said. "Are you sure?"

"Positive," Christopher said, wriggling a bare foot dubiously into a striped stocking. "I'm only doing this while I'm on my way to something quite different. When I find what I want, I shall leave at once."

I was at that moment standing on one foot while I tried to put a stocking on, too. It was floppy and it twisted and the top kept closing up. I was so astonished to hear that Christopher was in exactly the same position as me, that I overbalanced. After a moment or so of frantic hopping about, I sat on the floor with a crash.

"I see your feelings overwhelm you," Christopher remarked. "You really needn't worry, Grant. Regard me as a complete amateur. I shall never be a serious footman, let alone a valet or a butler."

6

❧⚜❧

AFTER WHAT CHRISTOPHER had said, I expected
him to look all wrong in his new clothes. Not a bit of
it. As soon as he had tightened the straps of his
striped waistcoat, so that it sat trimly around his waist,
and tied the white neckcloth under his chin, he looked
a perfect, jaunty young footman. I was the one who
looked wrong. I could see myself in the long stripe of
mirror on the back of the door looking, ever so
slightly, a mess. This was odd *and* unfair, because my
hair was as black as Christopher's and I was not fat
and there was nothing wrong with my face. But I
looked as if I had stuffed my head through a hole on
the top of a suit of clothes meant for someone else, the
way you do for trick photographs.

"Seven minutes up," Christopher said, folding
back the frill at the wrist of his shirt to look at his
watch. "No time to admire yourself, Grant."

As we left the room, I remembered that I had
left the port wine cork in the pocket of my own
trousers. Mayor Seuly had said to carry it with me at
all times. I had to dive back to get it and stuff it

into . . . Oh. The wretched breeches turned out not to have pockets. I crammed the cork into a narrow waistcoat pocket as I followed Christopher out. I was going to tell him it was a keepsake from home, if he asked, but he never seemed to notice.

Hugo had his watch out when we found him. "You'll have to keep better time than this," he said. "My father insists on it." He put his watch away in order to tweak at my neckcloth, then at Christopher's. Everyone at Stallery was *always* trying to rearrange our neckcloths, but we didn't know that then, and we both backed away in surprise. "Follow me," Hugo said.

We didn't go down in the lift. Hugo led us down narrow, creaking stairs to the next floor. Here the ceilings were higher and the corridors wider, with matting on them, but everywhere was rather dark. "This is the nursery floor," he said. "At the moment, we use some of the rooms for the housekeepers and the sort of guests who don't eat with the Family, valets, the accountant, and so on."

On the way to the next flight of stairs, he opened a door to show us a long, dark, polished room with a rocking horse halfway down it, looking rather lonely. "Day nursery," he said.

The next flight of stairs was wider and had matting for carpet. At the bottom, the ceilings were a bit higher still, and there was carpet everywhere, new and pungent and dove gray. There were pictures on the walls. "Guest rooms?" Christopher guessed brightly.

"*Overflow* guest rooms." Hugo corrected him. "My father has his quarters on this floor," he added, taking us to the next flight of stairs. These stairs were quite broad and carpeted rather better than the best hotel in Stallchester.

Below this, it was suddenly opulent. Christopher pursed his mouth and whispered out a whistle as we stared along a wide passageway with a carpet like pale blue moss, running through a vista of gold-and-crimson archways, white statues, and golden ornaments on marble-topped tables with bent gold legs. There were vases of flowers everywhere here. The air felt thick and scented.

Hugo took us right along this passage. "You'll need to know this floor," he said, "in case you have to deliver anything to one of the Family's rooms." He pointed to each huge white double door as we came to it, saying, "Main guest room, red guest room, Count Robert's rooms, blue guest room, painted guest room. The Countess has the rose rooms, through here. This one is the white guest room, and Lady Felice has the rooms on this corner. Round beyond there are the lilac room and the yellow room. We don't use these so often, but you'd better know. Have you got all that?"

"Only vaguely," Christopher admitted.

"There's a plan in the undercroft," Hugo said, and he led us on, down wide, shallow steps this time, blue and soft like the passage, to a floor more palatial yet. My head was spinning by this time, but I sort of aimed my face where Hugo pointed and tried to look intelligent. "Ballroom, banquet room, music room, Grand Saloon," he said, and I saw vast spaces, enormous chandeliers, vistas of gold-rimmed sofas, and one room with about a hundred yards of table lined with flimsy gold chairs. "We don't use these more than two or three times a year," Hugo told us, "but they all have to be kept up, of course. There was going to be a grand ball here for Lady Felice's coming-of-age, but it had to be canceled when the Count died. Pity. But we'll be using them again in a couple of weeks to celebrate Count Robert's engagement. We had a spectacular ball here four years ago when the present Count was eighteen. Almost all the titles in Europe came. We used ten thousand candles and nearly two thousand bottles of champagne."

"Quite a party," Christopher remarked as we went past the main grand stairway. We craned and saw it led down into a huge hall with a streaky black marble floor.

Hugo pointed a thumb down the stairway. "The rooms down there are used by the Family most of the time—drawing rooms, dining rooms, library, and so on—but Staff are not allowed to use these stairs. Don't forget."

"Makes me want to slide down those banisters at once," Christopher murmured as Hugo took us to a much narrower flight of stairs instead, which came out into the hall behind the Family lift. He pointed to the various big black doors and told us which was which, but he said we couldn't look inside the rooms because Family might be using any

74

one of them. We nodded, and our feet skidded in our new shoes on the black, streaky floor.

Then we thudded through a door covered with green cloth, and everywhere was suddenly gray stone and plain wood. Hugo pointed, "My father's pantry, Family china scullery, silver room, flower room, Staff toilets. We go down here to the undercroft."

He went galloping down a flight of steep stone steps. As we clattered down after him, I suddenly felt as if I were back at school. It had that smell, rather too warm and mixed with chalk and cooking, and like school, there was that feeling of lots of people about, many voices in the distance and large numbers of feet shuffling and hurrying. A girl laughed, making echoes, and—again like school—a bell rang somewhere.

The bell was ringing in the large stone lobby at the bottom of the stairs. There was a huge board there with row upon row of little round lights on it. One was flashing red more or less in the middle of it. A lady in a neat brown-and-yellow-striped dress and a yellow cap on her gray hair was looking up at the light rather anxiously.

"Oh, Hugo," she said gladly as we clattered off the stairs. "It's Count Robert."

Hugo strode across to the board. "Right," he said, and unhooked a sort of phone from the side, which seemed to stop the light flashing at once. I looked up at it as it went off. White letters under the light said *CR Bdm*. All the lights had similar incomprehensible labels. *Stl Rm*, I read. *Bkfst Rm*,

Dng Rm, *Hskpr*, *C Bthrm*, *Stbls*. The only clear one was in the middle at the bottom. It said *Mr. Amos*.

Meanwhile, a voice was distantly snapping out of the phone thing. It sounded nervous and commanding. "Coming right away, my lord," Hugo said to it. He hung the phone up and turned to us. "I've got to go. I'll have to leave you here with Miss Semple. She's our Under-Housekeeper. Do you mind showing these Improvers round the undercroft?" he asked the lady.

"Not at all," she said. "You'd better go. He's been ringing for three minutes now." Hugo grinned at all of us and went racing up the stone steps again. We were left with Miss Semple, who smiled a mild, cheerful smile at us. "And your names are?"

"Conrad T—Grant," I said. I only remembered my alias just in time.

Christopher was just the same. He said, "Christopher—er, er—Smith," and backed away from her a little.

"Conrad and Christopher," she said. "Two Cs." Then she made us *both* start backward by pouncing on us and straightening our neckcloths. "*That's* better!" she said. "I've just been putting your duty rosters up on our bulletin board. Come and look."

It was really more like school than ever. There was a long, long board, taking up all the wall beside the stairs. This was divided into sections by thick black lines, with black headings over each section: *Housemaids*, *Footmen*, *Parlor Staff*, *Stillroom*,

Laundry, *Kitchen*, we read, and right at the end beside the stairs, we found *Improvers*. There were lists and timetables pinned under each heading, but it was like school again in the way there were other, less official notices scattered about the board. A big pink one said, "*Housemaids' KneesUp, 8:30 Thurs. All Welcome.*" Miss Semple tut-tutted and took that one down as we came to it. Another one read, in dark blue letters, "*Chef wants that hat returned NOW!!*" Miss Semple left that one up. She also left a yellow paper that said, "*Mrs. Baldock still wants to know who scattered those pins in the Conservatory.*"

When we came to the *Improvers* column, we saw two large sheets of paper neatly ruled into seven and labeled with the days of the week. Times of the day, from six in the morning until midnight, were written on the left, and lines ruled for each hour. Almost every one of the boxes made like this was filled with neat gray spidery writing. "*6:00,*" I read on the left-hand sheet, "*Collect shoes to take to Blacking Rm for cleaning. 7:00, Join Footmen in readying Breakfast Rm. 8:00, On duty in Breakfast Rm . . .*" My eyes scudded on, with increasing dismay, to things like "*2:00, Training session in Laundry, 3:00, Training sessions in Stillroom and Kitchen annex 3 with 2nd Underchef.*" It was almost a relief to find a square labeled simply "*Mr. Amos*" from time to time. On down my eyes went, anxiously, to the last box, "*11:00–12:00.*" That said, "*On call in Upper Hall.*" Bad, I thought. I couldn't see one spare minute in which I might manage to summon a Walker, once I knew who was causing my Fate. And there didn't seem to be any boxes with meals marked in them either.

Christopher seemed to be trying to hide even worse dismay than I felt. "This is a *disaster*!" I heard him mutter as he scanned the closely filled right-hand sheet. He put a finger out to one of the only empty squares there was. "Er, someone seems to have forgotten to fill this square in."

"No mistake," Miss Semple said, in her high, cheerful voice. She was one of those nice, kind people who have no sense of humor at all. "You both have two hours off on Wednesday afternoons and two more on a Thursday morning. That's a legal requirement."

"Glad to hear it!" Christopher said faintly.

"And another hour to yourselves on a Sunday, so that you can write home," Miss Semple added. "Your full day off comes every six weeks and you can—" A bell began to ring on the board across the lobby. Miss Semple whirled around to look. "That's Mr. Amos!" She hurried over and unhooked the phone.

While she was busy saying, "Yes, Mr. Amos . . . No, Mr. Amos . . . ," I said to Christopher, "Why did you say this was a disaster?"

"Well, er," he said. "Grant, did you *know* we were going to be kept this busy when you applied for the job?"

"No," I said dolefully.

Christopher was going to say more, but Miss Semple hooked the phone back and hastened across the lobby again, saying confusingly, "You can take two free days together every three months if you prefer, but I shall have to show you the undercroft later. Hurry upstairs, boys. Mr. Amos wants a word with you before Tea is Served."

We ran up the stone stairs. As Christopher said late that night, if we had grasped one thing about Stallery by then, it was that you did what Mr. Amos said, and you did it fast. "Before he's said it, if possible," Christopher added.

Mr. Amos was waiting for us in the wood-and-stone passage upstairs. He was smoking a cigar. Billows of strong blue smoke surrounded us as he said, "Don't pant. Staff should never look hurried unless Family particularly tells you to hurry. That's your first lesson. Second— Straighten those neckcloths, both of you." He waited, looking irritated, while we fumbled at the white cloths and tried not to pant and not to cough in the smoke. "Second lesson," he said. "Remember at all times that what you really are is living pieces of furniture." He pointed the cigar at us three times, in time to the words. "Living. Pieces. Of furniture. Got that?" We nodded. "No, *no!*" he said. "You say, 'Yes, Mr. Amos— '"

"Yes, Mr. Amos," we chorused.

"Better," he said. "Say it smarter next time. And like furniture, you stand against the walls and seem to be made of wood. When Family asks you for anything, you give it them or you do it, as gracefully and correctly as possible, but you do not speak unless Family makes a personal remark to you. What would you say if the Countess gives you a personal order?"

"Yes, your ladyship?" I suggested.

"No, *no*!" Mr. Amos said, billowing smoke at me. "Third lesson. The Countess and Lady Felice are to be addressed as 'my lady' and Count Robert as 'my lord.' Now bear these lessons firmly in mind. You are about to be shown to the Countess while we Serve Tea. You are there for this moment simply to observe and learn. Watch me, watch the footman on duty, and otherwise behave like two chairs against the wall."

His stone-colored eyes stared at us expectantly. After a moment we realized why and chorused again, "Yes, Mr. Amos."

"And chairs would be slightly more use," he said. "Now, repeat back to me—"

Luckily at that moment a bell shrilled downstairs in the lobby.

"Ah," said Mr. Amos. "The Countess has Rung for Tea." He stubbed out his cigar on a piece of wall that was black and gray with having cigars stubbed on it and put the dead cigar into a pocket of his striped waistcoat. Then he stuck out both arms, rather like a penguin, to make his shirt cuffs show and shook his thick shoulders to settle his coat. "Follow me," he said, and pushed through the green cloth door into the hall.

We followed his solemn pear-shaped back out into the middle of the huge black-floored hall. There his voice rang around the space. "Wait here." So we waited while he went to one of the large doors on the other side of the hall and pushed the two halves of it gently open. "You rang, my lady?" His voice came to us, smooth and rich and full of respect.

Probably someone said something in the room beyond. Mr. Amos bowed and backed away into the hall, gently closing the doors. For a moment after that, I could hardly see or hear anything, because I knew I was now actually going to see the person causing my bad karma. I was going to *know* who they were and I was going to have to summon a Walker. My heart banged, and I could hardly breathe. My face must have looked odd, because I saw Christopher give me a surprised, searching look, but he had no time to say anything. At that moment the footman called Andrew backed out through the distant green door, carefully towing a high-tea trolley.

Later that day Christopher said this was when he began to feel he might be in church. Mr. Amos gestured to us to fall in on either side of Andrew, while he walked in front of the trolley himself and threw the double door wide open so that we could all parade into the room beyond in a solemn procession, with the trolley rattling among us. But it didn't go quite smoothly. Just as we got to the doorway, Andrew had to stop the trolley to let a young blond lady go through first.

She was very good-looking. Christopher and I agreed on that. We both stared, although we noticed that Andrew very carefully didn't look at her. But she did not seem to see me, or Christopher, or

Andrew, though she nodded at Mr. Amos and said, "Oh, good. I'm in time for Tea." She went on into the room, where she sat bouncily on one of the several silk sofas, opposite the lady who was already there. "Mother, guess what—"

"Hush, Felice dear," the other lady said.

This was because the church service was still going on, and the other lady—the Countess—did not want it interrupted. She was one of those who had to have everything exactly so and done in the right order.

If you looked at her quickly, this Countess, you thought she was the same age as the good-looking one, Lady Felice. She was just as blond and just as slender, and her dark lilac dress made her face look pure and delicate, almost like a teenager's. But when she moved, you saw she had studied for years and years how to move gracefully, and when she spoke, her face took on expressions that were terribly *sweet*, in a way that showed she had been studying expressions for years, too. After that, you saw that the delicate look was careful, careful, expert makeup.

By this time two small jerks of Mr. Amos's chin had sent me and Christopher to stand with our backs against the wall on either side of the doorway. Andrew stopped the trolley and shut the doors—practically soundlessly—and Mr. Amos gently produced a set of little tables, which he placed out beside the ladies. Then back and forth he and Andrew went, back and forth from trolley to tables, setting a thin gold-rimmed plate and a fluted cup and saucer on three of the tables, then napkins and little forks and spoons. Then there was the teapot to place on its special mat on another table, a strainer in a bowl, a gold-edged jug of cream, and a boat-shaped thing full of sugar cubes. All just so.

Then there was a pause. The ladies sat. The teapot sat, too, steaming faintly.

Christopher, who was staring ahead looking so totally blank that he seemed to have no brain at all, said that at this point he was thinking the tea in the pot would soon be cold. Or stewed. So was I, a bit. But mostly I was feeling really let down. I stared and stared at the Countess, hoping I would suddenly *know* that she was the person causing my Fate. I even looked at Lady Felice and wondered, but I could tell she was just a normal, happy kind of person who was having to behave politely in front of the Countess. The Countess was a sort of hidden dragon. That was why I thought she might be the one. She was very like a teacher we had in my third year. Mrs. Polak *seemed* very sweet, but she could really give you grief, and I could see the Countess was the same. But I didn't get any *knowing* off her at all.

It has to be Count Robert, then, I thought.

"Amos," the Countess said in a lovely, melodious voice, "Amos, perhaps you could tell my son, the Count, that we are waiting to have tea."

"Certainly, my lady." Mr. Amos nodded at Andrew, and Andrew scudded out of the room.

We waited some more, at least five minutes to judge from the way my feet ached. Then Andrew slithered back between the doors and whispered to Mr. Amos.

Mr. Amos turned to the Countess. "I regret to tell you, my lady, that Count Robert left for Ludwich some twenty minutes ago."

"Ludwich!" exclaimed the Countess. I wondered why she didn't know. "What on earth does he need to go to Ludwich for? And did he give *any* indication of how long he proposed to be away?"

Mr. Amos's pear-shaped body bent in a bow. "I gather he intended a stay of about a week, my lady."

"That's what I was going to tell you, Mother," Lady Felice put in.

At this, something happened to the Countess's face, a hard sort of movement under the delicate features. She gave a tinkly little laugh. "Well!" she said. "At least the tea has had time to brew. Please pour, Amos."

Ouch! I thought. The Count's going to be in for it when he gets back!

This was the signal for the church service to go on. Mr. Amos poured tea as if it were the water of life. It was steaming so healthily that Christopher said later that he was sure there was a keep-warm spell in the mat. Andrew offered cream. The Countess waved him away and got given lemon in transparent-thin slices by Mr. Amos instead. Then Andrew moved in with the sugar boat, and the Countess let him give her four lumps.

While the show moved on to Lady Felice, the Countess said, as if she were covering up an awkward pause, "I see we have two new page boys, Amos."

"Improvers, my lady," Mr. Amos said, "who will function as pages until they learn the work." His head jerked sharply at Christopher. "Christopher, be good enough to hand the sandwiches."

Christopher jumped. I could see his mind had been miles away, but he pulled himself together and heaved the sandwiches up off the trolley. There were scores of them, tiny, thin things with no crusts and thick, savory-smelling fillings, heaped up on a vast oval silver plate. Christopher sniffed at them yearningly as he hoisted the plate up, but he went and held the plate out to the Countess very gallantly, with a flourishing bow that matched the way he looked. The Countess seemed startled, but she took six sandwiches. Mr. Amos frowned as Christopher brought the plate to Lady Felice and went on one knee to hold it out to her.

Christopher had to go back and forth. It was amazing how much those two slim ladies ate. And all the while Mr. Amos stood back like a stuffed penguin and frowned. I could see he thought Christopher was too fancy.

"Ludwich!" the Countess complained after about her fifteenth sandwich. "Whatever does Robert *mean* by it? Without warning, too!"

She went on about it rather. Eventually Lady Felice dumped her eighteenth sandwich back on her plate in an irritated way and said, "Really, Mother, does it *matter*?"

She got a stare. The Countess had ice blue eyes, big ones, and the stare was glacial. "Of course it matters, dear. It's extreme discourtesy to *me*."

"But he was probably called away on business," Lady Felice said. "He was telling me that his bonds and shares—"

I could see this was quite a cunning thing to say, a bit like the way Anthea and I used to ask Uncle Alfred for money to stop him raging when we'd broken something. The Countess held up a small, gentle hand all over rings to stop Lady Felice. "Please, darling! I know nothing about finance. Amos, are there cakes?"

It was my turn to jump. Mr. Amos said, "Conrad, hand the cakes now, please."

They were at the bottom of the trolley on another huge silver plate. I almost staggered as I heaved it up. The plate was truly heavy and made heavier still by being piled so with all the tiniest and most delicious pastries you could imagine. Scents of cream, fruit, rosewater, almond, meringue, and chocolate hit my nose. I felt my stomach whir. It sounded so loud to me that I couldn't think of any elegant way to hand those cakes. I simply walked over to the Countess and held the plate out to her.

Mr. Amos frowned again. I could tell he thought I was too plain.

Luckily I didn't have to heave the plate about for very long. The Countess had just wanted to change the subject, I think. She only took three cakes. Lady Felice had one. How they could bear not to eat the lot, I shall never know.

After that we had the church service again, with everything being cleared back onto the trolley in the proper religious order. Mr. Amos and Andrew bowed. Both glared sideways at us until we realized we had to bow, too. Then we were allowed to push the trolley away into the hall.

"Tea ceremony over," Christopher muttered, under the clattering.

But it was not, not quite. In the middle of the hall Mr. Amos stopped and told us off. He made me at least feel quite awful. "In front of *Family*!" he kept saying. "One of you flounces like a pansy, and the other plods like a yokel!" Then he went on to the way we stood. "You do *not* gaze like half-wits; you do *not* stand to attention like common soldiers. You are in a proper household here. You behave *right*. Watch Andrew next time. He stands against a wall as if it were *natural*."

"Yes, Mr. Amos," we said miserably.

He allowed us to go away down the stone stairs in the end. And there the bewildering day went on and on. Miss Semple was waiting to show us the undercroft. Christopher tried to sidle off then, but she turned and shot him a mild but all-seeing look and shook her head. He came glumly to heel. I followed her resignedly anyway. It was clear to me that I was here for a week, until Count Robert came back, so I thought I might as well learn my way about.

The undercroft was vast. I had to be shown all over it again the next day because it was too big to take in that first time. All I remembered was a confusion of steams and scents from several kitchens and a laundry, and people in brown-and-gold uniform rushing about. There were cold stores and dry stores full of food, and a locked door leading to the cellars. There was at least one room dedicated entirely to crockery, where two girls seemed to be washing up all the time. I was very surprised when Miss Semple told us this was just crockery for Staff. The good china for the Family was upstairs in another pantry with another set of maids to wash it. Family and Staff were like two different worlds that only linked together at certain times and places.

Christopher became fascinated by this. "It's my amateur status, Grant," he told me. "It allows me to take a detached view of the tribal customs here. You must admit it's a strange setup when all these people chase about in the basement, just to look after two women."

He was so fascinated that he asked question after question at supper. Our part of the Staff had supper in the Upper Hall at seven, so that we would be ready to wait on the Family when they dined at eight. Their food was called Dinner and was very formal, but ours was fairly formal, too. A whole lot of Staff gathered round a big table at one end of a large sort of sitting room. There were chairs and magazines in the other end, and a smaller board with lights, in case anyone needed us while we were there, but no television. Andrew told me rather sadly that you couldn't get a signal up in Stallery, not for any money. Andrew was the nicest of the footmen by far.

Anyway, there were six footmen, and us, and a dismal old man with a snuffle (he was steward or accountant or something) and a whole lot of women. Miss Semple was there, of course, and she told me that the very smart elderly woman was the Countess's maid, and the almost as smart younger one was Lady Felice's. Those two weren't very nice. They only spoke to each other. But there were the Upper Stillroom Maid, the Head of Housemaids, the Head of Parlormaids, and several other Heads of Somethings. Apparently there should have been Hugo, too, but he had gone to Ludwich with Count Robert. All the other Staff ate in the Lower Hall, except Mr. Amos, who had his meals alone, Miss Semple said.

There was also Mrs. Baldock. She was Housekeeper, but I kept thinking of her as the Headmistress. She was the largest woman I had ever seen, a vast six-footer with iron gray hair and a huge bosom. The most noticeable thing about her was the purple flush up each side of her large face. Christopher said this didn't look healthy to him. "Possibly she drinks, Grant," he said, but this was later. At that supper she swept in after all the rest of us. Everyone stood up for her. Mrs. Baldock said a short grace, then looked down the table until she saw Christopher and me.

"I'll expect you two in the Housekeeper's Room promptly at nine-thirty tomorrow," she said.

This sounded so ominous to me that I kept my head down and said nothing for most of the meal. But Christopher was another matter. When supper came——and it was steak pie and marvelous, with massive amounts of potatoes in butter——it was brought in by four maids. Mrs. Baldock cut the pie, and the maids carried it around to us. Nobody started eating until Mrs. Baldock did.

"What is this?" Christopher said as the maid brought his slice.

"Steak pie, sir," the girl said. She was about Christopher's age, and you could see she thought he was ever so handsome.

"No, I mean, the way there are Staff to wait on Staff," Christopher said. "When do *you* get to eat?"

"We have high tea at six-thirty, sir," the girl said, "but——"

"What a lot of meals!" Christopher said. "Doesn't that take another whole kitchen and a whole lot more Staff to wait on *you*?"

"Well, only sort of," the girl said. Her eyes went nervously to Mrs. Baldock. "Please, sir, we're not supposed to hold conversations while we're serving."

"Then I'll ask *you*," Christopher said to Andrew. "Do you see any reason why this serving business should ever stop? *We* have supper now, so as to wait on the Family, and these charming young ladies have theirs at six-thirty in order to wait on *us*. And when *they* are waited on, those people must have to eat at six, and before that some *other* people have to eat earlier still in order to wait on *them*. There must be some Staff who have supper at breakfast time in order to fit all this serving *in*."

Andrew laughed, but some of the other footmen were not amused. The one called Gregor growled, "Cheeky little beggar!" and the one called Philip said, "You think you're quite a card, don't you?" Behind them all four maids were trying not to giggle, and from the head of the table, Mrs. Baldock was staring. Well, everyone was staring. Most of the Head Maids were annoyed, and the two Lady's Maids were scandalized, but Mrs. Baldock stared with no expression at all. There was no way of knowing if she approved of Christopher or was about to sack him on the spot.

"Someone must be cooking all the time," Christopher said. "How do you manage with only three kitchens?"

Mrs. Baldock spoke. She said, "*And* a bakery. That will do, young man."

"Yes, ma'am," Christopher said. "Delicious pie, whichever kitchen it came from." He and Mrs. Baldock eyed each other down the length of the table. Everyone's heads turned from one to the other like people's at a tennis match. Christopher smiled sweetly. "Pure curiosity, ma'am," he said.

Mrs. Baldock just said, "Hmm," and turned her attention to her plate.

Christopher kept a wary eye on her, but he went on asking questions.

7

❦

WE HAD TO jump up as soon as we had finished supper. We left the maids clearing plates and giggling at Christopher's back and hurried upstairs with the footmen to the dining room. This was a tall, gloomy room that matched the black-floored hall. Mr. Amos was waiting there to show us how to fold stiff white napkins into a fancy boat shape and then to instruct us in the right way to make two little silver islands of cutlery and wineglasses on the shiny black table. We had to put each knife, fork, and spoon exactly in its right place.

Christopher went rather pale while we were trying to get it right. "Indigestion, Grant," he told me in a sorrowful whisper. "Bolting pie and then running upstairs is not what I'm used to."

"That won't be the only thing that disagrees with you if Mr. Amos hears you," the surly footman—Gregor—said to him. "Hold your tongue. Put this cloth over that arm, both of you, and stand by that wall. Don't move, or I'll belt you one."

We spent the next hour doing just that. We were

supposed to be attending to what Mr. Amos and the footmen did as they circled in and out around the two Ladies sitting each at their little island of glass and silver, but I think I dozed on my feet half the time. The rest of the time I stared at a big picture of a dead bird and some fruit on the opposite wall and wished I could be at home in the bookshop. The two Ladies bored me stiff. They talked the whole time about the clothes they were going to buy as soon as the time of mourning was over and where they would stay in Ludwich while they were shopping. And they seemed to go on eating forever.

When at last they were finished, we were allowed to go back to the undercroft, but we had to stay in the Upper Hall in case we were needed to bring things to the Ladies in the drawing room. Gregor watched us to make sure we didn't try to slip away. We sat side by side on a hard sofa as far away from Gregor as we could get, trying not to listen to the two Lady's Maids, who were doing embroidery quite near to us and whispering gossipy things to each other.

"She's got a whole drawerful of keepsakes from him by now," said one.

The other one said, "If that gets found out, they'll *both* be in trouble."

"I wouldn't be in her shoes for any money," the first one said.

I yawned. I couldn't help it.

"Come, come, Grant," Christopher said. "On these occasions you have to keep going by taking an interest in *little* things, like those two maids do. We've been here a good seven hours by now. I know they seem the longest we've ever known, but you must have found *some* little thing to be amazed about *somewhere*."

I had, now he came to remind me. "Yes," I said. "How do the Countess and Lady Felice eat so much and stay so *thin*?"

"Good question," Christopher replied. "They fair put it away, don't they? The young one probably rushes about, but the old one is slightly stately. She ought by rights to be the size of Mrs. Baldock. Perhaps the chef charms her food. But my guess is she takes slim spells. I dare you to go over and ask her Lady's Maid if I'm right."

I looked across at the two gossiping women. I laughed. "No. You do it."

Christopher didn't dare either, so we went on to talk about other things we had noticed. This was when Christopher told me his theory that Mrs. Baldock drank. But right at the end, just before Andrew came in and said we could go off to bed, Christopher astounded me by asking, "By the way, what or where is this Ludwich that the Countess is so peeved with the Count for vanishing to?"

I stared at him. How could he not know? "It's the capital city, of course! Down in the Sussex Plains, beside the Little Rhine. Everyone knows that!"

"Oh," said Christopher. "Ah. So the Count's gone on a spree, has he? The fact is, Grant, that one gets a little confused about geography, living with the Travelers. They never bother to say where we are or where we're going. So what part of the country are we in now?"

"The English Alps," I said. "Just above Stallchester." I was still astonished.

Christopher repeated, "The English Alps. Ah," looking grave and wise. "What other Alps are there, then—as a matter of interest?"

"French, Italian, Austrian," I said. "Those Alps sort of run together. The English Alps are divided off by Frisia." Christopher looked quite bewildered. He didn't seem to know any geography at all. "Frisia's the country on the English border," I explained. "The whole of Europe is quite flat between Ludwich and Mosskva, and the Alps make a sort of half-moon round the south of that. The English Alps are to the north of the plains."

Christopher nodded to himself. I thought I heard him murmur, "Series Seven—no British Isles here, of course."

"What?" I said. "What are you on about now?"

"Nothing," he said. "I'm half asleep."

I don't think he was, although I certainly was. When Andrew said we could go, I tottered into the lift, then out of it, and fell into the nightshirt and into bed and went to sleep on the spot. I dimly heard Christopher get up later in the night. I assumed he was visiting the toilet up at the end of the corridor, and I waited, mostly asleep, for him to come back. But he was away for so long that I went properly back to sleep and never heard him returning. All I knew was that he was in bed and asleep the next morning.

They woke us up at dawn.

We got used to this in the end, but that first morning was awful. We had to put on aprons and go around with a big basket collecting shoes to be cleaned, from the attics downward. Most doors had at least one set of shoes outside them. But Mr. Amos put out four pairs of small black shoes. The Countess put out a dozen pairs, all fancy. Lady Felice put out a stack of riding boots. We had to stagger down to the undercroft with the lot, where we were very relieved to discover that they employed someone else to clean them all. I could hardly clean my face that morning, let alone shoes.

Then we were allowed to have breakfast with a crowd of red-eyed, grumpy footmen. Andrew was off duty that morning, and Gregor was in charge, and he didn't like either of us and had it in for Christopher particularly. He sent us upstairs to the Family breakfast room before we'd really finished eating. He said it was important to have someone on duty there in case one of the Family came down early.

"I bet that was a lie!" Christopher said, and he rather shocked me by helping himself to bread and marmalade from the vast sideboard. We found out that all the footmen did the same, when they finally loitered in.

And it was just as well they deigned to turn up. Lady Felice came in before seven, looking pale and pensive and wearing riding clothes. No one had expected her. Gregor had to shove the bread he was eating under the sideboard in a hurry, and his mouth was so full that one of the other footmen had to ask Lady Felice what she fancied for breakfast. She said, a bit sadly, that she only wanted rolls and coffee. She was going out riding, she said. And would Gregor go to the stables and ask them to get Iceberg saddled. Gregor couldn't speak still, or he would have sent Christopher. He had to go himself, scowling.

By the time the Countess stalked in, obviously seething for some reason, the sideboard had been lined with dishes under dome-shaped silver covers, most of them fetched from the food lift by Christopher or me, and she had a choice of anything from mixed grill to smoked kidneys and fish. She ate her way through most of them while she was interviewing the poor snuffly old accountant man.

His name was Mr. Smithers, and I think he had only just started his own breakfast when she rang for him. He kept eyeing her plates sorrowfully. But he was a long time arriving, and Gregor sent Christopher to look for him, while the Countess drummed her long pearly nails angrily on the tablecloth.

Christopher marched smartly out of the room and marched smartly in again almost at once with Mr. Smithers, who behaved as if Christopher had dragged him there by his coat collar. Gregor looked daggers at Christopher. And honestly, that was one of a good many times that I didn't blame Gregor. Christopher was so pleased with himself. When he looked like that, I usually wanted to hit him as much as Gregor did.

Mr. Smithers was in trouble with the Countess. She had an awful way of opening her ice blue eyes wide, wide, and saying in a sweet, cold, cooing voice, "*Explain* yourself, Smithers. *Why* is this so?" Or sometimes she just said, "*Why?*" which was worse.

Poor Mr. Smithers snuffled and shifted and tried to explain. It was about some part of her money that was late coming in. We had to stand there and listen while he tried.

And it was odd. It was all quite ordinary stuff, like the income from the home farms and the inn she owned in Stallstead and her property in Ludwich. I kept thinking of Uncle Alfred telling me about Stallery's worldwide dealings and the huge markets that needed the possibilities pulled to work them, and I began to wonder if Uncle Alfred had got this right. He had told me about *millions* on the stock exchange, and here was the Countess asking about sixties and eighties and hundreds. I was really confused. But then I thought it had to be the Count who dealt in the big money. *Someone* had to. You only had to look at Stallery to see it cost a bomb to run the place.

But I didn't have much time to think. Mrs. Baldock rang for us the moment the Countess had polished off Mr. Smithers and her breakfast. Christopher and I had to pelt off to the Housekeeper's Room. By the time we got there, Mrs. Baldock was pacing about among her pretty floral chairs and little twiddly tables. The purple bits down the sides of her face were almost violet with impatience.

"I can only spare you five minutes," she said. "I have to be at my daily conference with the Countess after this. There's just time to outline the nature of your training to you now. We aim, you see, to ensure that whichever of you attains the post of valet to the Count is completely versed in all aspects of domestic science. You'll be learning, first and foremost, the correct care of clothing and the correct fashion for everything a gentleman does. Proper clothes for fishing are just as important as evening dress, you know, and there are six types of formal evening wear. . . ."

She went on about clothes for a good minute. I couldn't help thinking that the Count would have had to hire a lorry when he went to Ludwich if he really did take all the clothes Mrs. Baldock said he needed. I watched her feet tramping about on the floral carpet. She had huge ankles that draped over the sides of her buckled shoes.

"But just as important are laundering, housecleaning, and bed making," she said. "And in order to learn to care for your gentleman in every way, you'll be having courses on flower arranging, haircutting, and cookery, too. Do either of you cook?"

While I was saying, "Yes, ma'am," I had the briefest glimpse of absolute horror on Christopher's face. Then he somehow managed a beguiling smile.

"No," he said. "And I couldn't arrange flowers if my life depended on it. It's beginning to look as if Conrad's going to be the next valet, isn't it?"

"The Count will shortly marry," Mrs. Baldock pointed out. "The Countess is insisting on it. By the time *his* son is of an age to require a valet, even *you* should have learned what is necessary." She gave Christopher one of her long, expressionless looks.

"But why *cooking*?" he said despairingly.

"It is the custom," Mrs. Baldock said, "for the Count's son to be sent to university accompanied by both his tutor and his valet. They will take lodgings together, and the valet will create their meals."

"I'd far rather *create* a meal than *cook* one," Christopher told her frankly.

Mrs. Baldock actually grinned. She seemed to have taken to Christopher. "Get along with you!" she said. "I can see well enough that you can do anything you set your mind to, young man. Now go and report to the Upper Laundrymaid and tell her I sent you both."

We blundered our way through the stone warren of the undercroft and finally found the laundry. There the woman in charge looked at us doubtfully, then straightened our neckcloths, and then stood back to see if this had changed her opinion of us. She sighed. "I'll start you on ironing," she said pessimistically. "Things that don't matter too much. Paula! Take these two to the pressing room, and show them what to do."

Paula materialized out of the steam and took us

in tow, but unfortunately, she turned out to be no good at explaining things. She showed us to a bare stone room with various sizes of ironing tables in it. She gave Christopher a damp linen sheet and me a pile of wettish neckcloths. She told us how to turn the irons on. Then she left.

We looked at each other. Christopher said, "Penny for them, Grant."

"It's a bit like," I said, "that story where they had to turn straw into gold."

"It is!" Christopher agreed. "And no Rumpelstiltskin to help." He pushed his iron experimentally across the sheet. "This makes no difference—or possibly more wrinkles than before."

"You have to wait for the iron to get hot," I said. "I *think*."

Christopher lifted the iron and turned it this way and that in front of his face. "A touch of warmth now," he said. "How do these things work anyway? They don't plug in. Is there a salamander inside, or something?"

I laughed. Christopher's ignorance was truly amazing. Fancy thinking a fire lizard could heat an iron! "They have a power unit inside—just like lights and cookers and tellies do."

"*Do* they? Oh!" said Christopher. "A little light came on at the end of this iron!"

"That *may* mean it's hot enough," I said. "Mine's got a light now. Let's try."

We got going. My first idea—that you could save time and effort by doing ten neckcloths at once—didn't seem to work. I cut the pile down to five, to two, and then to just one, which promptly turned yellowish and smelled. Christopher kept muttering, "I don't seem to be living up to Mrs. Baldock's high opinion of me—not at *all*!" until he startled me by crying out, "Great heavens! A *church window*! Look!"

I looked. He had a dark brown iron shape burned into the middle of his sheet.

"I wonder if it will do that again," he said.

He tried, and it did. I watched, fascinated, while Christopher printed a whole row of church windows right across the sheet. Then he went on to make a daisy shape in the lower half of it.

But at this point I was recalled to my own work by a cloud of black smoke and a very strong smell. I looked down to find that my iron had burned a neckcloth right in two and then gone on to burn its way into the ironing table beneath. I had a very deep black church window there. I found red cinders in it when I snatched the iron up.

"Oh, help!" I said.

"Panic ye not, Grant," Christopher said.

"I can't *help* it!" I said, trying to fan away rolls of brown smoke. "We're going to get into awful trouble."

"Only if things stay like this," Christopher said. He came across and looked at my disaster. "Grant," he said, "this is too deep for a church window. What you have here is probably a dugout canoe." He switched his own iron off and wagged it in my face. "I congratulate you," he said.

I nearly screamed at him. "It's not *funny*!"

"Yes, it is," he said. "Look."

I looked, and I gaped. The smoke had gone. The black boat shape was not there anymore. The ironing table was flat and complete, with its brown-blotched surface quite smooth, and on top of it lay a plain, white, badly ironed neckcloth. "How . . . ?" I said.

"No questions," Christopher said. "I shall just get rid of my own artwork." He picked up a corner of his ruined sheet and shook it. And all the church windows simply disappeared. He turned to me, looking very serious. "Grant," he said, "you didn't see me do this. Promise me you didn't, or your dugout canoe comes back deeper and blacker and smokier than ever."

I looked from him to the restored ironing table. "If I promise," I said, "can I ask you how you did it?"

"No," he said. "Just promise."

"All right. I promise," I said. "It's obvious anyway. You're a magician."

"A magician," Christopher said, "is someone who sets out ritual candles round a pentangle and then mutters words of power. Did you see me do that?"

"No," I said. "You must be a very advanced kind."

Then I was half frightened, half pleased, because I thought I had made Christopher annoyed enough to tell me about himself. "*Piffle!* Pigheaded *piffle!*" he began. "Grant—"

To my great disappointment, Miss Semple hurried in and interrupted him. "You have to stop this now, boys," she said. "Make sure the irons are switched off. Mr. Avenloch has just brought in the produce for today, and Mr. Maxim wants you to start your cookery course by learning to pick out the best."

So off we hurried once more, to a chilly stone storeroom that opened off the yard, where Mr. Avenloch was standing watching a gang of lower gardeners carry in baskets of fruit and boxes of vegetables. One of the gang was the boy with the handmade boots. He grinned at us, and we grinned back, but I didn't envy him. Mr. Avenloch was one of those tall, thin, eagle-faced types. He looked a total tyrant.

"Wipe that smile off your face, Smedley," he said, "and get you gone back to that hoeing."

When the whole gang had gone scurrying out again, Mr. Maxim pranced forward. He was almost as full of himself as Christopher was. He was Second Underchef and he had been given the extra responsibility of teaching us, and this had made him really cocky. He rubbed his hands eagerly together and said to Christopher, "You are choosing for the table of the Countess herself. Pick me out—by sight only—all the best vegetables for her."

From the look on Christopher's face, I was fairly sure he had never seen a raw vegetable in his life before this. But he made a confident pounce toward a basket of gooseberries. "Here," he said, "are some splendid peas, really big ones. Oh no, they're hairy. It can't be good for peas to have bristles, can it?"

"Those," Mr. Maxim said, "are gooseberries for the Stillroom. Try again."

A little more cautiously, Christopher approached a small box of bright red chilies. "Now here are some fine, glossy carrots," he suggested. "They probably fade a bit when you cook them." He looked at Mr. Maxim. Mr. Maxim nearly dislodged his tall white hat by clutching at his head. "No?" Christopher asked. "What are they then? Pipless strawberries? Long, thin cherries?"

By this time I was leaning against the wall bent over with laughter. Mr. Maxim rounded on me. "This is no joke!" he shouted. "He's winding me up, isn't he?"

I could see he was furious. Cocky people hate being made fun of. I shook my head and managed to pull myself together. "No, he's not," I said. "He really doesn't know. He—you see—he's lived all his life as heir to a great estate—a bit like Stallery, really—but the family fell on hard times, and he had to get a job." I looked sideways at Christopher. He put on a modest look and did not try to deny what I said. Interesting.

Mr. Maxim was instantly sorry for Christopher. "My dear boy," he said, "I quite understand. Please go round with Conrad and let him identify the produce for you." He was wonderfully kind to Christopher after that and even *quite* kind to me when I mistook a pawpaw for a vegetable marrow.

"Thanks," Christopher murmured to me while we were arranging the fruit I had chosen in a great cut glass bowl. "I owe you one, Grant."

"No, you don't," I whispered back. "Dugout canoe."

But he did end up owing me one later that day. This was after we had stood against the wall in yet another eating room, each of us with a useless white cloth draped over one arm, watching the Countess and Lady Felice eat lunch. Part of the meal was actually the bowl of fruit we had arranged that morning. This gave me a good feeling, as if I had really *done* something at last. The Countess attacked the fruit heartily, but Lady Felice took one grape, and that was all.

"Darling," said the Countess, "you've hardly eaten anything. *Why?*"

It was the bad *"Why?"* with the stare. Lady Felice looked at her plate in order not to meet the stare and muttered that she wasn't hungry. This did not satisfy the Countess at all. She went on and on about it. Was Felice ill? Should she call a doctor? What were the symptoms? Or had breakfast disagreed with her? All in the sweet, high voice.

In the end Lady Felice said, "I just don't feel like food, Mother. All right?" Her face went pink, and she almost glared at the Countess.

And the Countess said, "There's no need to be coy, dear. If you're trying to lose weight, you're welcome to borrow my pills."

Christopher's eyes went sideways and met mine. She *does* take spell pills! his look said. Both of us nearly burst, trying not to laugh. Mr. Amos shot us a dirty look. So did Gregor. And by the time we had a grip on ourselves, Lady Felice had flung down her napkin and rushed out of the room, leaving the Countess looking annoyed and mystified.

"Amos," she said, "I shall *never* understand the young."

"Naturally not, my lady," Mr. Amos replied.

She smiled graciously, folded her napkin neatly, and walked elegantly to the door. "Tell Smithers to come to my boudoir with his revised accounts," she said as she left.

For some reason—I think it was watching her walk—I remembered Mrs. Potts saying that the Countess used to kick up her legs in a chorus line. I was staring after her, trying so hard to imagine her doing it—and I couldn't—that I jumped a mile when Mr. Amos shouted at me. He was really angry. He planted himself on the carpet face-to-face with us, and he told us off thoroughly for daring to laugh in front of the Ladies. He made me at least feel awful. It didn't seem to matter that he was the same height as I was and inches shorter than Christopher. He was like a prophet or a saint or something, hating us for being ungodly and thundering out of heaven at us.

"Now you will learn to be mannerly," he said in the end. "Both of you are to go out of this door and come in again as softly and politely as you can. Go on."

Even Christopher was quite cowed by then. We crept to the double door, crept out into the hall, and tiptoed apologetically in again. And of course that was not right. Mr. Amos made us do it over and over again, while Gregor kept shooting us mean smiles as he cleared the lunch away. We must have gone in and out fifty times, and Mr. Amos was just promising us that we would go on doing it until we got it right, when one of the other footmen came to say that Mr. Amos was wanted on the telephone.

"*What* a relief!" Christopher muttered.

"Gregor," said Mr. Amos, "set these two to cleaning the silver until we Serve Tea. If this is the call I was expecting, I shall be busy all afternoon, so you are to make sure they keep at it." And he hurried away on his small, shiny feet.

"I spoke too soon," Christopher said as Gregor came toward us.

"This way. Hurry up," Gregor said. He was positively gloating. Among his other drawbacks, Gregor was big. Hefty. He had the meaty sort of hands you could rather easily imagine giving you a wallop on the ear. We scuttled after him without a word, with our three sets of feet ringing, *clack-clack-clack*, around the hall. He led us through the green cloth door and along the wood-and-stone passage to a room right at the end, where there was a long table covered with newspapers. "Right," Gregor said. "Aprons behind the door. Roll your sleeves up. Here are the rags, and this is the polish. Get going." He whipped the newspaper away. "I shall be back to check," he said, "and I need to see my face in all this when I do."

He left us staring at two deep boxes of cutlery, silver teapots, silver coffeepots, several jugs, ladles, and two rows of the huge silver plates, all laid out on more newspaper. Rearing behind those were bowls, tureens, urns, and complicated twiddly candlesticks, most of them enormous.

"Straw into gold again, Grant," Christopher said, "and I think that would be easier."

"Most of it's quite shiny already," I said. "Look on the bright side."

"I *hate* bright sides," said Christopher.

But we knew Gregor would love to catch us slacking, and we got to work. I let Christopher rub on the pink, strong-smelling polish—because that was the easy part, and I was fairly sure that cleaning silver was another thing Christopher had never done before—while I took a pile of rags and rubbed and rubbed. After a while I got into the swing of it and began to read the newspapers under the silver and to think of other things. The cleaning room must have been next door to Mr. Amos's pantry. I could hear his voice as I worked, droning on in blasts and occasionally giving out a sort of booming bark, but I couldn't hear the words, just his voice. It got me down.

I mentioned this to Christopher. He sighed.

I made several other remarks to Christopher, and he did not answer any of them. I turned and looked at him. He was drooping over the table, panting a bit, and his face was almost the gray and white color of the newspaper on the table. He had turned his neckcloth back to front in order not to get polish on it, and I noticed that there was a gold chain with a ring threaded on it hanging out of his shirt. It kept tinking on the candlestick he was working on because he was all bowed over.

I remembered a boy called Hamish at my school who could never do Art because the paints gave him asthma. It looked as if something the same was wrong with Christopher. "What's the matter? Is the polish making you ill?"

Christopher put the candlestick down and held himself up with both hands on the table. "Not the polish," he said. "The silver. There's something about Series Seven that makes it worse than usual. I don't think I can go on, Grant."

Gregor, luckily, was lazy enough not to keep dropping in on us. But he was going to come in at some point. And Christopher was the one he disliked most. "All right," I said. "You keep a lookout by the door so that you can look busy when Gregor turns up, and I'll do it. There's no point making yourself ill."

"Really?" said Christopher.

"Truly," I said, and waited. Now he really did owe me one.

Christopher said, *"Thanks!"* gratefully, and backed away from the silver. He went a better color almost at once. I saw him glance down and notice the gold ring dangling out of his shirt. He looked quite horrified for an instant. He tucked the ring and its chain out of sight, double quick, and pulled his neckcloth around to hide it. "I owe you, Grant," he said as he went to the door. "What can I do for you?"

Success! I thought. I was so curious about Christopher by now that I very nearly blurted out that I wanted him to tell me all about himself. But I didn't. Christopher was the kind of person that you needed to go cautiously with. So I said, "I don't want anything at the *moment*. I'll let you know when I do."

"Fair enough," Christopher said. "What's this droning sound coming through the wall?"

"Mr. Amos phoning," I said, picking up the candlestick and starting to rub.

"What could a butler find to phone about all this time?" Christopher said. "The exact vintage of champagne? Or has he an old mother who insists on a daily report? Amos, dear, are you using those corn plasters I sent you? Or is it his wife? Hugo must have a mother, after all. I wonder where they keep her."

I grinned. I could tell Christopher was feeling all right again now.

"Talking of mothers," he said, "I don't care for the Countess at all, do you, Grant?"

"No," I said. "Mrs. Potts, who cleans the book-shop, says she used to be a chorus girl."

Christopher was absolutely delighted. "No? *Really?* Tell me every word Mrs. Potts said about her."

So I told him as I polished. From there I some-how went on to tell him about the bookshop, too, and about Mum and Uncle Alfred, and how Anthea had left. As I talked, it occurred to me that, instead of *me* finding out about Christopher, *he* was finding out about *me*. And I thought that was just typical of Christopher. Anyway, I didn't mind telling him, as long as he didn't get to know about my Evil Fate and what I had to do, and it did help the silver cleaning along wonderfully. By the time Gregor put his head around the door—and Christopher dashed to the table and pretended to buff up a jug—it was almost all done. Gregor was really annoyed.

"Tea is Served in ten minutes," he said, scowling. "Get washed. You two are pushing the tea trolley in today."

"Never an idle moment here, is there?" Christopher said.

8

THERE WAS NEVER an idle moment. We were kept so hard at it that I never managed to read one word of my Peter Jenkins book. Most nights I fell into bed and went straight to sleep. But I did notice, that second night, while we were getting into the night-shirts, that there was no sign of the ring or the chain around Christopher's neck. Hidden by magic, I thought, and then fell fast asleep.

Then—you know how it is—after three more days I began to get into the rhythm of things and to know my way about. Everything started to feel much more leisurely. I had time that day to be maddened with curiosity about what Christopher was really doing at Stallery and about where he had come from. In fact I had time to be maddened by Christopher generally. He would keep calling me Grant in that superior way, and there were times when I wanted to hit him for it, or shout that it was only my alias, or—anyway, he really annoyed me. Then he would say something that doubled me up with laughter, and I discovered I liked him again. It was truly confusing.

There was a full moon that fifth night. Christopher said, "Grant, this darned moon is shining right in my eyes," and he pinned our curtains together so that the room was almost completely dark.

As I lay down and shut my eyes, I thought, Ah! He wants me to be asleep while he goes off like he did before. I was annoyed enough to do my best to stay awake.

I didn't manage it. I was sound asleep when I somehow realized that the door had just shut softly behind Christopher.

By then I was so maddened with curiosity that I more or less tore myself out of sleep. I stumbled out of bed. It was cold. Stallery didn't provide you with dressing gowns or slippers, so I was forced to climb quickly into my velvet breeches and drag the bedspread off my bed to make a sort of cloak. With the undone buckles of the breeches banging at my knees, I raced out into the corridor just as Christopher flushed the toilet and came out of the bathroom. I dodged back into our room again and waited to see where he would go.

And a right idiot I shall look if he just comes back to bed! I thought.

But Christopher went straight past our room and on in the direction of the lift. I tiptoed quietly after him, trying to tread on the parts of the chilly floorboards that didn't creak. But Christopher himself was making the floor creak so much that I almost need not have bothered. He strode on as if he thought he was the only person awake in the attics.

He marched straight past the lift and toward the clothing room. He stood there in front of the slatted doors for a moment, in moonlight blazing down on him from the big skylights, and I heard him mutter, "No, it *is* farther on, then." Then he swung half around and marched off down the corridor that led to the line painted on the wall and the women's rooms beyond.

I must admit I nearly didn't follow him. It would be a disaster to be sacked from Stallery before I had met Count Robert and settled my Evil Fate. But then I thought that there was no point in getting up half dressed in order to follow Christopher if I *didn't* follow him. So I went after him.

When I caught up with Christopher, he was in a wide bare space where moonlight shone bright and white through a row of windows. He was shivering in his nightshirt as he turned slowly around on the spot. "It *is* here," he was saying to himself, quite loudly. "I *know* it is! So why can't I *find* it, then?"

"What are you looking for?" I said.

He made a noise like "Eek!" and jumped around to face me. It was the nearest to undignified that I had ever seen Christopher be. "Oh," he said. "It's you. For a moment I thought you were the ghost of a hunchback. What are you doing here? I left a really strong sleep spell on you."

"I made myself wake up," I said.

"Bother you!" he said. "You must have a bigger talent for magic than I realized."

"But what are you *doing* here?" I said. "You'll get the sack. This is the women's part."

"No, it isn't," Christopher said. "The women's part is along there." He pointed. "There's a painted line there, too, that I suppose they're forbidden to go past as well. Go and look if you like. This part of the attics is empty, right from the front to the back, and there's something very odd about it. Can't you feel it?"

I was going to say, "Nonsense!" I was quite sure he was just trying to distract me from my curiosity. But when I had my breath all drawn in ready to say it, I let it out again without speaking. There *was* an oddness. It was not unlike the peculiar buzzing I used to feel in Uncle Alfred's workroom after Uncle Alfred had been doing magic, except that this strange vibration felt old and stale. And it did not feel as if it had been made by a person. It felt like a sort of earth tremor, only it was magical instead of natural.

"Yes, and it feels pretty creepy," I said.

"It goes right down through the building," Christopher said, "though it's strongest up here. I've been all over this beastly mansion by now, so I know."

I was distracted, even though I knew he meant me to be. "What, even into the women's part and Mr. Amos's pantry?" I said. "You can't have."

"I couldn't get into the wine cellar,"

Christopher said regretfully, "but I've been every-where else. Mr. Amos's pantry stinks of cigars and booze, and Mrs. Baldock's room is full of crinoline dolls. Mr. Amos's bedroom is even more spectacular than the Countess's is. He has a circular bed. In mauve silk."

I was even more distracted. I tried to see Mr. Amos rolling about in a round mauve bed. It was nearly as hard as seeing the Countess in a row of cho-rus girls. "You're joking," I said. "I've been with you all the time."

Christopher gave a chuckle that was half a shiver. He wrapped his arms around his nightshirt and said, "Ah, Grant, what an innocent you are! It's not difficult to make an image of yourself. I simply made an illusion of me standing by the wall while the Countess wolfs down her dinner. It's the one time I *know* Mr. Amos is busy waiting on her. Think about it, Grant. Have I looked at you or talked to you much during these last few dinnertimes?"

I realized that he hadn't. I was amazed. It was hard not to be even more distracted and pester Christopher to tell me how he did it, but I took a stern grip on myself. "Yes, but what have you been looking *for*? Tell me. You owe me."

"Grant," Christopher said, "you're a pest. You keep your nose to my trail like a bloodhound. All right. I'll tell you. But let's go back to our room first. I'm getting frostbite."

Back in our room, Christopher put on his smart linen jacket and wrapped himself in his bedclothes.

"That's better," he said. "Why does it get so cold at night? Because this place is up in the mountains? How high *is* Stallery, Grant?"

"Three thousand feet, and you're trying to distract me again," I said.

Christopher sighed. "All right. I was just wondering where to start, really. I suppose I'd better begin by admitting that I don't come from this world of yours. I come from another one, a different universe entirely, that we call Series Twelve. This one, where *you* live, we call Series Seven. Do you have trouble believing that yours is not the only world in the world, Grant?"

"Not really," I said. "Uncle Alfred told me there might be other ones. He says it's all to do with possibilities."

"Right. Good," said Christopher. "One hurdle cleared. The next thing you should know is that I was born a nine-lifed enchanter—and that, believe me, Grant, is a *great* deal more than just being a magician—and although I only have a few lives left now, that doesn't make any difference to the kind of powers I have. And it means that, at home in my own world, I'm being trained to take over as what we call the Chrestomanci. The Chrestomanci is an enchanter appointed by the government to control the use of magic. Are you with me so far?"

"Yes," I said. "And what happens if you don't want the job?"

"Shrewd point," said Christopher. "I take off to Series Seven, I suppose." He laughed in a way that was not quite happy. "To be truthful," he said, "I was almost looking forward to being the Chrestomanci until I had a bad disagreement with my guardian, who happens to be the present Chrestomanci. He's a very serious and correct person, my guardian—one of those who *knows* he's always right, if you follow me, Grant."

"Then can't he train up someone else that he gets on with better?" I asked.

Across the dark room I could just see Christopher shaking his head. "No. As far as we know," he said, "there *is* no one else he can train up. Gabriel de Witt and I seem to be the only nine-lifed enchanters in all the known worlds. So we're stuck with each other. He disapproves of me, and I think he's boring. But the disagreement wasn't really about that. He's guardian to a lot of people my age— most of us live with him in Chrestomanci Castle— but one of us, an enchantress from Series Ten who likes to be called Millie, is a sort of special case. She only lives with us in the holidays because the people she came from insisted on her going to boarding school. Her latest school's in Switzerland—"

"Where's that?" I asked.

"You don't have it in Seven," Christopher said. "It's in the Alps, squashed in among France, Germany, and Italy—"

"I don't know of a Germany either," I said.

"The Teutonic States, then?" Christopher guessed.

"Oh, you mean the *Slavo*-Teutonic States!" I

said. "I know about those. Mum says the Tesdi—my father's ancestors—came from there during the Conquest."

"You don't have to tell me history and geography are different here," Christopher said. "I *have* been educated. Do you want to hear the rest or not?"

"Go on," I said.

"Well," Christopher said, "Millie was really unhappy at this Swiss school. She said the girls and the teachers were horrible and she didn't *learn* anything and they were always punishing her just for being different, and she didn't want to go back last term. But of course our guardian sent her back because it was *right*. She cried. She's not one who usually cries, so I knew she was having a really horrible time. I tried to tell our guardian she was, but he wouldn't listen, and we had our first row. So then Millie got desperate, and she ran away from this school. Being an enchantress, she did it very cleverly, in a way that made the school and my guardian think she was hiding somewhere in Series Twelve. But I knew, right from the start, that she was in a different Series. I told my guardian, but he told me he wasn't going to listen to juvenile maunderings. That was our second row."

There was a short silence here. I could feel Christopher brooding. I knew it had been a very bad row. At length Christopher sighed and went on.

"Anyway, soon after that, I began to be sure that wherever Millie was hiding, she was in some kind of trouble. I even got worried enough to go to my guardian again. He more or less told me to shut up and go away." There was another short, brooding silence here. "That made our third row," Christopher said. "*He* said they were doing all they could to find Millie and I was to stop wasting his time, and *I* said, no, they weren't because he wouldn't *listen* to me. Honestly, Grant, if he hadn't been a nine-lifed enchanter, too, I'd have turned him into a *slug*, I was so angry!"

"So you came to look for her yourself," I said.

"That," said Christopher, "makes it sound much easier than it was. It's taken me *weeks* just to get this far. Finding out—secretly, of course—where Millie had gone was hard enough, and I now see that was the *simple* part. I got her pinned down in this part of Series Seven in a couple of days, and I worked out what *I* had to do to stop them coming after me in a matter of *hours*. My guardian thinks I'm hiding in Twelve B, but that's just cover for the way I cadged a lift from the Travelers. That's what started the delays. Travelers, you see, are some of the few people who are always moving from world to world—"

"You mean those two—three—five—caravans and that horse go to other worlds!" I said.

"All the time, Grant," Christopher said, "and there are tribes more of them and much better organized than they let you see. They go in a sort of spiral around the worlds—that was something I didn't know either, and I nearly went mad while they did. And they're more important than anyone thinks. You wouldn't believe the delays and disasters there were, while they coped with crises in Series One and so on, and I chewed my nails. It's been over a month before we even got into smelling distance of Series Seven. Then we had to get here. Luckily they always go to Stallery. There's something about Stallery that they need to keep contained, they tell me. The only good thing is that my guardian is probably as confused as I am about where I've been."

"You'll be in awful trouble with him, won't you?" I said.

"Grant, you are putting that too mildly," Christopher replied. "*Trouble* is not the word for what will happen if he catches up with me. You see . . ." Christopher paused, and this time he seemed to be seething with bottled-up misery, rather than brooding. "You see, Grant, when I was younger, I kept losing my lives. And my guardian, in his usual high-handed way, tried to stop me losing any more of them by taking one of my lives away and locking it in his safe under nine high-power charms that only he was allowed to break. As long as he had that life, I knew he could trace me wherever I went. Anyway, I felt I had a right to my own life. So, before I left with the Travelers, I broke the charms, opened the safe, and took my life away with me. He's not going to forgive me for that, Grant."

That gold ring! I thought. I bet that's his life. This guardian of his sounded to be a total monster. "So what are you going to do," I asked, "when you find Millie?"

"I don't *know*! That's just the problem, Grant. I

can't find her!" There were pounding noises across the room, where I could dimly see Christopher's fist rising and falling, beating at his knees. "I can *feel* her," he said. "She's *here*, I *know* she is! I felt her when we were coming here across the park, and I *keep* feeling her inside this house. When I get to that queer part beyond that line of paint, it almost feels as if I'm *treading* on her! But she's not *there*! I don't understand it, Grant, and it's driving me *mad*!"

He was pounding away at his knees in a frenzy by then. I was surprised because Christopher always seemed so cool. "Take it easy," I said. "Does she seem unhappy—as if she was a prisoner or something?"

"No, not really." Christopher calmed down, enough to stop beating his knees and think about this. "No, I don't think she's a prisoner—exactly. But she's not happy. It's—it's more as if she was stuck somehow, in a way she didn't expect to be—in a maze, or somewhere like that—and can't work out the turnings to find the exit. I think she panics quite often. My first idea was that she was working as a maid here and had signed a fifty-year contract or something, but I've seen all the girls who work here now, and none of them is Millie, not even in disguise."

"And the only place you *haven't* looked is the wine cellar?" I said.

"Yes, but I couldn't feel her at all when I stood outside the cellar door," Christopher said. "Though—come to think of it—that cellar door *is* right in the center of the strange bit of the house. . . ."

"We'd better get inside it, then," I said. "We

could get round Mr. Maxim to take us in there for a wine tasting. And have you looked out-of-doors yet? There could be a maze in the gardens where she's stuck. Don't forget it's our free afternoon tomorrow. Let's go out and search the grounds then."

"Grant, you are a genius," Christopher said. "It *feels* like a maze, where she is—although she would have been inside it for months. There must be magic in it, or she would have starved to death by now."

"There *is* lots of magic in Stallery," I said. "Everyone in Stallchester complains about it. We can't receive television because of it."

"Oh, I know there's lots of magic here all right," Christopher agreed. "It's all over the place, but I haven't a clue what most of it's doing. Some of it's to keep trespassers out, so that the *rest* of the magic won't be interrupted, but—"

I think I fell asleep at this point. I don't remember anything else Christopher said, and the next thing I knew, beastly Gregor was battering on our door, shouting that we were lazy lumps and to get out and get those shoes collected or he'd tell Mr. Amos.

"I hate Gregor," I said while we were going down in the lift with the shoe basket. "You couldn't do some magic to make him fall face first into the sandwiches at Tea, could you?"

Christopher was pale and tired and thoughtful that morning. "It's tempting," he said. But I could tell that his mind was on this Millie he was looking for. If it was me, I'd have been worrying more about that dreadful guardian of his, but I could see that Christopher was just angry, really, and hardly scared of his guardian at all.

Oh well, I thought, and got on with the day.

9

❧•❧

At breakfast, Lady Felice looked more cheerful than usual, even though she did nothing but scrunch her bread all over the table and make a mess that Gregor made me clear up before the Countess arrived.

It was spotting with rain that morning. Lady Felice looked at it and said she would do her riding later on, when the rain had stopped. Andrew had to run all the way to the stables to stop them getting her horse ready. I wished she had sent Gregor. Andrew came back red in the face and quite wet.

We were supposed to go to Mr. Maxim straight after the Countess had finished breakfast, but Mrs. Baldock sent for us first.

"Have you looked in the stables?" I asked Christopher on our way to the Housekeeper's Room.

"Not really," he said. "Just felt about there. I don't get on with horses. But you're right, Grant. We'd better investigate there, too, this afternoon."

It was about our afternoon off that Mrs. Baldock wanted to see us. "You'll have time to go up to

Stallstead," she said, "and if you want to do that, I'll advance you some pay. But remember—you have to be back here at six o'clock promptly."

I was relieved. I was afraid she was going to tell us off for being up half the night. Christopher said, with great courtly politeness, "No, thank you, ma'am. We hoped to look round the gardens and perhaps take a tour of the stables, if that's all right."

"Oh, well, in that case," Mrs. Baldock said, and she smiled at Christopher. He was a real favorite with her by then. "There's no problem about the stables. Just ask one of the grooms. But the gardens and the park are another matter. Staff are not allowed to be seen there by the Family. In the gardens you must take care not to go where you can be seen from the windows, and if you see any member of the Family in the gardens or the park, you must get out of sight at once. If I get a complaint about that from the Family, there's nothing I can do but give you notice on the spot, and you wouldn't want that, would you?"

"No, indeed, ma'am," Christopher said, very seriously. "We'll be extremely careful." As we went back along the stone passage to find Mr. Maxim, he said, "You know, Grant, I was just getting really angry about the Family hogging all these acres of gardens, when I realized that I've never once seen a footman or a housemaid in the gardens at home. I think they must have the same rule there. Oh, and Grant, don't forget we're trying to persuade Mr. Maxim to take us into the wine cellar. That's urgent."

This turned out to be difficult. Mr. Maxim had us cooking eggs that day. "The simplest, quickest, and most nutritious form a light meal can take," he said, rubbing his hands together in his usual irritating way. "How many ways do you know of cooking an egg?"

"Poached, boiled," Christopher said, "er, omelets. What wine goes best with an egg, Mr. Maxim?"

"Later, later," Mr. Maxim said. "Conrad?"

"Scrambled," I said. "Fried. My sister sometimes used to do them in little pots in the oven. When she did, my uncle used to open a bottle of red wine—"

"Let's leave your family history out of this," Mr. Maxim retorted, "and come and look at the stove instead. I have a small pan of water boiling here and another full of melted butter. What is your next step? Christopher?"

He held a large bowl of eggs out to Christopher. Christopher thought hard for a moment. "Marinade!" he said. "That's the word! If I poured wine over these . . ."

"You could try boiling them in wine instead of water," I suggested, backing Christopher up. "Sort of poached de luxe?"

"Or we could put wine in the butter," Christopher said. "If I knew which wine—"

It was a wonder Mr. Maxim didn't throw all the eggs on the floor. I could see he wanted to. "Give me patience!" he all but screamed. "*Forget* wine! Learn the basics *first*! Christopher, how would you make me a plain boiled egg?"

"Um. I think I'd drop it in and let it boil for an hour or so," Christopher said. "But I do want to learn about wine, too," he added, looking hopeful.

Mr. Maxim said, with his teeth clenched together, "I . . . said . . . forget . . . wine. Wine is Mr. Amos's business, not yours. Conrad, what do you think of Christopher's suggestion?"

"He'd end up with a sort of poached bullet," I said. "Honestly, Mr. Maxim, we were hoping you'd let us do a little wine tasting today."

"Well, you can't," said Mr. Maxim. "Now boil me an egg."

The best thing about these lessons was that we were allowed to eat what we cooked. I suppose it was a good way to keep our minds on what we did. We ate boiled eggs—or I did. Christopher left his because he said his spoon bounced off it. We did omelets next. I think Christopher was hungry. He was very careful and attentive to his omelet. They were coming along beautifully, and I was really looking forward to eating mine, when there was a most peculiar feeling. It was as if the world jerked violently sideways.

Christopher cried out, "What was *that*?" His omelet flew out of his pan and fell on his feet. I only just saved mine—except that when I looked down at it, it was bacon and fried eggs. Christopher had a fried egg on each shoe and bacon caught on the buckles.

"What do you mean, *What was that?*" Mr. Maxim asked angrily. "You are a nightmare, boy, a cook's despair! I ask you to cook me the simplest meal there is, and you tip it on your shoes! Pick it up. Throw it away and try again."

Christopher's eyes met mine in a mystified stare. Instead of the big bowl of eggs waiting on the table to be cooked, there were rashers of bacon and four cups, each with an egg already broken into it. But Mr. Maxim simply had not noticed.

"There's been a change, Mr. Maxim," I explained. "We were cooking omelets a moment ago. Someone's pulled the possibilities, I think."

Christopher's stare turned into an enlightened grin. "Really, Grant? A probability shift? I never knew they felt like *that.*"

Mr. Maxim looked at us gloomily. "*My* memory is that I decided yesterday to teach you bacon and eggs," he said. "But I take your word for it. Staff are always telling me things have changed. I never notice." Then he went all suspicious and demanded, "You're not pulling my leg, are you?"

"No, I promise," I said. "The books in our shop used to change like this, too."

An idea struck Christopher. "If he really doesn't remember . . ." he murmured to me. And he said to Mr. Maxim, "I'd like to ask you about wine—"

"*Stop that!*" Mr. Maxim shrieked. "I tell you for once and for all that there is *no* wine that goes with bacon and eggs! Now clean up your shoes."

"Hmm," said Christopher. He delicately slid a

fried egg off each shoe into the waste bucket and shook the bacon off after them. "We obviously wanted a wine tasting in this probability as well. I think that means the cellar is important."

"What are you muttering about?" Mr. Maxim yelled.

"Nothing, nothing," Christopher said. "Just something we'd do on our afternoon off—I suppose *that* hasn't changed, has it, Grant?"

It hadn't. To our relief, as soon as the Countess had folded her napkin and left, Mr. Amos solemnly gave us leave to go. Because he was watching us, we walked soberly across the black floor of the hall, but once we were through the green door, we ran. We clattered down the stone steps and charged through the undercroft to the nearest outside door. It felt good just to run. The drizzle had stopped outside, and we galloped out into sun, laughing.

The stables, across the yard beyond the kitchens, were an enormous place like two barns joined together by a clock tower. I let Christopher talk to the groom on duty there. He could turn on the charm far better than I could. And he did. In next to no time we were walking on a soft passageway inside the big dim barn, gazing into spacious stalls lined with even softer stuff. The horses in the stalls put their faces over the doors and gazed back at us.

I found myself gripped with a sort of fierce wistfulness. If *only* I had not happened to be born and brought up in a bookshop, if *only* I had happened to be born a stableboy like the one who was showing us

131

around, then I could have spent all day with these huge, beautiful horses. The smell of them went to my head, and the *look* of them turned my heart over. There was one really big horse, almost red-colored, who had a white streak down his bent and noble nose, that I liked particularly. He was called Teutron. All the horses had their names on a board outside their stalls.

The stableboy said Teutron had belonged to the old Count and would probably be sold soon. I wished I were rich enough to buy him. The new Count liked a different style of horse, the boy said, and showed us two smaller, darker horses that moved like cats, which he said were Count Robert's. They were called Dawn and Dusk. Christopher, whose nose was wrinkled in disgust and who was definitely not enjoying it here, said those were sissy names. Lady Felice had three horses, Iceberg, Pessimist, and Oracle. They were putting a saddle on Oracle, down at the end of the barn, ready for Lady Felice to ride. Lucky thing.

We watched them doing that, me with interest, Christopher yawning, until the boy happened to mention that the next barn was where they kept the cars.

"Ah," Christopher said, suddenly coming awake. "Lead me to the cars."

I took this to mean that Christopher had not found any trace of Millie in the horse barn. I followed him rather sadly into the barn next door, where the lovely hay and animal smell was replaced by fumes of motor fuel. A row of gleaming saloons there were being polished by six dapper mechanics.

"Better," Christopher said. "Penny for them, Grant. You look mournful."

I sighed. "I was thinking I made a mistake not getting reborn in this life as a stable hand. But perhaps they don't let you choose. Maybe whatever I did to get my bad karma meant I had to be born in the bookshop instead."

Christopher gave me one of his long, vague looks as we edged along by the cars. "Why are you so sure that your soul has been recycled, Grant? There's no evidence of it that I can see."

"My Uncle Alfred knows," I said. "He said I was. I had a bad former life."

"Your Uncle Alfred's word is not law," Christopher said. "Oh, look. Here's a car with all its guts showing."

We leaned on the wall next to this car, and Christopher watched with ridiculous interest while a mechanic did things inside its open front. I yawned. "Can you tear yourself away, Grant?" Christopher said after an endless five minutes. "We must have a look at the gardens."

The man working on the car told us that the quickest way to the park was through the small door across the yard outside the car barn. Christopher sauntered off there beside me. I was just opening the small door when there was a terrific noise from a car—a really *bad* noise, like *pop-pop-pop BOOM*— and a small red sports car came bellowing into the yard through the big open gates. It stopped with a squeal, in a spray of stones and a gust of blue, smelly smoke. The two young men in it were laughing their heads off.

"That was quite horrible!" one of them said as the engine died with a final *pop*.

"At least it got us here," said the one who was driving.

Christopher, like lightning, pushed us both through the small door and then held it not quite shut, so that we could only see a slit of the yard with the red car in it. "Family, Grant," he said.

The two young men came vaulting out of the car, still laughing. The one who had been driving called out, "Lessing! I'm afraid we need you. This is a very sick car."

The mechanic we had been watching walked into view, saying, "What is it *this* time, my lord?"

The other young man swallowed a giggle and said, "A piece dropped off in the middle of Stallchester. Robert said it was only a piece of trim, but it obviously wasn't. I said if he was that sure, there was no point stopping and picking it up. A mistake."

"Yes, blame Hugo," said the driver. "He couldn't wait to get home, so we've had to push the darn thing up all the steepest Alps." Both young men laughed again.

I stared at them through the gap Christopher was holding open. They were both in ordinary sort of clothes, and medium tall, and thin, with fairish hair. They might have been a pair of students, laughing and joking after a day out together. But the one with the fairer hair had to be Count Robert himself, and the other one, now I looked properly, was indeed Hugo. I just hadn't known him without his valet's clothes.

I looked at the Count then, expecting to *know* that he was the one causing my Evil Fate. But I had no feeling at all. The Count might have been any cheerful, healthy young man, like one of the students who came to Stallchester to ski. I put my hand into my waistcoat pocket and took hold of the port wine cork, hoping that would help me to *know*, but it made no difference at all. The Count was still nothing but a normal, good-looking young man. I couldn't understand it.

While I stared, Lessing was saying something about the pair of them only having to *look* at a car for it to go wrong and he'd better see what they'd done *now*. He shrugged humorously and went to fetch his tools.

When he was gone, the Count and Hugo turned to each other, not laughing anymore, and stood for a moment looking sober and rueful. "Ah, well, Hugo," the Count said. "Back to real life, I suppose." And they both followed Lessing into the car barn.

"Interesting," Christopher remarked, gently shutting the small door. "No sign of Millie here, Grant. We have to look elsewhere."

We followed a path around to the gardens at the back of the mansion. These were massive. We went through steep ferny parts, flat places with pools and water lilies, fountains and rose arches, and a huge stretch that was all gravel and trees carved into silly shapes, and came to the part directly behind the house. There the garden was like one of those jigsaws that are almost impossible to do, with flowers of all kinds stacked into acres of long beds and grass and paths between.

I hung back, rather. "We aren't supposed to be seen from the windows."

"I assure you," Christopher said, "that not a soul will see us, Grant. I'm not a nine-lifed enchanter for nothing, you know."

He strode on, and I followed much less boldly. We marched down an endlessly long path slap in the middle of the jigsaw, with frothy walls of flowers on both sides of us and our ears filled with the buzzing of bees. We were in full view from the rows of windows behind us, but nobody came after us with yells of anger, so I supposed it was all right.

"I can feel that strangeness here, too," Christopher said, "but not as strongly as at the top of the house."

As he said this, we came out into a wider bit, where the flowers bent outward to make a circle around a sundial. "Can you feel Millie here at all?" I asked him.

Christopher frowned. "Ye-es," he said, "and no." He went and leaned on the sundial. "She's here and *not* here," he said. "Grant, I don't understand this at *all*."

"You said a maze," I was beginning, when there came that sideways jerk that had changed the eggs that morning. Christopher was suddenly leaning against a statue of a chubby boy with wings. He sprang away with a squawk. "The Count," I said. "He's back. He must have done that."

"Nonsense," Christopher said. "Use your head, Grant. Someone was messing with the probabilities this morning, long before the Count got home. Come along, and let's look for a maze."

There didn't seem to be a maze. The nearest we found to one was where the jigsaw puzzle petered out into a place where stone pillars stood in rows, hung with flowering creepers. Beyond that the gardens stopped. There was drop of about ten feet down into a ditch, and after the ditch, the parklands began, rolling away for miles ahead of us.

"A ha-ha," Christopher said.

"Nothing's funny," I said. I was too hot by then, and sick of searching for a girl who didn't seem to exist. I was beginning to think Christopher was imagining Millie was near.

"I mean that this drop into a ditch at the end of a garden is called a ha-ha," Christopher explained. "At least it is in my world."

"I don't think it is here," I said. The new gardener's boy, Smedley, was sitting in the ditch, a few yards along from us. He had his boots off, and he looked as hot and sulky as I felt. "Why not ask him?" I said.

"Good idea." Christopher bounded along the

row of pillars and stuck his head through the creepers above where the boy was sitting. "I say! Smedley!"

The poor kid jumped a mile. His sweaty face went white, and he scrambled to his bare feet in a hurry. "Just coming, sir— Oh, it's *you*!" he said when he saw Christopher's face sticking out from the creepers above his head. "Don't call out at me in posh voices like that! Do you want to give me a heart attack?"

"This is my normal voice," Christopher said coldly. "What are you doing in that ditch anyway?"

"Skiving off, of course," said Smedley. "I'm supposed to be looking for that damn guard dog—the one you tamed when we was walking here. Brute disappeared this morning, and park security's doing his nut, thinking someone may have poisoned it. All us garden staff are out looking for it." He scowled. "I'm not risking getting bitten, thanks."

"Very sensible," Christopher said. "Tell me, does this garden have a maze?"

"No," said Smedley. "Oriental garden, rose garden, four flower gardens, water garden, shrubbery, topiary garden, fern garden, hedged garden, vegetable garden, fruit garden, six hothouses, one orangery, big conservatory, but no maze. Or it may have got caught in a trap, see."

"What—the maze? Or the whole garden?" Christopher asked.

"The dog, stupid!" Smedley said.

"We'll keep a look out for it for you,"

Christopher told him. "What do you call this ditch and wall at the end of this garden? Apart from a good place to lurk, that is."

"This? This is the ha-ha," Smedley said.

Christopher shot me a superior look. "There you are, Grant. Come along now." He jumped down into the ditch beside Smedley, who flinched away. "Fear me not," Christopher said. "Grant and I are merely going for a stroll in the park. We will not give you away."

I jumped down and went *squelch*. One of my buckled shoes came off. I took the other one off, too, and my striped stockings. Smedley seemed to me to have the right idea. The grass felt deliciously cool and wet as we climbed the bank and set off into the parklands.

"Your funeral if you tread on a bee!" Smedley shouted after me. Evidently Christopher's superior manner annoyed him as much as it annoyed me, because he added, "Poncy footmen!" when we were almost too far away to hear.

"Take no notice," Christopher said—as if I would have done. "Our friend Smedley has clearly been told that house staff are nothing but mincing lackeys and that gardeners do all the real work." We walked a little way. I curled my toes luxuriously into the grass and thought that Christopher *would* think this. He had no idea how irritating he could be. "Smedley may be right," Christopher added. "I've never minced so much in my life before." We walked some more, and Christopher began to frown. "The oddness is getting fainter," he said. "Can you feel?"

"Not really," I confessed. "I only properly felt it in the attics."

"Pity. Well, let's go as far as that clump of trees and see," Christopher said.

The clump of trees was more like a small bushy wood on top of a little hill. We pushed our way through, up the hill and down in a straight line. I had forgotten it had rained earlier. Willows wept on us, and bushes sprayed us. Christopher hardly seemed to notice. He pushed on, murmuring, "Fainter, fainter." I put my shoes back on my muddy feet, wishing we'd taken the time to put on ordinary clothes. We would both need to change into dry uniforms for this evening, or Mr. Amos would have our guts for garters. Count Robert would be there for Dinner, I supposed. Maybe the reason I hadn't *known* he was causing my Fate was because I hadn't been close enough to him. I could get to stand right beside him at Dinner. Then I'd surely *know*.

We were both so busy thinking of other things that we nearly missed seeing Lady Felice riding toward the wood on Oracle.

I said, "Oh-oh! Family!" and pulled Christopher back among the wet willows.

He said, "Thanks, Grant." Then we had to stand there, because Lady Felice was cantering straight toward the hill where we were. Water ran down our necks, along with itchy bits of willow, while we waited for her to swerve around the hill and ride out of sight.

Instead, she came careering straight toward the edge of the wood and pulled the horse to a stop there. Hugo came out of the bushes just below us, still in his everyday clothes, and stood there with his hair as wet as ours was, looking up at her. She stared down at Hugo. Everything went tense and still.

Hugo said, "The car nearly broke down. I thought I was *never* going to get back."

Lady Felice said, "I wish you or Robert had *warned* me. It felt like a hundred years!"

"For me, too," Hugo said. "Robert didn't want any questions asked, you see. At least he didn't find Ludwich as dreary as I did. It was like being half *dead*."

Lady Felice cried out, "Oh, Hugo!" and jumped down off Oracle. Hugo sort of plunged forward to meet her, and the two of them flung their arms around each other as if it really had been a hundred years since they last met. Oracle wandered peacefully off and then stood, with the look of a horse that was used to this.

I stared at them and then stared at Christopher, who looked quite as uncomfortable as I felt. He made a very slight gesture and said, in his normal voice, "Spell of silence, Grant. They won't hear us. I guess we're looking at something here that mustn't get back to the Countess *or* Mr. Amos either."

Not altogether believing in the spell of silence, I was just nodding when there was another of those sideways jerks. It was quite strong, but nothing much seemed to change. It did not seem to affect Hugo and Lady Felice in the least, and we were still draped in trees—except that they were not willows now, but some other kind, just as drooping and just as wet. I noticed that my striped stockings were not in my hand anymore. When I looked down, I saw they were on my legs instead.

Christopher backed away out of sight of Hugo and his Lady, looking very excited. "That *definitely* came from the house!" he said. "Come on, Grant. Let's get back there quickly and find out what's doing it."

10

CHRISTOPHER SET OFF through the wet wood at a gallop. On the level grass beyond I had to work hard to keep up. He had such long legs. But he had to stop in the ditch in front of the ha-ha and wait for me to boost him up the wall.

"Found the dog?" Smedley called out from farther along.

"No," I panted, boosting hard.

Christopher held down his hands to help me scramble up and hauled me up as if I weighed nothing.

"What's the hurry, then?" Smedley said as my feet met the top of the wall and we both set off running again. "I thought the dog was after you!"

We were too breathless to answer. Christopher dropped to a jog-trot and kept on in a straight line toward the house, past yew hedges and tiny box hedges, and then between the banks of flowers. I had a feeling that some of this was new, but it all jogged past so fast that I was not really sure anything had changed until we came to the open circle where

Christopher had leaned on the sundial. The chubby boy statue was now a stately stone young lady carrying an urn, which was spouting water.

I couldn't help laughing. "Lucky it didn't do that while you were leaning on it!"

"Save your breath," Christopher panted.

We jogged on, pounding on gravel, then clattering up stone steps, and more stone steps, until we were charging across a wide paved platform in front of the house itself. I tried to stop here. It was obviously a place where Staff were not allowed. But Christopher trotted on, into the house through an open glass door, across a parquet floor in a room that was lined with books. While Christopher was wrestling open the heavy door, I saw there was a ladder up to a balcony where there were more books, under a fancy ceiling, and I knew this was the library and we shouldn't be there.

The heavy door brought us out into the hall, with the main stairway ahead in the distance. Andrew was just crossing the black floor, carrying a tray. He said, *"Hey!"* as we dashed past him. I knew then that Christopher, in his hurry to discover what was making the changes, had clean forgotten to make us invisible—and forgotten that he had forgotten. Andrew stared after us as Christopher skidded around the banisters and led me charging up the forbidden stairway. I was just glad it was Andrew and not Gregor. Gregor would have reported us to Mr. Amos.

At the top, outside the ballroom, Christopher had

to stop and bend over to get his breath. But as soon as he could stand up again, he stared around in a puzzled way and then pointed toward the lofty ceiling.

"I don't understand, Grant. I thought we'd be on top of it here. Up again."

So up we went again, to the floor where the Family bedrooms were. Here the next lot of stairs were not in a straight line from the lower lot. We had to tear along the palatial passage to get to them and around a corner. When we whirled around that corner, I thought for a moment we were in a riot. There were squeals and screams and girls in brown-and-gold uniforms pelting everywhere. They all froze when they saw us. Then one of them said, "It's only the Improvers," and there were sighs of relief all around. I could see they were all the younger maids. None of them were much older than me or Christopher.

"It's line-tig," one of them explained breathlessly. "Want to play?"

"Love to," Christopher said, quite as breathlessly. "But we have to take a message." And he charged on to the next stairs and up those. "I suppose . . . have to have . . . fun . . . somewhere," he panted as we pounded upward.

"If I was them, I'd go and chase about in the nurseries where it's empty," I said.

"No . . . excuse for . . . being there," Christopher suggested.

He did not pause on the next floor with its smell of new carpets. He just shook his head, chased along to the next stairs, and clattered up them to the nursery floor. "Getting warmer," he gasped, and we trotted along to the creaking wooden stairs to the attics.

By this time I could feel the strangeness, too. It was buzzing actively. It did not surprise me in the least when, as soon as we panted into the attics, Christopher plunged away past the lift toward the center of the house. I knew we were going to end up in that space beyond the line painted on the wall.

Christopher was galloping along, excitedly puffing out, "Warm, warmer, almost *hot*!" when we both more or less ran into Miss Semple coming away from the clothes stores.

"Steady *on*!" she said. "Don't you know the rule about not running?"

"Sorry!" we both said. Then, without having to think, I added, "We need new clothes. Christopher got mud on his breeches."

Christopher looked down at himself. He was covered in brick dust and moss as well as mud. "And Conrad's ruined his stockings," he said.

I looked at my striped legs and discovered that at least four of the stripes had converted into ladders, with my skin showing through. There were willow leaves stuck behind the buckles of my shoes.

"So I see," Miss Semple said, looking, too. "Come along, then." She marched us into the clothes room, where she made us change practically everything. It was such a waste of time. Miss Semple said we were a disgrace to Stallery. "And those stockings will have to come out of your wages," she told me. "Silk stockings are costly. Be more careful in future."

Christopher scowled and sighed and fretted. I whispered to him, "If we hadn't met her, she'd have gone down and caught those girls playing tig. Or she might have caught *us* going past the painted line."

"True," Christopher muttered. "But it's still maddening. The changes have *stopped* now, damn it!" He was right. I couldn't feel the strangeness buzzing at all now.

When we were clean and neat and crisp again, Miss Semple picked up the pile of towels she had been carrying and sailed away to the lift with them.

"Now, hurry," Christopher said, "before anything else interferes."

We tiptoed speedily and cautiously toward the center of the attics. In the distance, floors creaked and someone banged a door, but no one came near. I think we both gasped with nervous relief when we passed the line painted on the wall. Then we sprinted to the wide space with the row of windows.

"Here—it *is* here, the center of things!" Christopher said. He turned slowly around, looking up, looking down. "And I still don't understand it," he said.

There really did seem to be nothing but flaking plaster ceiling above and wide old floorboards underfoot. In front of us, the rather dirty row of windows looked out over the distant blue mountains above Stallchester, and behind us was just wall, flaking like the ceiling. The dark passage on the other side that led to the women's side was identical to one we had come along.

I pointed to it. "What about Millie? Is she along there?"

Christopher shook his head impatiently. "No. Here. *Here* is the only place she feels anywhere near at the moment. It looks as if these changes are somehow connected to the way she's not here, but that's all I know."

"Under the floor, then?" I suggested. "We could take one of the floorboards up."

Christopher said, in an unconvinced way, "I suppose we could *try*," and we had, both of us, knelt down near the windows to look at the boards, when another sideways jolt happened. It was lucky we were kneeling. Up here the shift was savage. We were both thrown over by it. My head cracked against the wall under the windows. I swore.

Christopher reached out and hauled me up. "I see the reason for these painted lines now," he said, rather soberly. "If you'd been standing up, Grant, you'd have gone straight through the window. I shudder to think how far it is to the ground from here."

He was pale and upset. I was annoyed. I looked around while I was rubbing my head, and it was all exactly the same, wide floorboards, distant mountains through the windows, flaky plaster, and the feeling of something strange here as strong as ever. "What *does* it?" I said. "And *why*?"

Christopher shrugged. "So much for my clever

ideas," he said. "If I have a fault, Grant, it's being too clever. Let's go down and check the nursery floor. Nothing seems to have changed at all this time."

Famous last words, my sister Anthea used to say. Christopher strode away down the passage, and there was a door blocking his way, a peeling red-brown door.

"Oh!" he said. "This is new!" He rattled at it until he found the way it opened.

It blew inward out of his hands. We both went backward.

Wind howled around us, crashing the door into the wall and flapping our neckcloths into our faces. We both knew at once we were somewhere different and rickety and very, very high up. We could feel the floor shaking under our feet. We clutched at each other and edged cautiously forward into the stormy daylight beyond the door.

There Christopher said, "Oooh!" and added airily, "Not afraid of heights, I hope, Grant?"

I could hardly hear him for the wind and the creaking of wood. "No," I said. "I like them." The door led out onto a small wooden balcony thing with a low, flimsy-looking rail around it. Almost at our feet, a square hole led into a crazy old wooden stairway down the side of what seemed to be a tall wooden tower. Our heads both bent to look through the hole. And we could see the stairway zigzagging giddily away, down and down, getting smaller and smaller, outside what was definitely the tallest and most unsafe-looking wooden building I had ever seen. It could have been a lighthouse—except that it had slants of roof sticking out every so often, like a pagoda. It swayed and creaked and thrummed in the wind. Far, far below, something seemed to be channeling the gale into a melancholy howling.

I tore my eyes from that tottering stairway and looked outward. Where the park should have been, the ground was all gray-green heathery moor, but beyond that—this was the creepy part to me—there were the hills around Stallery, the exact same craggy shapes that surrounded Stallchester. I could see Stall Crag over there, plain as plain.

After that I stood by the railing and looked upward. There was a very small slanting roof above us, made of warped wooden tiles, with a sort of spire on top that ended in a broken weathercock. It was all so old that it was groaning and fluttering in the wind. Behind and around us, the moor just went on. There was no sign of Stallery at all.

Christopher was white, nearly as white as the neckcloth that kept fluttering across his face. "Grant," he said, "I've got to go down. Millie feels quite near now."

"We'll both go," I said. I didn't want to be up at the top of this building when Christopher's weight brought the whole thing down, and besides, it was a challenge.

I don't think Christopher saw it as a challenge. It took him an obvious effort to unclench his hand from the doorjamb, and when he had, he turned around very quickly and clenched the same hand even harder on the rail beside the stairs. The whole balcony swayed. He kept making remarks—nervous, joky remarks—as he went carefully down out of sight, but the wind roared too hard for me to hear them.

As soon as Christopher was far enough down that I wouldn't kick his face, I scrambled onto the stairs, too. A mistake. Everywhere groaned, and the staircase, together with the balcony, swayed outward away from the building. I had to wait until Christopher was farther down and putting weight on a different part of it. Then I had to go slowly because he was. I could tell he was scared silly.

I was quite scared, too. I'd rather climb Stall Crag any day. It stays still. This place swayed every time one of us moved, and I kept wondering what lunatic had built the thing, and why. As far as I could tell, nobody lived in it. It was all cracked and weathered and twisted. There were windows without glass in the wooden walls. When Christopher was being particularly slow, I leaned over with the wind thundering around me and peered into the nearest window, but they were always just empty wooden rooms inside. There was a door on each balcony we came to, but when I looked down past my own legs—not a clever thing to do: I went quite giddy— I saw that Christopher was not trying to open any of the doors, so I left them alone, too. I just went on to the next flight, slanting the opposite way.

About halfway down, the sticking-out roofs were much wider. The stairs went out over the roofs there, to mad little spidery balconies hanging on the very edge, and then there would be another stair going down under that roof to the next one. When Christopher came to the first of these balconies, he just stopped. I had to hang on to the ladder and wait. I thought he must have found Millie, and that the howling sound I could still hear was being made by an injured girl in mortal agony. But Christopher went on in the end. And when I got to that balcony, I knew why he had stopped. You could see through the floor of it, down and down, and it was rocking. And the howling was still going on, below somewhere.

I got off that balcony as quick as I could. So did Christopher after that. We had to climb over three more of the horrible things before we came to a longer, thicker stair, where there was actually a handrail. I caught up there. We were only one floor up by then.

"Nearly there," Christopher said. He looked ghastly.

"Millie?" I asked.

"I can't feel her at all now," he said. "I hope I don't understand."

As we clattered down the last few steps, the howling became a sort of squeaking. At the bottom, a great brown shape hurled itself at us, slavering. Christopher sat down, hard. I was so scared that I went up half the flight again without even noticing. "They left a wild beast on guard!" I said.

"No, they didn't," Christopher said. He was sitting on the bottom step with his arms around the creature, and the creature was licking his face. Both of them seemed to be enjoying it. "This is the guard dog that went missing today. Its name is"—he reached around the great tongue and found the name tag on the dog's collar—"Champ. I think it's short for Champion and not a description of its habits."

I went down the stairs again, and the dog seemed glad to see me, too. I suppose it had thought it was permanently lost. It put great paws on my shoulders and squeaked its joy. Its massive tail thumped dust out of the ground, which whirled in the wind, stingingly. "No, you've got it wrong," I told it. "We're lost, too. We are, aren't we?" I asked Christopher.

"For the moment," he said. "Yes. Stallery seems to have been built on a probability fault, I *think*—a place where a lot of possible universes are close together and the walls between them are fairly weak. So when whoever—or *whatever*—keeps shifting to another line of possible events, it shifts the whole mansion across a *bit*, and that bit at the top of the house gets moved a *lot*. The top gets jerked somewhere else for a while. At least, I'm hoping it's just for a while. Now we know why those painted lines are *really* there."

"Do you think it's the Countess doing it?" I said. "Or the Count?"

"It may be no one," Christopher said. "It could just happen, like an earthquake."

I didn't believe that, but there was no point

arguing until I met the person causing my Evil Fate and *knew*. Come to think of it, my Fate must have landed us here anyway. In order not to feel too bad about it, I said to Christopher, "You worked out what had happened on the way down?"

"In order not to think of dry rot and planks snapping," he said, "or the distance to the ground. And I realized that Millie must be stuck in one of the other probabilities, just beyond this one. Maybe she hasn't noticed which part of the mansion moves— Oh dear!"

We both understood the same thing at the same moment. In order to get ourselves back to the Stallery we knew, we had to be at the top of the tower when another sideways shift happened. We looked at each other. We got up, towing the dog, and backed away to where we could see the whole unpainted wooden height of the thing, moving and quivering in the wind, and the crazy stairway zigzagging up it. It looked worse from the ground even than from at the top.

"I don't think," Christopher admitted, "I can bring myself to climb that again."

"And we'd never get the dog up it anyway— Hang on!" I said. "The dog *can't* have been in the attics when it got here. It lives in the grounds."

"Oh, *what* a relief!" Christopher said. "Grant, you're a genius! Let's sit on the right line and wait, then."

So we did that. Christopher very carefully paced from side to side, and then back and outward, until he found the spot where the strangeness felt strongest. He decided that a lump of rock about forty feet from the tower was the place. We sat leaning against it—with the dog between us for warmth and the wind hurling our hair and neck-cloths sideways—staring at the derelict front door of the tower and waiting. Gray clouds scudded overhead. An age passed.

"It's funny," Christopher said. "I have no desire at all to explore that building. Do you, Grant?"

I shuddered. The wind sort of moaned in the twisted timber, and I could hear doors opening and slamming shut somewhere inside. I *hoped* it was only the wind doing it. "No," I said.

Later on, Christopher said, "My stockings have turned into ladders held together by loops. If they take them out of our wages, how much do the things cost?"

"They're silk," I said. "You've probably worked all last week for nothing."

"Bother," he said.

"So have I," I said, "only I've ruined two pairs now. How long have we sat here?"

Christopher looked at his watch. It was nearly five-thirty. We were going to be late back on duty if another shift didn't happen soon. A whole set of doors slammed inside the tower, making us jump.

"I suppose I deserve this," I said.

"Why?" Christopher demanded.

"Because . . ." I sighed and supposed I might as

155

well confess. "This is all probably my fault. I have this bad karma, you see."

"*What* bad karma?" he said.

"There's something I didn't do in my last life," I said, "and now I'm not doing it in this life either—"

"You're talking perfect codswallop," Christopher said.

"Maybe it's something you don't have in your world," I said.

"Yes, we do. I was studying it, as it happens, just before I came away, and I assure you, my dear Grant—"

"If you're only in the middle of learning—" I started to say when we both realized that the wooden tower was now a dark stone building. Without any kind of warning, or blurring, or any sort of sideways jerk, it had become twice as wide, though no less derelict. It seemed to be built of long blocks of dark slate, sloping inward slightly, so that it tapered up to a square top, high, high above us. Its square stone doorway gaped in front of us, breathing out a dank and rather rotten smell. There were no stairs anymore.

"That's odd," said Christopher. "I didn't feel it change, did you? What do you say, Grant? Do we risk looking inside?"

"It looks more like a house than the wooden place," I said, "and we're stuck here if we don't do *something*."

"True," said Christopher. "Let's go."

We got up and lugged the dog over to the empty square doorway. The place smelled horrible inside, and it was absolutely empty in there. Light came in through enough small windows—just gaps between slabs of slate, really—to show us that the stairs were now indoors. They went zigzagging up one of the walls, and they were simply steps, with nothing to stop a person falling off the outside edge. They were made of slate like all the rest, but they were so old that they sort of drooped outward toward the empty middle of the place. And the trouble was, this building was as high as ever the wooden tower had been.

I told myself that it was no worse than Stall Crag. Christopher swallowed, rather. "One slip," he said, "one stumble, and we'll be dogmeat for Champ here. But I *think* I can keep us stuck to them by magic if we stay close together."

The dog refused to go inside at first. I knew it was the smell combined with the sight of those stairs, but Christopher explained cheerfully that poor Champ lived out-of-doors and was probably forbidden to go inside a house. It could have been true. Anyway, he towed the resisting beast to the bottom of the stairs. There Champ braced all four gigantic paws and would not budge. We tried climbing up a short way and calling beguilingly, but he simply went out into the middle of the dark, smelly floor and began to howl again.

Christopher said, "This is hopeless!" and he went down and tied his neckcloth into Champ's collar for a lead. He hauled. The neckcloth stretched. Champ stopped howling, but he shook all over and still refused to move.

"Do you think he knows something we don't?" I suggested. I was resting a hand on a step two stairs up, and it was slimy. It would be nice to have an excuse not to climb the things.

"He knows exactly what we know. He's a coward, that's all," Christopher said. "Champ, I refuse to put a compulsion spell on a mere dog. Come *on*. It's getting late. Supper, Champ. Supper!"

That did the trick. Champ came up the steps in a rush. I was barged into the slate wall, first by the dog and then by Christopher as Christopher was towed upward, and I had to scramble like a maniac to keep up with them. We took the first three zigzags at a mad run, but after that, when the hollow building was like a deep, smelly well around us, Champ seemed to realize he might need to save his breath, and he slowed down.

It was worse like that. I climbed sliding my back up the rough wall and hoped hard that Christopher's spell was a good strong one. Some of the steps higher up were broken and slanted outward more than ever. To take my mind off it, I asked, "Why did you say my bad Fate was codswallop—my karma?" My voice made a dead sort of booming around the place.

Christopher's voice made more dead echoes as he called downward, "I don't think you have any. You have a new, fresh feel to me. Either this is your very first life or your earlier ones were blameless."

I knew he was wrong. He was making me seem so childish. "How do you mean?" I boomed up at him.

And he echoed back, "Like Lady Felice. I don't think she's been around more than once at the most. Compare her with the Countess, Grant. *There's* an old soul if ever I met one!"

"You mean she has bad karma?" I boomed.

"Not particularly," he echoed down. "Not anything very bad from before, I think, though mind you she's laying up a bit this time round, if you ask me."

This made me sure he was just guessing. "You don't know really, do you?" I shouted back. "*Other* people can see my Fate! They *told* me!"

"Like who?" Christopher called down.

"Like my Uncle Alfred and the Mayor of Stallchester," I yelled upward. "So!"

By now it was getting hard to hear. The place was filling with echoes, and Champ, up ahead, was rasping out breaths as if Christopher's neckcloth were throttling him, but I am fairly sure Christopher said, "If you ask me, Grant, they were probably smelling their own armpits."

"Will you *stop* calling me Grant in that superior way!" I shouted at him.

I don't think he heard. Champ at that moment dived away sideways. I thought he was simply diving up the next zigzag, but it turned out to be the top of the stairs. Christopher, with his arm stretched out to hang on to the neckcloth, was jerked after Champ and out of sight. I thought for a moment that they had disappeared, but when I sidled up after them, I found a square slate passage leading through the top of the wall. There was light at the end of the passage, lighting up every slimy slab, and Champ was towing Christopher along it at full gallop. I sprinted after them, expecting to come out on the roof.

But we all burst out onto big floorboards, in a place full of the warm smell of wood, where I saw that the light had been coming from a row of dusty windows looking out to the mountains above Stallchester. The ceiling was flaking plaster, and all around us was the feel, like an engine in the distance, of other people living and moving around here.

"Grant," Christopher whispered, "I believe we're back." He looked ghastly. It wasn't just that he was white and shaking and his stockings were laddered. He was covered with dark slime and cobwebs, too. And if the back of his waistcoat was anything to go by, mine was ruined. I could see my breeches were. And my stockings. Again.

"Let's go and check," I said.

We tiptoed back along the passage we seemed to have just come in by. It was wooden now. At the end of it we came to the streak of paint on the wall. Then we had only to peep around the corner to see we were certainly in Stallery. Andrew and Gregor were just coming out of the clothes store, adjusting crisp new neckcloths. People were hurrying and calling things and coming in and out of doors in the distance. We could tell that everyone was getting smartened up for supper and Dinner after that.

We dodged back into the part with the windows.

"We'd better let them go downstairs before we get more clothes," I said.

"I approve of the first part of your plan," Christopher said, "but you're forgetting Champ. We have to account for him, too. We must go down as we are. Then, if anyone sees us, we can say that we found him stuck in the drains. And if nobody does see us, we let him out of the nearest door for Smedley to find and *then* sneak up here for more clothes."

"Drains right up *here*?" I said.

"There have to be," he said firmly. "Where does our bathwater go—and so forth?"

I supposed it might work. It seemed to me a recipe for trouble. "Can't you magic our clothes?"

"Not for a whole evening," Christopher said. "It would be an illusion, and illusions wear thin after an hour or so."

I sighed. "Anyway, thanks for keeping us on those stairs."

Just for a second Christopher had such a blank, dumbfounded look that I knew he had forgotten to work any magic on those steps. I was glad I had not known while I was on them. "Think nothing of it, Grant," he said airily.

Then we hung about for a boring ten minutes. Champ did not help. He whined and drooled and made little rushes toward the passage. Either he knew he was not meant to be here or he could smell all the suppers cooking.

At length the bell went for maids' supper,

making us all jump. Champ turned his jump into another surge down the passage. This time we followed him. There were still people about in the distance, and we could hear the lift working. That meant we had to go down the stairs, trying not to let Champ tow us down them too fast.

He took us in an eager rush down onto the matting of the nursery floor. Here he broke into a gallop whatever we said. Perhaps he thought the matting was grass and he was allowed to run on it. Anyway, he ran us straight past the top of the next stairs and dragged us on down the passage, to where the door was open on that long, empty nursery.

As we hurtled up to it, a young man in evening dress came out of the nursery. The dim light there showed his fair hair and the lost, rather drooping way he looked. But the look changed as he saw us. His head went back, and he went ramrod straight, with his face all firmed into haughty surprise.

"What the devil do you think you're doing?" he said.

It was quite obvious to all three of us that he was Count Robert.

11

❧━◆━❧

CHRISTOPHER MUST HAVE used some magic then. He and the dog both stopped as if they had run into a wall. I overran a little and stopped myself on a doorknob on the other side of the corridor. The Count turned himself so that his frosty look could hit me as well as Christopher.

I had no idea what to do, but Champ had no doubt. His tail thumped. He crawled forward, quivering with shame, to the full stretch of Christopher's neckcloth, and tried to get into licking distance of the Count's beautiful, shiny shoes. Christopher just stood and looked at the Count as if he were summing him up. This was where being an amateur was a big help. Christopher would not have minded being sacked on the spot. He had more or less found Millie now, and he could make himself invisible and come back to finish the job, but I still had my Evil Fate to think of. I stared at the Count, too, hoping and hoping to *know* he was the one causing my Fate, but all I could see was a young fellow in expensive evening dress who had every right to stare at us in outrage.

"Come on," Count Robert said. "Explain. Why are you dragging poor old Champ around up here?"

"It's more that *he* was dragging *us*," Christopher said. "From the look of him, I think he caught your scent, my lord."

"Yes, he did, didn't he?" Count Robert agreed, looking thoughtfully down at Champ, who wagged and groveled more than ever. "But that doesn't explain why he's here or why all of you are covered with black gunk." At this, Christopher drew breath, presumably to begin on the drains story. "No," said the Count. "Not you. I can see you'd just tell me something glib and untrue." Christopher looked hurt and indignant, and the Count turned to me. "*You* tell me."

It seemed to me that I'd nothing more to lose. I knew I was about to be sacked and sent home in disgrace. Wondering what Uncle Alfred would say, and then thinking dismally that I would be dead by next year anyway, so what did Uncle Alfred matter either, I said, "We went past the painted line in the attics. Champ was at the bottom of a wooden tower there, but we couldn't have got him back up it, so we waited until it changed into an empty slate building."

Christopher muttered, "Believe it or not, I was going to tell you that, too." The Count gave him a disbelieving sideways look. "Honestly," Christopher said. "I thought you'd probably guessed."

"More or less," said Count Robert. His frosty look tipped up at the edges and became a slight grin.

"You were unlucky to get those two towers straight off. Hugo and I didn't run into them for years. Well, now what shall we do about it? I don't think any of you should be seen as you are. Amos is prowling round the next floor in a rage—"

"About us?" I said anxiously.

"No, no—about something I told him," the Count said. "But he'd certainly better not see you or Champ as you are. He'd fire you both on the spot if he knew where you'd been, so . . ." He considered for a second. "Give me the dog. Hugo and I can get him cleaned up in my rooms—luckily Champ is well known to be a friend of mine—and then I can take him down to the stables. You two go and get fresh clothes, or you'll be in real trouble."

We both said, with real gratitude, "Thank you, my lord."

Count Robert smiled. There was a sad sort of look to him, smiling. "No problem. Here, Champ!"

Christopher let go of the neckcloth. It was an ex-neckcloth really, more of a dirty string by this time. Champ immediately sprang to his hind legs and attempted to put both his paws on the shoulders of the Count's evening jacket. The Count caught the paws just in time, in a way that showed he had had a lot of practice, and said, "No, *down*, Champ! I love you, too, but there's a time and a place for everything." He put Champ down on all four feet and took firm hold of the ex-neckcloth. "Off you go," he said to us.

We scurried away to the attic stairs. I looked

around as we went and saw Count Robert using one of his gleaming shoes to urge Champ into the Family lift. "Get on, stupid!" he was saying. "It's quite safe. Or do you *want* to meet Amos in a rage?"

Christopher was very excited as we sped back to the clothes store. "My guess was right, Grant! You heard the Count, did you? There are lots more places beside those two frightful towers. Millie must be in one. Will you come with me to look for her tomorrow on our morning off?"

Well, of course I would. I could hardly wait to explore. Next time, I thought, I would take my camera with me, too, and collect some real evidence of other worlds, or dimensions, or whatever they were.

Before that, of course, we had to get into new clothes, hide the gunky ones in an empty room, and rush off to our supper. Then we had to stand by the dining room wall with those stupid cloths over our arms while Mr. Amos, Andrew, and two other footmen served the Family with their Dinner. Neither of us dared do a thing wrong. Mr. Amos was still in a rage. Whatever Count Robert had said to him, fury about it was bottled into Mr. Amos, so that he was like a huge pear-shaped balloon full of seething gas. Andrew and the other two tiptoed around him. Christopher and I tried our best to look like part of the wall.

The Countess was in a rage, too, but she wasn't doing nearly such a good job of bottling it as Mr. Amos was. I suppose she had no need to bother.

Nothing was right for her that evening. There was a thumbprint on her wineglass, she said, a speck of dirt on her fork, she said, and iron mold on her napkin. Then she found a smear of pink polish on the salt cellar. Each time one of us was sent whizzing away to fetch a new one of whatever was wrong, and then, while she waited for it, she turned to Count Robert, opened her eyes wide, and did her *"Why?"* at him. When I came back with a shiny new salt cellar, she was saying, "Really, darling, you *must* grow out of this habit of only pleasing yourself."

Count Robert stood up to it better than I would have done. He smiled and said, "But *you* asked me to arrange it, Mother."

"But not *now*, Robert. Not when we've got company coming to celebrate your engagement!" the Countess said. "Amos, this plate is dirty. See this speck on the edge here?"

Mr. Amos leaned over her shoulder and inspected the plate. "I believe that is part of the pattern, my lady." He shot Count Robert a mean look while he said it. "I'll have it replaced at once," he said, and snapped his fingers at Christopher.

By the time Christopher whizzed back with a fresh plate, Count Robert was really getting it in the neck. "And you haven't even considered where this hireling of yours will eat," the Countess said. "When I think of all the trouble I went to, to teach you that a gentleman should consider others, I quite despair of you, Robert! You behave like a greedy child.

Greedy and selfish. Me, me, me! Your character is so weak. Why can't you learn to be strong, just for once? Why?"

Christopher rolled his eyes at me as he took up his place by the wall again. And it really was amazing the way the Countess went on at Count Robert, who after all *owned* Stallery, as if he were about six years old, just as if there were no footmen standing like wooden statues, or us listening to her, or Mr. Amos by the serving table looking meanly glad that the Count was in trouble. I was quite embarrassed. But I was also pretty curious to know what Count Robert had done to annoy the Countess and Mr. Amos so.

By this time the Countess was on about the way the weaknesses of Count Robert's character had shown up when he was a toddler and kept reminding him of bad things he had done when he was two and four and ten years old. The Count just sat there, bearing it. Lady Felice kept her head down over her plate. But the Countess noticed her, too.

"I'm glad to see that your silly little eating disorder is over, dear."

"It was nothing, Mother," Lady Felice said.

So then the Countess decided that the fish was overcooked and told Mr. Amos to send it back to the kitchen. Mr. Amos snapped his fingers at me to take it. "And be sure," he said, handing me the loaded tray, "to tell Chef exactly what her ladyship found wrong with it."

I missed the next bit, while I went away through the hall and the swing door, down the steps to the undercroft, and on to the kitchen, but Christopher said it was just more of the same. In the kitchen the Chef put his hands on his hips and stared at me humorously. All the footmen called him the Great Dictator, but I thought he was quite a nice man. "And what's supposed to be wrong with it?" he asked me.

"She says it's overcooked," I said. "She's in a really bad mood."

"One of *those* evenings, eh?" the Chef said. "Slimming spells disagreed with her, and she's saving herself for the roast, is she? All right, get back and tell her that yours truly grovels all over the carpet and you needn't mention that this fish was perfect."

Back I went, all the way to the dining room, where I managed to go in almost exactly as I was supposed to, slipping in sideways with nearly no noise. Mr. Amos was waiting there for me. Behind his bulky pear shape the room felt like a thunder-storm. "And what has Chef to say for himself?" he demanded, low and urgent.

"He grovels on the carpet and I'm not to say the fish was perfect," I said.

That was stupid of me. I think it was Christopher's influence that made me say it. Mr. Amos had the perfect opportunity to get rid of some of *his* bad temper on me. He gave me a glare from his stone-colored eyes that made my knees go weak.

Luckily for me, Lady Felice chose that moment to jump up from her chair and fling her big white napkin onto the table. Two wineglasses went over.

"Mother!" she said, almost in a scream. "Will you *stop* going on at Robert as if he'd committed a crime! All he's done is hire the librarian you *asked* him to hire! So leave him *alone*, will you!"

The Countess turned to Lady Felice. Her eyes went wide, and her lips began shaping the "Wh—" of one of her dreadful *"Why?"*s.

"And if you say, 'Why, dear?,' *once* more," Lady Felice screamed, "I shall pick up this candlestick and *brain* you with it!" She gave out a sound like a laugh and a sob mixed, and rushed for the door. Mr. Amos and I both had to dodge. Lady Felice stormed past us and crashed out of the room like a warm, scented hurricane and slammed the door behind her.

In the rest of the room she left a feverish dead silence. Andrew and the other footmen sprang into action, silently and on tiptoe, mopping up spilled wine, taking away the fallen glasses, and whipping away all the knives, forks, and spoons still there at Lady Felice's place. The other two at the table simply sat there, while—just as if nothing had happened—Mr. Amos walked around to speak gently in the Countess's ear.

"Chef sends his profound apologies, my lady, and says it will not occur again. Allow me to bring on the next course, my lady."

The Countess, in a frozen way, nodded. Because the footmen were still busy wiping up wine, Mr.

Amos beckoned Christopher and me over to the food lift and passed us tureens and sauceboats to carry over to the table. I was not sure where to put things, but Christopher whirled everything across and dumped them any old where and then bowed and patted the mats with both hands, as if he knew just what he was doing. Mr. Amos glowered at him over his shoulder as he picked up a massive platter piled with meat.

The Countess, still looking frozen, said to Count Robert, "Felice is so tiresome these days. I think it's high time she was married. I shall invite that nice Mr. Seuly to dinner with our other guests. I feel sure I can induce Felice to marry him."

Count Robert said, "Are you making some kind of a joke, Mother?"

"Not at all. I never joke, dear," said the Countess. "Mr. Seuly *is* Mayor of Stallchester, after all. He is wealthy, and widowed, and he has a very respectable position in life—and it's not important who Felice marries, the way it is for *you*, dear. *You* are engaged to a title, but—"

"*Give me patience!*" Count Robert suddenly shouted out. He leaped to his feet, whacked his napkin on the table and—like Lady Felice—made for the door with great strides just as Mr. Amos arrived with the platter of meat.

I never could work out how Mr. Amos missed Count Robert. The Count did not seem to see either Mr. Amos or the meat. He just charged out through the door and banged it shut behind him. Mr. Amos somehow managed to raise the vast platter above both their heads and then to twirl himself away. The Countess sat, still frozen, watching Mr. Amos waltzing around with the great steaming dish.

When at last he stopped twirling, she said, "I don't understand, Amos. What is making my children so very tiresome lately?"

"I believe it is their extreme youth, my lady," Mr. Amos replied, laying the platter reverently down on the table. "They are mere adolescents, after all."

Christopher's eyes swiveled to mine in amazement. As he said to me afterward, you called people adolescents at his age and mine. "Lady Felice has come of age," he said, "even if they did have to cancel the party for it. And Count Robert must be in his twenties! Grant, do you think that the Countess is mad and Mr. Amos humors her?"

He said that much later, though. At that time we had to stand there while the Countess obstinately plowed through three more courses, half a bottle of wine, and dessert, and looked angrier with every mouthful. Mr. Amos's bottled rage grew so huge that even Christopher hardly dared move. The footmen all pretended they were invisible, and so did I.

And it did not stop there. The Countess laid down her napkin and went to the Grand Saloon, telling Mr. Amos that the Improvers could bring her coffee there. This meant that Christopher and I had to race upstairs after her with trays of comfits and chocolates, while Mr. Amos followed us with coffee, herding us like a rather heavy sheepdog.

The Grand Saloon was vast. It stretched from the front to the back of the house and was full of things to fall over, like golden footstools and small, shiny tables. The Countess sat in the middle of it, where Christopher and I had to keep dribbling coffee for her into a cup so small that it reminded me of the crucibles Uncle Alfred did his experiments in. I drizzled in coffee, and Christopher dripped in cream, while Mr. Amos stood by the distant door, rocking on his small, shiny feet and waiting for us to make a mistake so that he could vent some of his rage on us. We knew that the very least that could happen was that Mr. Amos would cancel our morning off, so we were very, very careful. We tiptoed and poured for what seemed a century, until the Countess said, "Amos, I wish to be alone now." By that time my arms were shaking and my calves ached with tiptoeing, but we hadn't made any mistakes, so Mr. Amos had to let us go.

"Whew!" I said when we were safely out of hearing. "What *has* Count Robert done to make them both so angry? Did you find out?"

"Well," Christopher said, scratching at his head so that his sleek hair separated into curls, "you probably know as much as I do, Grant. But while you were away with the fish, the Countess *did* say something about hiring penniless students to catalog the library here. Though why that should make anyone angry, I haven't a clue. After all, she's supposed to have *asked* Count Robert to hire someone. The Librarian at Chrestomanci Castle says you have to have a proper list of the books you've got or you can't find any of them. And I can't see why that should make Mr. Amos angry as well."

I felt suddenly full of an idea. "Could it be," I said, "that they have *secret* books in there? You know, books about pulling the possibilities or explaining how to work the changes at the top of the house?"

Christopher stood still in the passage outside our room. "Now that *is* a notion!" he said. "Grant, I think we ought to take a look at this library when we're free tomorrow morning."

❦

12

NATURALLY THAT NEXT morning we went to look at the top of the mansion first. Christopher was seriously anxious about this girl Millie, and I was really excited about what we'd see there next. We went to the attics as soon as we were free.

On the way, I dodged into our room and got my camera. I wanted to have proof that we weren't imagining the strange towers. As it was a dull sort of day, with fog down in Stallchester valley and only Stall Crag sticking up out of it, I made sure the flash was working.

Christopher jumped at the sudden brightness. "Don't count your chickens, Grant," he said while we crept along to the streak of paint on the wall. "You may not have anything to photograph."

This made me sure that my bad karma would cancel out any chance of the mansion changing. But we were in luck. Just as we passed the stripe of paint, there was the most almighty sideways wrench. Christopher and I were thrown against each other and sort of staggered around in a half circle, with me hanging on to Christopher's neckcloth for balance. And as soon as we were facing the other way, we realized that the passage we had just come through was now a tall pointed archway made of stone. Beyond it was somewhere so shadowy and stony that I was glad I'd remembered my camera flash.

"Looks like that tower we hauled the dog up again," Christopher said as we went through the archway.

It was nothing like the slate tower. The archway opened into a stone-floored gallery held up on one side by fancy stone pillars, each pillar a different shape. The roof was a basketwork of stone vaulting, and the other wall was blank stone. The vaulting and the carvings on the pillars must have been picked out in gold paint once, but a lot of the gold had flaked off, leaving the patterns hard to see. From the space beyond the pillars there came vast, soft, shuffling echoes. It felt huge out there, but not as if people were living in it. It was more like the time my school had gone around Stallchester Cathedral, when the guide had taken us up into the passages in the dome.

Christopher said, "Millie's here! Quite near!" and set off at a run to the other end of the gallery, where the gloomy light came from.

I raced after him with my camera bouncing on my chest. The gallery opened into a big curving stone staircase, leading down into the gray light. Christopher went plunging down the stairs, and I followed. And as soon as we came around the first curve, we realized we were on an enormous spiral—a *double* spiral, we realized after the next curve. There was another staircase opposite ours, sort of wrapped around the one we were on. When we leaned over the high stone side, we could see the two staircases spiraling down and down. When we looked up, we saw the inside of a tower overhead. It had fancy windows in it, but they were so dirty that it was no wonder the place was in such gloom.

Footsteps rang, like an echo of ours. We looked over at the other staircase, and there was a girl there, hurrying down to get to the same level as us. *"Christopher!"* she shouted. "What are *you* doing here?"

It was hard to see what the girl was like because of the gloom and because the staircases were so big and so wide apart, but her voice sounded nice. She seemed to have a rounded face and straight brownish hair, but that was all I could see. I swung up my camera and photographed her as she dashed down opposite us, which made her stop and try to cover her eyes.

"Meet us at the bottom!" Christopher shouted at her. His voice boomed around in a hundred echoes. "I'll tell you then."

In fact he tried to tell her as we dashed on down and around, the two of us circling around Millie and Millie circling around us, while the space rang with our hurrying feet and the voices of the other two. They kept shouting at each other as they went, trying to explain what they were doing here, but I don't think either of them could hear properly because of the echoes. I could tell they were truly glad to see each other. I took several more photos as we went. It was such an amazing place.

I think Millie shouted something like "I'm so pleased you came! I've been having such a frustrating time! This house keeps changing, and I can't seem to get *out*!"

"Me, too!" Christopher bellowed back. "I had to take a job as a lackey. What do you get to eat?"

"There's always food downstairs," Millie yelled in reply, "but I don't know where it comes from."

"How did you get *in*?" Christopher roared. The echoes got worse and worse. Neither of us could hear what Millie shouted in answer to this. Christopher roared again, "You know the main changes happen at the top of the house, do you?" I think Millie yelled back that of *course* she did, she wasn't a fool, but she never seemed to *get* anywhere. And she seemed to try and describe her frustrations as we all hammered down several more spirals. Then Christopher began bellowing, across her description, that *one* of the places was bound to be the perfect place for the two of them to live in secret—but we shot down the last curve at this point, and there was ceiling over the staircase. The echoes quite suddenly cut off. And we found ourselves in a plain stone hallway. Christopher stopped shouting and turned to me. "Quick, Grant. Where's the other stairway?"

We both ran along the hall to the place we thought the other spiral ought to come out, but there was only wall there. It had little windows in it that looked out on to woodland, so it was obviously wrong.

"We got turned around," Christopher panted, and he dashed back the other way so fast that I could barely keep up.

There was a door at the end of the hall that way. Christopher thundered through it and on into the middle of a largish room, where he stopped dead beside a pile of sofas and armchairs with a sheet draped on top of them. Beyond that, big windows showed a garden that was mostly weeds. Rain was falling on the weeds. There were more windows, showing more weeds, in the left-hand wall, a harp or something in one corner, and nothing but a big empty fireplace in the right-hand wall.

"Not here," Christopher said in a defeated way.

I only had time to take one photo of the harp thing before he was off again, back the way we had come, to the hall and the staircase again. "I think I saw a door," his voice said in the distance. "Ah, yes."

The door was behind the stairs. Christopher had opened it and rushed through before I caught up, but when I did, he was moving slowly and cautiously down the dark stone passage beyond. There was a door on each side and a door at the end. The door on the right was open, and we could see it was a sort of big cloakroom with a row of dusty boots on the floor, several grimy coats on pegs, and a cobwebby window that looked out onto wet woodland. Christopher made angry noises and barged me aside to open the door across the passage. The room there was a dining room, as neglected and dusty as the cloakroom, and its window looked on to the weedy garden.

Christopher expressed his feelings by slamming that door before I could take a photo. He plunged on to the door at the end of the passage.

There were kitchens beyond that, two quite cozy-looking places with rocking chairs and big scrubbed tables and some kind of a stove in the farther one. There was a scullery beyond that which opened into a rainy yard with red tumbledown sheds all around it. By this time even Christopher was having to admit that this house we were in was much, much smaller than the place with the double staircase.

"I don't *understand* it!" he said, standing miserably beside the table in the second kitchen. "I didn't *feel* any change. Did you?" He looked almost as if he might cry.

I wished he would keep his voice down. There were definite signs that someone had been in this kitchen recently. Warmth was coming from the stove, and there was a bag of knitting on one of the rocking chairs. I could see crumbs on the table around a magazine of some kind, as if someone had been reading while they had breakfast. "Maybe the change happened while you were shouting at Millie," I said, very quietly, to give Christopher a hint.

He looked around at the stove, the knitting, and the table. "This must be where Millie comes to eat," he said. "Grant, you stay here in case she turns up. I'm going back up the stairs to see if she's there anywhere."

"Does Millie do much knitting?" I asked, but he had dashed off again by then, and he didn't hear me. I sighed and sat in the chair by the table. It was clear to me, if not to Christopher, that the two staircases split apart somehow on the last spiral. Millie must have ended up somewhere as different from this house as the wooden tower was from Stallery. And I didn't like this house. People lived here. They had left furniture, coats, and knitting about, and they might come back at any moment and accuse me of trespassing. I had no idea what I would say if they did. Ask if they'd seen Millie, perhaps?

In order not to feel too nervous, I pulled the magazine across and looked through it while I waited for Christopher. It was quite, quite strange, so strange that it fascinated me—so very strange, in fact, that I was not surprised to find it was dated 1399, February issue. It could not have been anything like that old. It smelled new. It was printed on thick, furry paper in weird washed-out blues and reds, in the kind of round, plain letters you get in books in infant school. *Gossip Weekly*, it was called. There were no photographs or advertisements in it at all, and it was full of quite long articles that had titles like "From Rags to Riches" or "Singer's Lost Honeymoon" or "Scandal in Bank of Asia." Each article was illustrated by a drawing. Blue and red drawings. I had never seen such bad drawings in my life. They were so bad that most of them looked like caricatures, though I could see that the artist had put in lots of red and blue shadings, trying to make the drawings look like real people. And here was the really queer thing—about half of them looked like people I knew. The lady at the top of "Rags to Riches" could almost have been Daisy Bolger, and one of the drawings for the bank scandal looked exactly like Uncle Alfred. But it *must* have been bad drawing. When I turned to the big picture beside an article called "Royal Occasion," the picture looked like our king, except the caption called him "Prince of Alpenholm." One of the courtiers bowing to him might almost have been Mr. Hugo.

Now come on, I thought. This is, actually and truly, a magazine from another world. For all I know, in this world someone just like Hugo really is a royal courtier. How amazing. And I started reading about the royal occasion. I had got most of the way down one washed-out blue column, without understanding what the occasion was, or why it happened, when I heard heavy, slow footsteps coming in through the scullery.

They were the footsteps of a person you definitely did not want finding you sitting in their house. They stamped. There was angry puffing with them, and bad-tempered grunting. I dropped the magazine and tried to slide quietly away into the farther kitchen. Unfortunately, my foot knocked the chair as I slid out of it, and it scraped on the floor, quite loudly. The person in the scullery put on speed and arrived in the doorway while I was still in the middle of the room. This is my Evil Fate at work again, I thought.

She was a heavily built woman with a blunt, mauve face. I could see at a glance she was the kind of woman who *knows* you're up to no good, even if you aren't, and calls the police. She had a rubber sheet over her head against the rain, and she was wearing big rubber boots and carrying a can of milk. And she was a witch. I knew this the moment she put the milk can down and said, "Who are you? What are you doing here?" I could feel the witch-craft buzzing off her as she spoke.

"A mistake," I said. "Just going."

I backed away toward the door as fast as I could. She came trudging toward me in her big boots with her hands hanging, ready to grab. "They always find me," she said. "They send spies, and they find me wherever I hide."

She was saying this to make me think she was mad and harmless. I knew she was because I could feel her casting a spell. It buzzed in my ears under her words until I could hardly think or see. So I did the only thing I could manage. I raised my camera and took her picture. She was nearer than I realized. The flash went off right in her face. She screamed, and her rubber sheet fell off as she put her hands up to hide her face. I heard her fall over the chair I had kicked as I pelted away through the other kitchen.

I ran like mad, through the corridor and out into the stone hall. I raced up those stone stairs, around and up, around and up, with the other set of stairs spinning dizzily past as I climbed, until my breath was almost gone, but I still hardly slowed up when I met Christopher coming down.

"*Run!*" I shrieked at him. "There's a *witch* in that kitchen! *Run!*"

He said, "We can do better than that, Grant," and seized hold of my elbow.

Before I could shake him off, we were somehow at the top at the stairs in a strong buzzing of magic. This buzzing was somehow wider and cleaner feeling than the buzzing the witch had made. As Christopher pulled me by my elbow along the gallery I remembered that he was supposed to be a nine-lifed enchanter, which made me feel a little safer, but I didn't really feel safe until we came out through the archway into the smell of warm wood and plaster in the attics of Stallery.

"*Phew . . . !*" I began.

Christopher said, "In our room first, Grant," and turned me around. The archway had gone then, and we were able to scurry along the attic passages to our room, where we both sat heavily on our beds, me panting fit to burst and Christopher all limp, white and dejected. "Tell," he said, with his head hanging.

So I told him about the witch.

Christopher's head came up, and he said, "Hmm. I wonder if *she's* the reason Millie can't get out of there. Millie's an enchantress, you know. She *ought* to be able to leave. Instead, she seems to keep being shunted on to another probability. There was no sign of her on those stairs, and it could well be the witch doing it. We'd better go back and deal with the witch, then."

He got up. I got up, too, although my legs were weak and shaking, and followed him out beyond the stripe of paint again. Christopher groaned when we got there. There was no archway—nothing but the ordinary attics we had just come through. We sat on the floorboards for quite some time, waiting, but there was no change.

"You panicked me, Grant," Christopher said. "We should have gone down, not up. Oh, damn it! We were so close!"

"It was probably my bad karma," I said.

"Oh, don't talk nonsense!" he said. "Let's go and look for secret books in the library. I'm sick of sitting here. One of the maids is going to see us breaking the rules if we're not careful."

He was probably right. There seemed to be a lot of female noise coming from the other end of the attics suddenly, as if all the maids had arrived there at once. The empty space by the windows echoed to shrieks and giggles, and I could feel the floorboards creaking under me, the way they always did when everyone came up to bed. When we got up and went through our side of the attics, we found there was a fair amount of noise there, too. There were doors being slammed, running feet, and men laughing. A big deep man's voice was singing inside the nearest bathroom. It was so out of tune that I giggled.

Christopher raised his eyebrows at me. "Gregor?" he asked.

"Mr. Amos?" I said.

Christopher laughed then. It seemed to do him good. He was a lot more cheerful as we went down in the lift. He nodded at my camera, still hanging around my neck. "Are you intending to photograph the books, Grant?"

"No," I said. "I'd need a different lens. I just forgot I'd got it. Why are we getting off at floor two? The library's on the ground floor."

"Ah. Admire my forethought and cunning, Grant," Christopher said. "That library has a sort of minstrel's gallery, and the door to it is on this floor. We can sneak in and make sure the Countess isn't in there consulting a cookery book or something."

"Ha, ha," I said. I was glad Christopher had cheered up, but there were times when his jokes really annoyed me.

But there *was* a woman in the library. When we softly opened the low wooden door and crept through onto a high balcony lined with shelves of books, we could see her through the carved wooden bars at the front of it. We both ducked down and knelt on the carpet, but she could have seen us through the bars, even so. She was sitting at the top of a long wooden stepladder, reaching for a book on a high shelf. The one good thing was that she wasn't the Countess, because she had dark hair, but that didn't alter the fact that she only needed to turn her head to see us there.

I grabbed for the door, ready to crawl out through it at once. "Never fear, Grant," Christopher said. I judged from the buzzing feeling I was getting that he had put a spell of invisibility around us on the spot. Then I gathered it was probably a spell of silence, too, because Christopher first sat down comfortably with his arms around his knees and then spoke in his normal voice. "We wait, Grant. Again. Honestly, Grant, I've never *done* so much waiting around as I have in this place."

"But she could be here for *ages*," I whispered. The stepladder was so close to the balcony that I couldn't help whispering. "I think she must be the penniless student who's supposed to catalog the books."

Christopher looked critically through the bars of the balcony. "She doesn't look penniless to me," he said.

I had to admit that she didn't. She was wearing a dark blue dress that was both flowing around her and clinging to her in an expensive way, and her feet, hooked on a rung of the ladder, were in soft red boots, really nice ones. Her dark hair fell to her shoulders in the same sort of costly hairstyle that Lady Felice had.

"She's a friend of the Family come to borrow a book," Christopher said.

While he was saying it, the lady took down a book and opened it. She looked at the title page, nodded, and made a note on the pad on her knee. Then she leafed through the book, shut it, looked at the binding, and shook her head. She slipped some kind of card into the front and turned to put the book carefully into a box that was fastened to the back of the ladder.

She was my sister, Anthea.

I stood up. I couldn't help it. I nearly called out. I would have done if Christopher had not grabbed me and pulled me down. "Someone else coming!" he said.

13

❧❦❧

CHRISTOPHER WAS RIGHT. The big main door of the library opened, and Count Robert came in. He shut the door behind him and stood smiling up at my sister. "Hallo, love," he said. "Are you on the job already? It was only a pretext, you know."

And my sister Anthea cried out, "Robert!" and came galloping down the ladder. She flung herself into Count Robert's arms, and the two of them began hugging and kissing each other frantically.

At this point Christopher got cramp in one leg. I think it was embarrassment, really. Or it could have been running up and down those stairs. But it was real cramp. He whipped himself into a ball and rolled about, clutching his left calf, with his face in a wide grin of agony. I was forced to park my camera on the lowest bookshelf and lean over him, pounding and kneading at his striped silk leg. I could feel the muscles under the stocking in a hard ball, and you know how much that hurts. It used to happen to me after skiing sometimes. I tried to make Christopher take hold of his own foot and pull his toes upward, but he didn't seem to understand that this was the way to cure cramp. He just rolled and clutched.

I kept glancing through the bars in case my sister or Count Robert had noticed us, but they didn't seem to. They were now leaning backward with their arms around each other's waists, laughing and saying, "Darling!" rather often.

"Ooh—ow! Ooh—ow!" Christopher went.

"Pull your *toes*!" I kept whispering.

"Ooh—*ow*!" he said.

"Then use some magic, you fool!" I said.

I heard the main door open again and looked. This time it was Hugo who came in. He stood and smiled at Anthea, too, all over his puggy face. "Good to see you, Anthea," he said, and then something that sounded like "Join the club." But Christopher's knee hit my chin just then, and I went back to kneading. When I next looked, the three of them had gone to the leather chairs by the window, where Count Robert and Anthea each sat on the arm of the same chair, while Hugo leaned on the back of it. Hugo was talking quickly and urgently, and Count Robert and Anthea looked up at him and nodded anxiously at what he said.

I wanted to know what Hugo was saying. I took hold of Christopher's ear, put my mouth to it, and more or less shouted, "Use some *magic*, I said!"

That seemed to get through. There was some frantic buzzing. Then Christopher abruptly straightened out and lay with his face in the carpet, panting. "Oh, horrible!" he gasped. "And deaf in one ear, too."

I looked down into the library again in time to see Count Robert kiss Anthea and get up. Hugo kissed her, too, a friendly kiss on one cheek, and they both turned to go. But the library door opened yet again. This time it was Mr. Amos who came in, looking anything but friendly. Christopher and I both froze.

"Has this young person got everything she requires?" Mr. Amos asked, with truly dreadful politeness.

"Well, not really," my sister said, cool as a cucumber. "I was just explaining that I need a computer if I'm to do this job properly."

Hugo said, with an anxious look, "I told you, miss. Atmospheric conditions here in Stallery mean that your programming is liable to random changes."

Count Robert turned to Mr. Amos with his chin up, all lordly. "*Have* we a computer, Amos?"

It was a splendid cover-up from all three. Mr. Amos gave Count Robert a small bow and said, "I believe so, my lord. I will see to it personally." Then he went away, very slow and stately.

Count Robert and Hugo grinned at each other and then at Anthea. Hugo gave her a wink over his shoulder as he followed Count Robert out of the library.

"Phew!" said my sister. Then she swung around in a swirl of expensive skirt and came marching toward the balcony, looking really angry. "Come down out of there," she said, "whoever you are!"

I hardly needed to look at Christopher's face, squashed against the carpet, to know that he had forgotten all about his spells of invisibility and silence from the moment he got cramp. I stood up. "Hallo, Anthea," I said.

She caught hold of the stepladder and stared. She was really astonished. "*Conrad!*" she said. "What on *earth* are you doing here dressed like a lackey?"

"I *am* a lackey," I said.

"But that's ridiculous!" she said. "You ought to be at school."

"Uncle Alfred said I could go to Stall High as soon as I had expiated my Evil Fate," I explained.

"What evil fate? What are you *talking* about? Come down here this instant, and tell me properly," Anthea said. I had to smile. Anthea pointed over and over at the carpet in front of her as she gave her commands. It was so exactly what she used to do in the bookshop when she was annoyed with me that I felt almost happy as I climbed down the steep stair from the balcony. "And your friend," Anthea commanded, jabbing her finger toward another place on the carpet.

Christopher got up, quite meekly, and limped down the stair after me. Anthea looked from him to me.

"This is Christopher," I said. "He's a nine-lifed enchanter, and he's here on false pretenses like I am."

"Really?" Anthea said suspiciously. "Well, I

felt someone doing magic, so I suppose that *could* be true. Now stand there, Conrad Tesdinic, and tell me all about this nonsense that Uncle Alfred's been putting into your head."

"I knew it was nonsense," Christopher said. "But I thought his name was Grant. Are you his sister? You look quite alike."

"Yes. Shut up, you!" Anthea said. "Conrad?"

Christopher, to my surprise, did what Anthea said. He stood there attentively, looking slightly amused, while I told her what Uncle Alfred had said about my bad karma and how it was going to kill me unless I dealt with the person who was causing it. Anthea sighed and looked at the ceiling. So I told her that Mayor Seuly and the rest of the Magicians' Circle had seen my Evil Fate clinging to me, too, and how they had given me the way to *know* the person responsible before Uncle Alfred sent me to Stallery. Anthea frowned heavily at this, and Christopher looked even more amused. But he seemed quite surprised when Anthea said, "Oh dear! I feel really guilty! I shouldn't have left you. And Mother? Didn't she even *try* to tell you Uncle Alfred was talking nonsense?"

"She's always busy writing," I said uncomfortably. "We never talked about my Fate. And it isn't nonsense, is it? Mayor Seuly thought it was true."

"Everyone knows he's a crook. He just wants his chance to make money the way Stallery does," my sister said. "I think he lied to you, Conrad, in order to find out how to pull the probabilities himself." She looked from me to Christopher. "Have you discovered yet who's doing it, and how?"

"No," we both said, and Christopher asked, "So it doesn't happen naturally, then?"

"Some of it does," Anthea said. "But someone is helping it along somehow. This is something Robert and I would really like to know about. It's one reason why I'm here. And what were you supposed to do, Conrad, when you found out who was doing it?"

"Summon a Walker," I said.

Christopher and Anthea both looked utterly puzzled.

"They gave me this wine cork," I said, fetching it out. I was feeling awful by then, stupid and taken in and, well, sort of pointless. If I didn't have a Fate, then what *was* I?

I felt worse when Christopher said, "I did try to tell him he hasn't any bad karma."

"But he might have an awful lot if he does what Mayor Seuly and Uncle Alfred seem to want!" Anthea said. She gave me a worried, puzzled look. It made me feel worse than ever. "Conrad, for goodness' sake, what stopped Mother paying for you to go on at school?"

"She hasn't any money," I said. "Uncle Alfred owns the bookshop and—"

"But he *doesn't*!" Anthea exclaimed. "Oh, I should have written and *told* you! I admit that puzzled me, too, so I went and looked up Father's Will in the Record Office as soon as I got to Ludwich, and he'd left the entire shop to Mother."

"What? All of it?" I said.

"All of it," she said. "And to you and me after that. He left Uncle Alfred some money, but that's all. Come to think of it, I do remember Father saying to me when he was dying that he hoped Alfred would take his money and go, because he didn't trust him as far as he could throw him. . . ." She tailed off in an uncertain way. "Now why didn't I remember that before?"

She was looking vaguely at Christopher as she said this. He must have thought she was asking him because he said, "If he's a magician, this uncle, he could cast a selective forget spell quite easily. They're not difficult."

"He *must* have cast one," Anthea said, and went on decisively, "Conrad, I'm going to ring Mother up—I was going to anyway, and this makes it urgent—and see what she says."

There was a telephone in the corner of the library. Anthea marched across to it and dialed the number of our bookshop. I hurried after her and tried to listen in. Anthea turned the receiver so that I could distantly hear a bored woman's voice say, "Grant and Tesdinic. How can I help?"

Anthea mouthed at me, asking, "Who?" I said, "Daisy. New assistant after you left."

Anthea nodded. "Could I speak to Franconia Grant, please?" she said.

Daisy said, "Who?"

"The famous feminist writer," Anthea said. "I

believe she married a Mr. Tesdinic, but we feminists don't mention that."

"Ooh!" Daisy went in the distance. "I get you. Just a minute and I'll see if she's free."

There were muffled footsteps running about and voices calling murkily. I heard Uncle Alfred, faint and far off, saying, "Not me—I don't have anything to do with those harpies!" Finally there was a clatter, and my mother's voice said, "Franconia Grant speaking."

From then on it was much easier to hear. Christopher was leaning over us, wanting to hear, too.

Anthea said cheerfully, "Hallo, Mother. This is Anthea."

My mother said, "Good heavens," which was not surprising. It *had* been four years. "I thought you'd left here for good," she added.

"I have, really," Anthea said. "But I thought you ought to know when your daughter gets married."

"I don't believe it," my mother said. "No daughter of mine would ever even think of enslaving herself to a male ethic—"

"Well, I am," Anthea said. "He's wonderful. I knew you'd disapprove, but I had to tell you. And how's Conrad?" There was a blank pause on the other end of the line. "My little brother," Anthea said. "Remember?"

"Oh," said my mother. "Oh yes. But he's not here now. He insisted on leaving school as soon as he was old enough, and he took a job right outside this district. I—"

"Did Uncle Alfred tell you that?" Anthea interrupted.

"No, of course not," my mother said. "You know as well as I do that Alfred is a compulsive liar. *He* told me Conrad was staying on at school. I even signed the form, and then Conrad went off without a word, just like you did. I don't know what I've done to deserve two children like you." Then, while Anthea was trying to say that it was not true about me at least, my mother suddenly snapped, "Who is this wonderful man who has lured you into female bondage, Anthea?"

"If you mean marriage, Mother," Anthea said, "it's Count Robert of Stallery."

At this, my mother uttered something that sounded like "That impostor!," though it was more of a strange wailing yelp, and dropped the phone. We heard it clatter onto a hard surface. There was some kind of distant commotion then, until someone firmly put the phone back and cut us off.

As Anthea hung the whirring receiver back on its rest, I had the hardest job in the world not to burst into tears. Tears pushed and welled at my eyes, and I had to stand rigid and stare at the shelves of books in front of me. They bulged and swam. I felt utterly let down and betrayed. Everyone had lied to me. By now I didn't even know what the truth *was*.

Anthea put her arm around me, hard. Christopher said, "I know how you feel, Grant. Something a bit like this happened to me, too, once."

Anthea asked him, "*Is* our mother under a spell, do you think?"

"She just doesn't care!" I managed to say.

"No, Grant, I think it's a bit more complicated than that," Christopher said. "Think of it as a mixture of lies and very small spells done by someone who knows her very well and who knows she'll go where she's pushed if she's pushed often enough and gently enough. It sounds as if much the same was done to you, Grant. What's this Walker you were supposed to summon? Why don't you try summoning it now and see what happens?"

The same dry-mouthed fear seized me that I had felt in the Magicians' Circle. I was horrified. "No, no!" I cried out. "I'm not supposed to do that until I *know*!"

"Know what?" my sister asked.

"The—the person who's—the one who I should have killed in my last life," I stammered.

I felt Anthea and Christopher look at each other across my head. "Fear spell," Christopher said. "And you *don't* know, do you, Grant? Then it's much safer to summon the thing now, before there's any real danger."

"Yes, do that. Do it at once, Conrad," Anthea said. "I want to know what he's making you do. And you," she said to Christopher, "if you really *are* an enchanter, you can stand guard on the door, in case that butler comes back with a computer."

Christopher's face was such a mixture of surprise and outrage that I nearly laughed. "*If* I am an enchanter!" he said. "*If!* I've a good mind to turn you into a hippopotamus and see how Count Robert likes you then!" But he went and stood with his shoulders against the door all the same, glowering at my sister. "Summon away, Grant," he said. "Do what the hippopotamus tells you."

Anthea still had her arm around me. "I won't let it hurt you," she said, just as if I were six years old again and she was putting plaster on my knee.

I leaned on her as I took the wine-blotched cork out of my waistcoat pocket. I still felt miserably ashamed of myself for believing all those lies, but the dry-mouthed fear seemed to have gone. And the cork was so ordinary. It had *Illary Wines 1893* stamped on it, and it smelled faintly sour. I began to feel silly. I even wondered if the Magicians' Circle had been playing a joke on me. But I pointed the cork at the end wall of the library and said, "I hereby summon a Walker. Come to me, and give me what I need. I think it's a hoax," I added to Anthea.

"No, it *isn't*," Anthea said, sounding sharp and stern. Her arm went tight around my shoulders.

There was a sudden feeling of vast open distances. It was a very odd feeling, because the library was still all around us, close and warm and filled with the quiet, mildewy scent of books, but the distances were there, too. I could smell them. They brought a sharp, icy smell like the winds over frozen plains. Then I realized I could *see* the distance, too. Beyond the books, farther off than the edge of any world, there was a huge curving horizon, faintly lit by an icy sunrise, and winds that I couldn't feel blew off it. I knew those were the winds of eternity. And real fear gripped me, nothing to do with any fear spell.

Then I realized that I could see the Walker

coming. Across the huge horizon, lit from behind by the strange hidden sunlight, a dark figure came walking. He or she walked in an odd, hurried, careful way, bending a little over the small thing it carried in both hands, as if whatever it was might spill or break if it was jogged in any way. So it walked smoothly but quickly in little steps, and the winds blew its hair and its clothes out sideways—except that the hair and the clothes never moved at all. On it came, and on. And all the time I could see the shelves of books in front of me, in ordinary daylight, and yet I could see the distance and the Walker just as clearly.

Anthea's arm was clamped around me. I could feel her trembling. Christopher's shoulders thumped against the library door as he tried to back away, and I heard him mutter, "Gracious heavens!" We all knew there was nothing we could do to stop the Walker coming.

It came nearer and nearer with its strange pattering strides, and the winds blew its clothes and its hair and they still never moved, and it still bent over the small thing in its hands. When it was only yards away, and the room filled with gusts of arctic scent that we could smell but not feel, I could have sworn the Walker was taller than the library ceiling—and that was two stories high. But when it came right up to me, it was only a foot or so taller than Anthea. It was properly inside the room then, and I was numbed with the cold that I couldn't feel, only smell. It sort of bent over me. I saw a sweep of dark hair blown unmovingly away from a white face and long dark eyes. The eyes looked at me intently as it held out one hand to me. I had never seen any eyes so intent. I knew as I looked back that this was because the Walker was bound to get whatever it gave me exactly right. *Exactly* right. But I had to give it the cork first in exchange.

I put the cork into the hand it was holding out. That hand closed around the cork, and the other hand came out and passed me something else, something cold as ice and about twice as long and a good deal heavier. My face felt stiff and numb, but I managed to say, "Thanks," in a mumbling sort of way. The intent white face in front of me nodded in reply, once.

Then the Walker walked on past Anthea and me.

All our breaths, Christopher's, Anthea's, and mine, came out in a *Whoosh!* of pure relief. As soon as the Walker had gone past me, it had gone. The icy smell and the horizon of eternity had gone, too, and the library was once more an enclosed, warm room.

Christopher said, in a voice that was trying not to sound too awed, "Was it a man or a woman? I couldn't tell at all."

"I'm not sure that applies to a being like that," Anthea said. "What did it give you, Conrad?"

I looked at the thing in my hand. It felt quite warm now, or only cold the way metal always feels. I looked at it and puzzled. It seemed to be a small corkscrew—very like the one I used to struggle with when the Magicians' Circle wanted a bottle of port opened——one of those with an open handle that you hook two fingers through, with little curls at either side for two more fingers. But there was a key sticking out from the top of the handle. If I held the thing one way up, it was a corkscrew, but if I turned it around, the corkscrew became the handle of the key.

I held the thing up to Anthea and twiddled it at Christopher. "Look. I'm supposed to *need* this. What do you think I *do* with it?"

Anthea leaned over me to look. "It *could* be the key to a wine cellar."

Christopher slapped the side of his velvet breeches. "That's *it*! The hippopotamus has got it in one! I *knew* it was important to get into that wine cellar! Come on, Grant. Let's go and do it before we have to go back on duty."

He rushed off to the gallery staircase. I followed him slowly, feeling upset and puzzled and let down. I had expected the Walker to give me something much more dangerous than a key or a corkscrew.

"Get a move on, Conrad," Anthea said. "That butler . . ."

So I hurried a bit, and lucky that I did. I had only just climbed into the gallery when the door below opened again. Mr. Amos came importantly in, followed by a line of footmen carrying a viewscreen, a tower, a keyboard, drums of flex, armloads of disks, a stack of power cells, a printer, boxes of paper, and a load of other accessories.

"I shall supervise the setting up of the equipment personally, miss," Mr. Amos said to Anthea.

Christopher dragged me through the door at the back of the balcony. "Good," he said when we were safely out in the corridor. "If he's busy in there, he can't possibly be in the wine cellar. Let's *go*, Grant!"

14

❧❦

WE GALLOPED DOWNSTAIRS, and down again to the undercroft. "Funny," I said to Christopher as we tiptoed toward the stairs that led to the cellar. "I didn't know any of those footmen with Mr. Amos. Did you?"

"Hush," he said. "Utmost caution, Grant."

Actually there was no one about, and it was quite safe. Christopher was just being dramatic because it was all so easy. There were nice broad steps curving down to the cellar and a light switch beside the door at the bottom so that I could see to put the corkscrew key into the keyhole. The keyhole looked far too big, but the key went in, fitted exactly, and unlocked the door when I turned it. The door swung open easily and silently, and lights came on in the cellar as it opened.

"Lock it after you," Christopher said.

"No," I said. "We may need to get out quickly."

Christopher shrugged. I pushed the door shut, and we walked on into a set of low, cold rooms lined with wine racks and barrels. There were

204

dusty bottles and shiny new bottles, rank on rank of them, little kegs labeled *Cognac* in foreign letters, bigger barrels labeled *herez* that Christopher said meant sherry, and whole walls of champagne.

"One could get awfully drunk here," Christopher remarked, surveying a dusty wall of bottles marked *Nuits d'éte 1848*. "I have quite a mind to drown my sorrows, Grant. I *saw* Millie. I talked to her. Do you know how to open champagne?"

"Don't be a fool," I said. I pulled him away and led him on, and on, past thousands of bottles, until we came to another locked door in a wall at the end.

"Ah," said Christopher. "This may be it—whatever *it* is. Does your gadget work on this door, too?"

I tried the corkscrew key again, and it worked. This door creaked a bit as it opened, as if it were not used very much, and we saw why as soon as we were inside. Lights came on and showed another, newer-looking staircase that led to a trapdoor in the ceiling. Christopher looked up at the shiny new metal of the trapdoor very thoughtfully.

"I do believe," he said, "that we may be right under the butler's pantry here, Grant. In which case the important stuff is just round this corner."

The walls here were of quite new brick. It looked as if an extra room had been built, off at an angle to the main cellars. We edged around the corner to it. There we both stopped, quite bewildered. This room was lined—as closely as the wine cellars were lined with bottles—with lighted, flickering viewscreens. From floor to ceiling they were stacked in rows. Most were covered with green columns of figures that ran and jumped and changed all the time, but about a third of them, mostly on the end wall, were full of strange swirlings or colored jagged shapes. The jumping and flickering made me seasick. Worse than that was the peculiar buzzing of magic in the room, electric and alien and feeling like metal bars vibrating. I had to look at the floor for a while, until I got used to it. But Christopher walked up and down the room, watching the screens with interest.

"Do you understand this, Grant?" he asked.

"No," I said.

"I almost do," Christopher said, "but I'm going to need your help to be sure." He pointed to a screen of jumping numbers. "For instance, what does Coe-Smith mean?"

"Stock market," I said. "I think."

"Right!" Christopher said triumphantly. He pointed to another screen, where blue columns of numbers raced so fast that I couldn't read them. "What's Buda-Parich?"

"That's a city," I said, "over in the middle of the continent. It's where all the big banks are."

"And here's Ludwich," Christopher said, at another screen. "I know that one. More big banks and a stock exchange in Ludwich, am I right? But there can't be a city called Metal Futures, can there? This lot of screens must be stocks and shares, then. Yes, Chemics, Heavy Munitions, Carbon Products—

it sort of makes sense. And . . ." He paused at a clump of screens where green and red lines zigzagged, bent, and climbed. "These lot have to be graphs. But the really puzzling ones"—he went on, moving around to the end wall—"are *these*. They just seem to be patterns. What do you think this one is? The one that's all jagged moving shapes."

"Fractals?" I suggested.

"I wouldn't know a fractal if it jumped up and bit me," Christopher said. "Which it almost looks as if it could do. Oh, *look*. These must be the controls."

Under the possible fractals there was a sloping metal console. Rows of buttons took up the top half of it. The bottom part held a very used-looking keyboard. The lights from the screens painted winding colored patterns on Christopher's attentive face as he leaned both hands on the edge of the console and stared at the rows of buttons.

"Interesting," he said. "When controls are used a lot, you can see which the important ones are. This keyboard thingy is quite filthy with finger grease. Used every day, I should think. And this one on its own at the top has been used almost as much." His thin white finger pointed to a square button up on the right above all the others. The metal around this button was worn shiny and ribby, with a ring of grease around the shiny part. The label under it was all but worn away. As far as I could see, it said "shift."

"That must be—" I began, but Christopher turned to me, looking almost unholy in the colored lights.

207

"What do you think?" he said. "Dare we, Grant? Dare we?"

"No, we daren't," I said.

Christopher simply grinned and pressed the used square button firmly down.

We felt the shift like an earthquake down there. Our feet seemed to jerk sideways under us. All the screens blinked and began to flicker away madly in new configurations. Above the console, the strange patterns wove and writhed into quite different shapes and colors.

"*Now* you've done it!" I said. "Let's get out."

Christopher made a face, but he nodded and began to tiptoe away from the console. I had just turned to follow him, when a voice spoke. It was a woman's voice, very cultivated and rather deep. "Amos!" it said, and stopped both of us in our tracks. We stood, bent and on tiptoe, craning to look up at the round grid in the ceiling where the voice had come from. "Amos," it said. "Do pay attention. I don't think we can afford to make changes at the moment. We may have trouble this end. I told you about the ratty little fellow we caught sneaking around the office. Security locked him up, but he must have been some kind of magic user because he got away in the night. *Amos!* Are you listening?"

Christopher and I waited for no more. I clutched his arm and he grabbed my shoulder and we bundled each other around the corner and out through the door. I could scarcely turn the corkscrew key in the lock for giggling. Christopher giggled, too. It was the silly way you behave when you feel you have almost been caught.

As we sped back past the ranks of wine, Christopher said in a giggling whimper, "That was never the Countess, was it?"

"No," I said. "Mrs. Amos?"

"A bit la-di-da for that," Christopher said.

We were still laughing when we came to the outer door and I locked that after us, and we didn't really get a grip on ourselves until we came to the lobby of the undercroft and I tried to fit the corkscrew key into my waistcoat pocket. It wouldn't go. It was more than twice as long as the wine cork, and it stuck out whatever I did.

Christopher said, "Here. Let me." He whipped a piece of string out of thin air, threaded it through the corkscrew handle, knotted the ends together, and hung the lot around my neck. "Under your shirt with it, Grant," he said.

While I was stuffing it out of sight under my cravat, Miss Semple came into the lobby, full speed ahead, striped skirts flying. "I've been looking all over for you two!" she said. "You're eating in the Middle Hall from now on, with the new Staff—" She stopped, went back a step, and put her hands up in horror. She was the sort of person who did that. "My goodness!" she said. "Go and get into clean uniforms at *once*! You've got two minutes. You'll be late for lunch, but it will serve you right."

We fled up the undercroft steps and dodged into the Staff toilets at the top. Christopher sagged against the nearest wall inside. "This has been quite the busiest morning of my life," he said. "*Damned* if I go all the way up to the attics again!"

This was my feeling, too. But when I looked over at the mirror, I saw why Miss Semple had been so horrified. We were both filthy. Christopher was covered in dust and carpet fluff. One of his stockings had come down, and his cravat looked like a gray string again. I had cobwebs all over me, and my hair stuck up. "Then work some magic," I said.

Christopher sighed and flapped one hand. "There." And we were once more smart flunkeys in crisp, clean shirts and neat cravats. "Drained," he said. "I'm exhausted, Grant. You've forced me to do permanent magic on us. At this rate, I shall be old before my time."

I could see he was all right, really, but he kept saying this sort of thing all the way back into the undercroft. I didn't mind. Neither of us wanted to talk about the Walker, or about the screens in the cellar and the voice from the ceiling. It was all too big to face just then.

We opened the door of the Middle Hall to find it almost entirely full of strangers, maids in yellow caps and footmen in waistcoats and striped stockings, who all seemed more than usually good-looking. Andrew, Gregor, and the other footmen we knew were sitting in a row down at the end of the long, low room, staring in a stunned way. One of the best-looking maids was standing on the table among the glasses and cutlery. As we came in, she held one hand up dramatically and said, "Oh when, oh when comes azure night and brings my love to me?"

And a fellow in a dark suit who was kneeling on the floor between the chairs said, "E'en before the twilight streaks the west with rose, I come, I come to thee!"

"Most rash," replied the young lady on the table.

"EH?" said Christopher.

Everyone jumped. Before I could believe it possible, every new maid and every strange footman was sitting demurely in a chair at the table, except for the man in the suit, who was standing up and pulling his coat sleeves down. And the girl—she really was *very* pretty—was still standing on the table.

"You *rats*!" she cried out. "You might have helped me down. Now I'm the one in trouble!"

"It's all right," I said. "We're only the Improvers."

Everyone relaxed. The man in the suit bowed to us. He was almost ridiculously tall and thin, with a sideways sort of hitch to his face. "Prendergast," he said. "Temporary underbutler. Temporary name, too," he added, hitching his face to the other side. "My stage name is Boris Vestov. Perhaps you have heard of me? No," he said sadly, seeing Christopher looking as blank as I felt. "I mostly play in the provinces anyway."

"We're all actors here, darlings," another good-looking maid explained.

"How? Why?" Christopher said. "I mean . . ."

"Because Mr. Amos is an extremely practical person," said the girl on the table. She knelt down and smiled at Christopher. She was blond and, face-to-face, quite stunning. Christopher looked as stunned as Andrew and the rest. Her name, I found out, was Fay Marley, and she was a rising star. I'd seen her last year on a friend's television, when I came to think about it.

I nudged Christopher. "It's true," I said. "She was in *Bodies* last year."

"So?" he said. "What has it got to do with Mr. Amos being practical?"

Fay Marley scrambled off the table and explained. They all explained. Nobody could have been friendlier than those actors. They laughed and joked and called us "darling," and they went on explaining while the ordinary maids came in with lunch. The ordinary maids were full of giggles and goggles. They kept whispering to me or to Christopher, "She's that young nurse in *Bodies*!" and "He's the one who jumps through the window in the chocolate ad!" and "He was the lost elf in *Chick-Chack*!" Mr. Prendergast/Vestov had more or less to push them out of the room.

Anyway, it seemed that practical Mr. Amos had, a long time ago, made an agreement with the Actors' Union that when Stallery needed more maids or footmen in a hurry, he would hire any actors who were not at that moment working.

"Being out of work is something actors are quite often," a glamorous footman said.

"But the Union makes strict conditions," a dark maid, who was quite as glamorous, told us. "If we get stage or film work while we're here, we're allowed to leave Stallery at once."

"And we take our meals together," a beautiful parlormaid said. "We're only allowed to work so many hours a day here. You'll be doing much longer hours than us, darlings."

"But," said Christopher, "what makes you think you can do the work at all?"

They all laughed. "There's not a soul among us," Mr. Prendergast told him, "who has not, at one time in his or her career, walked onto a stage and said, 'Dinner is served, madam,' or carried on a tray of colored water and wineglasses. We know the part quite well."

"And we've a day or so to rehearse in anyway," said another glamorous footman. He was Francis, and fair-haired like Fay. "I'm told that the guests don't arrive until the ladies get back from Ludwich."

They told us that they had all arrived by coach earlier that morning. "Along with that lovely wench who's checking the library," a pretty parlormaid added. "I'd give my eyeteeth for a complexion like that girl has."

We got told this bit more than once. This was because there were at least two more of those sideways changes during lunch. At each one, the conversation did a sort of jolt and went back a few stages. Christopher began to look just a little guilty. He rolled his eyes at me each time, hoping I would not say anything. By the end of lunch he was quite quiet and anxious.

Then the bell rang. Christopher and I had to go back on duty, along with Andrew, Gregor, and two of the actor footmen. And Mr. Amos was waiting at the top of the stairs, stubbing his cigar out in the usual place. I was sure he knew that we had been in his secret cellar. I almost ran away. Christopher went white. But it was the new footmen Mr. Amos wanted. He sent us on to the dining room ahead.

Whatever Mr. Amos said to the actors, it made them very nervous. They were awful. They got in one another's way all the time. Francis broke two plates, and Manfred fell over a chair. Andrew and Gregor were very scornful. And when the Countess came in, followed by Lady Felice and Count Robert, it was to the long clattering of knives pouring out of a drawer that Francis had pulled open too far. The Countess stopped and stared. She was all beautifully got up for her trip to Ludwich.

"I do beg pardon, my lady," Mr. Amos said. "The new Staff, you know."

"Is that what it was?" Count Robert said. "I thought it was a war."

The Countess gave him a disgusted look and stalked to her chair, while Francis, redder in the face than I thought a person could be, crawled about, scooping knives out of her path. Mr. Amos nodded me and Christopher off to help him. I was crawling about on the floor, and Manfred had just managed to slop soup over half the knives, when there came the most majestic clanging from somewhere, like someone tolling for a funeral in a cathedral.

"The front door," Mr. Amos said. "I beg you will excuse me, my ladies, my lord. Mr. Prendergast is not yet practiced in his duties." He seized Andrew's arm and whispered, "Put those two idiots against the wall until I get back." Then he fairly whirled out of the room.

Gregor gave me a sharp kick—typically—and made me serve the soup instead of Manfred. By the time I had given all three of them a bowlful, and the Countess, spoon poised at her lips, was saying, "Now, Felice, dear, you and I are going to have a very serious talk about Mr. Seuly on the way to Ludwich," Mr. Amos came hurrying back. He looked almost flustered. As he shut the door in his soundless way, I could hear the voice of Mr. Prendergast outside it.

"I tell you I'm quite capable of opening a door, you pear-shaped freak!"

Everyone pretended not to hear.

Mr. Amos came and bent over Count Robert. "My lord," he said, "there is a King's Courier in the hall asking to speak with you."

The Countess's head snapped up. Her spoon clanged back into the soup. "What's this? Asking to speak to Robert? What nonsense!" She sprang up.

Count Robert got up, too. "Sit down," she said to him. "There must be some mistake. *I'm* in charge here. *I'll* speak to this courier."

She pushed Count Robert aside and marched to the door. Manfred tried to make up for his mistakes by rushing to open it for her, but he slipped in the spilled soup and sat down with a thump. Christopher whisked the door open instead, and the Countess sailed out.

Count Robert simply shrugged, and while Francis and Christopher were hauling Manfred up, he walked around the struggle and went to talk to Lady Felice. She was sitting with her head hanging, looking really miserable. I didn't hear most of what Count Robert said to her, but when Gregor shoved me over to wipe up the soup from the floor, the Count was saying, "Bear up. Remember she can't *force* you to marry anyone. You can say no at the altar, you know."

Lady Felice looked up at him ruefully. "I wouldn't bet on that," she said. "Mother's a genius at getting her own way."

"I'll fix something," Count Robert said.

The Countess came back then, very crisp and angry. *"Well!"* she said. "Such impertinence! I soon sent that man packing."

"What did he want, my lady?" Mr. Amos asked.

"There's a Royal Commissioner coming to the district," the Countess said. "They want me to entertain him as a guest at Stallery, of all things! I told the man it was out of the question and sent him away."

Mr. Amos went a little white around his pear-shaped jowls. "But, my lady," he said, "this must have been a request from the King himself."

"I know," the Countess said as Andrew pulled her chair out for her and she sat down. "But the King has no right to interfere with *my* plans."

Mr. Amos gulped. "Forgive me, my lady," he said. "It is mandatory for peers of the realm to extend hospitality to envoys of the King when required. We would not wish to annoy His Majesty."

"Amos," said the Countess, "this person wishes to plant himself here, in my mansion, at the precise time when we have a house full of eminent guests. Lady Mary, the Count's fiancée, will be here with all her family and the people I have chosen to meet her. *All* the guest rooms will be full. The valets and lady's maids will be filling both upper floors. This Commissioner has a staff of ten *and* twenty security men. Where, pray, am I supposed to *put* them? In the stables? No. I told them to go to a hotel in Stallchester."

"My lady, I think that was most unwise," Mr. Amos said.

The Countess looked stonily at her soup and then across to the chops Andrew was fetching from the food lift. "I don't want this," she said. She slapped her napkin down and stood up again. "Come, Felice," she said. "We'll set off for Ludwich *now*. I'm not going to stay here and have my authority questioned all the time. Amos, tell them to bring the cars round to the door in five minutes."

She and Lady Felice hurried away in a brisk clacking of heels. Suddenly everyone else was rushing about as well. Andrew raced off with a message to the garage, Christopher was sent to fetch the two Lady's Maids, who were going to Ludwich, too, and the other footmen rushed away to bring down the luggage. Mr. Amos, looking thunderously upset, turned to Count Robert. "Will you wish to continue lunch now, my lord, or wait until the ladies have departed?"

Count Robert was leaning on the back of a chair, and I swear he was trying not to laugh. "I think you should go and lie down, Amos," he said. "Forget lunch. No one's hungry." Then, before Mr. Amos could send me off to the kitchens, he turned and beckoned me over to him. "You," he said, "go to the library and tell the young lady waiting there to meet me in the stable yard in ten minutes."

As I left, he was giving Mr. Amos a sweet, blank smile.

I found Anthea in the library sitting rather crossly in front of a computer screen. "They were quite right about the disturbances here," she said to me. "Everything keeps hopping sideways, and when I get it back, it says something quite different."

When I gave her Count Robert's message, she jumped up, beaming. "Oh good! How do I find the stables in this barracks?"

"I'll take you there," I said.

We went the long way around, talking the whole way. I told her about the screens Christopher and I had found in the cellar. "And I think your computer went wrong when Christopher pressed the shift button," I said. "It felt magic to me."

"Very probably," she said. "So it's that pear-shaped butler messing up the world's finance, is it? Thanks. Robert will be very glad to know that."

"How did you meet Count Robert?" I asked.

My sister smiled. "At university, of course. And Hugo, too—though he was always popping off to visit Felice in her finishing school. I met Robert at a magic class on my first day, and we've been together ever since."

"But," I said, "the Countess says Count Robert has to marry a Lady Mary Something who's coming here soon."

Anthea smiled, happily and confidently. "We'll see about that. You'll find Robert's just as strong-minded as his awful mother. So am I."

I thought about this. "And what do *I* do, Anthea? I can't stay on here as an Improver, and Uncle Alfred won't let me go to school, because I didn't use the cork like he said—anyway, he'll know I know he's told me all those lies now. What do I *do*?"

"It's all right, Conrad," Anthea said. "Just hang on. Hang on and wait. Robert will make everything all right. I promise."

Then we got to the stable yard, where Count Robert was waiting in his red sports car. My sister rushed over to it, waving happily. I went away. She had an awful lot of faith in him. I didn't. I couldn't see someone like Count Robert ever sorting out this mess. Anthea's faith was just love, really.

15

❧✦❧

THE NEXT COUPLE of days were strange and hectic.

I hardly saw Anthea, except when she was dashing away from the Upper Hall after breakfast. She was out with Count Robert in his sports car almost all the time. I don't think she went into that library at all. And Count Robert didn't come in to meals, so I never set eyes on him either. Hugo, now, he was another matter. I seemed to run into him everywhere, wandering about, missing Lady Felice.

Because none of the Family were using the dining room, Mr. Amos used it to train the actor footmen in. He had me and Christopher and Andrew and Gregor in there all that first afternoon, sitting at the table, pretending to be Family, so that Manfred and the rest could pour us water into wineglasses and hand us plates of dried fruit and cold custard. To do those actors justice, they learned quickly. By the evening, Francis only dropped one spoon the last time he served me with custard, and Manfred was the only one still falling over things. But, none of us really fancied our supper.

Christopher summed up my feelings, too, when he poked his potato cheese with a fork and said, "You know, Grant, I find it hard not to see this as custard." The food turned into liver and cauliflower as he poked it. Christopher shot me a glum, guilty look. Since Mr. Amos had been giving the actors a hard time in the dining room all afternoon, we knew he had not been down to the cellar to push the shift button. So this change was Christopher's fault. I quite expected him to start persuading me to go to the cellar again with him that night. I was determined to say no. One time in that place was enough. The thought of its alien, technological magics made my flesh creep—and the thought of Mr. Amos discovering us there was even worse.

But all Christopher said was, "Things must be changing like this where Millie is, too. She could be lost for good if I don't get to her soon." And I half woke up in the night to hear him tiptoeing away to the forbidden part of the attics.

I don't know how long he stayed out there, but he was very hard to wake in the morning. "No luck?" I asked as we collected the shoes.

Christopher shook his head. "I don't understand it, Grant. There were no changes at all, and I sat there for hours."

Here the lift opened, and we found it crowded with actors acting a scene from *Possession*. This was the strange thing about actors. They loved acting so much that they did it all the time. They spoke in funny voices and imitated people if they didn't do scenes from plays. And the lift made a good place to act in, because Mr. Amos and Mrs. Baldock couldn't see them at it there. From then on, the lift was always liable to have a scene going on in it or someone saying, "No, darling, the best way to see the part is like *this*," and then doing it. In between, Hugo rode broodingly up and down, looking as if he did not want to be disturbed. Christopher and I got used to taking the stairs instead.

The undercroft was crowded with the regular Staff, up early in hopes of catching one or other of the actors. The maids had all got it badly for the footmen. Francis was most popular, and Manfred next, because he looked dark and soulful, but even Mr. Prendergast got his share of giggles and fluttered eyelashes and shy requests for his autograph——and he was really odd-looking.

"It's something about greasepaint, Grant," Christopher said. "It acts like a love potion. What did I tell you?" he added as we ran into four of the regular footmen, Mr. Maxim, and the bootboy, who all wanted to know if we had seen Fay Marley that morning. "In the lift," Christopher told them, "pretending to be possessed by a devil or something."

Stallery echoed with rehearsals that day, not only actors acting, but with official ones. Mrs. Baldock and Miss Semple tore the maids away from the actor-footmen and the actor-maids out of the lift and drilled them all in their duties upstairs. Mr. Amos took Mr. Prendergast and all the footmen to the hall, where he trained them in how to receive the guests. Mr.

Smithers was roped in to pretend to be a guest, and sometimes Christopher was, too. Christopher was good at grand entries. I was on the stairs, mostly, learning what to do with the dozens of empty suitcases Mr. Amos had found to be luggage for the pretend guests. Mr. Amos made me stack them in pairs in the lift and then take each one to the right bedroom. This always took ages. If Hugo was not in the lift, then it was two of the actresses, looking exhausted.

"If I have to make one more bed or lay out one more breakfast tray, I shall *drop*, darling!"

"Why does Miss Semple *insist* on *counting* everything? Does she think I'm a *thief, darling?*"

And when I arrived in the right bedroom with my empty luggage, Mrs. Baldock usually grabbed me and trained me in all the other things I might have to bring to people's bedrooms. I was made to carry in trays, newspapers, drinks, and towels. Mrs. Baldock seemed to think she had as much right to me as Mr. Amos did. I several times caught myself thinking that this must be my Evil Fate at work—in fact I *kept* thinking it and then realizing all over again that Uncle Alfred had probably invented it. It gave me a strange, hectic feeling at the back of my mind all day. On top of that, I kept waiting for Mr. Amos to discover that Christopher had pressed that shift button.

Luckily, Mr. Amos was too busy in the hall just then. I came back to my station on the main stairs to find a full-scale rehearsal just starting.

"Right, *go!*" Mr. Amos shouted. He was standing in the middle of the hall like the director of a film.

The great doorbell solemnly clanged. At this signal, footmen in velvet breeches and striped waistcoats and stockings came rushing from behind the stairs and formed up in two slanting rows on either side of the front door.

"Like a flipping *ballet*," Mr. Prendergast said, gloomily standing beside me with his arms folded and too much wrist showing beyond the sleeves of his smart dark coat.

Mr. Amos paced solemnly toward the front door. He took hold of the handles. He stopped. He called over his shoulder, "Prendergast! Where are you *this* time?"

"Coming, coming," Mr. Prendergast called back, walking slowly and importantly down the stairs.

"Hurry it up, can't you?" Mr. Amos boomed up at him. "Do you think you're the King, or something?"

Mr. Prendergast stopped. "Ah, no indeed," he said. "It's these stairs, you see. No actor can ever resist a fine flight of stairs. You feel you have to make an entrance."

Mr. Amos, for a second, seemed about to burst. "Just . . . hurry . . . up," he said, slowly, quietly, and carefully.

Mr. Prendergast went on down the stairs, in a sort of royal loiter, and crossed the hall to stand behind Mr. Amos's left shoulder.

"My *right* shoulder, you fool!" Mr. Amos practically snarled.

Mr. Prendergast took two measured steps sideways.

"*Now!*" said Mr. Amos, and threw open the two halves of the door. Francis jumped forward and grabbed one half and Gregor took the other and they each dragged their half wide open. Mr. Amos bowed. Mr. Prendergast did a much better bow. And Mr. Smithers edged apologetically indoors. Christopher followed him, airily strolling, looking every inch an important guest. . . .

But here one of the sideways changes happened, and the show broke down. Everyone was suddenly in a different position, milling around, with Mr. Amos in the midst of the chaos almost screaming with rage. "No, no, *no*! Francis, why are you over there? Andrew, it is *not* your job to fetch luggage in. *You* take Mr. Smithers's coat."

Mr. Amos really did not seem to see that there had been a change. It began to dawn on me that he might be as insensitive to the shifts as Mr. Maxim was. It was an odd thing, because Mr. Amos must have been some sort of a magician, and I would have thought he ought to have known when his own magic machinery was working, but I could see that he didn't. That was a relief! Christopher was looking at Mr. Amos consideringly, as if he was thinking the same things as me. Beside him, Mr. Smithers stared around anxiously for the right footman to hand his imaginary coat to.

"Start again," Mr. Amos said. "And *try* this time."

"I try, I try!" Mr. Prendergast said, arriving beside me again. "I am exercising every thew and sinew to persuade that man to give me the sack, but *will* he?"

"Why?" I said.

"The union must have been right when they told me that a reasonable-looking underbutler was very hard to find at short notice," Mr. Prendergast said dolefully.

"No, I meant why do you want to be sacked?" I said.

Mr. Prendergast grabbed each of his elbows in the opposite hand and hitched his face mournfully sideways. "I don't like the man," he said. "I don't like this house. It strikes me as haunted."

"You mean the changes," I said.

"No," said Mr. Prendergast. "I mean haunted. As in ghosts."

And the strange thing was that by lunchtime everyone was saying that Stallery was haunted. Several agitated people told me that that someone— or something—had thrown a whole shelf of books on the library floor. I tried to find Anthea to ask her, but she was out with Count Robert. By teatime all the maids were saying that things in the bedrooms kept being moved. Some of them had heard strange hammerings and knockings there, too. By the end of the day Mr. Prendergast was not the only actor who was talking about leaving.

"It's just the changes," Christopher said as we climbed the stairs that night; the lift was full of a courtroom drama just then, with Mr. Prendergast as the judge and a very glamorous dark girl called Polly Varden being accused of murdering Manfred. "Actors are some of the most superstitious people there are."

"I'm glad Mr. Amos doesn't seem to notice the changes," I said.

"It is lucky," Christopher agreed. Here he began looking very anxious and raced ahead to the attics.

He didn't go into our room at all. I think he spent all night out in the forbidden part of the attics. I woke up to find him already dressed and bending over me urgently. "Grant," he said, "there were no changes last night either. I think that fat swindler turns his machines off before he goes to bed. I'm going to have to look for Millie by day. Be an absolute cracker and cover up for me, will you?"

"How do you mean?" I asked sleepily.

"By saying I'm ill. Pretend I'm up here covered in green and yellow spots. Please, Grant." Christopher had been learning from the actors. He went down on one knee and raised his hands to me as if he were praying. "Pretty please, Grant! There's a *witch* out there—remember?"

I woke up enough to start thinking. "It won't work," I said. "Miss Semple is bound to come up and check on you, and when you're not there, I'll be in trouble, too."

Christopher went, *"Oooh!"* desperately.

"No, wait," I said. "The way to work it is for you to *show* Mrs. Baldock that you're really not well.

Can't you work some magic to make yourself look ill? Give yourself bubonic plague or something? Then stagger into her room looking like death."

Christopher stood up. "Oh," he said. "Thanks, Grant. I wasn't thinking, was I? It's easy, really. All I have to do is to get hold of some silver, and Series Seven will do the rest. But you'll have to be the one who brings meals and medicines to my sickbed. Will you do that, Grant?"

"All right," I said.

So, when we took the boots and shoes down, we took them by way of the big main staircase. There was no one about to see us at that hour. This made it all the more puzzling when we found a big red rubber ball, which must have come from the nurseries, bouncing slowly down the stairs in front of us.

"I wonder if there *is* a ghost after all," Christopher murmured.

We were too busy with our plan to get hold of something silver to bother much about it. When the ball rolled away across the black marble floor of the hall, we simply dumped our baskets of footgear outside the breakfast room and sneaked in through the door. Christopher went on a rapid search of the sideboard in there. In no time he selected a very small silver spoon from one of the big cruet sets and stuffed it into his waistcoat pocket. "This'll do," he said.

The effect was almost instant. His face went bluish white, and by the time he was back at the door, his legs were staggering. "Perfect," he said. "Come on."

We dodged out into the hall again, where, as far as I could see, the red rubber ball had vanished. But I didn't have any opportunity to look for it because Christopher was now—honestly and completely— too weak to carry his basket. He panted and he wavered and I had to carry one handle of it for him.

"Don't look so concerned, Grant," he told me irritably. "It's only a sort of magical allergy."

Actually, I was staring anxiously after the vanished rubber ball with shudders creeping up my back, but I didn't like to say so. I helped Christopher to the undercroft, and to dump the baskets in the bootroom, and then to the Middle Hall for breakfast. By the time everyone else arrived there, he was looking like death warmed up.

All the actors exclaimed. Fay Marley took Christopher along to Mrs. Baldock herself, and Mrs. Baldock believed he was at death's door like everyone else did. Christopher reappeared in the Middle Hall doorway, blue pale and staggering between Fay on one side and Mrs. Baldock on the other.

"I must have Grant!" he gasped. "*Grant* can take me upstairs!"

I knew he meant that we had to put the silver spoon back before Mr. Amos noticed it was missing. I jumped up at once and draped Christopher's arm artistically across my shoulders. Christopher collapsed against me, so that I staggered, too.

To my surprise, everyone protested. "You're not his servant!" several actors said. Most of the others added, "Let Fay help you take him!" and

Gregor said, "I could probably carry him." Mrs. Baldock said anxiously, "Are you sure you're strong enough, Conrad? He's a big lad. Let someone else try."

"Grant!" Christopher insisted expiringly. *"Grant!"*

"Not to worry," I said. "I can get him as far as the lift, and we can go up in that."

They let us go, rather doubtfully. I heaved Christopher along to the lift, which was about as far as I could manage. Christopher was looking so unwell by then that I was quite alarmed. I took the spoon out of his waistcoat pocket and put it in mine, before I opened the lift, in case anyone was listening for me to do that. Hugo was in the lift, sitting on the floor with his arms around his knees, staring at nothing. So I shut the lift again. When I turned to Christopher, there was color back in his face and he was standing on his own—it was as quick as that.

"Keep tottering," I said, and we pretended to stagger to the lobby.

We met Anthea there, dashing past us from the stairs. "What's wrong with him?" she wanted to know.

"Muscular dysfunctional debilitation," Christopher said. "MDD, you know. I've had it from the cradle."

"You look pretty healthy to me," Anthea said, but she was, luckily, in too much of a hurry to ask any more.

We tottered artificially on, up into the hall and across it to the breakfast room, where Christopher took a swift look around to make sure that nobody was there. "You put it back, Grant," he said. "I have to get going." And he went dashing away up the main stairs.

I was a bit annoyed, but I sighed and slipped into the breakfast room.

As soon as I was inside, I was quite positive there was a ghost in there. The room had a heavy *occupied* feeling, and the air seemed thicker than it ought to be. It smelled of damp and dust instead of the usual coffee and bread smell. I stood for a moment wondering which was worse, facing a ghost or being accused of stealing the silver. Facing Mr. Amos, I thought. Definitely worse. But my back shuddered all over when I finally made myself scuttle over to the sideboard. As quick as I could, I laid the shiny little spoon back where I thought it came from.

There was a thudding sound behind me.

I whirled around to see the big bowl of fruit in the middle of the table in the act of tipping over. The thud had been the orange that tipped out first. It was followed by apples, pears, nectarines, and more oranges, which went rolling across the table and off its edges, while the bowl stood on its edge to shake out a floppy bunch of grapes.

"Don't *do* that!" I shouted.

The bowl thumped back to its right position. Nothing else happened. I stood there for what must have been five minutes, feeling as if my hair was trying to pull itself up by its roots. Then I made myself scramble to pick up the fruit and put it back.

"I'm only doing this because of what Mr. Amos will say," I said as I crawled after apples. "I'm not helping you. Go and annoy Mr. Amos, not me. *He's* the one that needs a fright." I crammed the last handful of apples in anyhow, on top of the grapes, and then I ran. I don't remember anything on my way to the Middle Hall. I was too scared.

The next thing I remember is being *in* the Hall and being greeted merrily by the actors. "Come and sit down," they called. "We saved your breakfast. Do you want my sausage?"

Polly Varden said, "I'm glad you're not ill, too. We enjoy having you here, Conrad."

"But you're too humble with Christopher, you know," Fay Marley said. "Why did it have to be *you* who hauled him to the attics?"

I couldn't answer that. All I could think of to say was, "Well, Christopher's—er—special."

"No, he's not, no more than you are," Francis said.

"Darling, he just *thinks* of himself as a star," Fay said. "Don't get taken in by the posing."

And Mr. Prendergast explained, "A person may have the *quality*, but he still has to earn his right to be a star, see. What has young Christopher done that makes him so special?"

"It's—more the way he was born," I said.

They didn't like that either. Mr. Prendergast said he didn't hold with aristocracy, and the rest said, in different ways, that it was *work* that made you a star. Polly made me really embarrassed by saying,

"But you don't put on airs, Conrad. We *like* you."

I was quite glad when it was time to go and stand against the wall while Count Robert bolted his breakfast—he seemed to be in as much of a hurry as Anthea. The ghost was still in there. I think it was the ghost that made Manfred drop a steaming squashy haddock on his feet—but it could have been Manfred on his own, of course.

❧•❦

16

THAT MORNING MR. Amos had us all up on the ball-room floor, first in the great Banqueting Hall, learning how to lay it out for a formal dinner, and after that in the Grand Saloon, where he made half of us pretend to serve coffee and drinks to the other half. It did not go well. There was change after change, sideways jerk after sideways jerk, and each change caused someone to make a mistake. There was a golden footstool that turned up in so many places that even Mr. Amos noticed. I suppose it was hard to miss after Manfred had booted it across the room six times. Mr. Amos thought it was me playing practical jokes.

"No, no, you wrong the lad," Mr. Prendergast said, stepping up between me and Mr. Amos. "There is a ghost in this place. You need an exorcist, not a lecture. You need a divine with bell, book, and candle. As I have played the part of a bishop many times, I would be happy to stand in the role of cleric and see what I could do."

Mr. Amos gave him an even nastier look than he

had been giving me. "There has never," he said, "been a ghost at Stallery, and there never will be." But he gave up lecturing me.

Despite what Mr. Prendergast said, the maids told me that they thought the ghost had been busy in the bedrooms all morning, making loud thumps on the walls and rolling soap about. Mrs. Baldock had had to go and lie down. The maids were scared stiff. And they may have been right, and it *may* have been the ghost. The trouble was, it was so difficult to tell, with all the changes. The sideways jerks seemed to be happening twice as often that day.

The maids crowded around and told me all about it when I went to the kitchens at lunchtime to fetch a tray of food for Christopher. I had to push my way through them. I knew that if I didn't take the food to Christopher quickly, then Fay or Polly would tell me I was being too humble and take the tray up herself. And either she would find Christopher looking perfectly healthy, or he would not be there at all.

Mr. Maxim handed me the tray with a wonderful domed silver cover on it and whispered, "You'll never guess! Mr. Avenloch has gone missing! The garden staff don't know what to do!"

"You mean, like the dog, Champ?" I asked.

"*Just* like that," Mr. Maxim said. "A real mystery!" He was loving it, I could see.

I rushed off to the lift with the tray before any of the actors could start acting in there. And it was just as well I took it. Christopher was not in our room.

There was no sign of him anywhere in the attics. I wondered what to do for a while. Then it occurred to me that the silver dome would make Christopher ill anyway, and so would the silver cutlery Mr. Maxim had given him, so I might as well eat the lunch myself. I sat on my bed and ate it all, peacefully.

I was finishing with the trifle when there was a really big sideways jerk. I sat there feeling a little sick, wondering if the trifle had changed into something else on the way down. As long as it wasn't sardines! I was thinking, when I heard footsteps clattering on bare boards in the distance.

Christopher's back! was my first, rather guilty thought. I laid the tray on my bed and hurried out to explain that I had eaten his lunch, but he could pretend to get well and go down and eat mine. By the time I reached the bathroom on the corner, I could clearly hear that there were two separate sets of footsteps, one heavy and one lighter. He's found Millie! I thought. Now we're going to have problems!

I shot anxiously through into the forbidden middle of the attics.

Mr. Avenloch, the head gardener, was there, along with the new gardener's boy, Smedley. They were clattering around, both of them looking tired, sweaty, and bewildered. "*Now* where have we got to?" Mr. Avenloch was saying, in an angry sort of moan. "This is different *again*!"

Smedley saw me. He shook Mr. Avenloch's earthy tweed sleeve. "Sir, sir, here's Conrad! We must be back in Stallery!" His face was bright red, and he was almost crying in his relief. "This *is* Stallery, isn't it?" he implored me.

"Yes, of course it is," I said. "Why? Where have you been?" I had a fair idea, of course.

"Half the morning outside a ruined castle," Mr. Avenloch said disgustedly. "With a lake to it, all weeds. Ought to have been drained and replanted years ago, but I suppose there was no one there to do it. Can you show us the way down from here, boy? I was only ever in the undercroft before now."

"Certainly," I said, in my best flunkey manner. "This way." I took them along toward the lift, collecting the tray on the way. They thumped along after me in their great crusty boots.

"It wasn't only a castle," Smedley said. "It was never the same castle anyway. It kept turning different. Then it was a huge place made of glass——"

"All cracked and dirty," said Mr. Avenloch. "Such neglect I never saw."

"And after that there were three palaces with white marble everywhere," Smedley chattered on. I knew how he felt. He had been having the sort of experience you just have to talk about. "And then there was this great enormous brick mansion, and when we went inside, it kept changing all the time. Stairs in all directions. Old furniture, ballrooms——"

"Didn't you see any people at all?" I asked, hoping to get news of Christopher.

"Only the one," Mr. Avenloch said repressively, "and she in the distance all the time." I could see he thought Smedley was talking too much.

I thought nervously of the witch. "What, like an old woman in rubber boots?" I asked.

"She seemed like a young girl to me," Mr. Avenloch replied, "and ran like a hare when we called out to her."

"That was what brought us up here," Smedley explained. "She ran away upstairs in the mansion—well, it was more like a cathedral by then—and we chased up after her, wanting to know what was happening and how to get out of there. . . ."

We were at the lift by then. Its door slid aside to show Mr. Prendergast pretending to be Mr. Amos. I hadn't realized that Mr. Prendergast was such a good actor. He was tall and thin, and Mr. Amos was short and wide, but he had Mr. Amos's way of holding his head back and slowly waving one hand so exactly that I almost saw him as pear-shaped. Mr. Avenloch and Smedley both gaped at him.

"Lunch is served," Mr. Prendergast said. "I require you to be furniture against the wall. Furniture with legs of flesh." Then he did a Mr. Amos stare at Mr. Avenloch and Smedley. "And what are you doing with a rake and a wheelbarrow, Conrad, may I ask?"

"It's a long story," I said. Hugo was in the lift, too, behind Mr. Prendergast, grinning all over his face. "Can we come down in the lift with you?" I asked.

"Feel free," Hugo said. "He came up looking for you anyway."

Mr. Prendergast waved the two gardeners

into the lift, like Mr. Amos ushering the Countess. "Enter. It is not your place to wait upon your fellow Improver, Conrad," he said to me, and I really felt for a moment as if it were Mr. Amos telling me off. "Enter, and place the rake in that corner and the wheelbarrow by the wall here. Hold your tray two inches higher. We will now descend." He pressed the lift button with a Mr. Amos flourish. "I will now," he said, "make use of our descent to instruct you upon the correct way to place chairs for a banquet. All chair legs must be exactly in line. Having placed them at the table, you must then crawl along behind them, measuring the distance of chair from chair, with a tape measure carried in the waistcoat pocket for the purpose."

He went on like this all the way down to the undercroft. Smedley could not help giggling—and kept getting a Mr. Amos glare, followed by "Know your place, wheelbarrow"—and even Mr. Avenloch began to grin after a while. Hugo was laughing as much as I was.

When we got to the undercroft, Mr. Prendergast announced, "Mr. Hugo will now repair to the Upper Hall, while I march Conrad off to his fate in the Middle Hall. You two implements—"

"Please, sir," Smedley interrupted imploringly, "have we missed our lunch, sir?"

"Take this tray," Mr. Prendergast said, removing it from me and dumping it on Smedley, "and proceed with your mentor to the kitchens, where you will find they have been anxiously awaiting your return. Off with you now." He pretended to look at his watch. "You have exactly two minutes before they feed your lunch to the dogs."

Smedley went racing off. Mr. Avenloch paused to say, "That was as good as a play. But don't let Mr. Amos catch you at it. You'd be in for it then."

"It's probably the one thing he wouldn't forgive me for," Mr. Prendergast agreed cheerfully. "Which is why I am rehearsing the part. Come, Conrad. Your lunch awaits."

I had to have another lunch. They really did not like me running after Christopher. And I really could not explain. I was half asleep for the rest of the afternoon, until around suppertime, when I was suddenly ravenous and wide-awake. And, I don't know why, I was quite convinced that Christopher was back. I sneaked off early to the kitchens and asked them to give me Christopher's tray now. I did not want Mr. Prendergast butting in again.

It was so early that the regular maids were all gathering there for their high tea. They told me that the ghost had been bouncing that red rubber ball up and down the corridors all afternoon. They weren't frightened by then, they said, just annoyed by it. Besides, who wanted to leave, one of them added, when there was a chance of getting to know Francis? Or Manfred, said another. A third one said, "Yes, if you want gravy poured down your neck!" and they all shrieked with laughter.

The men's end of the attics seemed very quiet after this. I went along to our room and got the door open—which is not easy when you're carrying a tray—and Christopher seemed to be there. At least he was in bed and asleep when I went in, but when I turned around from putting the tray on the chest of drawers, there was no one there. The bed was flat and empty.

"Oh, come *on*!" I said. "Don't be stupid. It's only me. What happened? Didn't you find Millie, then?"

A girl's voice answered, "Oh dear. What's gone wrong? You're not Christopher."

I spun about, looking for where the voice came from. Christopher's bed was still flat and unused, but there was a dip in the edge of my bed, the sort of dent a person makes sitting on the very edge. She was obviously very nervous. I said, "It's all right. I'm Conrad. I work here at Stallery with Christopher. You're Millie, aren't you? He said you were an enchantress."

She became visible rather slowly, first as a sort of wobble in the air, then as a blur that gently hardened into the shape of a girl. I think she was ready to whip herself invisible again and run away if I seemed to be hostile. She was just a girl, nothing like as glamorous as Fay or Polly, and a bit younger than Christopher. She had straight brown hair and a round face and a very direct way of looking at a person. I thought she seemed nice. "Not that *good* an enchantress," she said ruefully. "You're that boy who was with Christopher on those stairs, aren't you? I made a real mistake getting into all those mansions. There never seemed to be a way to get *outside* them."

"It may have been the witch keeping you in," I said.

"Oh, it *was*," she said. "I didn't realize at first. She was sort of kind, and she had food cooked whatever kitchen I got to, and she kept hinting that she knew all about the way the buildings changed. She said she'd show me the way out when things were ready. Then she suddenly disappeared, and as soon as she was gone, I realized that it was that knitting of hers—she was sort of knitting me in, trying to take me over, I think. I had to spend a day undoing her knitting before I could get anywhere."

"How did you get here?" I asked.

"Christopher shouted across those double stairs to go to the top and then find the room with his tie on the doorknob," Millie said. "I was so tired by then that I did."

"Then he's still out there?" I said.

Millie shrugged. "I suppose so. He'll be back in the end. He's good at that kind of thing—having nine lives and so on."

She seemed a bit cool about it. I began to wonder if the witch had grabbed Christopher instead, because he was stronger, and that this was how Millie got out. "Oh well," I said. "He's not here, and you are. He's supposed to be ill, and I'm supposed to bring his meals. Would you like this supper now I've brought it?"

Millie brightened up wonderfully. "Yes, *please*!

I don't know when I've *ever* been so hungry!"

So I passed her the tray. She arranged it on the bedside table, which she pulled in front of the bed, and began to eat heartily. The food changed from egg and chips to cottage pie while she ate, but she hardly seemed to notice. "I had nothing to buy food with, you see," she explained. "And the witch only did breakfast. The last breakfast was days ago."

"Did you run away from school without any money, then?" I asked.

"Pretty well," Millie said. "Money from Series Twelve wouldn't work in Series Seven, so I only took what was in my pocket. I was going to be a parlormaid and earn some money. Except when I got inside those mansions, there was nobody there to be a maid *for*. But . . ." She looked at me very earnestly. I could tell she was wanting me to believe the next bit particularly. "But I *had* to run away from that school. It really was an awful place— awful girls, awful teachers—and the lessons were all things like dancing and deportment and embroidery and how to make conversation with an ambassador, and so on. I told Gabriel de Witt that I was miserable and not learning a *thing*, but he just thought I was being silly."

"And you told Christopher," I said.

"In the end," Millie said. "Only as a last resort— Gabriel never listens to him either. And Christopher was just as overbearing as I knew he would be. *You* know, 'My dear Millie, set your mind at rest, and I will fix it,' and this time he was worse. He decided we were going to go and live together on an island in Series Five. And when I said I wasn't sure I wanted to go and live all alone with Christopher— Well, would *you* want to, Conrad?"

"No," I said, very definitely. "He's far too fond of his own way. And the way he makes superior jokes all the time—I want to hit him!"

"Oh, doesn't he just!" Millie said.

After that, all the while Millie was eating the pudding—which started as jam roly-poly and then became chocolate meringue—we both tore Christopher's character to shreds. It was wonderful fun. Millie, from having known Christopher for years, found two faults in him where I only knew one. His clothes, she told me, he fussed about his clothes being perfect *all* the time. He'd been like that for three years now. He drove everyone in Chrestomanci Castle mad by insisting on silk shirts and exactly the right kind of pajamas. "And he could get them right anyway by magic," Millie told me, "if he wasn't too lazy to learn how. He *is* lazy, you know. He hates having to learn facts. He knows he can get by just *pretending* to know—bluffing, you know. But the thing that *really* annoys me is the way he never bothers to learn a person's *name*. If a person isn't important to him, he *always* forgets their name."

When Millie said this, I realized that Christopher had never once forgotten *my* name— even if it was an alias. It suddenly seemed to me to be rather mean, talking about Christopher's faults when he wasn't here to defend himself.

"Yes," I said. "But I've never known him do anything really nasty. I think he's all right underneath. And he makes me laugh."

"Oh, me, too," Millie agreed. "I *do* like him. But you can't deny that he's *maddening* a lot of the time— Who's that?"

It was Mr. Prendergast again. We could hear him outside in the corridor, doing his Mr. Amos act. "Grant," he called out. "Conrad, stop lurking in sickrooms and descend to the undercroft immediately. Supper is being served!"

He was nearer than we realized. The next moment he flung the door open and stood looming in the doorway. Millie made a sort of movement, as if she was thinking of turning invisible, but then realized that it was too late, and stood up instead. Mr. Prendergast hitched his face sideways at her, and his eyebrows traveled up and down his forehead like two sliding mice. He looked at me, and then at the tray.

"What is this?" he said. "Is Christopher really a girl?"

"No, no," I said. "This is Millie."

"She's not another wheelbarrow," Mr. Prendergast said. "Is she?" And when Millie simply looked completely confused, he narrowed his eyes at her and said, "So where are you from, young lady?" For a moment he looked so utterly serious that he made goose bumps come up on my arms.

Millie probably felt the same. "Er, from Series Twelve, really," she admitted.

"Then I think I don't want to know," Mr. Prendergast said. He hitched his face the other way, and I remembered, with great relief, that he was simply a very good actor. "I think," he said to me, "that she'd better be a feather duster."

"What *are* you talking about?" Millie said, exasperated and frightened, but almost laughing, too. This was the effect Mr. Prendergast seemed to have on people.

"We can't have Conrad embarrassed," he said to her, "and he would be if you went on sharing his room like this. So I think you'd better come downstairs and get turned into another new housemaid. Luckily there are so many just now that one more will hardly be noticed. Come along to the lift, both of you. No, let *her* carry the tray, Conrad. It makes her look the part more."

Hardly able to believe it, we followed Mr. Prendergast to the lift. Hugo was in it. He stared at Millie with gloomy surprise.

"New feather duster," Mr. Prendergast told him airily. "She's the child star of *Baby Bunting*—you won't know it yet, it's on trial in the provinces, but it'll be a hit, I assure you."

Millie went bright red and gazed hard at her tray, biting her lip. I think she was trying not to laugh.

Mr. Prendergast said nothing more until the lift was nearly at the undercroft. Then he said suddenly. "By the way, where *is* Christopher?"

"Around," I said.

Millie added, "He went to the bathroom."

"Ah," said Mr. Prendergast. "Indeed. That accounts for it, then."

Rather to my surprise, he didn't ask any more. He just stalked with us to the Middle Hall, where he took Fay aside and murmured a few words to her. It was like magic, really. Fay and Polly and two other girls instantly took charge and hurried Millie off to the maids' cloakroom. When they came back, Millie was wearing a brown-and-gold-striped dress just like the other girls, and a proper maid's cap. She sat and chatted to them and the other actors while the rest of us had supper.

Fay and Polly must have found somewhere for Millie to sleep that night. When I saw her at breakfast the next morning, she had her hair up on top of her head, under her cap, and Fay or someone had done things to her face with clever makeup, so that Millie looked rather different and quite a bit older. I think she was enjoying herself. She had a surprised, happy look whenever I saw her.

I kept out of Millie's way on the whole. I dreaded the moment when Miss Semple spotted Millie. Miss Semple's mild, serious, distracted eyes didn't miss much, and I was sure she would realize that Millie was not a real maid before long. Then the fat would be in the fire, and Mr. Prendergast would probably get the sack. I was fairly sure he had made Millie into a feather duster in order to get sacked.

But Miss Semple—nor Mrs. Baldock—did not notice Millie all day. Some of the reason was the ghost. It distracted people by playing pranks, dragging the sheets off all the newly made beds on the nursery floor, smashing tooth glasses, and bouncing that red rubber ball down flights of stairs. It had done something new every time Mrs. Baldock took me over to train me upstairs. But some of the distraction was due to the changes Christopher had started by pressing that button in the cellar. Everything kept moving about, so that when you put something down and then turned around to pick it up again, it wasn't where you'd left it. Most people who noticed—and it was hard not to notice before long—thought this was the ghost's doing, too. They just sighed. Even when all the sheets and towels got shifted to quite different cupboards on different floors, they said it was the ghost again and sighed.

But no one could blame the ghost when, late in the afternoon, all our uniforms suddenly changed color. Instead of gold and brown stripes, we were suddenly wearing bright apple green and cream.

Miss Semple was really distressed by that change. "Oh Conrad!" she said, "what *is* going on? These are the colors we had in my mother's day. My mother changed them because they were thought to be unlucky. Green *is*, you know. Things had gone wrong then until Stallery had barely enough money to buy the new colors. Oh, I do hope we aren't in for any more bad luck!" she said, and went rushing off past me in her usual way.

We were all still rushing about exclaiming, when the Countess and Lady Felice came back unexpectedly.

17

THE COUNTESS AND Lady Felice were not expected until the next morning, just before all the guests arrived. But they had finished their shopping early, it seemed, and now there they were, in three cars drawing up outside the great front entrance.

Their arrival caused a general stampede. I had just arrived in the kitchens for my cookery lesson, but Mr. Maxim sent me away again, because he had to help get together a proper dinner for the ladies in a hurry. He told me to go and help in the hall instead. Hugo shot out of the lift as I went by and raced to the garage to find out where Count Robert had gone with Anthea, and to get him back if he could. In the black-floored hall, there was the main stampede, for what Mr. Prendergast called "the dress rehearsal for the real show tomorrow." Footmen raced down from the attics and up from the undercroft, and the marvel was that we all arrived there just as Mr. Amos—with Mr. Prendergast haunting his right shoulder like a skinny black scarecrow—threw open the huge front doors and Francis and Andrew pulled them wide.

The Countess sailed inside with a new fur wrap trailing from her shoulders. As she handed the wrap off to Manfred, she gazed around at us all with gracious satisfaction, but she seemed, for a second, a little puzzled to see us all in our green-and-cream stripes. "Amos . . ." she began.

Mr. Amos said, "Yes, my lady?"

"I forgot what I was going to say," said the Countess. Evidently she was as insensitive to the changes as Mr. Amos was. "Has all been well?"

"Naturally, my lady," said Mr. Amos. He turned and *looked* at the red rubber ball that came trundling out of the library as he spoke. Then he looked at me. I picked it up—and it felt just as if I was wrenching the ball out of someone's resisting hand. I shuddered and shoved it into the library and shut the door on it.

"Then where is Count Robert?" the Countess demanded.

"Mr. Hugo is currently searching for him, my lady," Mr. Amos replied.

"Oh," the Countess said ominously. She marched away to the stairs, saying, "See to the luggage, will you, Amos."

It needed all of us to see to it. The three cars were stuffed with boxes, carrier bags, and parcels. I could not believe that two ladies could have bought so much in such a short time—though I suppose there were four ladies at it, really. The two Lady's Maids came in with armfuls of parcels and made a great pother about things being handled *gently* and being carried *right way up*. You could see they had been enjoying themselves. But Lady Felice, who hurried through while we were all handing parcels and carrier bags along like a bucket chain, did not look happy. She kept her head down, but I could see she had been crying.

She still looked that way when I was waiting on the Family at Dinner that night. This was such a magnificent meal that you would never have guessed that the Great Dictator and Mr. Maxim had been taken by surprise like the rest of us and had— so Mr. Maxim told me—made it up as they went along, wrestling also with the way chickens became salmon and cream became parsley as the food was fetched to the kitchens. The changes were quite bad that evening.

"You know I never notice," Mr. Maxim told me, "but Chef *does*, and he sorrowed, Conrad."

It struck me as a pity that neither Lady Felice nor Count Robert seemed to feel much like eating. Count Robert, who arrived back from some inn outside Stallstead, had certainly had supper with my sister before Hugo found him. He pushed food about on his plate, while the Countess told him that he should have been in the hall to meet her and how discourteous he was not to be there. He didn't even point out that she had come home a day early. But he stopped even pretending to eat when she went on to describe all the things he was expected to do and say when Lady Mary Ogworth arrived tomorrow.

So much for Anthea's chances! I thought, standing against the wall on my own. Christopher was still missing, and I was beginning to worry about him. With all these changes happening, he could be in castles and towers and mansions moving farther and farther away from Stallery all the time, and if the witch had not caught him yet, she *would* catch him if he was stuck out there again when Mr. Amos turned his machines off for the night. But there seemed nothing I could do. . . .

"As for Felice," I heard the Countess say, "the very *least* I insist on is that she be polite to Mr. Seuly."

At this, Lady Felice threw her fork down with a clatter.

Count Robert leaned forward. "Mother," he said, "does this mean that you've made some kind of arrangement for this Mr. Seuly to marry Felice?"

"Of course, dear," said the Countess. "We called on him on our way to Ludwich, and we had a long talk. He has made a very handsome offer for Felice, financially speaking."

"As if I was a *horse*!" Lady Felice said violently.

The Countess ignored this. "As I *keep* telling Felice," she said, "Mr. Seuly is even richer than Lady Mary Ogworth."

"Then," said Count Robert, "why don't you marry him yourself?"

This caused an astonished silence. Mr. Amos stared, the Countess stared, Gregor's mouth came open, and even Lady Felice raised her face and looked at her brother as if she could not believe her ears. At length, the Countess said, in a fading, reproachful whisper, "Robert! *What* a thing to say!"

"*You* said it first. To Felice," Count Robert pointed out. And before the Countess could pull her wits together, he went on, "Tell me, Mother, why are you so very set on your children marrying for money?"

"*Why?*" gasped the Countess, with her eyes very wide and blue. "*Why?* But, Robert, I only want the best for you both. I want to see you properly settled—with plenty of money, naturally—so that if anything happens, you'll both be all right."

"What do you mean, 'if anything happens'?" Count Robert demanded. "What do you imagine *might* happen?"

The Countess looked to one side and then to the other and seemed not to know how to answer this. "Well, dear," she said finally, "all sorts of things might happen. We might lose all our money—or—or . . . This is a very uncertain world, Robert, and you *know* Mother knows best." She was so much in earnest, saying this, that big tears trembled on the ends of her eyelashes. "You've hurt me very much," she said.

"My heart bleeds," Count Robert answered.

"At all events," the Countess said, in a sort of imploring shriek, "you have to *promise* me, darlings, both of you, to behave properly to our guests!"

"You can count on us to behave," Count Robert

said, "but neither of us is going to promise more than that. Is that clear?"

"I *knew* I could count on you!" the Countess announced. She smiled lovingly from Count Robert to Lady Felice.

They both looked confused. I didn't blame them. It was really hard to tell what anyone had promised by then. I looked at Mr. Amos to see what he thought. He was scowling, but that might have been because he could see a speck of dust on the glass he was holding to the light. I wished Christopher were there. He would have known what was going on underneath this talk.

But Christopher was not there that night, and he did not turn up in the morning either. I had to make two journeys to collect all the boots and shoes. I was annoyed. After that I was working almost too hard to remember Christopher. But not quite. People are wrong when they say things like "I didn't have time to think." If you're really worried, or really miserable, those feelings come welling up around the edges of the other things you're doing, so that you are in the feelings even when you're working hard at something else. I was thinking—and feeling—a lot all the time the guests were arriving. Thinking about Christopher, worrying about Anthea, and feeling for myself, stuck here without even an Evil Fate to account for what I was doing.

The guests began arriving from early afternoon onward. Very stately people rolled up to the front doors in big cars and came in past the lines of footmen, wearing such expensive clothes that it seemed like a fashion parade in the hall. Then Mr. Prendergast would give out calls of "Lady Clifton's luggage to the lilac room!" or "The Duke of Almond's cases to the yellow suite!" and I would be rushing after Andrew and Gregor, or Francis and Manfred, with a heavy leather suitcase in each hand. When no guests were arriving, Mr. Amos had us measuring the spaces between the chairs at the banquet table to make sure they were evenly spaced. He really did that! And I'd thought Mr. Prendergast had been joking! Then the bells would clang, and it would be back to the black marble hall to carry more luggage.

And all the time I was more miserable and wishing Christopher would get back. Millie was quite as worried about him by then, too. I kept meeting her racing past with trays or piles of cloths. Each time, she said, "Is Christopher back yet?" and I said, "No." Then, as things got more and more frantic, Millie simply said, "Is Christopher?" and I shook my head. By the middle of the afternoon, Millie was just giving me a look as we shot past each other, and I hardly had time even to shake my head.

This was when Lady Mary Ogworth arrived. She came with her mother—who reminded me more than a little of the Countess, to tell the truth. Both of them were wearing floaty sort of summer coats, but the mother looked like just another guest in hers. Lady Mary was beautiful. Up till then I'd never expected to see anyone who was better-looking than Fay Marley, but believe me,

Lady Mary was. She had a mass of feathery white-fair curls, which made her small face look tiny and her big dark blue eyes look enormous. She walked like a willow tree in a breeze, with her coat sort of drifting around her, and her figure was perfect. Most of the footmen around me gasped when they saw her, and Gregor actually gave out a little moan. That was how beautiful Lady Mary was.

Count Robert was in the hall to meet her. He had been hanging about beside Mr. Prendergast on the stairs, fidgeting and shuffling and pulling down his cuffs, exactly like a bridegroom waiting by the altar for the bride. As soon as he saw Lady Mary, he rushed down the stairs and across the hall, where he took Lady Mary's hand and actually kissed it.

"Welcome," he said, in a choky sort of way. "Welcome to Stallery, Mary." Lady Mary kept her head shyly bent and whispered something in reply. Then Count Robert said, "Let me show you to your rooms," and he took her, still holding her hand, across the hall and away up the stairs. He was smiling at her all the way.

Gregor had to poke me in the back to remind me to pick up my share of her luggage. I was staring after them, feeling horrible. Anthea doesn't have a *chance*! I thought. She's deluding herself. Count Robert has simply been fooling about with her.

As soon as I'd dumped the suitcases, I sneaked to the library to find my sister, but she wasn't there. The ghost was. A book sailed at my head as soon as my face was around the door. But there was no sign of Anthea. I dodged the book and shut the door. Then I went to look for Anthea in the undercroft, but she was nowhere there either. And the undercroft was in an uproar because Lady Mary never stopped ringing her bell.

"Honestly, darling," Polly said, flying past, "you'd think we'd put her in a pigsty! *Nothing's* right for that woman!"

"The water, the sheets, the chairs, the mattress," Fay panted, flying past the other way. "This time it was the towels. Last time it was the soap. We've all been up there at least six times. Millie's up there now."

Miss Semple rushed down the stairs to the lobby, saying, "Mr. Hugo's fixed her shower—he thinks. But . . ."

Then the bell labeled *Ldy Ste* rang again, and they all cried out, "Oh, what is it *now*?"

Miss Semple got to the phone first and made soothing Yes madams into it. She turned away in despair. "*Oh*, I do declare! There's a spider in her water carafe now! Fay—no, you're finding her more shoe trees, aren't you?" Her mild, all-seeing eye fell on me. "Conrad. Fetch a clean carafe and glasses and take them up to the lady suite on one of the best gilt trays, please. Hurry."

If I had been Christopher, I thought, I would have found an amusing way to say that my arms had come out of their sockets from carrying luggage. As I was just me, I sighed and went to the glass pantry beside the green cloth door. While I loaded a tray with glittering clean glassware and took it up in the lift, I decided that it must be the changes that were upsetting Lady Mary. They were going on remorselessly now. Before I got to the second floor, the lift stopped being brown inside and became pale yellow. It was enough to upset anyone who wasn't used to it.

The lift stopped and the door slid back. Millie, still looking very smart and grown up in her maid's uniform, was waiting outside to go back down. She gave me another of her expressive looks.

"No," I said. "Still no sign of Christopher."

"I didn't mean that this time," Millie said. "Are you taking that trayful to Lady Mary?"

"Yes," I said. "Fay and them have had enough."

"Then I don't want to prejudice you," Millie said, "but I think I ought to warn you. She's a witch."

"Really?" I said as I got out of the lift. "Then . . ."

Millie turned sideways to go past me. I could see she was angry then, pink and panting. "Then nothing!" she said. "Just watch yourself. And, Conrad, forget all the mean things I said about Christopher—I was being unreasonable. Christopher never misuses magic the way that—that—*she* does!"

The lift shut then and carried Millie away downward. I went along the blue moss carpet and around the corner to the best guest suite, thinking about Christopher. He could be very irritating, but he was all right, really. And now I considered, he had set off to rescue Millie like a knight errant rescuing a damsel in distress. That impressed me. I wondered why I hadn't thought of Christopher that way before. I wished he would come *back*.

I knocked at the big gold-rimmed double door, but no one told me to come in. After a moment I knocked again, balanced the tray carefully on one hand, and went in.

Lady Mary was sitting sprawled in a chair that must have come from another room. Everything in the huge frilly room was pink, but the chair was navy blue, with the wrong pattern on it. Fay or Polly or someone must have lugged it in here from somewhere else. Lady Mary was clutching its arms with fingers bent up like claws and scowling at the fireplace. Like that, she looked almost as old as the Countess and not very beautiful at all. There was a half-open door beyond her. I could hear someone sobbing on the other side of it—her lady's maid probably.

"Oh, shut up, Stevens, and get on with that ironing!" Lady Mary snarled as I came in. Then she saw me. Her big blue eyes went narrow, unpleasantly. "I didn't say you could come in," she said.

I said, very smoothly, like Mr. Prendergast imitating Mr. Amos, "The fresh carafe and glasses you rang for, my lady."

She unclawed a hand and waved it. "Put them down over there." She waited for me to cross the room and put the tray on a small table, and then snapped, "Now stand there and answer my questions."

I was glad Millie had warned me. The hand waving must have been a spell. I found myself standing to attention beside the table, and the door

259

to the corridor seemed a mile off. Lady Mary waved her hand again. This time I felt as if there was a tight band around my head, so tight that it somehow gave me pins and needles down both arms. I couldn't loosen it however hard I tried. "Why are you doing that?" I said.

"Because I want to know what I'm taking on here," she said, "and you're going to tell me. What do you think of Count Robert?"

"He seems nice enough—but I really hardly know him," I said. By this time I was panting and sweating. The pressure around my head seemed to be worse every second. "Please take this off," I said.

"No. Is Count Robert a magic user?" Lady Mary said.

"I've no idea—I don't think so," I said. *"Please!"*

"But *someone* here is," she said. "Someone's using magic to change things all the time. Why?"

"To make money," I found myself saying.

"Who?" Lady Mary asked.

I thought of Christopher pressing that shift button. I thought of Mr. Amos. I thought my head was going to burst. And at the same time I knew I wasn't going to tell this horrible woman anything else. "I don't—I don't know anything about magic," I said.

"Nonsense," Lady Mary said. "You're stuffed with talent. For the last time, *who?"*

"Nobody taught me magic," I gabbled desperately. My head was going to crack like an egg any moment, I thought. "I *can't* tell you because I don't *know!"*

Lady Mary screwed her mouth up angrily and muttered, "Why don't any of them know? It's ridiculous!" She looked at me again and said, "What do you think of the Countess?"

"Oh, she's awful," I said. It was a relief to be able to tell her *something*.

Lady Mary smiled—it was more of a gloating grin really. "They all say that," she remarked. "So it must be true. I'll have to get rid of her first thing then. *Now* tell me . . ."

A change came just as she said this. I never thought I'd be glad of a change. The tightness around my head snapped—*ping!*—like a rubber band that had been stretched too much. I staggered for a moment, pins and needles all over, eyes all blurry, but I could just see that the carafe and glasses on the tray had turned into a teapot, an elegant cup and saucer, and a plate of sugary biscuits.

I took a look at Lady Mary. She was behaving as if the rubber band had snapped itself in her face, blinking her big eyes and gasping. "Enjoy your tea, my lady," I said. Then I turned and ran.

I went down in the lift feeling awful. The pins and needles went away, slowly, but they left me feeling very miserable indeed. Lady Mary was obviously going to take over Stallery the moment she was married to Count Robert—or maybe even sooner. She would give me the sack at once, because I knew what she was like. I had no idea what I would do then. It was no good asking Anthea—she was as badly off as I was. And Christopher was not here to ask.

That was the good thing about Christopher. He never seemed to think anything was hopeless. If something went wrong, he made one of his annoying jokes and thought of something to do about it. I really needed that at the moment. I stopped the lift and sent it upward instead, just in case the changes had brought Christopher back. But our room was empty. I looked at Christopher's tie dangling from the doorknob and felt so lost that I began to wonder if Uncle Alfred was right after all about my Evil Fate. Everything went wrong for me all the time.

18

MIDDLE HALL WAS crowded that evening. Mr. Smithers and quite a few Upper Maids were sent to eat with the actors, because Upper Hall was filled with valets and lady's maids who had come with the guests. They had to help the guests get dressed, of course, so they had supper later. Mrs. Baldock was holding a special cocktail party for them in her Housekeeper's Room before that. Polly, Fay, Millie, and another girl had to bolt their food in order to race off and wait on Mrs. Baldock and her guests. The rest of us hardly had time to finish before bells began pealing and Miss Semple came rushing in.

"Quick, quick, all of you! That's Mr. Amos ringing. The company will be down in five minutes. Mr. Prendergast, you're in the Grand Saloon in charge of drinks—"

"Oh, am I?" Mr. Prendergast said, unfolding to his feet. "Menial tasks, nuts, and pink gin, is it?"

"—with Francis, Gregor, and Conrad," Miss Semple rushed on. "All other menservants to the Banqueting Hall to make ready there. Maids to the ballroom floor crockery store and service hatches. Hurry!"

The undercroft thundered with our feet as we all raced away.

The part in the Grand Saloon is a bit of a blur to me. I was too anxious and upset to notice much, except that Mr. Prendergast plonked a heavy silver tray in my hands, which made my arms ache. The guests were mostly a roar of loud voices to me, fine silk dresses and expensive evening suits. I remember the Countess graciously greeting them all, in floating blue, with a twinkly thing in her hair, and I remember Count Robert coming and snatching up a glass from my tray, looking as if he really needed that drink—and then I noticed that the glass he had taken was orange juice. I wondered whether to call out to him that he had made a mistake, but he was off by then, saying hallo to people, chatting to them and working his way over to the door as if he expected Lady Mary to come in any minute.

Lady Mary didn't arrive until right near the end. She was in white, straight white, like a pillar of snow. She went to Count Robert almost at once and talked to him with her head bent and a shy smile. I could hardly believe she had spent the afternoon complaining and casting spells and making her maid cry.

"That," Mr. Prendergast said, looming up beside me, "is a classic example of a glamour spell. I thought you might like to know."

"Oh," I said. I wanted to ask Mr. Prendergast how he knew, but he said, "Your tray's slanting," and surged away to fetch Gregor a fresh soda siphon.

Lady Felice arrived, wearing white, too, and looking horribly nervous. She went nearly as white as her dress when Mr. Amos flung the door open and boomed, "The Mayor of Stallchester, Mr. Igor Seuly."

Mr. Seuly looked really out of place. He was just as well dressed as everyone else, but he seemed smaller somehow, a little sunken inside his good clothes. He walked in trying to swagger, but he looked as if he was crawling, really. When the Countess rustled graciously up to him, he took hold of her hand with a grab, as if she was rescuing him from drowning. Then he caught sight of me and my tray and came and took the largest glass as if that was a rescue, too.

"Have you found out how they pull the possibilities yet?" he asked me in a whisper.

"Not quite," I said. "I, er, we——"

"Thought not," Mr. Seuly said. He seemed relieved. "Not to worry now," he said. "When I'm spliced to Felice, I'll be part of the setup, and I'll be able to handle it for you. Don't you do anything until then. Understand?"

"But Uncle Alfred said——" I began.

"I'll fix your uncle," Mr. Seuly answered. Then he turned around and marched away into the crowd.

Shortly after that, Mr. Amos unfolded the double doors at the end of the room and said, in his grandest manner, "My lords, ladies and gentlemen, Dinner is served."

Everyone streamed slowly away into the Banqueting Hall, and it got quite peaceful. While

Francis, Gregor, and I were clearing up spilled nuts and piling glasses on trays to give to Polly and the other maids at the door, Mr. Prendergast stretched himself out with a sigh along the most comfortable sofa.

"An hour of peace at least," he said, and lit a long black cigar. "Pass that ashtray, Conrad. No, make that nearly three hours of peace. I'm told they're having ten courses."

The double doors opened again. "Prendergast," Mr. Amos said. "You're on front hall duty. Get on down there."

"But surely," Mr. Prendergast said, sitting up protestingly, "everyone's arrived who's going to arrive."

"You never can tell," Mr. Amos said. "Events like this often attract poor relations. Stallery prides itself on being prepared."

Mr. Prendergast sighed—it was more of a groan, really—and stood up. "And what do I do in the unlikely event that penniless Cousin Martha or drunken Uncle Jim turn up and start hammering at the front door? Deny them?"

"You use your discretion," Mr. Amos growled. "If you have any. Put them in the library, of course, man, and then inform me. And *you*—Gregor, Francis, Conrad—in the Banqueting Hall as soon as you've finished here. Service is slower than I would like. We need you."

So, for the next two and a half hours, I was hard at it, fetching dishes for other footmen to hand over elegant shoulders and carrying bottles for Mr. Amos to pour. Manfred had done quite well and only dropped one plate, but Mr. Amos would not let Manfred or me do any of the actual waiting at table. He said he was taking no chances. But we were allowed to go around with cheese boards, near the end. By this time the chinking of cutlery and the roar of voices had died down to a mellow rumble mixed with the occasional sharp *tink*. Mr. Amos sent Andrew back to the Grand Saloon to make coffee. And after I had carried around special wine for the speech and the toasts, he sent me to the Saloon, too.

Mrs. Baldock and Miss Semple were there, arranging piles of chocolates enticingly on silver plates. Mrs. Baldock seemed a little unsteady. I thought I heard her hiccup once or twice. And I remembered Christopher saying the first night we were here that he thought Mrs. Baldock drank— although she *had* just given a party, I suppose. I reached out to sneak a chocolate, thinking of Christopher. There had been no changes for hours now. Mr. Amos must have switched off his equipment, so Christopher was stuck for yet another night. Here Miss Semple slapped my reaching hand and brought me back to reality. She sent me hustling up and down the huge room, planting the piles of chocolates artistically on little tables. So I was able to snitch a chocolate anyway, before Andrew called me over to help him rattle out squads of tiny coffee cups and ranks of equally tiny glasses.

I was thinking of Christopher, so I said what Christopher might have said. "Are we having a dolls' tea party?"

"Liqueurs are served in small glasses," Andrew explained kindly, and showed me a table full of round bottles, tall bottles, triangular bottles, flat bottles, red, blue, gold, and brown bottles, and one big green one. He thought I didn't know about liqueurs. If he had been Christopher, he would have *known* I was joking. "The big round glasses are for brandy," Andrew instructed me. "Don't go making a mistake."

Before I could think of a Christopher-type joke about this, the Countess came sailing in through the distant doors, saying over her shoulder to a stout man with a beard, "Ah, but this is Stallery, Your Grace. We never have *new* brandy!" Other guests came slowly crowding after her.

Mrs. Baldock and Miss Semple vanished. Andrew and I went into furniture mode. The rest of the guests gradually filtered out across the room and settled into chairs and sofas. Mr. Seuly had a lot of trouble over this. He kept trying to sit in a chair next to Lady Felice, but Lady Felice always stood up just before he got to her and, with a sad, absentminded stare, walked away to another chair in another part of the room. Count Robert somehow got buried in the crowd. He was never anywhere near Lady Mary, who was sitting on a golden sofa beside her mother, looking lovelier than ever.

Then Mr. Amos arrived. He closed the double doors on a violent crashing—Manfred was dropping plates again, I think, as the rest of the footmen cleared away the feast—and beckoned me and Andrew over to the table with the coffee cups. I was kept very busy taking around tiny clattery cups. The main thing I remember about this part is when I had to take coffee to Lady Mary and her mother. As I got to their sofa, the mother put out her hand to take one of the chocolates on the table beside them. Lady Mary snapped at her, in a little grating voice, "Mother! Those are bad for you!"

The mother took her hand back at once, looking so sad that I was sorry for her. I handed Lady Mary a cup of coffee, and managed to make it rattle and clatter so much that Lady Mary put out both hands to it and turned to give me a dirty look. Behind her, I saw the mother's hand shoot out to the chocolates. I think she took about five. When I handed the mother her coffee, she gave me a look that said, Please don't give me away!

I was just giving her a blank, furniture look in reply that said, Give away *what*, my lady? when the door to the service area behind us opened and Hugo and Anthea came quietly into the Saloon. They were wearing evening dress, just like the guests. Hugo looked good in his, and far more natural than Mr. Seuly. My sister was in red, and she looked stunning.

Nobody seemed to notice them at first except me. They walked slowly side by side out into the middle of the room, both looking very determined. Hugo was so determined that he looked almost like a bulldog. Then Anthea made a small magical gesture, and the Countess looked up and saw them. She sprang up and swept toward them in a swirl of silky blue.

"*What* is the meaning of this?" she said in a fast, angry whisper. "I will *not* have my guests disturbed in this way!"

At this, Lady Mary looked up, looked at Anthea, and looked venomous. Beside my sister's black hair and glowing skin, Lady Mary hardly seemed to be there. She was like a faded picture, and she knew it.

Across by the little cups and glasses, Mr. Amos looked up, too. He stared. Then he glared. If looks could have killed, Hugo would have dropped dead then, followed by Anthea.

But Lady Felice was now standing up, slowly and nervously. She was so obvious in her white dress that most of the guests turned around to see what she was doing. They looked at her, and then they looked at Hugo and Anthea. The talk died away. Then Count Robert stood up and walked forward from the other end of the Saloon. Everyone stared at him, too. One lady got out a pair of glasses on a stick in order to stare better.

"I apologize for the disturbance," Count Robert said, "but we have a couple of announcements to make."

The Countess whirled around to him and began to make her *Why, dear?* face. She was sweetly bursting with rage. By the look of him, so was Mr. Amos, only not sweetly. But before either of them could speak, the main door at the far end of the Saloon opened and Mr. Prendergast stood and loomed there.

"The Honorable Mrs. Franconia Tesdinic," he announced, in his ringing actor's voice.

Then he backed out of the room, and my mother came in.

My mother looked even more unkempt than usual. Her hair was piled on her head in a big, untidy lump, rather like a bird's nest. She had found from some cupboard, where it must have hung for twenty years or more, a long yellow woolen dress. It had turned khaki with age. I could see the moth holes in it even from where I was. She had added to the dress a spangled bag she must have bought from a toy shop. And she sailed into that huge room as if she were dressed as finely as the Countess.

I have never been so embarrassed in my life. I wanted to get into a hole and pull it in after me. I looked at Anthea, sure that she must be feeling at least as bad as I was. But my sister was gazing at our mother almost admiringly. With an affectionate grin growing on her face, she said to Hugo, "My mother is a naughty woman. I know that dress. She saves it to embarrass people in."

My mother sailed on like a queen, through the room, until she came face-to-face with the Countess. "Good evening, Dorothea," she said. "You seem to have grown very fine since you married for money. What became of your ambition to go on the stage?" She turned to the lady with the glasses on a stick and explained, "We were at school together, you know, Dorothea and I."

"So we were," the Countess said icily. "What

became of your ambition to write, Fanny? I don't seem to have read any books by you."

"That's because your reading skills were always so low," my mother retorted.

"What are you doing here?" the Countess demanded. "How did you get in?"

"The usual way," my mother said. "By tram. The lodge keeper remembered me perfectly well, and that nice new butler let me into the house. He said he had had instructions about poor relations."

"But why are you here?" the Countess said. "You swore at my wedding never to set foot in Stallery again."

"When you married that actor, you mean?" said my mother. "You must realize that only the most pressing reason would bring me here. I came—"

She was interrupted by Mr. Amos. His face was a strange color, and he seemed to be shaking as he arrived beside my mother. He put a hand on her moth-eaten arm. "Madam," he said, "I believe you may be a little overwrought. Would you allow me to take you to our housekeeper?"

My mother gave him a short, contemptuous look. "Be quiet, Amos," she said. "This has nothing to do with you. I am here purely to prevent my daughter from marrying this Dorothea's son."

"What?" said the Countess.

From the other end of the room, Lady Mary said, "WHAT?" even louder and sprang to her feet. "There must be some mistake, my good woman," Lady Mary said. "Robert is going to marry *me*."

Count Robert gave a cough. "No mistake," he

said. "Or only slightly. Before the three of you settle my fate between you, I'd better say that I've already settled it myself." He went over to Anthea and pulled her hand over his arm. "This is one of the announcements I was about to make," he said. "Anthea and I were married two weeks ago in Ludwich."

There were gasps and whispers all over the room. My mother and the Countess stared at each other in almost identical outrage. Count Robert smiled happily at them and then at all the staring guests, as if his announcement was the most joyful thing in the world.

"And Hugo married my sister, Felice, this morning in Stallstead," he added.

"*What?*" thundered Mr. Amos.

"But she can't, dear," the Countess said. "I didn't give my consent."

"She's of age. She didn't need your consent," Count Robert said.

"Now look here, young lord," Mr. Seuly said, getting up and advancing on Count Robert. "I had an understanding——"

Mr. Amos cut him off by suddenly bellowing, "*I forbid this!* I forbid *everything*!"

Everyone stared at him. His face was purple, his eyes popped, and he seemed to be gobbling with rage.

"*I* give the orders here, and *I* forbid it!" he shouted.

"He's mad," some duchess said from beside me. "He's only the butler."

Mr. Amos heard her. "No, I am *not*!" he boomed. "I am Count Amos Tesdinic of Stallery, and I will *not* have my son marry the daughter of an impostor!"

Everyone's faces turned to the Countess then, my mother's very sardonically. The Countess turned and stretched her arms out reproachfully to Mr. Amos. "Oh, Amos!" she said tragically. "How *could* you? Why did you have to give us all away like this?"

"Too bad, isn't it?" Hugo said, with his arm around Lady Felice.

Mr. Amos turned on him, so angry that his face was purple. "*You . . . !*" he shouted.

Goodness knows what might have happened then. Mr. Amos threw a blaze of magic at Hugo and Lady Felice. Hugo flung one hand up and seemed to send the magic back. Lady Mary joined in, with a sizzle that shot straight at Anthea. My mother whirled around and sent buzzing lumps of sorcery at Lady Mary. Lady Mary screamed and hit back, which made my mother's bird's nest of hair tumble down into hanks on her shoulders. By then Mr. Seuly, Anthea, Count Robert, and some of the guests were throwing magics, too. The room buzzed with it all, like a disturbed wasps' nest, and there were screams and cries mixed in with it. Several chairs fell over as most of the guests tried to retreat toward the Banqueting Hall.

Mr. Prendergast threw open the door again. His voice thundered over the rest of the noise.

"My lords, ladies and gentlemen, your attention, please! Pray silence for the Royal Commissioner Extraordinary!"

19

❦

THE MAGICS AND the shouting stopped. Everyone
stared. Mr. Prendergast stood aside from the doorway and announced each person as he or she came
in. There was quite a crowd of them. The first two
were large solemn men in dark suits, who went at
once to stand on either side of Mr. Amos.

"Sir Simon Caldwell and Captain William
Forsythe," Mr. Prendergast boomed, "personal wizards to His Majesty the King."

Mr. Amos looked from Sir Simon to Captain
Forsythe in an astonished, hunted way and then
looked a little happier when two smartly dressed
ladies came to stand on either side of Count Robert.

"The Princess Wilhelmina and Madame
Anastasia Dupont, Sorceresses Royal," Mr.
Prendergast announced. Count Robert went very
pale, hearing this.

Quite a lot of the guests went pale, too, as the
next group was announced. Mr. Prendergast
intoned, "Mrs. Havelok-Harting, the Prosecutor
Royal; Mr. Martin Baines, Solicitor to His Majesty;

Lord Constant of Goodwell and Lady Pierce-Willoughby, King's High Justices. . . ." I forget the rest, but they were *all* legal people, and Mrs. Havelok-Harting in particular was an absolute horror, gray, severe, and pitiless. They all stared keenly at everyone in the Saloon as they spread out to make room for the next group of people.

"The Chief Commissioner of Police, Sir Michael Weatherby, Inspectors Hanbury, Cardross, and Goring," Mr. Prendergast boomed. This lot was in police uniform.

It dawned on me around then that *these* were all the people the Countess had told the courier to send to a hotel in Stallchester. I felt a trifle dizzy at the Countess's nerve. I tried to imagine them all crowded into the Stallchester Arms or the Royal Stag—probably both, considering how many of them there were—and I simply could not see it. The Countess obviously knew what she had done. She had both hands to her face. When the woman Inspector Goring came and stood stonily beside her, the Countess looked as if she might faint. The other two Inspectors went to stand by Hugo, who looked grim, and Mr. Seuly, who went a sort of yellow, and the Chief Commissioner marched through the Saloon and went to stand by the doors to the Banqueting Hall. Some of the guests who had been edging toward those doors went rather hastily to sit down again.

"The household wizards to the Royal Commissioner," Mr. Prendergast announced, and another group of sober-looking men and women filed in. They brought with them a cold, clean buzz of magic that reminded me somehow of the Walker.

"And," Mr. Prendergast proclaimed, "by special request of His Majesty the King, the Royal Commissioner Extraordinary, Monsignor Gabriel de Witt."

Oh no! I thought. Gabriel de Witt was every bit as terrifying as Christopher had led me to believe. He made Mrs. Havelok-Harting look ordinary. He was very tall, and dressed in foreign-looking narrow trousers and black frock coat, which made him seem about eight feet high. He had white hair and a gray, triangular face, out of which stared the most piercing eyes I had ever seen. He brought such strong age-old magic with him that he made my whole body buzz and my stomach feel as if it were plunging down to the center of the earth. I must warn Millie! I thought. But I didn't dare move.

After all this, I was not surprised when Mr. Prendergast swept his large right hand toward his own chest and added, "And also myself, the King's Special Investigator." Of course Mr. Prendergast was a detective, I thought. It made perfect sense.

Gabriel de Witt stepped slowly forward. "I must explain," he said. He had an old, dry voice, like a corpse speaking. "I came to Series Seven initially in search of two of my young wards, who seemed to have got themselves lost in this world. Naturally I went to the King first and asked his permission to continue my search in this country. But the King had problems of his own. It seemed that somebody in this country kept changing the probabilities for this world. There had been so many shifts, in fact, that *all* Series Seven was in danger of flowing into Series Six on one side and Series Eight on the other. The King's wizards were very concerned."

Mr. Amos, looking very startled, shook his head and made denying gestures. "It couldn't possibly have that effect!" he said.

"Oh yes, it could," Gabriel de Witt said. "I assure you that this is true. I noticed it from the moment I stepped into this world. There are beginning to be serious climate changes and even more serious disruptions to geography—mountains subsiding, seas moving about, continents cracking apart—as this Series tries to conform to the Series on either side. Altogether these changes constitute such a serious misuse of magic that when the King asked me for my help, I had no hesitation in agreeing. I and my staff started to investigate immediately. As a first result of our inquiries, a woman calling herself Lady Amos was arrested yesterday and her offices in Ludwich closed down."

"No!" Mr. Amos cried out.

"Yes," said Gabriel de Witt. "I fancy she is your wife. And"—he looked at Hugo—"your mother, I believe. We now have enough evidence to make further arrests here in Stallery. Mrs. Havelok-Harting, if you would be so good as to read out the charges."

The gray, pitiless lady stepped forward. She rattled open an official paper and cleared her throat with a rather similar rattle. "Robert Winstanley Henry Brown; Dorothea Clarissa Peony Brown, née Partridge; Hugo Vanderlin Cornelius Tesdinic; and Amos Rudolph Percival Vanderlin Tesdinic," she read, "you are all four hereby charged with treasonous imposture, the working of magic to the peril of the realm, fraud, conspiracy to defraud, and high treason. You are under arrest—"

"Not high treason!" Mr. Amos said. He had gone a queer pale mauve.

Count Robert—or plain Robert Brown, as I suppose he really was—had turned the same sort of color Christopher went when he touched silver. "I deny treason!" he said chokingly. "I told Amos I wasn't going along with his pretense anymore. I told him as soon as I got back from marrying Anthea."

My sister, who was clearly trying not to cry, opened her mouth to speak, but Mrs. Havelok-Harting simply turned implacably to one of the legal people. "Make a note," she said. "Tesdinic the elder and the male Brown enter pleas of not guilty as charged."

"And *I* am *innocent*!" the Countess said sobbingly. If she was not crying, she was doing a good job of pretending to. "I never did any of this!"

"No more did I," Mr. Amos said. "This is all some kind of trumped-up . . ."

He stopped and backed away as the red rubber ball came sailing through the Saloon. When it reached Mr. Amos, it began bouncing up and down vehemently in front of him.

"Mistake," Mr. Amos finished, eyeing the ball queasily.

"One moment." Gabriel de Witt held up his hand and strode toward the bouncing ball. "What is this?"

"It's a ghost, Monsignor," said one of the royal wizards beside Mr. Amos.

The other wizard added, hushed and shocked, "It says it's been murdered, sir."

Gabriel de Witt caught the ball and held it in both hands. There was dead silence in the Saloon as he stood there inspecting it, his face growing grimmer every second. "Yes," he said. "Indeed. A female ghost. It says the evidence for the murder will be found in the library. Sir Simon, would you be so good as to accompany this unfortunate ghost to the library and bring the evidence back here to me?"

He passed the wizard the ball. Sir Simon nodded and carried it away past Mr. Prendergast and out through the door.

"This has nothing to do with me," Mr. Amos declared. "You must understand, all of you!" He spread his arms pleadingly. The trouble was that everyone was so shocked and frightened by the presence of a murdered ghost that nobody really took Mr. Amos seriously. My thought was that Mr. Amos looked like a short pear-shaped penguin as he went on passionately. "You *must* understand! I only acted for the sake of Stallery. When my father, Count Humphrey, died, Stallery was bankrupt. The gardens were a wilderness, the roof was falling in, and I had to mortgage everything to pay what Staff we had—and they were a second-rate, slipshod lot anyway. It nearly broke my heart. I *love* Stallery. I wanted to have it as it *should* be, well run, restored, beautiful, full of properly respectful servants. I knew that would take millions, I knew it would take all my time and energy, I knew it would take magic—specially applied magic, magic I invented *myself*, I'll have you know, and secretly installed in the cellars! And in order to make my money, I had to have control of those cellars. The only person who has control of the cellars is the butler, so naturally I had to become the butler. You must see I had to be the butler! I paid a young actor to take my place—Rudolph Brown and I looked much alike in those days—"

"Yes, and you turned your own brother—my husband—out," my mother said, suddenly and bitterly. "So he wouldn't get in your way. Hubert never got over it."

Mr. Amos stared at her as if he had forgotten she was there. "Hubert was quite happy running a bookshop," he said.

"No, he wasn't," my mother retorted. "The bookshop was *my* idea."

"You are ignoring two things, Count Amos," Gabriel de Witt put in. "First, that your elevation of your actor friend meant you were deceiving the King, which is treason, and second, that your attempt to restore Stallery was bound to come to nothing."

"Nothing?" said Mr. Amos. He held up a hand

and flourished it around the Grand Saloon, the guests, the chandeliers, the beautifully painted ceiling, the golden chairs and sofas. "You call this nothing."

"Nothing," Gabriel de Witt repeated. "You must have seen that all the other buildings constructed over this probability fault are, without exception, empty ruins. This probability fault is like a sink. It would have pulled Stallery into the same ruined state in the end, however much magic you used, however much money you poured into it. I imagine this place costs more to run every year. . . . Ah, here is Sir Simon again."

He turned away from Mr. Amos's look of horrified disbelief as Sir Simon came striding among the lawyers and wizards. Of course, on this floor, he could go in through the balcony to the library and be there and back in minutes. Sir Simon came up to Gabriel de Witt, holding the rubber ball in one hand. With the other hand he was dangling my camera.

"Here we are, Monsignor," he said. "The victim claims that the murderer killed her by trapping her soul in this camera."

For a moment I could not breathe. I swear my heart stopped beating. Then, all of a sudden, my heart thundered into life again, hammering in my ears until everything went gray and blotchy and I thought I was going to pass out. I remembered then, I had parked that camera on a bookshelf when Christopher got cramp. I remembered the flashlight going off in the face of that witch as she started to put a spell on me. And I remembered that peculiar magazine, illustrated with bad drawings. Not photographs, *drawings*. The witch came from a world where nobody dared take a photo, because that trapped the person's soul inside the camera. I was a murderer. And I thought, I really do have an Evil Fate, after all.

I only dimly heard Gabriel de Witt saying, "I must ask every person here to wait, either in this room or in the Banqueting Hall with the servants. I or my staff or the police must question each of you under a truth spell."

Quite a number of the guests protested. I thought, I must get out of here! I looked around and realized I was quite near the service door. I had been pushed back toward it when all the people had come in with Gabriel de Witt. While Gabriel de Witt was saying, "Yes, it may indeed take all night, but this is a case of murder, madam," I began backing, very slowly and gently, toward that door. I backed while more guests protested. As I reached the door, Gabriel de Witt was saying, "I apologize, but justice must be done, sir." I went on backing until the door had swung open, just a small bit, behind me. Then, quite thankful that Mr. Amos had made me practice going in and out of rooms so much, I took hold of the door and slid myself around it. I let it close itself on top of my fingers so that it would not thump and then stood for a moment, hoping that no one had noticed me.

"Gabriel de Witt's in there, isn't he?" somebody whispered.

I shot sideways and saw Millie pressed against the wall beside the door. She looked almost as terrified as I was.

"And the house is full of policemen," she said. "Help me get away, Conrad!"

I nodded and tiptoed toward the service stairs. I told myself Millie would be much more frightened if I said why I needed to get away even more urgently than she did. I just whispered to her as she followed me, "Where are they mostly, these policemen?"

"Collecting all the maids and the kitchen staff and taking them to the Banqueting Hall to be questioned," she whispered back. "I kept having to hide."

"Good," I said. "Then we can probably get out through the undercroft. Can you make us both invisible?"

"Yes, but a lot of them are wizards," Millie whispered. "They'd *see* us."

"Do it all the same," I said.

"All right," she said.

We tiptoed on. I couldn't tell if we were invisible or not. I think we must have been, though, because we passed the lift before we got to the stairs and a policeman came out of it, pushing Mrs. Baldock and Miss Semple in front of him, and none of them saw us. Both housekeepers were crying, Mrs. Baldock in big, heaving sobs and Miss Semple noisy and streaming. "You don't *understand*!" Miss Semple wept. "We've both worked here most of our *lives*! If they turn us off over this, where do we *go*? What do we *do*?"

"Nothing to do with me," the policeman said.

Millie and I dodged around them and fled down the stairs to the ground floor. I pushed the green cloth door open a fraction there. There was a lot of noise in the entrance hall, where more policemen seemed to be marshaling gardeners, stablemen, and chauffeurs up the main stairs. Most of them were protesting that only Family were allowed to go up this way. I let the door shut itself, and we scudded away, down to the undercroft.

I had never seen the undercroft so deserted. It was dim, empty, and echoing. I could almost believe that the probability fault had already swallowed all the life down here. I led Millie as fast as I could toward the door between the kitchens and the cellars where the gardeners usually brought their vegetables and fruit.

This bit was not empty. Light was shining up the cellar steps from the open door at the bottom. There were sounds of people busy in the cellars. Millie and I both jumped violently when a strong, wizardly voice shouted upward, "Go and tell him that shift key is completely stuck at *on*! If I turn the power on, we'll have changes all over the place again. Go on. Hurry!"

I nearly laughed. Christopher stuck that key down! I thought. But somebody began coming up the steps at a run. Millie seized my wrist, and we sprinted past the top of the stairs and into the produce lobby, before the person could get to the top of the cellar steps and see us. I opened the door, and we tiptoed out. Really out, outside into the gardens.

I was very dismayed to find that it was pitch-dark out there, but I said, "Now, run!"

Actually we went at more of a lumbering trot, with our arms out in case we hit something, trying to follow the pale lines that were probably paths. I think that misled us a bit. We may have been following things that were accidentally pale. At any rate, after lumbering for what seemed half an hour, we found ourselves bursting out beyond some mid-night black bushes into the wide-open spaces of the park, not the garden as I had expected. It seemed much, much lighter out there.

"Oh, good, we can *see*!" Millie said.

And be seen! I thought. But we had to get outside the grounds somehow. I began to run, quite hard, toward where I thought the main gate was, taking a straight line over the driveway and across the mown turf of the parkland. I felt I couldn't get away from Stallery fast enough.

There was a deep *woof!* somewhere near us, followed by the pounding of mighty paws. I had forgotten Champ. I said a bad word and slowed down. So did Millie.

"Is that a guard dog?" she asked. She sounded even more nervous than I felt.

"Yes, but don't worry," I said, trying to sound thoroughly confident. "He knows me." And I called out, "Champ! Hey, Champ!"

We could trace Champ by the paws and the enormous panting at first. Then his huge dark shape appeared out of the gloom at a gallop. Millie and I both panicked and clutched at each other. But Champ simply swerved toward us, showing us he knew we were there, and went hurtling on, uttering another deep *woof*.

A second later there was the most terrible noise in the distance. Champ burst out barking, a deep, chesty baying, like thunder. Another dog joined in, this one high and ear-piercing, and yapped and yapped and yapped, making even more noise than Champ. A horse started whinnying, over and over, madly. Mixed in with the animal sounds were human voices shouting, some high, some low and angry. We had no idea *what* was going on until another human voice shouted ringingly. *"Shut up, the lot of you!"*

There was instant silence. This was followed by the same voice saying, "Yes, Champ, I love you, too. Just take your paws off my shoulders, please."

Millie shouted, *"Christopher!"* and ran toward the voice.

When I caught her up, she was hanging on to Christopher's hands with both hers, and I think she was crying. Christopher was saying, "It's all right, Millie. I only had a little bother with the changes. Nothing else was wrong. It's all *right*!"

Behind them, looming against the dark sky, was a Traveler's caravan drawn by an irritated-looking white horse. Beyond its twitching ears and flicking tail I could just see a man on the driving seat. His skin was so dark that I never saw him clearly. All I saw were his eyes, looking from me to

Millie. The small white dog sitting beside him was much easier to see. Last of all I picked out the faces of a woman and two children looking at us over the man's shoulders.

Here the small white dog decided I was an intruder and started yapping again. Champ, on the ground beside me, took this as a mortal insult and replied. The two yelled abuse at each other, fit to wake the dead.

"*Do* shut them up!" I bawled across the din. "The mansion's full of lawyers and police!"

"And *Gabriel's* here!" Millie yelled. She seemed to be having some kind of reaction to our narrow escapes. Anyway, she was shivering all over.

Christopher said to the dogs, "Shut *up*!" and they did. "I *know* he's here," he said to us. "Gabriel and his merry men were all over the towers and empty castles yesterday, having a good look at the changes. I had an awful job keeping out of sight."

"We *have* to get away," Millie said.

Christopher said, "I know," and looked up at the Traveler driving the caravan. "Is there any chance you can take us all a bit farther?" he asked.

The man gave a sort of mutter and turned to talk with the woman. They spoke quickly together in a language I had never heard before. When the man turned back, he said, "We can take you down to the town, but no farther. We have a rendezvous to make just after dawn."

"I suppose we can get a train there," Christopher said. "Fine. Thank you."

The woman said, "Climb in at the back, then."

So we all scrambled into the caravan, leaving Champ as a melancholy dark hump in the middle of the parkland, and the Traveler clicked to his horse and we drove away.

20

❦·❧

IT WAS STRANGE inside the caravan. I never saw it properly because it was so dark in there, but it seemed much bigger than I would have expected it to be. It was warm—at least it was warm to me, but Millie kept shivering—and full of warm smells of cloth and onions and spiciness, with a sort of tinny, metallic smell behind that. Things I couldn't see kept up a tinkling and chiming from somewhere in the walls. There were what seemed like bunks to sit on, where Christopher and I sat with Millie between us to keep her warm, looking across to the two children, who had hurried inside to stare at us through the dimness as if we were the strangest things on earth. But they wouldn't speak to us whatever we said.

"They've gone shy again. Take no notice," Christopher said. "Why are *you* fleeing Stallery, Grant?"

"I'm a murderer," I said, and told him about the ghost and the camera.

Christopher said, "Oh," very soberly. After a while, he said, "I could really almost believe you *do* have bad karma, Grant, although I know you don't. You certainly have vilely bad luck. Maybe it was the magic— Did you know you were absolutely covered in spells when I first met you? One of them *may* have been a death spell. But I thought I took them all off you while we were walking through the park."

It was my turn to say, "Oh." I explained, rather angrily, "One of those spells was supposed to make Mr. Amos give me a job."

"I know," Christopher said. "That's why I took them off you. I wanted the job. What was Gabriel doing in Stallery—besides looking for me and Millie, that is?"

"Arresting Mr. Amos," I said. "Did you know he was my uncle?"

"Gabriel *can't* be your uncle," said Christopher. "He comes from Series Twelve."

"No, stupid—Mr. Amos," I said. "My mother said she was married to Mr. Amos's brother."

"That usually does make a person your uncle," Christopher agreed.

"And Mr. Amos is really Count of Stallery," I told him. "Not Count Robert. *His* father was an actor called Mr. Brown. The Countess is really plain Mrs. Brown."

Christopher was delighted. "Tell me all, Grant," he said. So I did.

Millie said, with her teeth chattering, "Did they arrest that witch, too—Lady Mary?"

"I don't think so," I said, "but they may have been going to arrest Mr. Seuly."

"What a pity," Millie said. "Lady Mary *ought* to be arrested. She uses magic in the vilest way. But— No, shut up, Christopher. Stop making clever remarks, and tell me what happened to *you* now. How did you end up with the Travelers?"

"By using my brain," Christopher said, "at last. Before it rotted and fell out of my head. I confess that I got really stuck, out in all those empty towers and mansions. Every time there was a change—and there were plenty of those—I seemed to get farther and farther off from Stallery, and half the time there didn't seem to be a way to get anywhere, even when I went outside. I got really tired and hungry and confused. I was in a giant building made entirely of glass, when the whole scene suddenly filled with Gabriel's people. Have you ever tried to hide in a glass house? Don't. It can't be done. And they were between me and the way to the roof, so I couldn't go up there to wait for another change. So I panicked. And then I thought, There must be another way! Then I thought of Champ. Champ was never allowed into the house—"

"Just like Mr. Avenloch and Smedley!" I said. "The changes happen out in the park, too!"

"They do, Grant," Christopher said. "The probability fault has two ends, but one is out in the middle of nowhere, and nobody notices it. As soon as I realized that, I dodged out of the beastly greenhouse and went chasing out into the moors to look for the other end. But I don't think I'd ever have found it if the Travelers hadn't come through more or less as I got there. They gave me some food, and I asked them to get me to Stallery—I hoped you were there by then, Millie—and they didn't want to do that at first. They said they would come out in the middle of the park. But I said I'd get them out through the gatehouse, so they agreed to take me."

"How *do* we get out through the gate?" I asked.

The words were hardly out of my mouth when the regular clop of the horse's shoes stopped. The Traveler leaned back from the driver's seat and said, "Here is the gatehouse."

"Right." Christopher got up and scrambled to the front of the caravan.

I don't know what he did. The horse started walking again, and after a moment the inside of the caravan went so dark that the kids opposite me gave out little twitters of alarm. The next thing I knew, I was looking out of the back of the van at the tunnel of the gateway, with its gates wide open, and the horse was turning out into the road. I heard its hooves bang and slide on the tramlines as Christopher came crawling back, and then it must have found the space between the rails, because its feet settled into a regular clopping again.

"How did you do that?" Millie asked. It was a professional, enchantress sort of question, even though her teeth were still chattering.

"The gatekeeper wasn't there," Christopher said, "so it was easy to short out the defenses. They must have arrested him, too."

It was a long way down to Stallchester, and the

horse went nothing like so fast as the tram. The slow clopping of its feet was so regular and the inside of the caravan so cozy that I fell asleep and dreamed slow cloves-and-metal-scented dreams. From time to time I woke up, usually on the steep bits, where the horse went slower than ever and the Traveler put on the brake with a long, slurring noise and called out to the horse in his foreign language. Then I went to sleep again.

I woke up finally when white morning light was coming through both ends of the caravan. The clopping hooves seemed louder, with a lot of echo to them. I sat up and saw Stallchester Cathedral going past, very slowly, at the back of the caravan.

A moment later, the Traveler leaned backward to say, "This is where we must put you down."

Christopher jumped awake in a flurry, to say, "Oh. Right. Thanks." I don't think Millie woke up until we were down in the street, watching the caravan swiftly rumbling away from us, jingling and tinkling all over, with the horse now at a smart trot.

Millie started to shiver again. I was not surprised. Her striped Stallery uniform was not at all warm—neither was mine, for that matter. We looked very out of place, in the middle of the wet, slightly foggy street. Christopher's clothes must have been caught in one of the changes. He was wearing wide, baggy garments that could have been made of sackcloth, and he looked even odder than Millie and I did.

"Are you all right?" he said to Millie.

"Just freezing," she said.

"She lived most of her life in a hot country," Christopher explained to me. He looked anxiously around at the touristy boutiques on either side of the street. "It's too early for these shops to be open. I suppose I could conjure you a coat . . ."

Coat, I thought, sweaters, woolen shirts—I know where to find all these things. "Our bookshop is just down the end of this street," I said. "I bet my winter clothes are still there in my room. Let's sneak in and get some sweaters."

"Good idea," Christopher said, looking worriedly at Millie. "And then show us the way to the train station."

I led them down the street and into the alley at the back of our shop. Our yard gate opened in the usual way, with me climbing to the top of it, leaning over to slide the bolt back, and then jumping down and lifting the latch. Inside the yard, the key to the back door was hanging behind the drainpipe, just as usual. I might never have been away, I thought, as we tiptoed through the office. In the shop it was not quite as usual. The cash desk and most of the big bookcases were in different places. I couldn't tell whether this was from one of Uncle Alfred's reorganizations or because of all the changes up at Stallery. The place *smelled* the same, anyway, of book and floor polish and just a whiff of chemicals from Uncle Alfred's workroom.

"You two stay here," I whispered to Christopher and Millie. "I'll creep up and fetch the clothes."

"Will anyone hear?" Millie asked. She settled into the chair behind the cash desk with a weary shiver.

As far as I knew, my mother was still up at Stallery. She had missed the last tram by the time she came into the Grand Saloon, and the first tram in the morning didn't get down to Stallchester until eight-thirty. Uncle Alfred needed two large alarm clocks with double bells the size of teacups in order to wake up in the mornings. "No," I said, and ran up the stairs as lightly as I could.

It was strange. Our stairs seemed small and shabby after Stallery. The fizz of old magics coming from Uncle Alfred's workroom felt small and shabby, too, after the magic I had felt from Christopher and from Stallery itself. And I had forgotten that the private part of our house smelled so dusty. I hurried through the strangeness up to the very top, to my room.

And I could scarcely believe it when I got there. My mother had taken my room to write in. It was full of her usual piles of papers and copies of her books, and there by the window was her splintery old table with her typewriter on it. For a moment I thought it just might be one of the changes from Stallery, but when I looked closely, I saw the marks where my bed and my chest of drawers had been.

Still scarcely able to believe it, I shot down half a floor to Mum's old writing room. My bed was in there, upside down, and rammed in beside it was my chest of drawers with all its drawers open, empty. All my clothes were gone, and my model aircraft, and my books. They had truly not expected me to come back. I felt—well, *hurt* is the only word for it. Very, dreadfully hurt. But just in case, I went on down and looked into Anthea's room.

That was worse. When I left, there had still been Anthea's furniture in there, along with Mum's papers. Now that was all cleared away. Uncle Alfred had made it into a store for his magical supplies. There were new shelves full of bottles and packets on three of the walls and a stack of glassware in the middle. I stood and stared at it for a moment, thinking about Anthea. How did she feel at this moment, now they had arrested her new husband for fraud?

I felt quite as bad.

I pulled myself together and tiptoed across the landing to my mother's room. This was better. This room looked and smelled the same as always—though perhaps dustier—and her unmade bed was piled with heaps of her dusty, moth-eaten clothes. There were more clothes puddled in heaps on the floor. Mum had obviously thrown everything out of her cupboards when she hunted out that awful yellow dress to wear at Stallery. I picked up one of her usual mustard-colored sweaters and put it on. It smelled of Mum, which somehow made me feel more hurt than ever. The sweater looked awful over my green and cream uniform, but at least it was warm. I picked up another, thicker sweater for Millie and a jacket for Christopher and hurried away downstairs.

As I went, I thought I heard the shop door open, with its usual muffled tinkle. Oh no! I thought. Christopher is doing something cleverly stupid again! I put on speed and fairly charged out into the shop.

It was empty. I stood in the polished space beside the cash desk and stared around miserably. Christopher and Millie must have left without me.

I was just about to charge on out into the street, waving the clothes, when I heard the flop, flop of slippers hurrying down the stairs behind me. Uncle Alfred bustled out into the shop, tying his dressing gown over his striped pajamas.

"Someone in the shop," he was saying as he came. "I can't turn my back for a moment—never a wink of sleep—" Then he saw me and stopped dead. "What are *you* doing here?" he said. He pushed his spectacles up his nose to make sure it *was* me. When he was certain, he ran his hands through his tousled hair and seemed quite bewildered. "You're supposed to be up at Stallery, Con," he said. "Did your mother send you back here? Does that mean you've killed your Uncle Amos *already*?"

"No," I said. "I haven't." I wanted to tell him that Mr. Amos had been arrested. So there! But I also wanted to tell Uncle Alfred just what I thought of him for putting spells on me and pretending I had an Evil Fate, and I couldn't decide which I wanted to say first. I hesitated, and after that I had lost my chance. Uncle Alfred more or less screamed at me.

"You haven't killed him!" he shrieked. "But I sent

you up there with death spells all over you, boy! I sent you to summon a Walker! I sent you with spells to make you *know* it was Amos Tesdinic you had to kill! And you let me down!" He advanced on me in dreadful flopping of slippers and his hands sort of clutching like claws. "You'll pay for this!" he shouted. His face was wild, with strange blotches all over it, and his eyes glared at me through his glasses like big yellow marbles. "I might have had Stallery in my hands—*these* hands—but for you!" he screamed. "With *you* hanged and Amos dead, they'd give the place to your mother, and I can manage *her*."

"No, you're wrong," I said, backing away. "There's Hugo, you see. And Anthea."

He didn't listen to me. He almost never did, of course, unless I forced him to by going on strike about something. *"I could have been pulling the possibilities this moment!"* he howled. "Just let me get my hands on you!"

I could feel the fizz of his magic rising around me. I wanted to turn and run, but I didn't seem to be able to. I didn't know *what* to do.

"Summon the Walker again!" Christopher's voice whispered urgently in my ear. I could feel Christopher's breath tickling the side of my face and the invisible warmth of him beside me. I don't think I have ever been so glad to feel anything. "Summon it *now*, Grant!" The corkscrew key hung around my neck was tugged by invisible fingers and flipped out over Mum's mustard-colored sweater.

I dropped the jacket and the sweater for Millie and grabbed the corkscrew key gratefully. I held it up. The string it was hanging on lengthened helpfully so that I could more or less wave the thing in Uncle Alfred's glaring face. "I hereby summon a Walker!" I screamed. "Come to me and give me what I need!"

The cold, and the feeling of vast open distances, began at once. I could see the immense curving horizon beyond Uncle Alfred's untidy hair, glowing from the light that was out of sight below it. Uncle Alfred whipped around and saw it, too. His mouth opened. He started to back away toward the cash desk, but he did not seem to be able to. I could see dents on the sleeves of his dressing gown where two pairs of hands were hanging on to each of his arms. As the figure of the Walker crossed the huge horizon with its hurried, pattering steps, I could feel Christopher on one side of Uncle Alfred and Millie on the other, both holding on to Uncle Alfred like grappling irons.

Uncle Alfred shouted, "No, no! Let *go!*" and plunged and pulled to get free. His arms heaved as if there were lead weights on him as Christopher and Millie hung on.

The Walker approached with surprising speed, its hair and clothing blown sideways without moving, in the unfelt frozen wind it brought with it. In no time at all, it was towering into the shop and looming among the bookcases, filling the space with its icy smell. Then it was standing over us. Its intent white face and long dark eyes turned from Uncle Alfred to me.

"No, no!" Uncle Alfred cried out.

The Walker's long dark eyes turned to Uncle Alfred again. It held out to him the small crimson-stained wine cork labeled *Illary Wines 1893*.

"Don't point that at me!" Uncle Alfred shrieked, pulling away backward. "Point it at Con! It's got a really strong death spell on it!"

The Walker's white face nodded at him. Once. Both its arms swept out. It picked Uncle Alfred up bodily and pattered on past me, carrying Uncle Alfred as easily as if he had been a baby. The last I saw of him were his striped pajama legs kicking frantically as he was carried away beside my right shoulder. As the Walker itself passed me, there was a jerk at my neck, and the corkscrew key flew out of my hands and vanished. The feeling of wind and the horizon of eternity vanished at the same instant.

Millie and Christopher became visible then, staggering away sideways, both looking extremely shaken. Christopher said, in an unusually small, sober voice, "I don't think I like either of your uncles, Grant."

"That," said a deep, dry voice from behind me, "must be the first sensible notion you have had for months, Christopher."

Gabriel de Witt was standing there, gray and severe, and looking tall as the Walker in his black frock coat. He was not alone. All the staff who had come with him into the Grand Saloon were there, too, crowded up against bookcases and standing in the space where the Walker had been. Mr. Prendergast was with them, and the King's solicitor, and one of the Sorceresses Royal—Madame Dupont, it was—and the dreadful Mrs. Havelok-Harting as well. My mother and Anthea were standing beside Gabriel de Witt, both very weary and tearstained. But I was interested to see, looking around, that every single person there seemed as shaken as I was by the passing of the Walker. Even Gabriel de Witt was a little grayer than he had been in Stallery.

At the sight of him, and of all the other people, Christopher looked as dumbfounded as I had ever seen him. His face went as white as the Walker's. He gulped a bit and tried to straighten the tie he wasn't wearing. "I can explain everything," he said.

"Me, too," Millie whispered. She looked downright ill.

"I shall speak to the two of you later," Gabriel de Witt said. It sounded very ominous. "For now," he said, "I want to talk to Conrad Tesdinic."

This sounded even more ominous. "I can explain everything, too," I said. I was scared stiff. I thought I'd rather talk to Uncle Alfred, any day. "I come of a criminal family, you see," I said. "Both my uncles—and I'm sure I *do* have an Evil Fate, whatever Christopher says."

For some reason, this made Anthea give a weepy little laugh. My mother sighed.

"I need to ask you some questions," Gabriel de Witt said, just as if I had not said anything. He pulled a packet out of an inside pocket of his ink black respectable frock coat and passed it to me. It seemed to be a packet of postcards. "Please look through these pictures and explain to me what you see there."

Though I could not for the life of me see why Gabriel de Witt should be interested in picture postcards, I opened the packet and pulled them out. "Oh," I said. They were prints of the photographs I had taken of the double spiral staircase where we saw Millie. There was one of just the staircase, then two of Millie on the same staircase, shouting across at Christopher, and then one of the same staircase, looking up toward the dirty glass of the tower. But something had gone wrong with all of them. Behind each one, misty but quite distinct, were the insides of other buildings, dozens of them. I could see fuzzy hallways, other stairways, domed rooms in many different styles, ruined stone arches, and, several times, what looked like a giant greenhouse. They were all on top of one another, in layers. "I think I must have loaded a film that someone else had used first," I said.

Gabriel de Witt simply said, "Continue looking, please."

I went on down the pile. Here was the hall the double stairway had led down to, but the other person seemed to have photographed a marble place with a sort of swimming pool in it and somewhere dark, with statues, behind that. The next was the room with the harp, but this had literally dozens of rooms mistily behind it, blurred vistas of ballrooms and dining rooms and huge saloons, and a place with billiard tables on top of what looked like several libraries. The next two photographs showed the kitchens—with dim further kitchens behind them—including the knitting on the chair and the table with the strange magazine on it. The next . . .

I gave a sharp yelp. I couldn't help it. The witch had been even nearer than I'd thought. Her face had come out flat and round and blank, the way faces do when you push a camera right up to them. Her mouth was open in a black and furious crescent, and her eyes glared flatly. She looked like an angry pancake.

"I didn't mean to kill her," I said.

"Oh, you didn't kill her," Gabriel de Witt, to my astonishment, replied. "You merely trapped her soul. We found her body in a coma in one of those kitchens, while we were exploring the alternate buildings, and we returned it to Seven D, where I am pleased to say they promptly put it in prison. She was wanted in that world for killing several enchanters in order to obtain their magical powers."

Millie gave a small gasp at this.

One of Gabriel de Witt's tufty eyebrows twitched toward Millie, but he continued without interrupting himself, "We have of course returned the woman's soul to Seven D now, so that she may stand trial in the proper way. Tell me what *else* you see in those pictures."

I leafed through the pile again. "These two of

Millie on the stairs would be quite good," I said, "if it wasn't for all the buildings that have come out behind her."

"They were not there when you took the photographs?" Gabriel de Witt asked me.

"Of course not," I said. "I've never seen them before."

"Ah, but we *have*," said one of Gabriel de Witt's people, a youngish man with a lot of light, curly hair and a brown skin. He came forward and handed me a packet of differently shaped photographs. "I took these while we were searching the probabilities for Millie and Christopher," he said. "What do you think?"

These were photographs of two ruined castles, some marble stairs leading up from a pool, a ballroom, a huge greenhouse, and the double spiral staircase again, and the last one was of the rickety wooden tower where Christopher and I found Champ. All of them, to my shame, were clear and single and precise.

"They're much better than mine," I said.

"Yes, but just look," said the man. He took my first photograph of Millie on the stairway and held it beside four of his. "Look in the background of yours," he said. "You've got both these ruined castles in it and the glass house, and I think that blurred thing behind them is the wooden tower. And if you take yours with the harp, you can see my ballroom at the back of it quite clearly. See?"

The Sorceress Royal said, "In our opinion—and

Mrs. Havelok-Harting agrees with me—it's a remarkable talent, Conrad, to be able to photograph alternate probabilities that you can't even see. Isn't this so, Monsignor?" she asked Gabriel de Witt.

Mr. Prendergast added, "Hear, hear."

Gabriel de Witt took my photographs back from me and stood frowning down at them. "Yes, indeed," he said at last. "Master Tesdinic here has an extraordinary degree of untrained magical talent. I would like"—he turned his frown on my mother—"to take the lad back with me to Series Twelve and make sure that he is properly taught."

"Oh no!" Anthea said.

"I believe I must," Gabriel de Witt said. He was still frowning at my mother. "I cannot think what you were doing, madam, neglecting to provide your son with proper tuition."

My mother's hair was down all over the place, like an unstuffed mattress. I could see she had no answer to Gabriel de Witt. So she said tragically, "Now *all* my family is to be taken from me!"

Gabriel de Witt straightened himself, looking grim and dour even for him. "That, madam," he said, "is what tends to happen when one neglects people." And before my mother could think what to say to this, he added, "The same thing can be said to myself, if this is any consolation." He turned his grim face to Millie. "You were quite right about that Swiss school, my dear," he said to her. "I went and inspected it before I came on here. I should have done that before I sent you to it. It's a terrible place. We shall see about a better school as soon as we get home."

Millie's face became one jubilant, shivering smile.

Christopher said, "What did I tell you?"

It was clear that Christopher was still in bad trouble. Gabriel de Witt said to him, "I said I would speak to you later, Christopher," and then turned to Mrs. Havelok-Harting. "May I leave all outstanding matters in your capable hands, Prosecutor? It is more than time that I returned to my own world. Please present my compliments to His Majesty and my thanks to him for allowing me the freedom to investigate here."

"I shall do that," the formidable lady said. "We would have been quite at a stand without you, Monsignor. But," she added rather more doubtfully, "did your magics last night definitely *stop* those dreadful probability changes?"

"Very definitely," Gabriel de Witt said. "Some foolish person appeared to have jammed the shift key to *on*, that was all." I saw Christopher wince at this. Luckily Gabriel de Witt did not notice. He went on, "If you have any further trouble, please send a competent wizard to fetch me back. Now, is everyone ready? We must leave."

Anthea rushed at me and flung her arms around me. "Come back, Conrad, please!"

"Of course he will," Gabriel de Witt said, rather impatiently. "No one can leave his own world forever. Conrad will return to act as my permanent representative in Series Seven."

I have just come back to Series Seven to be Agent for the Chrestomanci here.

Before this I spent six blissfully happy years at Chrestomanci Castle, learning magic I never dreamed existed and making friends with all the other young enchanters being educated there—Elizabeth, Jason, Bernard, Henrietta, and the rest—although the first week or so was a little difficult. Christopher was in such bad trouble—and so annoyed about it—that the castle seemed to be inside a thunderstorm until Gabriel de Witt forgave him. And Millie turned out to have caught flu. This was why she had been feeling so cold. She was so ill with it that she did not go to her new school until after Christmas.

At the end of the six years, when I was eighteen, Gabriel de Witt called me into his study and explained that I must go home to Series Seven now or I would start to fade, not being in my own world. He suggested that the way to get used to my own world again was to attend Ludwich University. He also said he was sorry to lose me, because I seemed to be the only person who could make Christopher see sense. I am not sure anyone can do that, but Christopher seems to think so, too. He has asked me to come back next year to be best man at his wedding. He and Millie are using the gold ring with Christopher's life in it as a wedding ring, which seems a good way to keep it safe.

Anyway, I have enrolled as a student in Ludwich, and I am staying with Mr. Prendergast in his flat opposite the Variety Theater. Though Mr. Prendergast isn't really an actor, he never can stay away from theaters. Anthea wanted me to stay with her. She keeps ringing me up from New Rome to say I must live with her and Robert as soon as she gets back. She is in New Rome supervising her latest fashion show—she has become quite a famous dress designer. And Robert is away, too, filming in Africa. He took up acting as soon as the police let him go. Mrs. Havelok-Harting decided that as Robert only discovered Mr. Amos's fraud when his father died and then refused to be part of it, he could not be said to be guilty. Hugo had a harder time, but they released him, too, in the end. Now—and I could hardly believe this when Mr. Prendergast told me—Hugo and Felice are running the bookshop in Stallchester. My mother is still writing books in their attic. We are driving up to see them next weekend.

Mr. Amos is still in jail. They transferred him to St. Helena Prison Island last year. And the Countess is living in style in Buda-Parich, not wanting to show herself in this country. And—Mr. Prendergast is not sure, but he thinks this is so—Mr. Seuly went there to join her when he got out of prison. Anyway, Stallchester has a new mayor now.

No one has seen or heard of my Uncle Alfred since the Walker took him away. Now I have learned about such things, I am not surprised. The

Walkers are messengers of the Lords of Karma, and Uncle Alfred tried to use the Lords of Karma in his schemes.

And Stallery is falling into ruin, Mr. Prendergast told me sadly, and becoming just like all the other deserted probability mansions. I remembered Mrs. Baldock and Miss Semple coming weeping out of the lift and wondered what had become of all the Staff who had lost their jobs there.

"Oh, the King stepped in there," Mr. Prendergast told me cheerfully. "He's always on the lookout for well-trained domestics to man the royal residences. They've all got royal jobs. Except Manfred," Mr. Prendergast added. "He had to give up acting after he fell through the wall in a dungeon scene. I think he's a schoolteacher now."

The King wants to see me tomorrow. I feel very nervous. But Fay Marley has promised to go with me at least as far as the door and hold my hand. She knows the King well, and she says she thinks he may want to make me a Special Investigator like Mr. Prendergast. "You notice things other people don't see, darling," she says. "Don't worry so much. It'll be all right, you'll see."

THE PINHOE EGG

To Greer Gilman

1

❧

AT THE BEGINNING of the Summer holidays, while
Chrestomanci and his family were still in the south
of France, Marianne Pinhoe and her brother, Joe,
walked reluctantly up the steep main street of
Ulverscote. They had been summoned by Gammer
Pinhoe. Gammer was head of Pinhoe witchcraft in
Ulverscote and wherever Pinhoes were, from
Bowbridge to Hopton, and from Uphelm to Helm
St. Mary. You did not disobey Gammer's com-
mands.

"I wonder what the old bat wants this time," Joe
said gloomily, as they passed the church. "Some new
stupid thing, I bet."

"Hush," said Marianne. Uphill from the
church, the Reverend Pinhoe was in the vicarage
garden spraying his roses. She could smell the acid
odor of the spell and hear the *hoosh* of the vicar's
spray. It was true that Gammer's commands had
lately become more and more exacting and peculiar,
but no adult Pinhoe liked to hear you say so.

Joe bent his head and put on his most sulky

look. "But it doesn't make sense," he grumbled as they passed the vicarage gate. "Why does she want me too?"

Marianne grinned. Joe was considered "a disappointment" by the Pinhoes. Only Marianne knew how hard Joe worked at being disappointing—though she thought Mum suspected it. Joe's heart was in machines. He had no patience with the traditional sort of witchcraft or the way magic was done by the Pinhoes—or the Farleighs over in Helm St. Mary, or for that matter the Cleeves in Underhelm, on the other side of Ulverscote. As far as that kind of magic went, Joe wanted to be a failure. They left him in peace then.

"It makes sense she wants *you*," Joe continued as they climbed the last stretch of hill up to Woods House, where Gammer lived. "You being the next Gammer and all."

Marianne sighed and made a face. The fact was that no girls except Marianne had been born to Gammer's branch of the Pinhoes for two generations now. Everyone knew that Marianne would have to follow in Gammer's footsteps. Marianne had two great-uncles and six uncles, ten boy cousins, and weekly instructions from Gammer on the witchcraft that was expected of her. It weighed on her rather. "I'll live," she said. "I expect we both will."

They turned up the weedy drive of Woods House. The gates had been broken ever since Old Gaffer died when Marianne was quite small. Their father, Harry Pinhoe, was Gaffer now, being Gammer's eldest son. But it said something about their father's personality, Marianne always thought, that everyone called him Dad, and never Gaffer.

They took two steps up the drive and sniffed. There was a powerful smell of wild animal there.

"Fox?" Joe said doubtfully. "Tomcat?"

Marianne shook her head. The smell was strong, but it was much pleasanter than either of those. A powdery, herby scent, a bit like Mum's famous foot powder.

Joe laughed. "It's not Nutcase anyway. He's been done."

They went up the three worn steps and pushed on the peeling front door. There was no one to open it to them. Gammer insisted on living quite alone in the huge old house, with only old Miss Callow to come and clean for her twice a week. And Miss Callow didn't do much of a job, Marianne thought, as they came into the wide entrance hall. Sunlight from the window halfway up the dusty oak staircase made slices of light filled thick with dust motes, and shone murkily off the glass cases of stuffed animals that stood on tables round the walls. Marianne hated these. The animals had all been stuffed with savage snarls on their faces. Even through the dust, you saw red open mouths, sharp white teeth, and glaring glass eyes. She tried not to look at them as she and Joe crossed the hall over the wall-to-wall spread of grubby coconut matting and knocked on the door of the front room.

"Oh, come in, do," Gammer said. "I've been waiting half the morning for you."

"No, you haven't," Joe muttered. Marianne hoped this was too quiet for Gammer to hear, true though it was. She and Joe had set off the moment Aunt Joy brought the message down from the Post Office.

Gammer was sitting in her tattered armchair, wearing the layers of black clothing she always wore, with her black cat, Nutcase, on her bony knees and her stick propped up by the chair. She did not seem to have heard Joe. "It's holidays now, isn't it?" she said. "How long have you got? Six weeks?"

"Nearly seven," Marianne admitted. She looked down into the ruins of Gammer's big, square, handsome face and wondered if she would look like this when she was this old herself. Everyone said that Gammer had once had thick chestnutty hair, like Marianne had, and Gammer's eyes were the same wide brown ones that Marianne saw in the mirror when she stared at herself and worried about her looks. The only square thing about Marianne was her unusually broad forehead. This was always a great relief to Marianne.

"Good," said Gammer. "Well, here's my plans for you both. Can't have the pair of you doing nothing for seven weeks. Joe first, you're the eldest. We've got you a job, a live-in job. You're going to go and be boot boy to the Big Man in You-Know-Where."

Joe stared at her, horrified. "In Chrestomanci Castle, you mean?"

"Be quiet," his grandmother said sharply. "You don't say that name here. Do you want to have them notice us? They're only ten miles away in Helm St. Mary."

"But," said Joe, "I'd got plans of my own for these holidays."

"Too bad," said Gammer. "Idle plans, stupid plans. You know you're a disappointment to us all, Joseph Pinhoe, so here's your chance to be useful for once. You can go and be our inside eyes and ears in That Castle, and send me word back by Joss Callow if they show the slightest signs of knowing us Pinhoes exist—or Farleighs or Cleeves for that matter."

"Of course they know we exist," Joe said scornfully. "They can't think there's no one living in Ulverscote or—"

Gammer stopped him with a skinny pointing finger. "Joe Pinhoe, you know what I mean. They don't know and can't know that we're all of us witches. They'd step in and make rules and laws for us as soon as they knew and stop us from working at our craft. For two hundred years now—ever since they put a Big Man in That Castle—we've stopped them finding out about us, and I intend for us to go *on* stopping them. And you are going to help me do that, Joe."

"No, I'm not," Joe said. "What's wrong with Joss Callow? *He's* there."

"But he's an outside man," Gammer said. "We want you *inside*. That's where all the secrets are."

"I'm not—" Joe began.

"Yes, you *are*!" Gammer snapped. "Joss has you all fixed up and recommended to that harpy Bessemer that they call Housekeeper there, and go there you will, until you start school again." She snatched up her stick and pointed it at Joe's chest. "I so order it," she said.

Marianne felt the jolt of magic and heard Joe gasp at whatever the stick did to him. He looked from his chest to the end of the stick, dazed and sulky. "You'd no call to do that," he said.

"It won't kill you," Gammer said. "Now, Marianne, I want you with me from breakfast to supper every day. I want help in the house and errands run, but we'll give out that you're my apprentice. I don't want people thinking I need looking after."

Marianne, seeing her holidays being swallowed up and taken away, just like Joe's, cast around for something—anything!—that might let her off. "I promised Mum to help with the herbs," she said. "There's been a bumper crop—"

"Then Cecily can just do her own stewing and distilling alone, like she always does," Gammer said. "I want you *here*, Marianne. Or do I have to point my stick at you?"

"Oh, no. Don't—" Marianne began.

She was interrupted by the crunch of wheels and hoofbeats on the drive outside. Without waiting for Gammer's sharp command to "See who's there!" Marianne and Joe raced to the window. Nutcase jumped off Gammer's knee and beat them to it. He took one look through the grimy glass and fled, with his tail all bushed out. Marianne looked out to see a smart wickerwork pony carriage with a well-groomed piebald pony in its shafts just drawing up by the front steps. Its driver was Gaffer Farleigh, whom Marianne had always disliked, in his best tweed suit and cloth cap, and looking grim even for him. Behind him in the wicker carriage seat sat Gammer Norah Farleigh. Gammer Norah had long thin eyes and a short thin mouth, which made her look grim at the best of times. Today she looked even grimmer.

"Who is it?" Gammer demanded urgently.

"Gaffer Farleigh. In his best," Joe said. "And Gammer Norah. State visit, Gammer. She's got that horrible hat on, with the poppies."

"And they all look horribly angry," Marianne added. She watched a Farleigh cousin jump out of the carriage and go to the pony's head. He was in a suit too. She watched Gaffer Farleigh hand the whip and the reins to the cousin and climb stiffly down, where he stood smoothing his peppery whiskers and waiting for Gammer Norah, who was making the carriage dip and creak as she stood up and got down too. Gammer Norah was a large lady. Poor pony, Marianne thought, even with a light carriage like that.

"Go and let them in. Show them in here and

then wait in the hall," Gammer commanded. "I want *some* Pinhoes on call while I speak to them." Marianne thought Gammer was quite as much surprised by this visit as they were.

She and Joe scurried out past the stuffed animals, Joe with his sulkiest, most head-down, mulish look. The cracked old doorbell jangled, and Gaffer Farleigh pushed the front door open as they reached it.

"Come all the way from Helm St. Mary," he said, glowering at them, "and I find two children who can't even be bothered to come to the door. She in, your Gammer? Or pretending she's out?"

"She's in the front room," Marianne said politely. "Shall I show——?"

But Gaffer Farleigh pushed rudely past and tramped toward the front room, followed by Gammer Norah, who practically shoved Joe against the nearest stuffed animal case getting her bulk indoors. She was followed by her acid-faced daughter Dorothea, who said to Marianne, "Show some manners, child. They'll need a cup of tea and biscuits at *once*. Hurry it up."

"Well, I like that!" Joe said, and made a face at Dorothea's back as Dorothea shut the front-room door with a slam. "Let's just go home."

Raised voices were already coming from behind the slammed door. "No, stay," Marianne said. "I want to know what they're so angry about."

"Me too," Joe admitted. He grinned at Marianne and quietly directed a small, sly spell at the front-room door, with the result that the door shortly came open an inch or so. Gaffer Farleigh's voice boomed through the gap. "Don't deny it, woman! You let it out!"

"I did *not*!" Gammer more or less screamed, and was then drowned out by the voices of Norah and Dorothea, both yelling.

Marianne went to the kitchen to put the kettle on, leaving Joe to listen. Nutcase was there, sitting in the middle of the enormous old table, staring ardently at a tin of cat food someone had left there. Marianne sighed. Gammer always said Nutcase had only two brain cells, both of them devoted to food, but it did rather look as if Gammer had forgotten to feed him again. She opened the tin for him and put the food in his dish. Nutcase was so ecstatically grateful that Marianne wondered how long it was since Gammer had remembered that cats need to eat. There were no biscuits in any of the cupboards. Marianne began to wonder if Gammer had forgotten to feed herself, too.

As the kettle was still only singing, Marianne went into the hall again. The screaming in the front room had died down. Dorothea's voice said, "And I nearly walked into it. I was lucky not to be hurt."

"Pity it didn't eat you," Gammer said.

This caused more screaming and made Joe giggle. He was standing over the glass case that held the twisted, snarling ferret, looking at it much as Nutcase had looked at the tin of cat food. "Have you found out what it's about yet?" Marianne whispered.

Joe shrugged. "Not really. They say Gammer did something and she says she didn't."

At this moment the noise in the front room died down enough for them to hear Gaffer Farleigh saying, "Our sacred trust, Pinhoes and Farleighs both, not to speak of Cleeves. And you, Edith Pinhoe, have failed in that trust."

"Nonsense," came Gammer's voice. "You're a pompous fool, Jed Farleigh."

"And the very fact that you deny it," Gaffer Farleigh continued, "shows that you have lost all sense of duty, all sense of truth and untruth, in your work and in your life."

"I never heard anything so absurd," Gammer began.

Norah's voice cut across Gammer's. "Yes, you have, Edith. That's what we're here to say. You've lost it. You're past it. You make mistakes."

"We think you should retire," Dorothea joined in priggishly.

"Before you do any more harm," Gaffer Farleigh said.

He sounded as if he was going to say more, but whatever this was, it was lost in the immense scream Gammer gave. "What nonsense, what cheek, what an *insult*!" she screamed. "Get out of here, all of you! *Get out of my house, this instant!*" She backed this up with such a huge gust of magic that Joe and Marianne reeled where they stood, even though it was not aimed at them. The Farleighs must have gotten it right in their faces. They came staggering backward out of the front room and across the hall. At the front door, they managed to turn themselves around. Gaffer Farleigh, more furiously angry than either Joe or Marianne had ever seen him, shook his fist and roared out, "I tell you you've *lost* it, Edith!" Marianne could have sworn that, mixed in with Gammer's gust of magic, was the sharp stab of a spell from Gaffer Farleigh, too.

Before she could be sure, all three Farleighs bolted for their carriage, jumped into it, and drove off, helter-skelter, as if Chrestomanci himself was after them.

In the front room, Gammer was still screaming. Marianne rushed in to find her rocking back and forth in her chair and screaming, screaming. Her hair was coming down and dribble was running off her chin. "Joe! Help me stop her!" Marianne shouted.

Joe came close to Gammer and bawled at her, "I'm *not going* to Chrestomanci Castle! Whatever you say!" He said afterward that it was the only thing he could think of that Gammer might attend to.

It certainly stopped Gammer screaming. She stared at Joe, all wild and shaky and panting. "Filberts of halibuts is twisted out of all porringers," she said.

"Gammer!" Marianne implored her. "Talk *sense*!"

"Henbane," said Gammer. "Beauticians' holiday. Makes a crumbfest."

Marianne turned to Joe. "Run and get Mum," she said. "Quickly. I think her mind's gone."

By nightfall, Marianne's verdict was the official one.

Well before Joe actually reached Furze Cottage to fetch Mum, word seemed to get round that something had happened to Gammer. Dad and Uncle Richard were already rushing up the street from the shed behind the cottage where they worked making furniture; Uncle Arthur was racing uphill from the Pinhoe Arms; Uncle Charles arrived on his bicycle, and Uncle Cedric rattled in soon after on his farm cart; Uncle Simeon's builder's van stormed up next; and Uncle Isaac pelted over the fields from his smallholding, followed by his wife, Aunt Dinah, and an accidental herd of goats. Soon after that came the two great-uncles. Uncle Edgar, who was a real estate agent, spanked up the drive in his carriage and pair; and Uncle Lester, who was a lawyer, came in his smart car all the way from Hopton, leaving his office to take care of itself.

The aunts and great-aunts were not far behind. They paused only to make sandwiches first—except for Aunt Dinah, who went back to the Dell to pen the goats before she too made sandwiches. This, it seemed to Marianne, was an unchanging Pinhoe custom. Show them a crisis, and Pinhoe aunts made sandwiches. Even her own mother arrived with a basket smelling of bread, egg, and cress. The great table in the Woods House kitchen was shortly piled with sandwiches of all sizes and flavors. Marianne and Joe were kept busy carrying pots of tea and sandwiches to the solemn meeting in the front room, where they had to tell each new arrival exactly what happened.

Marianne got sick of telling it. Every time she got to the part where Gaffer Farleigh shook his fist and shouted, she explained, "Gaffer Farleigh cast a spell on Gammer then. I felt it." And every time, the uncle or aunt would say, "I can't see Jed Farleigh doing a thing like that!" and they would turn to Joe and ask if Joe had felt a spell too. And Joe was forced to shake his head and say he hadn't. "But there was such a lot of stuff coming from Gammer," he said, "I could have missed it."

But the aunts and uncles attended to Joe no more than they attended to Marianne. They turned to Gammer then. Mum had arrived first, being the only Pinhoe lady to think of throwing sandwiches together by witchcraft, and she had found Gammer in such a state that her first act had been to send Gammer to sleep. Gammer was most of the time lying on the shabby sofa, snoring. "She was screaming the place down," Mum explained to each newcomer. "It seemed the best thing to do."

"Better wake her up, then, Cecily," said the uncle or aunt. "She'll be calmer by this time."

So Mum would take the spell off and Gammer would sit up with a shriek. "Pheasant pie, I tell you!" she would shout. "Tell me something I don't know. Get the fire brigade. There's balloons coming." And all manner of such strange things. After a bit, the uncle or aunt would say, "On second thoughts, I think she'll be better for a bit of a sleep. Pretty upset, isn't she?" So Mum would put the sleep spell back on again and solemn peace would descend until the next Pinhoe arrived.

The only one who did not go through this routine was Uncle Charles. Marianne *liked* Uncle Charles. For one thing—apart from silent Uncle Simeon—he was her only thin uncle. Most of the Pinhoe uncles ran to a sort of wideness, even if most of them were not actually fat. And Uncle Charles had a humorous twitch to his thin face, quite unlike the rest. He was held to be "a disappointment," just like Joe. Knowing Joe, Marianne suspected that Uncle Charles had worked at being disappointing, just as hard as Joe did—although she did think that Uncle Charles had gone a bit far when he married Aunt Joy at the Post Office. Uncle Charles arrived in his paint-blotched old overalls, being a housepainter by trade, and he looked at Gammer, snoring gently on the sofa with her mouth open. "No need to disturb her for me," he said. "Lost her marbles at last, has she? What happened?"

When Marianne had explained once more, Uncle Charles stroked his raspy chin with his paint-streaked hand and said, "I don't see Jed Farleigh doing *that* to her, little as I like the man. What was the row about?"

Marianne and Joe had to confess that they

had not the least idea, not really. "They said she'd let a sacred trust get out and it ran into their Dorothea. I *think*," Marianne said. "But Gammer said she never did."

Uncle Charles raised his eyebrows and opened his eyes wide. "Eh?"

"Let it be, Charles. It's not important," Uncle Arthur told him impatiently. "The important thing is that poor Gammer isn't making sense anymore."

"Overtaxed herself, poor thing," Marianne's father said. "It was that Dorothea making trouble again, I'll bet. I could throttle the woman, frankly."

"Should have been strangled at birth," Uncle Isaac agreed. "But what do we do now?"

Uncle Charles looked across at Marianne, joking and sympathetic at the same time. "Did she ever get round to naming you Gammer after her, Marianne? Should you be in charge now?"

"I hope *not*!" Marianne said.

"Oh, do talk *sense*, Charles!" all the others said. To which Dad added, "I'm not having my little girl stuck with that, even for a joke. We'll wait for Edgar and Lester to get here. See what they say. They're Gammer's brothers, after all."

But when first Great-Uncle Edgar and then Great-Uncle Lester arrived, and Marianne had gone through the tale twice more, and Gammer had been woken up to scream, "We're infested with porcupines!" at Uncle Edgar and "I *told* everyone it was twisted cheese!" at Uncle Lester, neither great-uncle seemed at all sure what to do. Both pulled at their whiskers uncertainly and finally sent Joe and Marianne out to the kitchen so that the adults could have a serious talk.

"I don't like Edgar," Joe said, moodily eating leftover sandwiches. "He's bossy. What does he wear that tweed hat for?"

Marianne was occupied with Nutcase. Nutcase rushed out from under the great table demanding food. "It's what real estate agents wear, I suppose," she said. "Like Lester wears a black coat and striped trousers because he's a lawyer. Joe, I can't find any more cat food."

Joe looked a little guiltily at the last of Great-Aunt Sue's sandwiches. They had been fat and moist and tasty and he had eaten all but one. "This one's sardine," he said. "Give him that. Or—" He lifted the cloth over the one untouched plateful. These were thin and dry and almost certainly Aunt Joy's. "Or there's these. Do cats eat meat paste?"

"They sometimes have to," Marianne said. She dismantled sandwiches into Nutcase's dish, and Nutcase fell on them as if he had not been fed for a week. And perhaps he hadn't, Marianne thought. Gammer had neglected almost everything lately.

"You know," Joe said, watching Nutcase guzzle, "I'm not saying you *didn't* feel Gaffer Farleigh cast a spell—you're better at magic than I am—but it wouldn't have taken much. I think Gammer's mind was going anyway." Then, while Marianne was thinking Joe was probably right, Joe said coaxingly, "Can you do us a favor while we're here?"

"What's that?" Marianne asked as Nutcase backed away from the last of Aunt Joy's sandwiches and pretended to bury it. She was very used to Joe buttering her up and then asking a favor. But I think her mind *was* going, all the same, she thought.

"I need that stuffed ferret out there," Joe said. "If I take it, can you make it look as if it's still there?"

Marianne knew better than to ask what Joe wanted with a horrid thing like that ferret. Boys! She said, "Joe! It's Gammer's!"

"*She's* not going to want it," Joe said. "And you're much better at illusion than me. Be a sport, Marianne. While they're all still in there talking."

Marianne sighed, but she went out into the hall with Joe, where they could hear the hushed, serious voices from the front room. Very quietly, they inspected the ferret under its glass dome. It had always struck Marianne as like a furry yellow snake with legs. All *squirmy*. Yuck. But the important thing, if you were going to do an illusion, was that this was probably just what everyone saw. Then you noticed the wide-open fanged mouth, too, and the ferocious beady eyes. The dome was so dusty that you really hardly saw anything else. You just had to get the shape right.

"Can you do it?" Joe asked eagerly.

She nodded. "I think so." She carefully lifted off the glass dome and stood it beside the stuffed badger. The ferret felt like a hard furry log when she picked it up. Yuck again. She passed the thing to Joe with a shudder. She put the glass dome back over the empty patch of false grass that was left and held both hands out toward it in as near ferret shape as she could. Bent and yellow and furry-squirmy, she thought at it. Glaring eyes, horrid little ears, pink mouth snarling and full of sharp white teeth. Further yuck. She took her hands away and there it was, exactly as she had thought it up, blurrily through the dust on the glass, a dim yellow snarling shape.

"Lush!" said Joe. "Apex! Thanks." He raced back into the kitchen with the real ferret cradled in his arms.

Marianne saw the print of her hands on the dust of the dome, four of them. She blew on them furiously, willing them to go away. They were slowly clearing, when the door to the front room banged importantly open and Great-Uncle Edgar strode out. Marianne stopped doing magic at once, because he was bound to notice. She made herself gaze innocently instead at Edgar's tweed hat, like a little tweed flowerpot on his head. It turned toward her.

"We've decided your grandmother must have professional care," Great-Uncle Edgar said. "I'm off to see to it."

Someone must have woken Gammer up again. Her voice echoed forth from inside the front room. "There's nothing so good as a stewed ferret, I always say."

Did Gammer read other people's minds now? Marianne held her breath and nodded and smiled at Great-Uncle Edgar. And Joe came back from the kitchen at that moment, carrying Aunt Helen's sandwich basket—which he must have thought was Mum's—with a cloth over it to hide the ferret. Great-Uncle Edgar said to him, "Where are you off to?"

Joe went hunched and sulky. "Home," he said. "Got to take the cat. Marianne's going to look after him now."

Unfortunately Nutcase spoiled this explanation by rushing out of the kitchen to rub himself against Marianne's legs.

"But he keeps getting out," Joe added without a blink.

Marianne took in a big breath, which made her quite dizzy after holding it for so long. "I'll bring him, Joe," she said, "when I come. You go on home and take Mum's basket back."

"Yes," said Great-Uncle Edgar. "You'll need to pack, Joseph. You have to be working in That Castle tomorrow, don't you?"

Joe's mouth opened and he stared at Edgar. Marianne stared too. They had both assumed that Gammer's plans for Joe had gone the way of Gammer's wits. "Who told you that?" Joe said.

"Gammer did, yesterday," Great-Uncle Edgar said. "They'll be expecting you. Off you go." And he strode out of the house, pushing Joe in front of him.

2

MARIANNE MEANT TO follow Joe home, but Mum came out into the hall then, saying, "Marianne, Joy says there's still her plate of sandwiches left. Can you bring them?"

When Marianne confessed that there were no sandwiches, she was sent down to the Pinhoe Arms to fetch some of Aunt Helen's pork pies. When she got back with the pies, Aunt Joy sent her off again to pin a note on the Post Office door saying CLOSED FOR FAMILY MATTERS, and when she got back from that, Dad sent her to fetch the Reverend Pinhoe. The Reverend Pinhoe came back to Woods House with Marianne, very serious and dismayed, wanting to know why no one had sent for Dr. Callow.

The reason was that Gammer had no opinion at all of Dr. Callow. She must have heard what the vicar said because she immediately began shouting. "Quack, quack, quack! Cold hands in the midriff. It's cabbages at dawn, I tell you!"

But the vicar insisted. Marianne was sent to the vicarage phone to ask Dr. Callow to visit, and when the doctor came, there was a further outbreak of shouting. As far as Marianne could tell from where she sat on the stairs with Nutcase on her knee, most of the noise was "No, no, no!" but some of it was insults like "You knitted squid, you!" and "I wouldn't trust you to skin a bunion!"

Dr. Callow came out into the hall with Mum, Dad, and most of the aunts, shaking his head and talking about "the need for long-term care." Everyone assured him that Edgar was seeing to that, so the doctor left, followed by the vicar, and the aunts came into the kitchen to make more sandwiches. Here they discovered that there was no bread and only one tin of sardines. So off Marianne was sent again, to the baker and the grocer and down to Aunt Dinah's to pick up some eggs. She remembered to buy some cat food, too, and came back heavily laden, and very envious of Joe for having made his getaway so easily.

Each time Marianne came back to Woods House, Nutcase greeted her as if she were the only person left in the world. While she was picking him up and comforting him, Marianne could not help stealing secret looks at the glass dome that had held the ferret. Each time she was highly relieved to see a yellow smear with a snarl on the end of it seemingly inside the dome.

At long last, near sunset, the hooves, wheels, and jingling of Great-Uncle Edgar's carriage sounded in the driveway. Great-Uncle Edgar shortly strode into the house, ushering two extremely sensible-looking nurses. Each had a neat navy overcoat and a little square suitcase. After Mum, Aunt Prue, and Aunt Polly had shown them where to sleep, the nurses looked into the kitchen, at the muddle of provisions heaped along the huge table there, and declared they were not here to cook. Mum assured them that the aunts would take turns at doing *that*—at which Aunt Prue and Aunt Polly looked at each other and glowered at Mum. Finally the nurses marched into the front room.

"Now, dear"—their firm voices floated out to Marianne on the stairs—"we'll just get you into your bed and then you can have a nice cup of cocoa."

Gammer at once started screaming again. Everyone somehow flooded out into the hall with Gammer struggling and yelling in their midst. No one, even the nurses, seemed to know what to do. Marianne sadly watched Dad and Mum looking quite helpless, Great-Uncle Lester wringing his hands, and Uncle Charles stealthily creeping away to his bicycle. The only person able to cope seemed to be solid, fair Aunt Dinah. Marianne had always thought Aunt Dinah was only good at wrestling goats and feeding chickens, but Aunt Dinah took hold of Gammer's arm, quite gently, and, quite as gently, cast a soothing spell on Gammer.

"Buck up, my old sausage," she said. "They're here to *help* you, you silly thing! Come on upstairs and let them get your nightie on you."

And Gammer came meekly upstairs past Marianne and Nutcase with Aunt Dinah and the nurses. She looked down at Marianne as she went, almost like her usual self. "Keep that cat in order for me, girl," she said. She sounded nearly normal.

Soon after that, Marianne was able to walk home between Mum and Dad, with Nutcase struggling a little in her arms.

"Phew!" said Dad. "Let's hope things settle down now."

Dad was a great one for peace. All he asked of life was to spend his time making beautiful solid furniture with Uncle Richard as his partner. In the shed behind Furze Cottage the two of them made chairs that worked to keep you comfortable, tables bespelled so that anyone who used them felt happy, cabinets that kept dust out, wardrobes that repelled moths, and many other things. For her last birthday, Dad had made Marianne a wonderful heart-shaped writing desk with secret drawers in it that were *really* secret: no one could even find those drawers unless they knew the right spell.

Mum, however, was nothing like such a peace addict as Dad. "Huh!" she said. "She was born to make trouble as the sparks fly upward, Gammer was."

"Now, Cecily," said Dad. "I know you don't like my mother—"

"It's not a question of *like*," Mum said vigorously. "She's a Hopton Pinhoe. She was a giddy town girl before your father married her. Led him a proper dance, she did, *and* you know it, Harry! It was thanks to her that he took to going off into the wild and got himself done away with, if you ask—"

"Now, *now*, Cecily," Dad said, with a warning look at Marianne.

"Well, forget I said it," Mum said. "But I shall be very surprised if she settles down, mind or no mind."

Marianne thought about this conversation all evening. When she went to bed, where Nutcase sat on her stomach and purred, she sleepily tried to remember her grandfather. Old Gaffer had never struck her as being led a dance. Of course she had been very young then, but he had always seemed like a strong person who went his own way. He was wiry and he smelled of earth. Marianne remembered him striding with his long legs, off into the woods, leading his beloved old horse, Molly, harnessed to the cart in which he collected all the strange plants and herbs for which he had been famous. She remembered his old felt hat. She remembered Gammer saying, "Oh, *do* take that horrible headgear *off*, Gaffer!" Gammer always called him Gaffer. Marianne still had no idea what his name had been.

She remembered how Old Gaffer seemed to love being surrounded by his sons and his grandchildren—all boys, except for Marianne— and the way she had a special place on his knee after Sunday lunch. They always went up to Woods House for Sunday lunch. Mum couldn't have enjoyed that, Marianne thought. She had very clear memories of Mum and Gammer snapping at each other in the kitchen, while old Miss Callow did the actual cooking. Mum loved to cook, but she was never allowed to in that house.

Just as she fell asleep, Marianne had the most vivid memory of all, of Old Gaffer calling at Furze Cottage with what he said was a special present for her. "Truffles," he said, holding out his big wiry hand heaped with what looked like little black lumps of earth. Marianne, who had been expecting chocolate, looked at the lumps in dismay. It was worse when Gaffer fetched out his knife—which had been sharpened so often that it was more like a spike than a knife—and carefully cut a slice off a lump and told her to eat it. It tasted like *earth*. Marianne spat it out. It really hurt her to remember Old Gaffer's disappointed look and the way he had said, "Ah, well. She's maybe too young for such things yet." Then she fell asleep.

Nutcase was missing in the morning. The door was shut and the window too, but Nutcase was gone all the same. Nor was he downstairs asking for breakfast.

Mum was busy rushing about finding socks and pants and shirts for Joe. She said over her shoulder, "He'll have gone back to Woods House, I expect. That's cats for you. Go and fetch him back when we've seen Joe off. Oh, God! I've forgotten Joe's nightshirts! Joe, here's two more pairs of socks—I *think* I darned them for you."

Joe received the socks and the other things and secretively packed them in his knapsack himself.

Marianne knew this was because the stolen ferret was in the knapsack too. Joe had his very sulkiest look on. Marianne could not blame him. If it had been her, she knew she would have been dreading going to a place where they were all enchanters and out to stop anyone else doing witchcraft. But Joe, when she asked him, just grumbled, "It's not the magic, it's wasting a whole holiday. That's what I hate."

When at last Joe pedaled sulkily away, with a shirtsleeve escaping from his knapsack and fluttering beside his head, it felt as if a thunderstorm had passed. Marianne, not for the first time, thought that her brother had pretty powerful magic, even if it was not the usual sort.

"Thank goodness for that!" Mum said. "I hate him in this mood. Go and fetch Nutcase, Marianne."

Marianne arrived at Woods House to find the front door—most unusually—locked. She had to knock and ring the bell before the door was opened by a stone-faced angry nurse.

"What good are *you* going to do?" the nurse demanded. "We asked the vicar to phone for Mr. Pinhoe."

"You mean Uncle Edgar?" Marianne asked. "What's wrong?"

"She's poltergeisting us," said the nurse. "That's what's wrong." As she spoke, a big brass tray rose from the table beside the door and sliced its way toward the nurse's head. The nurse dodged. "See what I mean?" she said. "We're not going to stay here one more day."

Marianne watched the tray bounce past her down the steps and clang to a stop in the driveway, rather dented. "I'll speak to her," she said. "I really came to fetch the cat. May I come in?"

"With pleasure," said the nurse. "Come in and make another target, do!"

As Marianne went into the hall, she could not help snatching a look at the ferret's glass dome. There still seemed to be something yellow inside the glass, but it did not look so much like a ferret today. Damn! she thought. It was fading. Illusions did that.

But here Gammer distracted her by coming rushing down the stairs in a frilly white nightdress and a red flannel dressing gown, with the other nurse pelting behind her. "Is that you, Marianne?" Gammer shrieked.

Maybe she's all right again, Marianne thought, a bit doubtfully. "Hallo, Gammer. How are you?"

"Under sentence of thermometer," Gammer said. "There's a worldwide epidemic." She looked venomously from nurse to nurse. "Time to leave," she said.

To Marianne's horror, the big longcase clock that always stood by the stairs rose up and launched itself like a battering ram at the nurse who had opened the door. The nurse screamed and ran sideways. The clock tried to follow her. It swung sideways across the hall, where it fell across the ferret's dome with a violent twanging and a crash of breaking glass.

Well, that takes care of *that*! Marianne thought. But Gammer was now running for the open front door. Marianne raced after her and caught her by one skinny arm as she stumbled over the brass tray at the bottom of the steps.

"Gammer," she said, "you can't go out in the street in your nightclothes."

Gammer only laughed crazily.

She *isn't* all right. Marianne thought. But she's not so *un*-all right as all that. She spoke sternly and shook Gammer's arm a little. "Gammer, you've got to stop *doing* this. Those nurses are trying to *help* you. And you've just broken a valuable clock. Dad always says it's worth hundreds of pounds. Aren't you *ashamed* of yourself?"

"Shame, shame," Gammer mumbled. She hung her head, wispy and uncombed. "I didn't *ask* for this, Marianne."

"No, no, of course not," Marianne said. She felt the kind of wincing, horrified pity that you would rather not feel. Gammer smelled as if she had wet herself, and she was almost crying. "This is only because Gaffer Farleigh put a spell on you—"

"Who's Gaffer Farleigh?" Gammer asked, sounding interested.

"Never mind," Marianne said. "But it means you've got to be *patient*, Gammer, and let people help you until we can make you better. And you've really *got* to stop throwing things at those poor nurses."

A wicked grin spread on Gammer's face. "They can't do magic," she said.

"That's why you've got to stop doing it to them," Marianne explained. "Because they can't fight back. Promise me, Gammer. Promise, or—" She thought about hastily for a threat that might work on Gammer. "Promise me, or I shan't even think of being Gammer after you. I shall wash my hands of you and go and work in London." This sounded like a really nice idea. Marianne thought wistfully of shops and red buses and streets everywhere instead of fields. But the threat seemed to have worked. Gammer was nodding her unkempt head.

"Promise," she mumbled. "Promise Marianne. That's you."

Marianne sighed at a life in London lost. "I should hope," she said. She led Gammer indoors again, where the nurses were both standing staring at the wreckage. "She's promised to be good," she said.

At this stage, Mum and Aunt Helen arrived hotfoot from the village, Aunt Polly came in by the back door, and Great-Aunt Sue alighted from the carriage behind Great-Uncle Edgar. Word had got round, as usual. The mess was cleared up, and to Marianne's enormous relief, nobody noticed that there was no stuffed ferret among the broken glass. The nurses were soothed and took Gammer away to be dressed. More sandwiches were made, more Pinhoes arrived, and, once again, there was a solemn meeting in the front room about what to do now. Marianne sighed again and thought Joe was lucky to be out of it.

"It's not as if it was just anyone we're talking about, little girl," Dad said to her. "This is our head of the craft. It affects all of us in three villages and all the country that isn't under Farleighs or Cleeves. We've got to get it right and see her happy, or we'll *all* go to pot. Run and fetch your Aunt Joy here. She doesn't seem to have noticed there's a crisis on."

Aunt Joy, when Marianne fetched her from the Post Office, did not see things Dad's way at all. She walked up the street beside Marianne, pinning on her old blue hat as she went and grumbling the whole way. "So I have to leave my customers and lose my income—and it's no good believing your Uncle Charles will earn enough to support the family—all because this spoiled old woman loses her marbles and starts throwing clocks around. What's wrong with putting her in a Home, I want to know."

"She'd probably throw things around in a Home too," Marianne suggested.

"Yes, but I wouldn't be dragged off to deal with it," Aunt Joy retorted. "Besides," she went on, stabbing her hat with her hatpin, "my Great-Aunt Callow was in a Home for years and did nothing but stare at the wall, and she was just as much of a witch as your Gammer."

When they got to Woods House, Marianne escaped from Aunt Joy by going to look for Nutcase in the garden, where, sure enough, he was, stalking birds in the overgrown vegetable plot. He seemed quite glad to be taken back to Furze Cottage and given breakfast.

"You stupid old thing!" Marianne said to him. "You have to have your meals here now. I don't think Gammer knows you exist anymore." To her surprise, Marianne found herself swallowing back a sob as she spoke. She had not realized that things were as upsetting as that. But they were. Gammer had never done anything but order Marianne about, nothing to make a person fond of her, but all the same it was awful to have her screaming and throwing things and being generally like a very small child. She hoped they were deciding on a way to make things more reasonable, up at Woods House.

It seemed as if it had not been easy to decide anything. Mum and Dad came home some hours later, with Uncle Richard, all of them exhausted. "Words with the nurses, words with Edgar and Lester," Mum said while Marianne was making them all cups of tea.

"Not to speak of Joy rabbiting on about that nursing home she stuck old Glenys Callow in," Uncle Richard added. "Three spoonfuls, Marianne, love. This is no time for a man to watch his weight."

"But what *did* you decide?" Marianne asked.

It seemed that the nurses had been persuaded to stay on another week, for twice the pay, provided one of the aunts was there all the time to protect them.

"So we take it in turns," Mum said, sighing. "I've drawn tonight's shift, so it's cold supper and rush off, I'm afraid. And after that—"

"It's my belief," Dad said peacefully, "that they'll settle in and she'll get used to them and there'll be no more need to worry."

"In your dreams!" Mum said. Unfortunately, she was right.

The nurses lasted two more nights and then, very firmly and finally, gave notice. They said the house was haunted. Though everyone was positive the haunting was Gammer's doing, no one could catch her at it and no one could persuade the nurses. They left. And there was yet another Pinhoe emergency meeting.

Marianne avoided this one. She told everyone, quite reasonably, that you had to keep a cat indoors for a fortnight in a new place or he would run away. So she sat in her room with Nutcase. This was not as boring as it sounded because, now that Joe was not there to jeer at her, she was able to open the secret drawer in her heart-shaped desk and fetch out the story she was writing. It was called "The Adventures of Princess Irene" and it seemed to be going to be very exciting. She was quite sorry when everyone came back to Furze Cottage after what Uncle Richard described as a Flaming Row and even Dad described as "a bit of difficulty."

According to Mum, it took huge arguments for them even to agree that Gammer was not safe on her own, and more arguments to decide Gammer had to live with someone. Great-Uncle Edgar then cheerfully announced that he and Great-Aunt Sue would live in Woods House and Great-Aunt Sue would look after Gammer. This had been news to Great-Aunt Sue. She did not go for the idea at all. In fact, she had said she would go and live with her sister on the other side of Hopton, and Edgar could look after Gammer himself and see how *he* liked it. So everyone hastily thought again. And the only possible thing, Mum said, was for Gammer to come and live with one of Gammer's seven sons.

"Then," said Uncle Richard, "the fur really flew. Cecily let rip like I've never seen her."

"It's all very well for *you*!" Mum said. "You're not married and you live in that room over in the Pinhoe Arms. Nobody was going to ask you, Richard, so take that smug look—"

"Now, Cecily," Dad said peaceably. "Don't start again."

"I wasn't the only one," said Mum.

"No, there was Joy and Helen and Prue and Polly all screeching that they'd got enough to do, and even your Great-Aunt Clarice, Marianne, saying that Lester couldn't have his proper respectable lifestyle if they had to harbor a madwoman. It put me out of patience," Dad said. "Then Dinah and Isaac offered. They said as they don't have children, they had the room and the time, and Gammer could be happy watching the goats and the ducks down in the Dell. Besides, Dinah can manage Gammer—"

"Gammer didn't think so," said Mum.

Gammer had somehow gotten wind of what was being decided. She appeared in the front room wrapped in a tablecloth and declared that the only way she would leave Woods House was feet first in her coffin. Or that was what most Pinhoes thought she meant when she kept saying, "Root first in a forcing bucket!"

"Dinah got her back to bed," Uncle Richard said. "We're moving Gammer out tomorrow. We put a general call out for all Pinhoes to help and—"

"Wait. There was Edgar's bit before that," Mum said. "Edgar was all set to move into Woods House as soon as Gammer was out of it. Your Great-Aunt Sue didn't disagree with him on *that*, surprise, surprise. The ancestral family home, they said, the big house of the village. As the oldest surviving Pinhoe, Edgar said, it was his *right* to live there. He'd rename it Pinhoe Manor, he thought."

Dad chuckled. "Pompous idiot, Edgar is. I told him to his face he couldn't. The house is mine. It came to me when Old Gaffer went, but Gammer set store by living there, so I let her."

Marianne had had no idea of this. She stared. "Are *we* going to live there, then?" And after all the trouble I've been to, training Nutcase to stay *here*! she thought.

"No, no," Dad said. "We'd rattle about in there as badly as Gammer did. No, my idea is to sell the place, make a bit of money to give to Isaac to support Gammer at the Dell. He and Dinah could use the cash."

"Further flaming row," said Uncle Richard. "You should have seen Edgar's face! And Lester saying that it should only be sold to a Pinhoe or not at all—and Joy screeching for a share of the money. Arthur and Charles shut her up by saying, 'Sell it to a Pinhoe, then.' Edgar looked fit to burst, thinking he was going to have to *pay* for the place, when he thought it was his own anyway."

Dad smiled. "I wouldn't sell to Edgar. His side of the family are Hopton born. He's going to sell it for *me*. I told him to get someone rich from London interested, get a really good price for it. Now let's have a bit of a rest, shall we? Something tells me it may be hard work moving Gammer out tomorrow."

Dad was always given to understating things. By the following night, Marianne was inclined to think this was Dad's understatement of the century.

3

❧❦

EVERYONE GATHERED SOON after dawn in the yard
of the Pinhoe Arms: Pinhoes, Callows, half-
Pinhoes, and Pinhoes by marriage, old, young and
middle-aged, they came from miles around. Uncle
Richard was there, with Dolly the donkey harnessed to Dad's furniture delivery cart. Great-Uncle
Edgar was drawn up outside in his carriage, alongside Great-Uncle Lester's big shiny motor car.
There was not room for them in the yard, what with
all the people and the mass of bicycles stacked up
among the piles of broomsticks outside the beer
shed, with Uncle Cedric's farm cart in front of those.
Joe was there, looking sulky, beside Joss Callow
from That Castle, alongside nearly a hundred distant relatives that Marianne had scarcely ever met.
About the only people who were not there were
Aunt Joy, who had to sort the post, and Aunt Dinah,
who was getting the room ready for Gammer down
in the Dell.

Marianne tried to edge up to Joe to find out how
he was getting on among all the enemy enchanters,

but before she could get near Joe, Uncle Arthur climbed onto Uncle Cedric's cart and, with Dad up there too to prompt him, began telling everyone what to do. It made sense to have Uncle Arthur do the announcing. He had a big booming voice, rather like Great-Uncle Edgar's. No one could say they had not heard him.

Everyone was divided into work parties. Some were to clear everything out of Woods House, to make it ready to be sold; some were to take Gammer's special things over to the Dell; and yet others were to help get Gammer's room ready there. Marianne found herself in the fourth group that was supposed to get Gammer herself down to the Dell. To her disappointment, Joe was in the work party that was sent to Aunt Dinah's.

"And we should be through by lunchtime," Uncle Arthur finished. "Special lunch for all, here at the Pinhoe Arms at one o'clock sharp. Free wine and beer."

While the Pinhoes were raising a cheer at this, the Reverend Pinhoe climbed up beside Uncle Arthur and blessed the undertaking. "And may many hands make light work," he said. It all sounded wonderfully efficient.

The first sign that things were not, perhaps, going to go that smoothly was when Great-Uncle Edgar stopped his carriage outside Woods House slap in the path of the farm cart and strode into the house, narrowly missing a sofa that was just coming out in the hands of six second cousins. Edgar strode up to Dad, who was in the middle of the hall, trying to explain which things were to go with Gammer and which things were to be stored in the shed outside the village.

"I say, Harry," he said in his most booming and important way, "mind if I take that corner cupboard in the front room? It'll only deteriorate in storage."

Behind him came Great-Uncle Lester, asking for the cabinet in the dining room. Marianne could hardly hear him for shouts of "Get out of the *way*!" and "Lester, move your car! The sofa's *stuck*!" and Uncle Richard bawling, "I have to back the donkey there! *Move* that sofa!"

"Right royal pile-up, by the sound," Uncle Charles remarked, coming past with a bookshelf, two biscuit tins, and a stool. "I'll sort it out. You get upstairs, Harry. Polly and Sue and them are having a bit of trouble with Gammer."

"Go up and see, girl," Dad said to Marianne, and to Edgar and Lester, "Yes, *have* the blessed cupboard *and* the cabinet and then get out of the way. Though mind you," he panted, hurrying to catch up with Marianne on the stairs, "that cupboard's only made of plywood."

"I know. And the legs on the cabinet come off all the time," Marianne said.

"Whatever makes them happy," Dad panted.

The shouts outside rose to screams mixed with braying. They turned around and watched the sofa being levitated across the startled donkey. This was followed by a horrific crash as someone dropped the glass case with the badger in it. Then they had to turn the other way as Uncle Arthur came pelting down the stairs with a frilly bedside table hugged to his considerable belly, shouting, "Harry, you've *got* to come! Real trouble."

Marianne and Dad squeezed past him and rushed upstairs to Gammer's bedroom, where Joss Callow and another distant cousin were struggling to get the carpet out from under the feet of a crowd of agitated aunts. "Oh, thank goodness you've come!" Great-Aunt Clarice said, looking hot and wild-haired and most unlike her usual elegant self.

Great-Aunt Sue, who was still almost crisp and neat, added, "We don't know what to do."

All the aunts were holding armfuls of clothes. Evidently they had been trying to get Gammer dressed.

"Won't get dressed, eh?" Dad said.

"Worse than that!" said Great-Aunt Clarice. "Look."

The ladies crowded aside to give Dad and Marianne a view of the bed. Dad said, "My God!" and Marianne did not blame him.

Gammer had grown herself into the bed. She had sunk into the mattress, deep into it, and rooted herself, with little hairy nightdress-colored rootlets sticking out all round her. Her long toenails twined like transparent yellow creepers into the bars at the end of the bed. At the other end, her hair and her ears were impossibly grown into the pillow. Out of it her face stared, bony, defiant, and smug.

"Mother!" said Marianne's dad.

"Thought you could get the better of me, didn't you?" Gammer said. "I'm not going."

Marianne had almost never seen her father lose his temper, but he did then. His round amiable face went crimson and shiny. "Yes, you *are* going," he said. "You're moving to Dinah and Isaac's whatever tricks you play. Leave her be," he said to the aunts. "She'll get tired of this in the end. Let's get all the furniture moved out first."

This was easier said than done. No one had realized quite how much furniture there was. A house the size of Woods House, that was big enough to have held a family with seven children once, can hold massive quantities of furniture. And Woods House did. Joss Callow had to go and fetch Uncle Cedric's hay wain and then borrow the Reverend Pinhoe's old horse to pull it, because the farm cart was just not enough and they would have been at it all day. Great-Uncle Edgar prudently left at this point in case someone suggested they use his fine, spruce carriage too; but Great-Uncle Lester nobly stayed and offered to take the smaller items in his car. Even so, all three vehicles had to make several trips to the big barn out on the Hopton Road, while a crowd of younger Pinhoes rushed out there on bikes and broomsticks to unload the furniture, stack it safely, and surround it in their best spells of preservation. At the same time, so many things turned up that people thought Gammer would need in her new home, that Dolly the donkey was going backward and forward nonstop between Woods House and the Dell, with the cart loaded and creaking behind her.

"It's so *nice* to have things that you're used to around you in a strange place!" Great-Aunt Sue said. Marianne privately thought this was rather sentimental of Aunt Sue, since most of the stuff was things she had never once seen Gammer use.

"And we haven't touched the attics yet!" Uncle Charles groaned, while they waited for the donkey cart to come back again.

Everyone else had forgotten the attics. "Leave them till after lunch," Dad said hastily. "Or we could leave them for the new owner. There's nothing but junk up there."

"I had a toy fort once that must be up there," Uncle Simeon said wistfully.

But he was ignored, as he mostly was, because Uncle Richard brought the donkey cart back with a small Pinhoe girl who had a message from Mum. Evidently Mum was getting impatient to know what had become of Gammer.

"They're all ready," small Nicola announced. "They sprung clent."

"They *what*?" said all the aunts.

"They washed the floor and they dried and they polished and the carpet just fits," Nicola explained. "And they washed the windows and did the walls and put the new curtains up and started on all the furniture and the pictures and the stuffed trout and Stafford and Conway Callow teased a goat and it butted them and—"

"Oh, they spring cleaned," said Aunt Polly. "Now I understand."

"Thank you, Nicola. Run back and tell them Gammer's just coming," Dad said.

But Nicola was determined to finish her narrative first. "And they got sent home and that Joe Pinhoe got told off for being lazy. I was good. I helped," she concluded. Only then did she scamper off with Dad's message.

Dad began wearily climbing the stairs. "Let's hope Gammer's uprooted herself by now," he said.

But she hadn't. If anything, she was rooted to the bed more firmly than ever. When Great-Aunt Sue said brightly, "Up we get, Gammer. Don't we want to see our lovely clean new home?" Gammer just stared, mutinously.

"Oh, come on, Mother. Cut it out!" Uncle Arthur said. "You look ridiculous like that."

"Shan't," said Gammer. "I said root downward and I meant it. I've lived in this house every single year of my life."

"No, you haven't. Don't talk nonsense!" Dad said, turning red and shiny again. "You lived opposite the Town Hall in Hopton for twenty years before you ever came here. One last time—do you get up, or do we carry you to the Dell bed and all?"

"Please yourself. I can't do with your tantrums,

Harry—never could," Gammer said, and closed her eyes.

"Right!" said Dad, angrier than ever. "All of you get a grip on this bed and lift it when I count to three."

Gammer's reply to this was to make herself enormously heavy. The bare floor creaked under the weight of the bed. No one could shift it.

Marianne heard Dad's teeth grind. "Very well," he said. "Levitation spell, everyone."

Normally with a levitation spell, you could move almost anything with just one finger. This time, whatever Gammer was doing made that almost impossible. Everyone strained and sweated. Great-Aunt Clarice's hairstyle came apart in the effort. Pretty little combs and hairpins showered down on Gammer's roots. Great-Aunt Sue stopped looking neat at all. Marianne thought that, for herself, she could have lifted three elephants more easily. Uncle Charles and four cousins left off loading the donkey cart and ran upstairs to help, followed by Uncle Richard and then by Great-Uncle Lester. But the bed still would not move. Until, when every possible person was gathered round the bed, heaving and muttering the spell, Gammer smiled wickedly and let go.

The bed went up two feet and shot forward. Everyone stumbled and floundered. Great-Aunt Sue was carried along with the bed as it made for the doorway and then crushed against the doorpost as the bed jammed itself past her and swung sideways into the upstairs corridor. Great-Aunt Clarice rescued Aunt Sue with a quick spell and a tremendous *POP!* which jerked the bed on again. It sailed toward the stairs, leaving everyone behind except for Uncle Arthur. Uncle Arthur was holding on to the bars at the end of the bed and pushing mightily to stop it.

"Ridiculous, am I?" Gammer said to him, smiling peacefully. And the bed launched itself down the stairs with Uncle Arthur pelting backward in front of it for dear life. At the landing, it did a neat turn, threw Uncle Arthur off, bounced on his belly, and set off like a toboggan down the rest of the stairs. In the hall, Nutcase—who had somehow gotten out again—shot out of its way with a shriek. Everyone except Uncle Arthur leaned anxiously over the banisters and watched Gammer zoom through the front door and hit Great-Uncle Lester's car with a mighty *crunch.*

Great-Uncle Lester howled, "My car, my *car!*" and raced down after Gammer.

"At least it stopped her," Dad said as they all clattered after Great-Uncle Lester. "She hurt?" he asked, when they got there to find a large splintery dent in the side of the car and Gammer, still rooted, lying with her eyes shut and the same peaceful smile.

"Oh, I do hope so!" Great-Uncle Lester said, wringing his hands. "*Look* what she's done!"

"Serve you right," Gammer said, without opening her eyes. "You smashed my dollhouse."

"When I was *five!*" Great-Uncle Lester howled.

"Sixty *years* ago, you dreadful old woman!"

Dad leaned over the bed and demanded, "Are you ready to get up and walk now?"

Gammer pretended not to hear him.

"All *right*!" Dad said fiercely. "Levitation again, everyone. I'm going to get her down to the Dell if it kills us all."

"Oh, it will," Gammer said sweetly.

Marianne's opinion was that the way they were all going to die was from embarrassment. They swung the bed up again and, jostling for a handhold and treading on one another's heels, took it out through the gates and into the village street. There the Reverend Pinhoe, who had been standing in the churchyard, vaulted the wall and hurried over to help. "Dear, dear," he said. "What a very strange thing for old Mrs. Pinhoe to do!"

They wedged him in and jostled on, downhill through the village. As the hill got steeper, they were quite glad of the fact that the Reverend Pinhoe was no good at levitation. The bed went faster and faster and the vicar's efforts were actually holding it back. Despite the way they were now going at a brisk trot, people who were not witches or not Pinhoes came out of the houses and trotted alongside to stare at Gammer and her roots. Others leaned out of windows to get a look, too. "I never knew a person could *do* that!" they all said. "Will she be like that permanently?"

"*God* knows!" Dad snarled, redder and shinier than ever.

Gammer smiled. And it very soon appeared that she had at least one more thing she could do.

There were frantic shouts from behind. They twisted their heads around and saw Great-Uncle Lester, with Uncle Arthur running in great limping leaps behind him, racing down the street toward them. No one understood what they were shouting, but the way they were waving the bed carriers to one side was quite clear.

"Everyone go right," Dad said.

The bed and its crowd of carriers veered over toward the houses and, on Marianne's side, began stumbling over doorsteps and barking shins on foot-scrapers, just as Dolly the donkey appeared, with her cart of furniture bounding behind her, apparently running for her life.

"Oh, *no!*" groaned Uncle Richard.

The huge table from the kitchen in Woods House was chasing Dolly, gaining on her with every stride of its six massive wooden legs. Everyone else in the street screamed warnings and crowded to the sides. Uncle Arthur collapsed on the steps of the Pinhoe Arms. Great-Uncle Lester fled the other way into the grocer's. Only Uncle Richard bravely let go of the bed and jumped forward to try to drag Dolly to safety. But Dolly, her eyes set with panic, swerved aside from him and pattered on frantically. Uncle Richard had to throw himself flat as the great table veered to charge at him, its six legs going like pistons. Gammer almost certainly meant the table to go for the bed and its carriers, but as it galloped near enough, Uncle Charles, Dad, Uncle Simeon, and the Reverend Pinhoe each put out a leg and kicked it hard in the side. That swung it back into the street again. It was after Dolly in a flash.

Dolly had gained a little when the table swerved, but the table went so fast that it looked as if, unless Dolly could turn right at the bottom of the hill toward Furze Cottage in time, or left toward the Dell, she was going to be squashed against the Post Office wall. Everyone except Marianne held their breath. Marianne said angrily, "Gammer, if you've killed poor Dolly I'll never forgive you!"

Gammer opened one eye. Marianne thought the look from it was slightly ashamed.

Dolly, seeing the wall coming up, uttered a braying scream. Somehow, no one knew how, she managed to throw herself and the cart sideways into Dell Lane. The cart rocked and shed a birdcage, a small table, and a towel rail, but it stayed upright. Dolly, cart and all, sped out of sight, still screaming.

The table thundered on and hit the Post Office wall like a battering ram. It went in among the bricks as if the bricks weighed nothing and plowed on, deep into the raised lawn behind the wall. There it stopped.

When the shaken bed carriers trotted up to the wreckage, Aunt Joy was standing above them on the ruins, with her arms folded ominously.

"You've done it now, haven't you, you horrible old woman?" she said, glaring down at Gammer's smug face. "Making everyone carry you around like this—you ought to be ashamed! Can you pay for all this? Can you? I don't see why *I* should have to."

"Abracadabra," Gammer said. "Rhubarb."

"That's right. Pretend to be balmy," said Aunt Joy. "And everyone will back you up, like they always do. If it was me, I'd dump you in the duck pond. *Curse* you, you old—!"

"That's enough, Joy!" Dad commanded. "You've every right to be annoyed, and we'll pay for the wall when we sell the house, but no cursing, please."

"Well, get this table out of here at least," Aunt Joy said. She turned her back and stalked away into the Post Office.

Everyone looked at the vast table, half buried in rubble and earth. "Should we take it down to the Dell?" a cousin asked doubtfully.

"How do you want it when it's there?" Uncle Charles asked. "Half outside in the duck pond, or on one end sticking up through the roof? That house is *small*. And they say this table was built inside Woods House. It couldn't have gotten in any other way."

"In that case," asked Great-Aunt Sue, "how did it get *out*?"

Dad and the other uncles exchanged alarmed looks. The bed dipped as Uncle Simeon dropped his part of it and raced off up the hill to see if Woods House was still standing. Marianne was fairly sure that Gammer grinned.

"Let's get on," Dad said.

They arrived at the Dell to find Dolly, still harnessed to the cart, standing in the duck pond shaking all over, while angry ducks honked at her from the bank. Uncle Richard, who was Dolly's adoring friend, dropped his part of the bed and galloped into the water to comfort her. Aunt Dinah, Mum, Nicola, Joe, and a crowd of other people rushed anxiously out of the little house to meet the rest of them.

Everyone gratefully lowered the bed to the grass. As soon as it was down, Gammer sat up and held a queenly hand out to Aunt Dinah. "Welcome," she said, "to your humble abode. And a cup of hot marmalade would be very welcome too."

"Come inside then, dear," Aunt Dinah said. "We've got your tea all ready for you." She took hold of Gammer's arm and, briskly and kindly, led Gammer away indoors.

"Lord!" said someone. "Did you know it's four o'clock already?"

"Table?" suggested Uncle Charles. Marianne could tell he was anxious not to annoy Aunt Joy any further.

"In one moment," Dad said. He stood staring at the little house, breathing heavily. Marianne could feel him building something around it in the same slow, careful way he made his furniture.

"Dear me," said the Reverend Pinhoe. "Strong measures, Harry."

Mum said, "You've stopped her from ever coming outside. Are you sure that's necessary?"

"Yes," said Dad. "She'll be out of here as soon as my back's turned, otherwise. And you all know what she can do when she's riled. We got her here, and here she'll stay—I've made sure of that. Now let's take that dratted table back."

They went back in a crowd to the Post Office, where everyone exclaimed at the damage. Joe said, "I *wish* I'd seen that happen!"

"You'd have run for your life like Dolly did," Dad snapped, tired and cross. "Everybody levitate."

With most of the spring-cleaning party to help, the table came loose from the Post Office wall quite quickly, in a cloud of brick dust, grass, earth, and broken bricks. But getting it back up the hill was not quick at all. It was *heavy*. People kept having to totter away and sit on doorsteps, exhausted. But Dad kept them all at it until they were level with the Pinhoe Arms. Uncle Simeon met them there, looking mightily relieved.

"Nothing I can't rebuild," he said cheerfully. "It took out half the kitchen wall, along with some cabinets and the back door. I'll get them on it next Monday. It'll be a doddle compared with the wall down there. That's going to take time, and money."

"Ah, well," said Dad.

Uncle Arthur came limping out of the yard, leaning on a stick, with one eye bright purple-black. "There you all are!" he said. "Helen's going mad in here about her lunch spoiling. Come in and eat, for heaven's sake!"

They left the table blocking the entrance to the yard, under the swinging sign of the unicorn and griffin, and flocked into the inn. There, although Aunt Helen looked unhappy, no one found anything wrong with the food. Even elegant Great-Aunt Clarice was seen to have two helpings of roast and four veg. Most people had three. And there was beer, mulled wine, and iced fruit drink—just what everyone felt was needed. Here at last Marianne managed to get a word with Joe.

"How are you getting on in That Castle?"

"Boring," said Joe. "I clean things and run errands. Mind you," he added, with a cautious look at Joss Callow's back, bulking at the next table, "I've never known anywhere easier to duck out from work in. I've been all over the Castle by now."

"Don't the Family mind?" Marianne asked.

"The main ones are not there," Joe said. "They come back tomorrow. Housekeeper was really hacked off with me and Joss for taking today off. We told her it was our grandmother's funeral—or Joss did."

With a bit of a shudder, hoping this was not an omen for poor Gammer, Marianne went on to the question she really wanted to ask. "And the children? They're all enchanters too, aren't they?"

"One of them is," Joe said. "Staff don't like it. They say it's not natural in a young lad. But the rest of them are just plain witches like us, from what they say. Are you going for more roast? Fetch me another lot, too, will you?"

Eating and drinking went on a long time, until nearly sunset. It was quite late when a cheery party of uncles and cousins took the table back to Woods House, to shove it in through the broken kitchen wall and patch up the damage until Monday. A second party roistered off down the hill to tidy up the bricks there.

Everyone clean forgot about the attics.

4

❧❦

ON THE WAY back from the south of France, Chrestomanci's daughter, Julia, bought a book to read on the train, called *A Pony Of My Own*. Halfway through France, Chrestomanci's ward, Janet, snatched the book off Julia and read it too. After that, neither of them could talk about anything but horses. Julia's brother, Roger, yawned. Cat, who was younger than any of them, tried not to listen and hoped they would get tired of the subject soon.

But the horse fever grew. By the time they were on the cross–Channel ferry, Julia and Janet had decided that both of them would die unless they had a horse each the moment they got home to the Castle.

"We've only got six weeks until we start lessons again," Julia sighed. "It has to be at *once*, or we'll miss all the gymkhanas."

"It would be a complete waste of the summer," Janet agreed. "But suppose your father says no?"

"You go and ask him now," Julia said.

"Why me?" Janet asked.

"Because he's always worried about the way he had to take you away from your own world," Julia explained. "He doesn't want you to be unhappy. Besides, you have blue eyes and golden hair—"

"So has Cat," Janet said quickly.

"But you can flutter your eyelashes at him," Julia said. "My eyelashes are too short."

But Janet, who was still very much in awe of Chrestomanci—who was, after all, the most powerful enchanter in the world—refused to talk to Chrestomanci unless Julia was there to hold her hand. Julia, now that owning a horse had stopped being just a lovely idea and become almost real, found she was quite frightened of her father too. She said she would go with Janet if the boys would come and back them up.

Neither Roger nor Cat was in the least anxious to help. They argued most of the way across the Channel. At last, when the white cliffs of Dover were well in sight, Julia said, "But if you *do* come and Daddy *does* agree, you won't have to listen to us talking about it anymore."

This made it seem worth it. Cat and Roger duly crowded into the cabin with the girls, where Chrestomanci lay, apparently fast asleep.

"Go away," Chrestomanci said, without seeming to wake up.

Chrestomanci's wife, Millie, was sitting on a bunk darning Julia's stockings. This must have been for something to pass the time with, because Millie, being an enchantress, could have mended most things just with a thought. "He's very tired, my loves," she said. "Remember he had to take a travel-sick Italian boy all the way back to Italy before we came home."

"Yes, but he's been resting ever since," Julia pointed out. "And this is urgent."

"All right," Chrestomanci said, half opening his bright black eyes. "What is it, then?"

Janet bravely cleared her throat. "Er, we need a horse each."

Chrestomanci groaned softly.

This was not promising, but, having started, both Janet and Julia suddenly became very eloquent about their desperate, urgent, crying need for horses, or at least ponies, and followed this up with a detailed description of the horse each of them would like to own. Chrestomanci kept groaning.

"I remember feeling like this," Millie said, fastening off her thread, "my second year at boarding school. I shall never forget how devastated I was when old Gabriel de Witt simply refused to listen to me. A horse won't do any harm."

"Wouldn't bicycles do instead?" Chrestomanci said.

"You don't under*stand*! It's not the *same*!" both girls said passionately.

Chrestomanci put his hands under his head and looked at the boys. "Do you all have this mania?" he asked. "Roger, are you yearning for a coal black stallion too?"

"I'd rather have a bicycle," Roger said.

Chrestomanci's eyes traveled up Roger's plump figure. "Done," he said. "You could use the exercise. And how about you, Cat? Are you too longing to speed about the countryside on wheels or hooves?"

Cat laughed. After all, he was a nine-lifed enchanter, too. "No," he said. "I can always teleport."

"Thank heavens! One of you is sane!" Chrestomanci said. He held up one hand before the girls could start talking again. "All right. I'll consider your request—on certain conditions. Horses, you see, require a lot of attention, and Jeremiah Carlow—"

"Joss Callow, love," Millie corrected him.

"The stableman, whatever his name is," Chrestomanci said, "has enough to do with the horses we already keep. So you girls will have to agree to do all the things they tell me these tiresome creatures need—mucking out, cleaning tack, grooming, and so forth. Promise me you'll do that, and I'll agree to one horse between the two of you, at least for a start."

Julia and Janet promised like a shot. They were ecstatic. They were in heaven. At that moment, anything to do with a horse, even mucking it out, seemed like poetry to them. And, to Roger's disgust, they still talked of nothing else all the way home to the Castle.

"At least I'll get a bicycle out of it," he said to Cat. "Don't you really want one too?"

Cat shook his head. He could not see the point.

Chrestomanci was as good as his word. As soon as they were back in Chrestomanci Castle, he summoned his secretary, Tom, and asked him to order a boy's bicycle and to bring him all the journals and papers that were likely to advertise horses for sale. And when he had dealt with all the work Tom had for him in turn, he called Joss Callow in and asked his advice on choosing and buying a suitable horse. Joss Callow, who was rather pale and tired that day, pulled himself together and tried his best. They spread newspapers and horsey journals out all over Chrestomanci's study, and Joss did his best to explain about size, breeding, and temperament, and what sort of price a reasonable horse should be. There was a mare for sale in the north of Scotland that seemed perfect to Joss, but Chrestomanci said that was much too far away. On the other hand, a wizard called Prendergast had a decent small horse for sale in the next county. Its breeding was spectacular, its name was Syracuse, and it cost rather less money. Joss Callow wondered about it.

"Go and look at that one," Chrestomanci said. "If it seems docile and anything like as good as this Prendergast says, you can tell him we'll have it and bring it back by rail to Bowbridge. You can walk it on from there, can you?"

"Easily can, sir," Joss Callow said, a little dubiously. "But the fares for horse travel—"

"Money no object," Chrestomanci said. "I need a horse and I need it now, or we'll have no peace. Go and look at it today. Stay overnight—I'll give you the money—and, if possible, get the creature here tomorrow. If it's no good, telephone the Castle and we'll try again."

"Yes, sir." Joss Callow went off, a little dazed at this suddenness, to tell the stableboy exactly what to do in his absence.

He reached the stableyard in time to discover Janet and Julia trying to open the big shed at the end. "Hey!" he said. "You can't go in there. That's Mr. Jason Yeldham's store, that is. He'll kill us all if you mess up the spells he's got in there!"

Julia said, "Oh, I didn't know. Sorry."

Janet said, "Who's Mr. Jason Yeldham?"

"He's Daddy's herb specialist," Julia said. "He's lovely. He's my favorite enchanter."

"And," Joss Callow added, "he's got ten thousand seeds in that shed, most of them from foreign worlds, and umpteen trays of plants under stasis spells. What did you think you wanted in there?"

Janet replied, with dignity, "We're looking for somewhere suitable for our horse to live."

"What's wrong with the stables?" Joss said.

"We looked in there," Julia said. "The loose box seems rather small."

"Our horse is special, you see," Janet told him.

Joss Callow smiled. "Special or not," he said kindly, "the loose box will be what he's used to. You don't want him to feel strange, do you? You cut along now. He'll be here tomorrow, with any luck."

"*Really?*" they both said.

"Just off to fetch him now," said Joss.

"*Clothes!*" Janet said, thoroughly dismayed. "Julia, we need riding clothes. *Now!*"

They went pelting off to find Millie.

Millie, who always enjoyed driving the big sleek Castle car, loaded Joss Callow into the car with the girls and dropped him at Bowbridge railway station before she took Julia and Janet shopping. Julia came back more madly excited than ever, with an armload of riding clothes. Janet, with another armload, was almost silent. Her parents, in her own world, had not been rich. She was appalled at how much riding gear *cost*.

"Just the hard hat on its own," she whispered to Cat, "was *ten years'* pocket money!"

Cat shrugged. Although it seemed to him to be a stupid fuss, he was glad Janet had new things to think about. It made a slight change from horses. Cat was feeling rather flat himself, after the south of France. Flat and dull. Even the sunlight on the green velvet stretch of the lawns seemed dimmer than it had been. The usual things to do did not feel interesting. He suspected that he had grown out of most of them.

Next morning, the Bowbridge carter arrived with Roger's gleaming new bicycle. Cat went down to the front steps with everyone else to admire it.

"This is something like!" Roger said, holding up the bike by its shiny handlebars. "Who wants a horse when they can have *this*?" Janet and Julia, naturally, glared at him. Roger grinned joyfully at them and turned back to the bicycle. The grin faded slowly to doubt. "There's a bar across," he said, "from the saddle to the handles. How do I—?"

Chrestomanci was standing with his hands in the pockets of a sky blue dressing gown with dazzling golden panels. "I believe," he said, "that you put your left foot on the near pedal and swing your right leg over the saddle."

"I do?" Roger said. Dubiously, he did as his father suggested.

After a moment of standing, wobbling and upright, Roger and the bicycle slowly keeled over together and landed on the drive with a crash. Cat winced.

"Not quite right," Roger said, standing up in a spatter of pebbles.

"I fancy you forgot to pedal," Chrestomanci said.

"But how does he pedal *and* balance?" Julia wanted to know.

"One of life's mysteries," Chrestomanci said. "But I have frequently seen it done."

"Shut up, all of you," Roger said. "I *will* do this!"

It took him three tries, but he got both feet on the pedals and pushed off, down the drive in a curvaceous swoop. The swoop ended in one of the big laurel bushes. Here Roger kept going and the bicycle mysteriously did not. Cat winced again. He was quite surprised when Roger emerged from the bush like a walrus out of deep water, picked up the bike, and grimly got on it again. This time his swoop ended on the other side of the drive in a prickly bush.

"It'll take him a while," Janet said. "I was three days learning."

"You mean you can *do* it?" Julia said. Janet nodded. "Then you'd better not tell Roger," Julia said. "It might hurt his pride."

The rest of the morning was filled with the sound of sliding gravel, followed by a crash, with, every so often, the hefty threshing sound of a plump body hitting another bush. Cat got bored and wandered away.

Syracuse arrived in the early afternoon. Cat was up in his room at the time, at the top of the Castle. But he clearly felt the exact moment when Joss Callow led Syracuse toward the stableyard gates and the spells around Chrestomanci Castle canceled out whatever spells Wizard Prendergast had put on Syracuse. There was a kind of electric jolt. Cat was so interested that he started running downstairs at once. He did not hear the mighty hollow bang as Syracuse's front hooves hit the gates. Nor the slam as the gates flew open. He did not see how Syracuse then got away from Joss Callow. By the time Cat arrived on the famous velvety lawn, Syracuse was out there too being chased by Joss Callow, the stableboy, two footmen, and most of the gardeners. Syracuse was having the time of his life dodging them all, skipping this way and that with his lead rein wildly swinging, and, when any of them got near enough to catch him, throwing up his heels and galloping out of reach.

Syracuse was beautiful. This was what Cat mainly noticed. Syracuse was a dark brown that was nearly black, with a swatch of midnight for his mane and a flying silky black tail. His head was shapely and proud. He was a perfect slender, muscly build of a horse, and his legs were elegant, long, and deft. He was not very large, and he moved like a dancer as he jinked and dodged away from the running, shouting, clutching humans. Cat could see Syracuse was having enormous fun. Cat trotted nearer to the chase, quite fascinated. He could not help chuckling at the clever way Syracuse kept getting away.

Joss Callow, very red in the face, called instructions to the rest. Before long, instead of running every which way, they were organized into a softly walking circle that was moving slowly in on Syracuse. Cat saw they were going to catch him any second now.

Then into the circle came Roger on his bicycle, waving both arms and pedaling hard to stay upright. "Look, no hands!" he shouted. "I can do it! I can do it!" At this point, he saw Syracuse and the bicycle wagged about underneath him. "I can't steer!" he said.

He shot among the frantically scattering gardeners and fell off in front of Syracuse.

Syracuse reared up in surprise, came down,

hurdled Roger and the bicycle, and raced off in quite a new direction.

"Keep him out of the rose garden!" the head gardener shouted desperately, and too late.

Cat was now the person nearest to the rose garden. As he sprinted toward the arched entry to it, he had a glimpse of Syracuse's gleaming brown rear turning left on the gravel path. Cat put on more speed, dived through the archway, and turned right. It stood to reason that Syracuse would circle the place on the widest path. And Cat was correct. He and Syracuse met about two-thirds of the way down the right-hand path.

Syracuse was gently trotting by then, with his head and ears turned slightly backward to listen to the pursuit rushing up the other side of the rose garden. He stopped dead when he saw Cat and nodded his head violently upward. Cat could almost hear Syracuse thinking, *Damn!*

"Yes, I know I'm a spoilsport," Cat said to him. "You were having real fun, weren't you? But they don't let people make holes in the lawn. That's what's annoyed them. They'll probably kill Roger. You made hoofprints. He's practically plowed it up."

Syracuse brought his head halfway down and considered Cat. Then, rather wonderingly, he stretched his neck out and nosed Cat's face. His nose felt very soft and whiskery, with just a hint of dribble. Cat, equally wonderingly, put one hand on Syracuse's firm, warm, gleaming neck. A definite thought came to him from Syracuse: *Peppermint*?

"Yes," Cat said. "I can get that." He conjured a peppermint from where he knew Julia had one of her stashes and held it out on the palm of his left hand. Syracuse, very gently, lipped it up.

While he did so, the pursuit skidded round the corner and piled to a halt, seeing Syracuse standing quietly with Cat. Joss Callow, who had been cunning too, and limping because Syracuse had trodden on him, came up behind Cat and said, "You got him, then?"

Cat quickly took hold of the dangling lead rein. "Yes," he said. "No trouble."

Joss Callow sniffed the air. "Ah," he said. "Peppermint's the secret, is it? Wish I'd known. I'll take the horse now. You better go and help your cousin. Got himself woven into that cycle somehow."

It took Cat quite serious magic to separate Roger from the bicycle, and then it took both of them working together to unplow the lawn where Roger had hit it, so Cat never saw how Joss got Syracuse back to the stables. He gathered it took a long time and a lot of peppermints. After that, Joss went to the Castle and asked to speak to Chrestomanci.

As a result, next morning when Janet and Julia came into the stableyard self-consciously wearing their new riding clothes, Chrestomanci was there too, in a dressing gown of tightly belted black silk with sprays of scarlet chrysanthemums down the back. Cat was with him because Chrestomanci had asked him to be there.

"It seems that Wizard Prendergast has sold us a very unreliable horse," Chrestomanci said to the girls. "My feeling is that we should sell Syracuse for dog meat and try again."

They were horrified. Janet said, "Not *dog meat*!" and Julia said, "We ought to give him a *chance*, Daddy!" Cat said, "That's not fair."

"Then I rely on you, Cat," Chrestomanci said. "I suspect you are better at horse magics than I am."

Joss Callow led Syracuse out, saddled and bridled. Syracuse reeked of peppermint and looked utterly bored. In the morning sunlight he was sensationally good looking. Julia exclaimed. But Janet, to her own great shame, discovered there and then that she was one of those people who are simply terrified of horses. "He's *enormous*!" she said, backing away.

"Oh, nonsense!" said Julia. "His head's only a bit higher than yours is. Get on him. I'll give you first go."

"I—I can't," Janet said. Cat was surprised to see she was shaking.

Chrestomanci said, "Given the creature's exploits yesterday, I think you are very wise."

"I'm not wise," Janet said. "I'm just scared silly. Oh, what a *waste* of new riding clothes!" She burst into tears and ran away into the Castle, where she hid in an empty room.

Millie found her there, sitting on the unmade

bed sobbing. "Don't take it so hard, my love," she said, sitting beside Janet. "A lot of people find they can't get on with horses. I don't think Chrestomanci can, you know. He always says he hates them because of the way they smell, but I think it's more than that."

"But I feel so ashamed!" Janet wept. "I went on and on about being a famous rider and now I can't even go *near* the horse!"

"But how could you possibly know that until you tried?" Millie asked. "No one can help the way they're made, my love. You just have to think of something you're good at doing instead."

"But," said Janet, coming to the heart of her shame, "I made such a fuss that I made Chrestomanci spend all that money on a horse, and all for *nothing*!"

"I think I heard Julia making quite as much fuss," Millie remarked. "We'd have bought the horse for her in the end, you know."

"And these clothes," Janet said. "So *expensive*. And I shall never wear them again."

"Now that is silly," Millie told her. "Clothes can be given to someone else. It will take me five minutes and the very minimum of magic to make them into a second set for Julia—or for anyone else who wants to ride. Roger might decide he wants to, you know."

Janet found herself giving a weak giggle at the thought of Roger sitting on Syracuse in her clothes. It seemed the most impossible thing in all the Related Worlds.

"That's better," said Millie.

Meanwhile, Chrestomanci said, "Well, Julia? You seem to have this horse all to yourself."

Julia happily approached Syracuse. She attended carefully to the instructions Joss Callow gave her, gathered up the reins, put her foot in the stirrup, and managed to get herself into the saddle. "It feels awfully high up," she said.

Syracuse contrived to hump his back somehow, so that Julia was higher still.

Joss Callow jerked the bit to make Syracuse behave and led Syracuse sedately round the yard with Julia crouching in a brave wobbly way on top. All went well until Syracuse stopped suddenly and ducked his head down. Cat only just prevented Julia from sliding off over Syracuse's ears, by throwing a spell like a sort of rope to hold her on. Syracuse looked at him reproachfully.

"Had enough, Julia?" Chrestomanci asked.

Julia clenched her teeth and said, "Not yet." She bravely managed another twenty minutes of walking round the yard, even though part of the time Syracuse was not walking regularly, but putting his feet down in a random scramble that had Julia tipping this way and that.

"It really does seem as if this animal does not wish to be ridden," Chrestomanci said. He went away indoors and quietly ordered two girl's bicycles.

Julia refused to give up. Some of it was pride and obstinacy. Some of it was the splendid knowledge that she now owned Syracuse all by herself.

None of this stopped Syracuse making himself almost impossible to ride. Cat had to be in the yard whenever Julia sat on the horse, with his rope spell always ready. Two days later, Joss Callow opened the gate to the paddock and invited Julia to see if she—or Syracuse—did better in the wider space.

Syracuse promptly whipped round and made for the stables with Julia clinging madly to his mane. The stable doors were shut, so Syracuse aimed himself at the low open doorway of the tack room instead. Julia saw it coming up fast and realized that she was likely to be beheaded. Shrieking out the words of a spell, she managed to levitate herself right up onto the stable roof. There, while Cat and Joss hauled Syracuse out backward, draped in six bridles and one set of carriage reins, Julia sat with big tears rolling down her face and gave vent to her feelings.

"I *hate* this horse! He *deserves* to be dog meat! He's *horrible*!"

"I agree," Chrestomanci said, appearing beside Cat in fabulous charcoal gray suiting. "Would you like me to try to get you a real horse?"

"I hate you too!" Julia screamed. "You only got this one because you thought we were silly to want a horse at all!"

"Not true, Julia," Chrestomanci protested. "I did think you were silly, but I made an honest try and Prendergast diddled me. If you like, I'll try for something fat and placid and elderly, and this one can go to the vet. What's his name?" he asked Joss.

"Mr. Vastion," Joss said, untangling leather straps from Syracuse's tossing head.

"*No!*" said Julia. "I'm sick of *all* horses."

"Mr. Vastion, then," said Chrestomanci.

Cat could not bear to think of anything so beautiful and so much alive as Syracuse being turned into dog meat. "Can I have him?" he said.

Everyone looked at him in surprise, including Syracuse.

"You want the vet?" Chrestomanci said.

"No, Syracuse," said Cat.

"On your head be it, then." Chrestomanci shrugged and turned to help Julia down off the roof.

Cat found he owned a horse—just like that. Since everyone seemed to expect him to, he approached Syracuse and tried to remember the way Joss had told Julia to do things. He got his foot stretched up into the correct stirrup, collected the reins from Joss, and jumped himself vigorously up into the saddle. He would not have been surprised to find himself facing Syracuse's tail. Instead, he found himself looking forward across a pair of large, lively ears beyond a tossing black mane, into Julia's tearful face.

"Oh, this is just not *fair*!" Julia said.

Cat knew what she meant. As soon as he was in the saddle, a peculiar kind of magic happened, which was quite unlike the magic Cat usually dealt in. He knew just what to do. He knew how to adjust his weight and how to use every muscle in his body. He knew almost exactly how Syracuse felt—which was surprise, and triumph at having gotten the right rider at last—and just what Syracuse wanted to do. Together, like one animal that happened to be in two parts, they surged off across the yard, with Joss Callow in urgent pursuit, and through the open paddock gate. There Syracuse broke into a glad canter. It was the most wonderful feeling Cat had ever known.

It lasted about five minutes, and then Cat fell off. This was not Syracuse's fault. It was simply because muscles and bones that Cat had never much used before started first to ache, then to scream, and then gave up altogether. Syracuse was desperately anxious about it and stood over Cat nosing him until Joss Callow raced up and seized the reins. Cat tried to explain to him.

"I see that," Joss said. "There must be some other world where you and this horse are the two parts of a centaur."

"I don't think so," Cat said. He levered himself up off the grass like an old, old man. "They say I'm the only one there is in any world."

"Ah, yes, I forgot," said Joss. "That's why you're a nine-lifer like the Big Man." He always called Chrestomanci the Big Man.

"Congratulations," Chrestomanci called out, leaning on the gate beside Julia. "It saves you having to teleport, I suppose."

Julia added, rather vengefully, "Remember you have to do the mucking out now." Then she smiled, a sighing, relieved sort of smile, and said, "Congratulations too."

❧·❧

5

CAT ACHED ALL over that afternoon. He sat on his bed in his round turret room wondering what kind of magic might stop his legs and his behind and his back aching. Or one part of him anyway. He had decided that he would make himself numb from the neck down and was wondering what the best way was to do it, when there was a knock at his door. Thinking it must be Roger being more than usually polite, Cat said, "I'm here, but I'm performing nameless rites. Enter at your peril."

There was a feeling of hesitation outside the door. Then, very slowly and cautiously, the handle turned and the door was pushed open. A sulky-looking boy about Roger's age, wearing a smart blue uniform, stood there staring at him. "Eric Chant, are you?" this boy said.

Cat said, "Yes. Who are *you*?"

"Joe Pinhoe," said the boy. "Temporary boot boy."

"Oh." Now Cat thought about it, he had seen

this boy out in the stableyard once or twice, talking to Joss Callow. "What do you want?"

Joe's head hunched. It was from embarrassment, Cat saw, but it made Joe look hostile and aggressive. Cat knew all about this. He had mulish times himself, quite often. He waited. At length Joe said, "Just to take a look at you, really. Enchanter, aren't you?"

"That's right," Cat said.

"You don't look big enough," Joe said.

Cat was thoroughly annoyed. His aching bones didn't help, but mostly he was simply fed up at the way *everyone* seemed to think he was too little. "You want me to prove it?" he asked.

"Yes," said Joe.

Cat cast about in his mind for something he could do. Quite apart from the fact that Cat was forbidden to work magic in the Castle, Joe had the look of someone who wouldn't easily be impressed. Most of the small, simple things Cat thought he could get away with doing without Chrestomanci noticing were, he was sure, things that Joe would call tricks or illusions. Still, Cat was annoyed enough to want to do *something*. He braced his sore legs against his bed and sent Joe up to the very middle of the room's round ceiling.

It was interesting. After an instant of total astonishment, when he found himself aloft with his uniformed legs dangling, Joe began casting a spell to bring himself down. It was quite a good spell. It would have worked if it had been Roger and not Cat who had put Joe up there.

Cat grinned. "You won't get down that way," he said, and he stuck Joe to the ceiling.

Joe wriggled his shoulders and kicked his legs. "Bet I can get down somehow," he said. "It must take you a lot of effort doing this."

"No it doesn't," Cat said. "And I can do this too." He slid Joe gently across the ceiling toward the windows. When Joe was dangling just above the largest window, Cat made the window spring open and began lowering Joe toward it.

Joe laughed in that hearty way you do when you are very nervous indeed. "All right. I believe you. You needn't drop me out."

Cat laughed too. "I wouldn't drop you. I'd levitate you into a tree. Haven't you ever wanted to fly?"

Joe stopped laughing and wriggling. "Haven't I just!" he said. "But boys can't use broomsticks. Go on. Fly me down to the village. I dare you."

"Er—*hem*," said someone in the doorway.

Both of them looked round to find Chrestomanci standing there. It was one of those times when he seemed so tall that he might have been staring straight into Joe's face, and Joe at that moment was a good fifteen feet in the air.

"I think," Chrestomanci said, "that you must achieve your ambition to fly by some other means, young man. Eric is strictly forbidden to perform magic inside the Castle. Aren't you, Cat?"

"Er—" said Cat.

Joe, very white in the face, said, "It wasn't his fault—er—sir. I told him to prove he was an enchanter, see."

"*Does* it need proving?" Chrestomanci asked.

"It does to me," Joe said. "Being new here and all. I mean, *look* at him. Do *you* think he looks like an enchanter?"

Chrestomanci turned his face meditatively down to Cat. "They come in all shapes and sizes," he said. "In Cat's case, eight other people just like him either failed to get born in the other worlds of our series, or they died at birth. Most of them would probably have been enchanters, too. Cat has nine people's magic."

"Sort of squidged together. I get you," Joe said. "No wonder it's this strong."

"Yes. Well. This vexed matter being settled," Chrestomanci said, "perhaps, Eric, you would be so good as to fetch our friend down so that he can go about his lawful business."

Cat grinned up at Joe and lowered him gently to the carpet.

"Off you go," Chrestomanci said to him.

"You mean you're not going to give me the sack?" Joe asked incredulously.

"Do you want to be sacked?" Chrestomanci said.

"Yes," said Joe.

"In that case, I imagine it will be punishment enough to you to be allowed to keep your doubtless very boring job," Chrestomanci told him. "Now please leave."

"Rats!" said Joe, hunching himself.

Chrestomanci watched Joe slouch out of the

room. "What an eccentric youth," he remarked when the door had finally shut. He turned to Cat, looking much less pleasant. "Cat—"

"I know," Cat said. "But he didn't believe—"

"Have you read the story of Puss in Boots?" Chrestomanci asked him.

"Yes," Cat said, puzzled.

"Then you'll remember that the ogre was killed by being tempted to turn into something very large and then something small enough to be eaten," Chrestomanci said. "Be warned, Cat."

"But—" said Cat.

"What I'm trying to tell you," Chrestomanci went on, "is that even the strongest enchanter can be defeated by using his own strength against him. I'm not saying this lad was—"

"He wasn't," said Cat. "He was just curious. He uses magic himself, and I think he thinks it goes by size, how strong you are."

"A magic user. *Is* he, now?" Chrestomanci said. "I must find out more about him. Come with me now for an extra magic theory lesson as a penalty for using magic indoors."

But Joe was all right, really, Cat thought mutinously as he limped down the spiral stairs after Chrestomanci. Joe had not been trying to tempt him, he knew that. He found he could hardly concentrate on the lesson. It was all about the kind of enchanter's magic called Performative Speech. *That* was easy enough to understand. It meant that you said something in such a way that it happened as you said it. Cat could do that, just about. But the *reason* why it happened was beyond him, in spite of Chrestomanci's explanations.

He was quite glad to see Joe the next morning on his way out to the stables. Joe dodged out of the boot room into Cat's path, in his shirtsleeves, with a boot clutched to his front. "Did you get into much trouble yesterday?" he asked anxiously.

"Not too bad," Cat said. "Just an extra lesson."

"That's good," said Joe. "I didn't mean to get you caught—really. The Big Man's pretty scary, isn't he? You look at him and you sort of drain away, wondering what's the worst he can do."

"I don't *know* the worst he can do," Cat said, "but I think it could be pretty awful. See you."

He went on out into the stableyard, where he could tell that Syracuse knew he was coming and was getting impatient to see him. That was a good feeling. But Joss Callow insisted that there were other duties that came first, such as mucking out. For someone with Cat's gifts, this was no trouble at all. He simply asked everything on the floor of the loose box to transfer itself to the muck heap. Then he asked new straw to arrive, watched enviously by the stableboy.

"I'll do it for the whole stables if you like," Cat offered.

The stableboy regretfully shook his head. "Mr. Callow'd kill me. He's a great believer in work and elbow grease and such, is Mr. Callow."

Cat found this was true. Looking after Syracuse

himself, Joss Callow said, could never be done by magic. And Joss was in the right of it. Syracuse reacted very badly to the merest hint of magic. Cat had to do everything in the normal, time-consuming way and learn how to do it as he went.

The other part of the problem with Syracuse was boredom. When Cat, now wearing what had been Janet's riding gear, most artfully adapted by Millie, had gotten Syracuse tacked up ready to ride, Joss Callow decreed that they go into the paddock for a whole set of tame little exercises. Cat did not mind too much, because his aches from yesterday came back almost at once. Syracuse objected mightily.

"He wants to gallop," Cat said.

"Well he can't," said Joss. "Or not yet. Lord knows what that wizard was up to with him, but he needs as much training as you do."

When he thought about it, Cat was as anxious to gallop across open country as Syracuse was. He told Syracuse, Behave now and we can do that soon. Soon? Syracuse asked. Soon, soon? Yes, Cat told him. Soon. Be bored now so that we can go out soon. Syracuse, to Cat's relief, believed him.

Cat went away afterward and considered. Since Syracuse hated magic so much, he was going to have to use the magic on himself instead. He was forbidden to use magic in the Castle, so he would have to use it where it didn't show. He used it, very quietly, to train and tame all the new muscles he seemed to need. He let Syracuse show him what was needed and then he used the strange unmagical magic that there seemed to be between himself and Syracuse to show Syracuse how to be patient in spite of being bored. It went slower than Cat hoped. It took longer than it took Janet, laughing hilariously, to teach Julia to ride her new bicycle. Roger, Julia, and Janet were all pedaling joyfully around the Castle grounds and down through the village long before Cat and Syracuse were able to satisfy Joss Callow.

But they did it quite soon. Sooner than Cat had believed possible, really, Joss allowed that they were now ready to go out for a real ride.

They set off, Joss on the big brown hack beside Cat on Syracuse. Syracuse was highly excited and inclined to dance. Cat prudently stuck himself to the saddle by magic, just in case, and Joss kept a stern hand on Cat's reins while they went up the main road and then up the steep track that led to Home Wood. Once they were on a ride between the trees, Joss let Cat take Syracuse for himself. Syracuse whirled off like a mad horse.

For two furlongs or so, until Syracuse calmed down, everything was a hardworking muddle to Cat, thudding hooves, loud horse breath, leaf mold kicked up to prick Cat on his face, and ferns, grass, and trees surging past the corners of his eyes, ears and mane in front of him. Then, finally, Syracuse consented to slow to a mere trot and Joss caught up. Cat had space to look around and to smell and see what a wood was like when it was in high summer, just passing toward autumn.

Cat had not been in many woods in his life. He had lived first in a town and then at the Castle. But, like most people, he had had a very clear idea of what a wood was like—tangled and dark and mysterious. Home Wood was not like this at all. Any bushes seemed to have been tidied away, leaving nothing but tall, dark-leaved trees, ferns, and a few burly holly trees, with long, straight paths in between. It smelled fresh and sweet and leafy. But the new kind of magic Cat had been learning through Syracuse told him that there should have been more to a wood than this. And there was no more. Even though he could see far off through the trees, there was no depth to the place. It only seemed to touch the front of his mind, like cardboard scenery.

He wondered, as they rode along, if his idea of a wood had been wrong after all. Then Syracuse surged suddenly sideways and stopped. Syracuse was always liable to do this. This was one reason why Cat stuck himself to the saddle by magic. He did not fall off—though it was a close thing—and when he had struggled upright again, he looked to see what had startled Syracuse *this* time.

It was the fluttering feathers of a dead magpie. The magpie had been nailed to a wooden framework standing beside the ride. Or maybe Syracuse had disliked the draggled wings of the dead crow nailed beside the magpie. Or perhaps it was the whole framework. Now that Cat looked, he saw dead creatures nailed all over the thing, stiff and withering and beyond even the stage when flies were interested in them. There were the twisted bodies of moles, stoats, weasels, toads, and a couple of long, blackened, tubelike things that might have been adders.

Cat shuddered. As Joss rode up, he turned and asked him, "What's this for?"

"Oh, it's nothing," Joss said. "It's just— Oh, good morning, Mr. Farleigh."

Cat looked back in the direction of the grisly framework. An elderly man with ferocious side whiskers was now standing beside it, holding a long gun that pointed downward from his right elbow toward his thick leather gaiters.

"It's my gibbet, this is," the man said, staring unlovingly up at Cat. "It's for a lesson. And an example. See?"

Cat could think of nothing to say. The long gun was truly alarming.

Mr. Farleigh looked over at Joss. He had pale, cruel eyes, overshadowed by mighty tufts of eyebrow. "What do you mean bringing one like him in my wood?" he demanded.

"He lives in the Castle," Joss said. "He's entitled."

"Not off the rides," Mr. Farleigh said. "Make sure he stays on the cleared rides. I'm not having him disturbing my game." He pointed another pale-eyed look at Cat and then swung around and trudged away among the trees, crushing leaves, grass, and twigs noisily with his heavy boots.

"Gamekeeper," Joss explained. "Walk on."

Feeling rather shaken, Cat induced Syracuse to move on down the ride.

Three paces on, Syracuse was walking through the missing depths that the wood should have had. It was very odd. There was no foreground, no smooth green bridle path, no big trees. Instead, everywhere was deep blue-green distance full of earthy, leafy smells—almost overpoweringly full of them. And although Cat and Syracuse were walking through distance with no foreground, Cat was fairly sure that Joss, riding beside them, was still riding on the bridlepath, through foreground.

Oh, please, said someone. *Please let us out!*

Cat looked up and around to find who was speaking and saw no one. But Syracuse was flicking his ears as if he, too, had heard the voice. "Where are you?" he asked.

Shut behind, said the voice—or maybe it was several voices. *Far inside. We've been good. We still don't know what we did wrong. Please let us out now. It's been so long.*

Cat looked and looked, trying to focus his witch sight as Chrestomanci had taught him. After a while, he *thought* some of the blue distance was moving, shifting cloudily about, but that was all he could see. He could feel, though. He felt misery from the cloudiness, and longing. There was such unhappiness that his eyes pricked and his throat ached.

"What's keeping you in?" he said.

That—sort of thing, said the voices.

Cat looked where his attention was directed and there, like a hard black portcullis, right in front of him, was the framework with the dead creatures nailed to it. It seemed enormous from this side. "I'll try," he said.

It took all his magic to move it. He had to shove so hard that he felt Syracuse drifting sideways beneath him. But at last he managed to swing it aside a little, like a rusty gate. Then he was able to ride Syracuse out round the splintery edge of it and on to the bridle path again.

"Keep your horse straight," Joss said. He had obviously not noticed anything beyond Syracuse moving sideways for a second or so. "Keep your mind on your road."

"Sorry," said Cat. As they rode on, he realized that he had really been saying sorry to the hidden voices. Even using all his strength, he had not been able to help them. He could have cried.

Or perhaps he had done something. Around them the wood was slowly and gently filling up with blue distance, as if it were leaking round the edge where Cat had pushed the framework of dead things aside. A few birds were, very cautiously, beginning to sing. But it was not enough. Cat knew it was not nearly enough.

He rode home, hugging the queer experience to him, the way you hug a disturbing dream. He thought about it a lot. But he was bad at telling people things, and particularly bad at telling something so peculiar. He did not mention it properly to anyone. The nearest he came to telling about it was when he said to Roger, "What's that wood like over on that hill? The one that's farthest away."

"No idea," Roger said. "Why?"

"I want to go there and see," Cat said.

"What's wrong with Home Wood?" Roger asked.

"There's a horrible gamekeeper," Cat said.

"Mr. Farleigh. Julia used to think he was an ogre," Roger said. "He's vile. I tell you what, why don't we both go to that wood on the hill? Ulverscote Wood, I think it's called. You ride and I'll go on my bike. It'll be fun."

"Yes!" said Cat.

Cat knew better than to mention this idea to Joss Callow. He knew Joss would say it was far too soon for Cat to take Syracuse out on his own. He and Roger agreed that they would wait until it was Joss's day off.

6

CAT WAS INTERESTED to see that Joss seemed to want to avoid Mr. Farleigh too. When they rode out after that, they went either along the river or out into the bare upland of Hopton Heath, both in directions well away from Home Wood. And here too, going both ways, Cat discovered the background felt as if it were missing. He found it sad, and puzzling.

Roger was hugely excited about going for a real long ride. He tried to interest Janet and Julia in the idea. They had now cycled everywhere possible in the Castle grounds and round and round the village green in Helm St. Mary too, so they were ripe for a long ride. The three of them made plans to cycle all of twelve miles, as far away as Hopton, although, as Julia pointed out, this made it twenty-four miles, there and back, which was quite a distance. Janet told her not to be feeble.

They were just setting out for this marathon, when a small blue car unexpectedly rattled up to the main door of the Castle.

Julia dropped her bike on the drive and ran toward the small blue car. "It's Jason!" she shrieked. "Jason's back!"

Millie and Chrestomanci arrived on the Castle steps while Julia was still yards away and shook hands delightedly with the man who climbed out of the car. He was just in time to turn around as Julia flung herself on him. He staggered a bit. "Lord love a duck!" he said. "Julia, you weigh a ton these days!"

Jason Yeldham was not very tall. He had contrived, even after years of living at the Castle, to keep a strong Cockney accent. "No surprise. I started out as boot boy here," he explained to Janet. He had a narrow, bony face, very brown from his foreign travels, topped by sun-whitened curls. His eyes were a bright blue and surrounded by lines from laughing or from staring into bright suns, or both.

Janet was fascinated by him. "Isn't it odd," she said to Cat, who came to see what the excitement was. "You hear about someone and then a few days later they turn up."

"It could be the Castle spells," Cat said. But he liked Jason too.

Roger morosely gathered up the three bicycles and put them away. The rest crowded into the main hall of the Castle, where Jason was telling Millie and Chrestomanci which strange worlds he had been to and saying he hoped that his storage shed was still undisturbed. "Because I've got this big hired van following on, full of some of the weirdest plants you ever saw," he said, with his voice echoing from the dome overhead. "Some need planting out straight-away. Can you spare me a gardener? Some I'll need to consult about—they need special soil and feed and so on. I'll talk to your head gardener. Is that still Mr. McDermot? But I've been thinking all the way down from London that I need a real herb expert. Is that old dwimmerman still around—the one with the long legs and the beard—*you* know? He always knew twice what I did. Had an instinct, I think."

"Elijah Pinhoe, you mean?" Millie said. "No. It was sad. He died about eight years ago now."

"I gather the poor fellow was found dead in a wood," Chrestomanci said. "Hadn't you heard?"

"No!" Jason looked truly upset. "I must have been away when they found him. Poor man! He was always telling me that there was something wrong in the woods round here. Must have had a presentiment, I suppose. Perhaps I can talk with his widow."

"She sold the house and moved, I heard," Millie said. "There's some very silly stories about that."

Jason shrugged. "Ah, well. Mr. McDermot's got a good head for plants."

Roger gloomed.

The van arrived, pulled by two cart horses, and everyone from the temporary boot boy to Miss Rosalie the librarian was roped in to deal with Jason's plants. Janet, Julia, the footmen, and most of the Castle wizards and sorceresses carried bags and pots and boxes to the shed. Millie wrote labels. Jason told Roger where to put the labels. Cat was told, along with the butler and Miss Bessemer the housekeeper, to levitate little tender bundles of root and fuzzy leaves to places where Mr. McDermot thought they would do best, while Miss Rosalie followed everyone round with a list. Anyone left over unpacked and sorted queer-shaped bulbs to be planted later in the year. Roger knew there was no question of cycling anywhere that day.

He almost forgave Jason that evening at supper when Jason kept everyone fascinated by telling of the various worlds he had been on and the strange plants he had found there. There was a plant in World Nine B that had a huge flower once every hundred years, so beautiful that the people there worshipped it as a god.

"That was one of my failures," Jason told them. "They wouldn't let me take a cutting, whatever I said."

But he had done better in World Seven D, where there was a remote valley full of medicinal crocuses. At first the old man who owned the valley could not think of anything he wanted in exchange for the bulbs, and he warned Jason that the crocuses were very bad for your teeth. Jason got round the old man and got a sackful of the crocuses by enchanting sets of false teeth for the old man and his family. And then he told of the mountain in World One F that was the only place in all the worlds where a dark green ferny plant grew that actually cured colds. Naturally, the man who owned the mountain was very rich from selling these plants—minus their roots, so that no one else could grow any—and quite determined that nobody else was going to get hold of one. He had guard beasts and armed men patrolling the mountain night and day. Jason had sneaked in at night, under heavy spells, and dug up several before he was spotted and forced to run for it. The guards pursued him right through World Two A before Jason skipped to World Five C and they gave up. There were now three of those plants at Chrestomanci Castle, in the care of Mr. McDermot.

"And we'll plant some of the rest tomorrow," Jason said gleefully.

Janet and Julia and most of the others were still helping Jason that next day. But that day was Joss Callow's day off. Roger looked at Cat. Cat went to the stables, where he fed Syracuse peppermints and saddled him up and led him through all the people busy around Jason and his shed. "I'm just going to ride him round the paddock," he explained. And he did that. He knew Syracuse would be unmanageable unless he had had a bit of exercise first.

Half an hour later, Cat and Roger were on the road to the distant hills.

Joss Callow meanwhile cycled down to Helm St. Mary, where he dropped in to see his mother, so that if anyone asked he could truthfully say he had been to visit his mother. But he only stayed half an hour before he pedaled on to Ulverscote.

In Ulverscote, Marianne's dad finished his work at mid-morning by packing the donkey cart with a set of kitchen chairs and sending Dolly the donkey and Uncle Richard off to deliver them in Crowhelm. Harry Pinhoe then walked up to the Pinhoe Arms to meet Joss. The two of them settled comfortably in the Private Snug with pints of beer. Arthur Pinhoe leaned amiably in through the hatch from the main bar, and Harry Pinhoe lit the pipe that he allowed himself on these occasions.

"So what's the news?" Harry Pinhoe asked, puffing fine blue clouds. "I hear the Family came back."

"Yes, and bought a horse," Joss Callow said. "Got diddled properly over it." Harry and Arthur laughed. "Me included," Joss admitted. "Wizard who sold it put half a hundred spells on it to make it seem manageable, see. About the only one who can ride it is the boy they're training up to be the next Big Man, and he gets on with it a treat. Odd, though. He doesn't seem to use any magic on it that I can see. But what I was getting round to with this was about Gaffer Farleigh. He turned up when I was out with the boy in Home Wood and gave us both a proper warning off. Seemed to think the boy was likely to interfere with our work. What do you think?"

Harry and Arthur exchanged looks. "Some of that may be about the row he had with Gammer," Arthur suggested, "before Gammer got took strange. All us Pinhoes are dirt to the Farleighs at the moment."

"They'll get over it," Harry said placidly. "But we can't have that boy riding all over the country. We'll have to stop that."

"Oh, I will," Joss assured him. "He's not going out without me any day soon."

Harry chuckled. "If he does, the road workings will take care of it." They drank beer peacefully for a while, until Harry asked, "Anything else, Joss?"

"Not much. Usual stuff," said Joss. "The Big Man got straight back to work when he wasn't buying horses and bicycles—magical swindle in London, some coven in the Midlands giving trouble, Scottish witches fussing about funds for Halloween, row of some kind two worlds away over the new tax on dragon's blood—business as usual. Oh, I nearly forgot! That enchanter's back from collecting plants all over the Related Worlds. The young one that used to be so thick with Old Gaffer. Jason Yeldham. He was asking after Gaffer. How much of an eye ought I to keep on him?"

"Shouldn't think he'd be much trouble," Harry said, emptying vile black dottle from his pipe into the ashtray. He scraped round the pipe bowl and thought about it. He shook his head. "Nah," he said. "He's not likely to come bothering us here, now Gaffer's gone all these years ago. I mean, it's all studying and book learning with him, isn't it? It's not like he *uses* the herbs the way we do. No need to interfere with him. But stay alert, if you follow me."

"Will do," said Joss.

They asked Arthur for more beer and refreshed themselves with pork pies and pickled onions for a while. After a bit, Harry remembered to ask, "How's Joe doing, then?"

Joss shrugged. "All right, I suppose. I scarcely ever see him."

"Good. Then he's not in trouble yet," Harry said.

Then Joss remembered to ask, "And how's Gammer settling in?"

"She's fine," Harry said. "Dinah looks after her a treat. She sits there and no one can get any sense out of her, not even our Marianne, but there you go, she's happy. She makes Marianne go round there every day and tells Marianne she has to look after that cat of hers every time, but that's all. It's all peace this end, really."

"I'd better go and pay my respects to her," Joss said. "She's bound to find out I was here if I don't." He drained off the rest of his beer and stood up. "See you later, Harry, Arthur."

He picked up his bicycle from the yard and coasted his way downhill through the village, nodding to the occasional Pinhoe who called out a greeting, shaking his head at the piles of brick and earth where the table had run into the Post Office wall. Wondering why nobody had done anything yet about mending that wall, he turned into Dell Lane and shortly arrived at the smallholding, where geese, ducks, and hens ran noisily out of his way as he went to knock at the front door.

"Come to see Gammer," he said to Dinah when she opened it.

"Now there's an odd thing!" Dinah exclaimed. "She's been on about you all this morning. She's said to me over and over, 'When Joss Callow comes, you're to show him straight in,' she said, and I'd no idea you were even coming to Ulverscote!" She dived back in and opened the door on the right of the tiny hallway. "Gammer, guess who! It's Joss Callow come to see you!"

"Well, they all say that," Gammer's voice answered. "They look and they spy on me all the time."

Joss Callow paused in the front doorway. Partly he was wondering what you said to that, and partly he was shaken by the strength of the spells Harry Pinhoe had put up to stop Gammer getting out. He pulled himself together and pushed his way through into the tiny front room, full of teapots and vases and boxes that people had thought Gammer might want. Gammer was sitting in an upright armchair with wings that almost hid her ruined face and tousled white hair, with her hands folded on the knee of her clean, clean skirt. "How are you today, then, Gammer?" he said heartily.

"Not so wide as a barn door, but enough to let chickens in," Gammer answered. "Thank you very much, Joss Callow. But it was Edgar and Lester who did it, you know."

"Oh?" said Joss. "Really?"

While he was wondering what else to say,

whether to give her news from the Castle or talk about the weather, Gammer said sharply, "And now you're here at last, you can go and fetch me Joe here at once."

"Joe?" Joss said. "But I can give you news of the Castle just as well, Gammer."

"I don't want news, I want Joe," Gammer insisted. "I know as well as you do where he is and I want him *here*. Or don't you call me Gammer anymore?"

"Yes, of course I do," Joss said, and tried to change the subject. "It's a bit gray today, but—"

"Don't you try to put me off, Joss Callow," Gammer interrupted. "I've told you to fetch me Joe here and I mean it."

"But quite warm—a bit warm for cycling, really," Joss said.

"Who *cares* about the weather?" Gammer said. "I said to fetch Joe here. Go and get him at once and stop trying to humor me!"

This seemed quite definite and perfectly sane to Joss. He sighed at the thought of a lost afternoon at the Pinhoe Arms, chatting to Arthur and maybe playing darts with Charles. "You want me to cycle all the way back to Helm St. Mary and tell Joe to come here, do you?"

"Yes. You should have done it yesterday," Gammer said. "I don't know what you young ones are coming to, arguing with the orders I give. Go and fetch Joe. Now. Tell him I want to speak to him and he's not to tell anyone else. Go on. Off you go."

Such was the awe all the Pinhoe family felt for Gammer that Joss didn't argue and didn't dare mention the weather again. He said, "All right, then," and went.

With Syracuse fighting to go faster, *faster!* Cat rode along the grass verge, while Roger pedaled beside them on the road. They were quite evenly matched going along the level, but whenever they came to a hill, Syracuse sailed up it, shaking his head and trying to gallop, and Roger stood on his pedals and worked furiously, puffing like a train. Roger's chubby face became the color of raspberries, and he still got left far behind.

They could see the woods they were making for, tantalizingly only two hills away, a spill of dark green trees with already one or two dashes of pure, sunlit yellow that signaled autumn coming. Every time Cat looked—usually while he was at the top of a hill waiting for Roger—those trees seemed farther and farther off, and more away to the left, and *still* two hills away. Cat began to think they had missed a turning, or perhaps even taken the wrong road to start with.

When Roger caught up next time, with his face beyond raspberry into strawberry color, Cat said, "We ought to take the next left turn."

Roger was too much out of breath to do anything but nod. So Cat took the lead and swung Syracuse into a nice broad road leading away left. SHALLOWHELM, the signpost said. UPHELM.

About half a mile later, when he could speak, Roger said, "This road can't be right. It should take us back to the Castle."

Cat could still see the wood, still in the same place, so he kept on. The road bent about, among nothing but empty countryside for what seemed miles, up and down, until Roger was more the color of a peony than anything else. Then it swung round a corner and went up a truly enormous hill.

Roger let out a wail at the sight of it. "*I can't*! I'll have to get off and push."

"No, don't," Cat said. "Let me give you a tow."

He used the same spell he had used to keep Julia from falling off Syracuse and flung it round Roger's bicycle. They went on, fast at first, because Syracuse still regarded every hill as a challenge to gallop, then slower—even when Cat allowed Syracuse to try to gallop—and then slower still. Halfway up, when Syracuse's front hooves were digging and digging and his back ones were scrambling, it dawned on Syracuse what was going on. He looked across at Roger and the bicycle, so uncannily keeping beside him. Then he threw Cat in the ditch and scrambled through the hedge into the stubble field beyond.

Roger only just saved himself and the bicycle from falling in the ditch too. "That horse," he said, kneeling in the grass beside his spinning front wheel, "is too clever by half. Are you all right?"

"I think so," Cat said, but he stayed sitting in the squashy weeds at the bottom of the ditch. It was not so much the fall. It was that Syracuse had broken

409

the spell quite violently. This had never happened to Cat before. He discovered that it hurt. "In a moment," he added.

Roger looked anxiously from Cat's white face to Syracuse pounding happily about in the field above them. "I wish I was old enough to drive a car," he said. "Or I wish that there was some way of moving this bike without having to pedal."

"Couldn't you invent a way?" Cat asked, to take his mind off hurting.

They were both sitting thinking about this, when a boy on a bicycle came past them up the hill. He was riding an ordinary bike, but he was humming smoothly upward at a good speed, and he was not pedaling at all. Roger and Cat stared after him with their mouths open. Cat was so amazed that it took him several seconds to recognize Joe Pinhoe. Roger was simply amazed. They both began shouting at once.

"Hey, Joe!" Cat shouted.

"Hey, you!" Roger shouted.

And they both yelled in chorus, "Can you stop a moment? Please!"

For a moment, it looked as if Joe was not going to stop. He had hummed his way about twenty yards uphill before he seemed to change his mind. He shrugged a bit. Then his hand went down to a box on his crossbar, where he appeared to move a switch of some kind, after which he turned in a smooth curve and came coasting back down the hill to them.

"What's the matter?" he asked, propping himself on the bank with one boot. "Want me to help catch the horse?" He nodded at Syracuse, who was now watching them across the hedge with great interest.

"No, no!" Cat and Roger said at once. "It's not the horse," Cat added.

Roger said, "We wanted to know how you make your bike go uphill without pedaling like that. It's *brilliant*!"

Joe was clearly very gratified. He grinned. But, being Joe, he also hung his head and looked sulky. "I only use it on hills," he said guardedly.

"That's what's so brilliant," Roger said. "How do you *do* it?"

Joe hesitated.

Roger could see Joe was very proud of his device, whatever it was, and was itching to show it off, really. He asked coaxingly, "Did you invent it yourself?"

Joe nodded, grinning his sulky grin again.

"Then you must be a brilliant inventor," Roger said. "I like inventing things too, but I've never come up with anything *this* useful. I'm Roger, by the way. Don't you work in the Castle? I know I've seen you there."

"Boot boy," said Joe. "I'm Joe." He nodded at Cat. "I've met him."

"Jason Yeldham used to be boot boy there too," Roger said. "It must go with brilliance."

"Herbs, I know," Joe said. "It's machines I like,

really. But this box—it's more of a dwimmer-thing, see." His hand went out to the box on his crossbar, and stopped. "What's in it for me, if I do show you?" he asked suspiciously.

Roger was commercially minded too. He sympathized with Joe completely. The problem was that he had no money on him and he knew Cat had none either. And Joe could be offended at being offered money anyway. "I wouldn't tell anyone else about it," he said while he thought. "And Cat won't either. I tell you what—when we get back to the Castle, I'll give you the address of the Magics Patent Office. You register your invention with them, and everyone has to pay you if they want to use it too."

Joe's face gleamed with cautious greed. "Don't I have to be grown up to do that?"

"No," said Roger. "I sent for the forms when I invented a magic mirror game last year, and they don't ask your age at all. They ask for a fifty-pound fee, though."

Cat wondered whether to point out that he, and not Roger, had invented the mirror game by accident. But he said nothing, because he was quite as interested in the box as Roger was.

Joe had a distant, calculating look. "I *could* be earning that much this summer," he decided. "They pay quite well at the Castle. All right. I'll show you."

Grinning his sulky grin, Joe carefully unhooked the small latch that held the box on his crossbar shut. The hinged lid dropped downward to show—Cat craned out of the ditch and then recoiled—of all things, a stuffed ferret! The bent yellow body had bits of wire and twisted stalks of plants leading from its head and its paws to the place where the box met the crossbar.

"Metal to metal," Joe explained, pointing to the join. "That's machinery, see. The dwimmer part is to use the right herbs for life. You have to use something that has once been alive, see. Then you can get the life power running through the frame and turning the wheels."

"Brilliant!" Roger said reverently, peering in at the ferret. Its glass eyes seemed to glare sharply back at him. "But how do you get the life power to flow? Is that a spell, or what?"

"It's some old words we sometimes use in the woods," Joe said. "But the trick is the herbs that go with the wires. Took me ages to find the right ones. You got to *blend* them, see."

Roger bent even closer. "Oh, I see. Clever."

Cat got up out of the ditch and went to catch Syracuse. He knew, now he had seen the box, that he could almost certainly make Roger one this evening, probably without needing a stuffed ferret. But he knew Roger would hate that. Cat's kind of magic made some things too easy. Roger would be wanting to make a box by himself, however long it took. As Cat pushed his way through the hedge, he wondered exactly what Joe's word "dwimmer" meant. Was it an old word for magic? It sounded more specialized than that. It must mean a special *sort* of magic, probably.

Syracuse was not very hard to catch. He was quite tired after hauling Roger uphill, and a little bored by now in the wide, empty stubble field. But when Cat finally had the reins in his hands again, he discovered that Syracuse only had three shoes. One shoe must have torn off while Syracuse was plunging through the hedge.

Finding the shoe was not a problem. Cat simply held his hand out and *asked*. The missing horseshoe whirled up out of a clump of grass, where no one would have found it for years in the ordinary way, and slapped itself into Cat's hand. The real problem was that Cat knew Joss Callow would be outraged if Cat tried sticking the shoe back on by magic. It was bound to go on wrong somehow. And Joss would be truly angry if Cat tried to ride Syracuse with one uneven foot. Cat sighed. He was going to have to levitate Syracuse all the way home, or conjure him along in short bursts, or—knowing how much Syracuse hated magic—most likely just walk. Bother.

He found a gate and led Syracuse out through it and down the hill, where Joe and Roger were sitting side by side on the bank, talking eagerly. Cat could see they were now fast friends. Well, they clearly had a lot in common.

"That's *women's* work, a machine for washing dishes," Joe was saying. "We can do better than that. If you get any good notions, you better come and tell me. I get in trouble if I wander round the Castle. You can find me in the boot room." He looked up as he heard Syracuse's uneven footfalls. "I have to be going," he said. "I've an errand to run for our Gammer, down in Helm St. Mary." He got up off the bank and picked up his bicycle. "And you'll never guess what it is," he said. "Take a look." He pulled a large glass jar with a lid on out of the basket on the front of his bicycle and held it up. "I'm to tip this in their village pond there," he said.

Cat and Roger leaned to look at the murky, greenish water in the jar. A few fat black things with tails were wiggling slowly around in it.

"Tadpoles?" said Roger. "A bit late in the year, isn't it?"

"Quite big ones," Cat said.

"I know," Joe said. "I could only find six, and some of those have their legs already. Know what they're for?" They shook their heads. "This is not a jar of tadpoles," Joe said. "It's a declaration of war, this is." He put the jar back in his basket and got astride his bike.

"Wait a moment," Cat said. "Do you know how far it is to Chrestomanci Castle?"

Joe shot him a slightly guilty look. "You can see it from the top of this hill," he said. "Got turned around, didn't you? Not my fault. But the Farleighs don't like people wandering around in their country, so they do this to the roads. See you."

He switched the toggle at the side of his box and went purring smoothly away up the hill.

7

⇛⋅⇚

NOT SURPRISINGLY, CAT got back to the Castle a long time after Joe or Roger did. Syracuse resisted Cat's attempt to levitate him and started to stamp and panic at the mere hint of teleportation. Cat was too much afraid he would split the unshod hoof to try either spell more than just the once. He could hardly bear to think of what Joss Callow would say if he brought Syracuse in with an injury. So he was reduced to plodding along by the grass verge, with Syracuse breathing playfully on his hair, happy that Cat was not trying to use magic anymore. That wizard who sold Syracuse, Cat thought glumly, must have frightened the horse badly by slamming spells on him. Cat would have liked to slam a few spells back on the wizard.

After a while, however, Syracuse's happiness made Cat cheerful too. He began to notice things in that special way Syracuse seemed to be training him to do. He sniffed the smells of the grass, the ditches, and the hedges, and the dustier smell of the crops standing in the fields. He looked up to see birds teeming across the sky to roost for the night; and, like Syracuse, he jumped and then peered at a rustling in the hedge that was certainly a weasel. They both glimpsed the tiny, brown, almost snake-like body. They both raised their heads to see rabbits bounce away from the danger in the pasture on the other side of the hedge.

But Syracuse was puzzled, because there should have been *more* than just these smells and sights. Cat knew what Syracuse meant. There was an emptiness to the countryside, where it should have been full—though quite what should have filled it, neither Cat nor Syracuse knew. It reminded Cat a little of that time in Home Wood, where the distance was so strangely missing. Things were not here, where they should have been joyful and busy. Even so, it was peaceful. They plodded on, quietly enjoying the walk, until they topped the hill and turned the long corner, and there was Chrestomanci Castle in the distance on the next hill.

Oh dear, Cat thought. Walking was so *slow*. He was going to miss supper.

In fact, it was still only early evening when they reached the stableyard gates. When Cat pushed one gate open and led Syracuse through, the yard was full of long golden light, with two long shadows stretching across it. Unfortunately, these shadows belonged to Chrestomanci and Joss Callow. They were waiting side by side to meet him, looking as unlike as two men more or less the same height could look. Where Chrestomanci was rake thin, Joss was wide and heavy. Where Chrestomanci was dark, Joss was ruddy. Chrestomanci was wearing a narrow gray silk suit, while Joss was in his usual rough leather and green shirt. But they both looked powerful and they both looked far from pleased. Cat could hardly tell which of them he wanted less to meet.

"At last," Chrestomanci said. "As I understand it, you had no business to be out alone on this horse at all. What kept you?"

Joss Callow simply ran his hand down Syracuse's leg and picked up the shoeless foot. The look he gave Cat across it made Cat's stomach hurt. He could think of nothing else to do but hold the missing horseshoe out to Joss.

"How come?" Joss said.

"He threw me off and went through a hedge," Cat said, "but it was my fault."

"Is he lame?" Chrestomanci asked.

"No more than you would be, walking with one bare foot," Joss said. "The hoof's sound, by some kind of a miracle. I'll take him to the stable now, if you don't mind, sir."

"By all means," Chrestomanci said.

Cat watched Joss lead Syracuse off. Syracuse drooped his head as if he felt as much to blame as Cat. From Syracuse's point of view this was probably true, Cat thought. Syracuse had *loved* their illegal outing.

"I am going to ask Joss to exercise that wretched horse himself for a while," Chrestomanci said. "I haven't decided yet if it's for a week or a month or a year. I'll let you know. But you are not to ride him until I say so, Cat. Is that clear?"

"Yes," Cat said miserably.

Chrestomanci turned round and started to walk away. Cat was relieved at first. Then he realized there was something he ought to tell Chrestomanci and ran after him.

"Did Roger tell you about the roads?"

Chrestomanci turned back. He did not look pleased. "Roger seems to be keeping out of my way. What about the roads?"

This made Cat see that, unless he was very careful, he would get not only Roger but Joe too into trouble. Joe should have been in the Castle, not riding about with a jar of tadpoles. He said, thinking about every word, "Well, Roger was with me on his bike—"

"And it jumped a hedge as well and perhaps lost a wheel?" Chrestomanci said.

"No, no," Cat said. Chrestomanci always confused him when he got sarcastic. "No, he's fine. But we were trying to get to Ulverscote Woods and we couldn't. The roads kept turning us back toward the Castle all the time."

Chrestomanci dropped his sarcastic look at once. His head came up, like Syracuse when he heard Cat coming. "Really? A misdirection spell, you think?"

"Something like that—but it was one I didn't know," Cat said.

"I'll check," Chrestomanci said. "Meanwhile, you are in disgrace, Cat, and so is Roger, when I find him."

Roger of course knew he was likely to be in trouble. He met Cat on his way down to the very formal supper they always had at the Castle. "Is he very angry?" he asked, nervously straightening his smart velvet jacket.

"Yes," Cat said.

Roger shivered a little. "Then I'll go on keeping out of his way," he said. "Oh, and keep out of the girls' way too."

"Why?" said Cat.

"They're being a *pain*," Roger said. "Particularly Janet."

The girls were already there, when Roger and Cat went into the anteroom where Chrestomanci, Millie, and all the wizards and sorcerers who made up the Castle staff were gathered before supper. Janet and Julia were pale and quiet but not particularly painful as far as Cat could see. Roger at once slid off along the walls, trying to keep a wizard or a sorceress always between himself and his father. It did not work. Wherever Roger slid, Chrestomanci turned and fixed him with a stare from those bright black eyes of his. At supper, it was worse. Roger had to be in plain view then, sitting at the table, since, being Roger, he seriously wanted to eat. Chrestomanci's vague, sarcastic look was on him most of the time. Jason Yeldham, for some reason, was not there that evening, so there was no one to distract Chrestomanci. Roger squirmed in his chair. He kept his head down. He pretended to look out of the long windows at the sunset over the gardens, but, whatever he did, that stare kept meeting his eyes.

"Oh *blast* it!" Roger muttered to Cat. "Anyone would think I'd murdered someone!"

As soon as supper was over, Roger jumped from his chair and rushed off. So too did Julia and Janet. Chrestomanci raised one of his eyebrows at Cat. "Aren't you going to run away as well?" he said.

"Not really. But I think I'll go," Cat said, getting up.

"Are you quite sure you won't join us for nuts and coffee?" Chrestomanci asked politely.

"You always talk about things I don't understand," Cat explained. "And I need to see Janet."

Whatever Roger said, Cat found this was one of the times when he felt a little responsible for Janet. She had been looking very pale. And she was only here in this world of Twelve A because Cat's sister Gwendolen had worked a thoroughly selfish spell and stranded Janet here. He knew there were still times when strangeness and loneliness overwhelmed Janet.

He thought, when he went into the playroom, that this was one of those times. Janet was sitting sobbing on the battered sofa. Julia had both arms round her.

"What is it?" Cat said.

Julia looked up, and Cat saw she was almost as woebegone as Janet. "Jason's *married*!" Julia said tragically. "He got married in London before he came here."

"So?" said Cat.

Janet flung herself round on the sofa. "You don't *understand*!" she said sobbingly. "I was planning to marry him myself in about four years' time!"

"So was I," Julia put in. "But I think Janet's more in love with him than I am."

"I know I shall hate his wife!" Janet wept. "*Irene!* What an *awful* name!"

Julia said, judicious and gloomy, "She *was* Miss Irene Pinhoe, but at least Irene Yeldham makes a better name. He probably married her out of kindness."

"And," Janet wailed, "he's gone to fetch her *here*, so that they can look at houses. They'll be here for *ages*, and I know I won't be able to go near her!"

Julia added disgustedly, "She's an *artist*, you see. The house they buy is going to have to be just right."

Cat knew by now exactly what Roger had meant. He began backing out of the playroom.

"That's right! Slide away!" Janet shouted after him. "You've no more feelings than a—than a chair leg!"

Cat was quite hurt that Janet should say that. He knew he was full of feelings. He was wretched already at being forbidden to ride Syracuse.

The next day, he missed Syracuse more than

ever. What made it worse was that he could feel Syracuse, turned out into the paddock, missing Cat too, and sad and puzzled when Cat did not appear. Cat moped about, avoiding Janet and Julia and not being able to see much of Roger either. Roger, possibly as a way of avoiding Chrestomanci, was spending most of his time with Joe. Whenever Joe was not working—which seemed to be more than half the day—he and Roger were to be found with their heads together, talking machinery in the old garden shed behind the stables. At least, Cat could find them, being an enchanter, but nobody much else could. They had a surprisingly strong "Don't Notice" spell out around the shed. But Cat was bored by machinery and only went there once.

The day after that, Jason Yeldham's small blue car thundered up to the front door of Chrestomanci Castle. This time, Janet and Julia refused to go near it. But Millie rushed through the hall to meet it and Cat went with her out of boredom. Jason sprang out of the car in his usual energetic way and ran around it to open the other door and help Irene climb out.

As Irene stood up and smiled—just a little nervously—at Millie and Cat, Cat's instant thought was, Janet and Julia can't possibly hate *her*! Irene was slender and dark, with that proud, pale kind of profile that Cat always thought of as belonging to the Ancient Egyptians. On Irene, it was somehow very beautiful. Her eyes, like those of the wives of the Pharoahs, were huge and slanted and almond shaped, so that it came as quite a shock when Irene looked at Cat and he saw that her eyes were a deep, shining blue. Those eyes seemed to recognize Cat, and know him, and to take him in and warm to him, like a friend's. Millie's eyes had the same knack, now Cat came to think of it.

He did not blame Jason for smiling so proudly as he led Irene up the steps and into the hall, where Irene looked at the huge pentacle inlaid in the marble floor, and up into the glass dome where the chandelier hung, and round at the great clock over the library door. "Goodness gracious!" she said.

Jason laughed. "I told you it was grand," he said.

By this time, all the wizards and sorceresses of Chrestomanci's staff were streaming down the marble stairs to meet Irene. Chrestomanci himself came behind them. As usual at that hour of the morning, he was wearing a dressing gown. This one was bronzy gold and green and blue, and seemed to be made of peacock feathers. Irene blinked a little when she saw it, but held out her hand to him almost calmly. As Chrestomanci took it and shook it, Cat could tell that Chrestomanci liked Irene. He felt relieved about that.

Julia and Janet appeared at the top of the stairs, behind everyone's backs as they crowded round Irene. Janet took one look and rushed away, crying bitterly. But Julia stayed, watching Irene with a slight, interested smile. Cat was relieved about that, too.

Altogether, the arrival of Irene made Cat's separation from Syracuse easier to bear. She was as natural and warm as if she had known Cat for years. Jason allowed Cat to show her round the Castle— although he insisted on showing Irene the gardens himself—and Irene strolled beside Cat, marveling at the ridiculous size of the main rooms, at the miles of green carpeted corridors, and at the battered state of the schoolroom. She was so interested that Cat even showed her his own round room up in the turret.

Irene much admired it. "I've always wanted a tower room like this myself," she said. "You must love it up here. Do you think there's a house in the neighborhood that's big enough to have a tower like this one?"

Cat was quite ashamed to say he didn't know.

"Never mind," said Irene. "Jason's found several for sale that I might like. You see, it's got to be quite a big house. My father left me money when he died, but he left me his two old servants as well. We have to have room for them to live with us without being cramped. Jane James insists she doesn't mind where we live or how much room we have—but I know that's not true. She's a very particular person. And Adams has set his heart on living in the country and I simply can't disappoint him. If you knew him, you'd understand."

Later, Irene sat in the vast Small Saloon and showed Cat a portfolio of her drawings. Cat was surprised to find that they were more like patterns than drawings. They were all in neatly ruled shapes, long strips and elegant diamonds. The strips had designs of ferns and honeysuckle inside them and the diamonds had fronds of graceful leaves. There were plaits of wild roses and panels of delicately drawn irises. It was a further surprise to Cat to find that each pattern sent out its own small, fragrant breath of magic. Each was full of a strange, gentle joy. Cat had had no idea that drawings could do this.

"I'm a designer really," Irene explained. "I do book decorations and fabrics, tiles and wallpaper and so forth. I do surprisingly well with them."

"But you're a witch too, aren't you?" Cat said. "These all have magic in."

Irene went the pink of the wild roses in the design she was showing Cat. "Not exactly," she said. "I always use real plants for my drawings, but I don't do anything else. The magic just comes out of them somehow. I've never thought of myself as a witch. My father, now, he could do real magic—I never knew quite what he did for a living, but Jason says he was a well-known enchanter—so maybe just a touch of it came down to me."

Later still, Cat overheard Irene asking Millie why Cat was so mournful. He went away before he had to hear Millie explain about Syracuse.

"Huh!" Janet said, catching him on the school-room stairs. "In love with Irene, aren't you? Now you know how I feel."

"I don't think I am," Cat said. He thought he probably wasn't. But it did strike him that when he was old enough to start being in love—pointless though that seemed—he would try to find someone not unlike Irene to be in love with. "She's just nice," he said, and went on up to his room.

Irene's niceness was real, and active. She must have spoken to Jason about Cat. The next morning, Jason came to find Cat in the schoolroom. "Irene thinks you need taking out of yourself, young nine-lifer," he said. "How do you feel about driving around with us this morning to look at a few houses for sale?"

"Won't I be in the way?" Cat asked, trying not to show how very much more cheerful this made him feel.

"She says she values your judgment," Jason said. "She assures me, hand on heart, that you'll only have to look at a house to know if we'll be happy there or not. Would you say that's true?"

"I don't know," Cat said. "It may be."

"Come along, then," Jason said. "It's a lovely day. It feels as if it's going to be important somehow."

Jason was right about this, although perhaps not quite in the way he or Cat thought.

8

❧·❦

OVER IN ULVERSCOTE, Nutcase was being a perfect nuisance to Marianne. Nothing seemed to persuade him that he was now living in Furze Cottage. Dad changed all the locks, and the catches on the windows, but Nutcase still managed to get out at least once a day. No one knew how he did it. People from all over the village kept arriving at Furze Cottage with Nutcase struggling in their arms. Nicola found him prowling in Ulverscote Wood. Aunt Joy sourly brought him back from the Post Office. Aunt Helen arrived at least twice with him from the pub, explaining that Nutcase had been at the food in the kitchen there. And Uncle Charles repeatedly knocked at the door, carrying Nutcase squirming under one paint-splashed arm, saying that Nutcase had turned up in Woods House yet *again*.

"He must think he still lives there," Uncle Charles said. "Probably looking for Gammer. Do try to keep him in. The wall's mended and I've nearly finished the painting. We put the back door in yesterday. He'll get locked in there when we leave and starve to death if you're not careful."

Mum's opinion was that Nutcase should go and live with Gammer in the Dell. Marianne would have agreed, except that Gammer was always saying to her, "You'll look after Nutcase for me, won't you, Marianne?"

Gammer insisted that Marianne walk over to see her every day. Marianne had no idea why. Often, Gammer simply stared at the wall and said nothing except that she was to look after Nutcase. Sometimes she would lean forward and say things that made no sense, like "It's the best way to get pink tomatoes." Most frequently Gammer just grumbled to herself. "They're out to get me," she would say. "I have to get a blow in first. They have spies everywhere, you know. They watch and they wait. And of course they have fangs and terrible teeth. The best way is to drain the spirit out of them."

Marianne grew to hate these visits. She could not understand how Aunt Dinah put up with these sinister grumbles of Gammer's. Aunt Dinah said cheerfully, "It's just her way, poor old thing. She's no idea what she's saying."

Nutcase must have learned the way to the Dell by following Marianne. He turned up there one day just after Marianne had left and got in among Aunt Dinah's day-old chicks. The slaughter he worked there was horrific. Uncle Isaac arrived at Furze Cottage, as Marianne was setting off to look for Nutcase, and threw Nutcase indoors so hard and far that Nutcase hit the kitchen sink, right at the other end of the house.

"Dinah's in tears," he said. "There's barely twenty chicks left out of the hundred. If that cat gets near the Dell one more time, I'll kill him. Wring his neck. I warn you." And he slammed the front door and stalked away.

Mum and Marianne watched Nutcase pick himself up and lick his whiskers in a thoroughly satisfied way. "There's no way he can go and live with Gammer after *this*," Mum said, sighing. "*Do* try to keep him in, Marianne."

But Marianne couldn't. She doubted if anyone could. She tried putting twelve different confinement spells on Nutcase, but Nutcase seemed as immune to magic as he was to locks and bolts, and he kept getting out. The most Marianne could manage was a weak and simple directional spell that told her which way Nutcase had gone *this* time. If he had set off in any way that led toward the Dell, Marianne ran. Uncle Isaac very seldom made threats, but when he did he meant them. Marianne could not bear to think of Nutcase with his neck wrung, like a dead chicken.

Each time she found Nutcase was missing, Marianne's heart sank. That particular morning, when she got back from another useless visit to Gammer and found that Nutcase had vanished yet again, she hastened to work her weak spell and did not feel comfortable until she had spun the kitchen knife three separate times and it had pointed uphill toward Woods House whenever it stopped.

That's a relief! she thought. But it's not fair! I never get any time to *myself*.

Upstairs, hidden in Marianne's heart-shaped desk, her story about the lovely Princess Irene was still hardly begun. She had made some headway. She knew what Princess Irene looked like now. But then she had to think of a Prince who was good enough for her and, with all these interruptions, she wondered if she ever would.

As she set off uphill to Woods House, Marianne thought about her story. Princess Irene had a pale Egyptian sort of profile, massive clusters of dark curls and fabulous almond-shaped blue eyes. Her favorite dress was made of delicate crinkly silk, printed all over with big blue irises that matched her eyes. Marianne was pleased about that dress. It was not your usual princess wear. But she could not for the life of her visualize a suitable Prince.

Typically, her thoughts were interrupted all the way up the street. Nicola leaned out of a window to shout, "Nutcase went that way, Marianne!" and point uphill.

Marianne's cousin Ron rode downhill on his bike, calling, "Your cat's just gone in the pub!"

And when Marianne came level with the Pinhoe Arms, her cousin Jim came out of the yard to say, "That cat of yours was in our larder. Our mum chased him off into the churchyard."

In the churchyard, the Reverend Pinhoe met Marianne, saying, "Nutcase seems to have gone

431

home to Woods House again, I'm afraid. I saw him jump off my wall into the garden there."

"Thanks," Marianne said, and hastened on toward the decrepit old gates of Woods House.

The house was all locked up by this time. Uncle Simeon and Uncle Charles had repaired the damage and gone on to other work, leaving the windows bolted and the doors sealed. Nutcase could not have gotten inside. Marianne gloomily searched all his favorite haunts in the garden instead. She wanted simply to go away. But then Nutcase might take it into his head to go down to the Dell by the back way, beside the fields, where Uncle Isaac would fulfill his threat.

Nutcase was not among the bushy, overgrown near-trees of the beech hedge. He was not sunning himself in the hayfield of the lawn, nor on the wall that hid the jungle of kitchen garden. He was not in the broken cucumber frame, or hiding in the garden shed. Nor was he lurking under the mass of green goosegrass that hid the gooseberry bushes by the back fence. Big, pale gooseberries lurked there instead. They had reached the stage when they were almost sweet. Marianne gathered a few and ate them while she went to inspect Old Gaffer's herb bed beside the house. This had once been the most lovingly tended part of the gardens, but it was now full of thistles and tired elderly plants struggling among clumps of grass. Nutcase often liked to bask in the bare patches here, usually beside the catmint.

He was not there either.

Marianne looked up and around, terribly afraid that Nutcase was now on his way to the Dell, and saw that the door to the conservatory was standing ajar.

"That's a relief— Oh, *bother*!" she said. Nutcase had almost certainly gone indoors. Now she had to search the house too.

She shoved the murky glass door wider and marched in over the dingy coconut matting on the floor. The massed Pinhoes had forgotten to clear the conservatory. Marianne marched past broken wicker chairs and dead trees in large pots and on down the passage to the hall.

There were four people in the hall—no, five. Great-Uncle Lester was just letting himself in through the front door. One of the other people was Great-Uncle Edgar in his tweed hat, looking unusually flustered and surprised. And as for the others—! Marianne stood there, charmed. There stood her Princess Irene, almost exactly, in her floating dress with the big irises printed on it to match her eyes. As she was a human lady and not part of Marianne's imagination, she was not quite as Marianne had thought. No one had the masses of hair that Marianne had dreamed up. But this Irene's hair *was* dark, though it was wavy rather than curly, and she had the right slender figure and exactly the right pale Egyptian profile. It was amazing.

Beside the Princess was a fair and cheerful young man with a twinkly sort of look to him that Marianne immediately took to. He was wearing a jaunty blazer and very smart, beautifully creased pale trousers, which struck Marianne as the sort of things a prince might put on for casual wear. He's just the Prince I ought to have given her! she thought.

There was a boy with them, who had that slightly deadened expression Joe often had when he was with adults he didn't like. Marianne concluded that he didn't care for Great-Uncle Edgar, just like Joe. Since the boy was fair haired, Marianne supposed he must be the son of Irene and her Prince. Obviously the story had moved on a few years. Irene and her Prince were in the middle of living happily ever after and looking for a house to do it in.

Marianne walked toward them, smiling at this thought. As she did so, the boy said, "*This* one's the right house."

Irene turned toward him anxiously. "Are you quite sure, Cat? It's awfully run-down."

Cat was sure. They had visited two shockers, one of them damp and the other where the ceilings pressed down, like despair, on your mind. And then they had gone to look at what was advertised as a small castle, because Irene had hoped it would have a tower room like Cat's, only it had had no roof. This one felt— Well, Cat had been confused for a moment, when the bulky man with a hat like a tweed flowerpot had come striding up to them booming, "Good *morning*. I'm Edgar Pinhoe. Real estate agent, you know." This man had looked at Jason and Irene as if they were two lower beings—

and they did seem sort of frail beside Edgar—and Jason had looked quite dashed. But Irene had laughed and held out her hand.

"How extraordinary!" she said. "My maiden name was Pinhoe."

Edgar Pinhoe was astonished and dismayed. He stepped backward from Irene. "Pinhoe, Pinhoe?" he said. "I had instructions to sell this house to a Pinhoe if possible." Upon this, he remembered his manners and shook Irene's hand as if he were afraid it would burn him, and dropped his superior, pitying look entirely. Cat realized that the man had been using some kind of domination spell on them up to then. Once it was gone, Cat was free to think about the house.

Jason said, "You might do that—sell it to a Pinhoe. My wife is the one with the money, not me."

While he was speaking, Cat was feeling the shape of the house with his mind. It was all big, square, airy rooms, lots of them, and though it echoed with emptiness and neglect, underneath that it was warm and happy and eager to be lived in again. Over many, many years, people had lived here who were friendly and full of power—special people—and the house wanted to be full of such people again. It was glad to see Irene and Jason.

Cat let them know it was the right house at once. Then he saw the girl walking up to them, as glad to see them as the house was. She was wearing villager sort of clothes, with the pinafore over them to keep them clean, the way most country girls did, but Cat did not think of her as a country girl because she had such very strong magic. Cat noticed the magic particularly, being used to Julia with her medium-sized magic and Janet with almost none at all. It seemed to blaze off this girl. He wondered who she was.

Edgar Pinhoe saw her. "Not now, Marianne," he said. "I'm busy with prospective buyers. Run along home, there's a good girl." His domination spell was back, aimed at Marianne. Cat wondered what good Edgar Pinhoe thought it would do, when his magic was only about warlock level and this girl's was pretty well as strong as Millie's. And Millie, of course, was an enchantress.

Sure enough, the domination bounced off Marianne. Cat was not sure she even noticed it. "I'm looking for Nutcase, Uncle Edgar," she said. "I think he got in through the conservatory door. It was open."

"Of course it was open. I unlocked it so that these good people could look round the garden," Edgar Pinhoe said irritably. "Never mind your wretched cat. Go home."

Here the pinstriped man who had just come in said, in a fussy, nervous way. "Please, Marianne. You've no right to come into this house now, you know."

Marianne's wide brown eyes turned to him, steady and puzzled. "Of course I've got the right, Uncle Lester. I know Gammer lived here, but the house belongs to my dad." A very good idea struck her. She turned to Jason and Irene. She was longing to get to know them. "Can I help show you round? If we go into all the rooms, we're bound to find Nutcase somewhere. He used to live here with Gammer, you see, and he keeps coming back."

"When he's not slaughtering day-old chicks," Great-Uncle Lester murmured.

He was obviously about to say no, but Irene smiled and interrupted him before he could. "Of course you can help show us round, my dear. Someone who knows the house would be really useful."

"You'll know where the roof leaks and so on," Jason said.

Both older men looked shocked. "I assure you this house is absolutely sound," Edgar said. He added, with a slightly defiant look at Uncle Lester, "Shall we start with the kitchen, then?"

They all went along to the kitchen. It was newly painted, and Cat could see new cupboards down the far end. Irene stood looking down the length of the huge scrubbed table, which seemed to have been carefully mended and planed smooth at her end. "This is lovely and light," she said. "And so much space. This table's enormous, and it still doesn't nearly fill the room. I can see Jane James loving it. We'd need to put in a new stove for her, though."

She went over to the old black boiler and cautiously took up one of its rusty lids, shaking her head and sprinkling soot down her iris-patterned dress. Marianne knew that Gammer's old cooker was now stored in the shed on the Hopton road. She had never seen that stove used since the old days before Gaffer died. She shook her head too and made her way down the kitchen, opening all the cabinets to make sure that Nutcase had not gotten himself shut inside one, and then looking into the pantry. Nutcase was not there either.

Jason meanwhile was rubbing his hand vaguely across the damaged end of the huge table. Cat could tell he was using a divining spell, but to the two elderly men who were rather tensely watching him, Jason probably looked like a man bored with womanish things like kitchens and stoves. "Seems to have got a bit bashed here, this table," he said. "Was there some trouble getting it in here?"

Edgar and Lester both flinched. "No, no, no," Lester said, and Edgar added, "I am told—family tradition has it—that this table was actually made inside this room."

"Ah!" said Jason. Cat could feel him quivering, hot on the scent of something. "Someone else told me about this table, quite a few years ago now. A dwimmerman called Elijah Pinhoe."

Edgar and Lester both jumped, quite violently. Lester answered gravely, "Passed away. Passed away these eight years now."

"Yes, but am I right in thinking he actually lived in this house?" Jason said.

"That's right," Edgar admitted. "Marianne's grandfather, you know."

"Right! Great!" Jason said. He whirled round

on Marianne as she came out of the empty pantry and seized her arm. "Young lady, come with me at once and show me where your grandfather's herb bed was."

"We-ell," said Marianne, who was wondering whether Nutcase had gone up to hide in the attics.

"You *do* know, don't you?" Jason said eagerly.

Good gracious, he's just like Gaffer, only young and Cockney! Marianne thought. And he has lovely bright blue eyes. "Yes, of course I do," she said. "It's outside the conservatory, so that he could take the weak ones inside. This way."

Jason cheered and rushed them all outside. Irene laughed heartily at his enthusiasm. "He's always like this about his herbs," she told Cat. "We have to humor him."

Jason stopped in dismay when he saw the thistles and the grass. "I suppose it *has* been eight years," he said, walking in among the weeds. Next moment he was down on his knees, quite forgetting his nice pale trousers, carefully parting a clump of nettles. "Hairy antimony!" he cried out. "Still alive! Well, I'll be——! And this is button lovage and here's wolfwort still going strong! This must be a strong spell on it, if it's alive after eight years! The ground's too dry for it, really. And here's—— What's this?" he asked, looking up at Marianne.

"Gaffer always called it hare's paws," she said. "And the one by your foot—— Oh, it's on the tip of my tongue! Do *you* know?" she asked Cat.

Cat surprised himself and everyone else by

answering, "*Portulaca fulvia*. Scarlet purslane's the English name." Evidently some of the herb lore he had been made to learn must have stuck in his brain somewhere. He rather thought it was Marianne's strong magic that had brought the name up out of a very deep, bored sleep.

"Yes, yes! And very rare. You get the green and yellow all the time, but the scarlet's the really magic one and you almost never find it!" Jason cried out, crawling across to another clump of plants. "Pinwort, golden spindlemans, nun's pockets, fallgreen—this is a *treasure house*!"

Edgar and Lester were standing in the grass, looking helpless, prim, and irritated. "Wouldn't you like to see the rest of the house?" Edgar said at last.

"No, no!" Jason cried out. "I'll buy it even if the roof's fallen off! This is *wonderful*!"

"But I'd like to see it," Irene said, taking pity on them. "Come and show me round." She led the pair of them away through the conservatory.

Marianne left Jason wrestling with a thistle and came over to Cat. "Will you help me look for Nutcase?" she asked him.

"What does he look like?" Cat said.

Marianne approved of this practical question. "Black," she said. "Rather fat, and one eye greener than the other. His coat grows in a ruff round his neck but the rest of him is smooth, except his tail. That's bushy."

"Have you tried a directional spell?" Cat said. "Or divining?"

More practical questions, Marianne thought approvingly. There was no nonsense about Cat. "Nutcase is pretty well immune to magic," she said. "I suppose he had to be, living with Gammer."

"But I bet he's not immune to a spell making a luscious fish smell down in the hall," Cat said. "Wouldn't that fetch him out?"

"Not fish. Bacon. He loves bacon," Marianne said. "Let's go and try."

They hurried through the house to the hall. It was empty, but they could hear hollow footsteps as Irene and the two great-uncles trod about on bare floorboards somewhere in the distance. Here Marianne set the bacon spell, going slowly and carefully, as if she did not quite trust her powers. Cat, while he waited, fixed the image of a black cat with odd eyes and a ruff in his mind and cast about for Nutcase.

"He went up," he said, pointing to the stairs when Marianne had finished. "We could go and catch him coming down."

"Yes," she said. "Let's."

They went up to the next floor. "This is nice," Cat said, looking through an open door into a square, comfortable bedroom.

The room was completely bare, but Marianne knew what Cat meant. "Isn't it?" she agreed. "You know, Gammer kept it all so dark and dusty that I never saw what a nice house this really is."

Cat found himself saying, "I think she kept *you* dark and dusty too. You do know your magic is pretty well enchanter standard, do you?" What made me say that? he thought.

Marianne stared at him. "*Is* it?"

"Yes, but you just don't trust it," Cat said.

Marianne turned away. Cat thought at first that she was upset, then that she didn't believe him, until she said, "I think you're right. It's hard to— to trust yourself when everyone's always telling you you're too young and to do what you're told. Thank you for telling me. I think Nutcase went to the attics. I've known he did all along really, but I didn't trust it."

They went along the bare passage to another set of stairs that were half hidden by a huge wooden hutch thing that must have had a hot-water tank inside. At any rate it was glopping and trickling as if it didn't work very well. The stairs were dark and splintery, and the door at the top was half open, on to brown dimness. Uncle Charles must have left it open, Marianne thought, as her foot knocked against a row of paint tins just inside.

Cat thought, There's been a really strong "Don't Notice" spell here! At least, it was more like a "Don't Want to Know" when he came to think about it—as if somebody had really disliked this place. He wondered why. Marianne seemed to have broken the spell as she went inside.

He followed Marianne into a glorious smell like the ghosts of mint sauce, turkey stuffing, and warm spiced wine. This came, he saw, from bundles and bundles of dry herbs hanging from the beams in the roof, most of them too old and dry to be any good now. Nearly all the floor space was filled with boxes, bundles, and old leather suitcases, but there were old-fashioned chairs and sofas there too, rows of pointed boots, tin trunks, and what looked like clumps of rusty garden tools. Everything was lit by a dim light coming in under the eaves of the house. Cat could see a dusty toy fort down by his feet, which made him feel sorry that he seemed to be too old for such things these days.

The place turned a corner, he saw, and went on out of sight. There was something exciting round there.

Cat was stepping forward in the narrow space between the piles of junk, to find out just what it was round that corner, when Marianne said, "Nutcase *was* here."

"How do you know?" said Cat.

Marianne pointed to what was left of a mouse, lying beside the paint cans. "He always only eats the front end and leaves the tail," she said.

This gave Cat the perfect excuse to explore the attic. He edged his way on along the strip of floor between the bundles and boxes.

"But he's not here now," Marianne said.

"I know, but I need an excuse," Cat said, and shuffled on. Marianne followed him.

The first recognizable thing they met as they turned the corner was a box of Christmas ornaments, really old-fashioned ones: carved wooden angels, heavy round glass balls, and masses of thick golden paper stamped into shapes and letters.

"Oh, I remember these!" Marianne cried out. "I used to help Gaffer put them on the tree in the hall."

She knelt by the box. Cat left her shaking out the gold paper, so that it fell into a long MERRY CHRISTMAS and an equally long YULETIDE IS COME, and groped his way onward. It was darker in this part of the attic and there were no more herbs, but Cat was now convinced that there was something truly precious and exciting stored down near the end. He shuffled and groped—and occasionally put an arm up over his face as something that did not seem quite real fluttered at his head. His feeling grew, and grew, that there was something enormously magical along there, something so important that it needed to be protected with nearly real illusions.

He found it right at the end, where it was so dark that he was in his own light and could barely see it at all. It was large and round and it sat in a nest of old moth-eaten blankets. At first Cat thought it was just a football. But when he put his hands on it, it seemed to be made of china. The moment Cat touched it, he knew it was very strange and valuable indeed. He picked it up—it was quite heavy—and shuffled carefully back to where Marianne was kneeling beside the box of decorations.

"Do you know what this is?" he asked her. He found his voice was shaking with hidden excitement, like Jason's when he knew that this was the herbman's house.

Marianne looked up from laying a row of golden bells out on the floor. "Oh, is that still here? I don't know what it is. Gammer always said it was one of Gaffer's silly jokes. She said he told her it was an elephant's egg."

It *could* be an egg, Cat supposed. He turned the thing round under what little light there was. It was *possibly* more pointed at one end. Its smooth, shiny surface was mauvish and speckled with darker mauve. It was not particularly lovely—just strange. And he knew he had to have it.

"Can—can I have it?" he said.

Marianne was doubtful. "Well, it's probably Gammer's," she said. "Not mine to give." But if everyone hadn't forgotten the attics, she thought, it would have been cleared out with all the other things up here and probably thrown away. And the house was Dad's really, together with all the things left in it. In a *way*, Marianne had a perfect right to give some of the junk away, since nobody else was going to want it. "Oh, go on, take it," she said. "You're the only person who's ever been interested in the thing."

"Thanks!" Cat said. Marianne could have sworn that his face literally glowed, as if a strong light had been shone on it. For a second his hair looked the same gold as the Christmas bells.

Great-Uncle Edgar's voice floated up to them,

peevish and distant, from somewhere downstairs. "Marianne! Marianne! Are you and the boy up there? We want to lock the house up."

Marianne bundled the bells back into the box, in a strong, high chiming. "Lord!" she said. "And I've still not found Nutcase! Let's hope that bacon spell fetched him down."

It had. When they clattered down the bare stairway to the hall, Cat carefully carrying the strange object in both arms, the first thing they saw was Nutcase's smug face peering at them over Irene's shoulder. Nutcase's tail was wrapped contentedly over Irene's arm, and he was purring. Irene was walking about the hall with him, saying, "You big fat smug thing you! You have no morals at all, do you? You wicked cat!" Jason was watching her with an admiring smile and a brown patch of earth on both knees.

"I knew she was bound to be a cat person!" Marianne said, at which the faces of both great-uncles turned up to her, irritably. Cat put a good strong "Don't Notice" around the thing he was carrying.

Great-Uncle Lester had enough magic to know that Cat was carrying *something*, but he must have thought it was the box of Christmas decorations. "Has Marianne given you those?" he said. "Rubbishy old stuff. I wouldn't be seen dead with those on my tree." Then, while Cat and Marianne both went red trying not to laugh, Uncle Lester turned to Jason. "If you and your good lady can be at my office in Hopton at eleven tomorrow, Mr. Yeldham, we'll have the paperwork ready for you then. Marianne, collect your cat and I'll give you a lift down to Furze Cottage."

9

∗≽∗≼∗

ALL THE WAY back to Chrestomanci Castle, Jason and Irene were far too excited at having actually bought a real house, with a bed full of rare herbs, to pay much attention to Cat and the strange object he was holding on his knees. When they got to the Castle, there was no one to ask Cat what it was or to tell him he shouldn't have it. There was some kind of panic going on.

Staff were rushing anxiously around the hall and up and down the stairway. Tom, Chrestomanci's secretary, was with Millie beside the pentacle on the floor. As Cat went past carrying his object, Tom was saying, "No, *none* of the usual spells have been tripped. Not one!"

Millie replied, "And I'm quite certain he didn't leave by this pentacle. Has Bernard finished checking the old garden yet?"

It seemed nothing to do with Cat. He carried the object carefully away by the back stairs and on up to his room. His room was in a mess, as if Mary, the maid who usually did the bedrooms, had been sucked into the panic too. Cat shrugged and took his new possession over to the windows to have a good look at it.

It was the chilly sort of mauve that his own skin went when he was too cold for too long. It was heavy and smooth and not at all pretty, but Cat still found it the most exciting thing he had ever owned in his life. Perhaps this feeling had something to do with the mysterious dark purple spots and squiggles all over its china surface. They were like a code. Cat thought that if only he knew this code, it would tell him something hugely important that nobody else in the world knew. He had never seen anything like this thing.

But the mauve color kept making him think it was too cold. He carefully put a spell of warmth around it. Then, because it looked as if it would break rather easily, and he knew how careless Mary could be, he surrounded the warmth with a strong protection. To keep it properly safe beyond that, he made a sort of nest for it out of his winter scarf and hat and put the lot on his chest of drawers so that he could look at it from wherever he was in the room. After that, he had to tear himself away from it and go down to the playroom for lunch.

Cat had meant to tell them all—or Roger at least—that he had just been given this amazing new object, but the three of them looked so worried that he said, "What's the matter?"

"Daddy's disappeared," Julia said.

"But he's *always* disappearing!" Cat said. "Whenever someone calls him."

"This is different," Roger said. "He has a whole string of spells set up so that the people here know who's called him and roughly where he's gone—"

"And," said Janet, who was still glum and red-eyed over Jason, "there are more spells to say if he's run into danger, and none of them have been set off."

"Mummy thinks he might not have had any clothes on when he went," Julia chipped in. "Today's dressing gown was thrown over a chair and none of the rest of his clothes seem to have gone."

"That's silly," Cat said. "He can always conjure clothes from somewhere."

"Oh, so he can," said Julia. "What a relief!"

"I think it's *all* silly," Cat told her. "He must have forgotten to set off the spells." He got on with his lunch. It was liver and bacon, and the smell reminded him of Marianne's spell. He thought about that cat, Nutcase. Cats were queer animals. This one had struck him as unusually magical.

"Oh, I wish you weren't so *calm* about things!" Janet said passionately. "You're even worse than Chrestomanci is! Can't you *see* when things are serious?"

"Yes," Cat said, "and this isn't."

But by suppertime, when Chrestomanci had still not reappeared, even Cat was beginning to wonder. It was odd. When Cat thought about

Chrestomanci, he had a calm, secure feeling, as if Chrestomanci was quite all right, wherever he was, but possibly wishing he could be there to supper; but when he looked at Millie, he saw desperate worry in her face, and in all the faces round the table, even Jason's. Cat almost began thinking he ought to worry too. But he knew that would make no difference.

Still, when he went to bed that night and lay staring proudly at the big speckled mauve sphere sitting in his scarf across the room, Cat found himself hanging a piece of his mind out to one side, so that he would know in his sleep if Chrestomanci came back in the night. But all that piece of his mind caught was Syracuse, out in the paddock under the moon, wistfully eating grass and wondering why Cat had deserted him.

In the middle of the night, he had a strange dream.

It started with something tapping at his biggest window. Cat turned over in his sleep and tried to take no notice, but the tapping grew more and more insistent, until he dreamed that he woke up and shambled across the room to open the window. He could see a face through the glass, upside down, looking at him with shining purple-blue eyes. But he never saw it clearly, because a great white moon was directly behind it, dazzling him.

"Enchanter," it said, muffled by the glass. "Enchanter, can you hear me?"

Cat put his hand on the catch and slowly pushed the window open. The face retreated upward to give the window room to open. Cat heard its feet shuffle on the roof and what were probably its wings flap and spread for balance. By the time he had the window wide open, he knew that a great shadowy dragonlike thing was sitting on the round turret roof above him.

"What do you want?" he said.

The face came down again and put itself through the window upside down. It was huge. Cat backed away from it, feeling a faint, dreamlike brush of what seemed to be feathers against his ear.

"You have my child in there," the creature said.

Cat looked over his shoulder to where the moonlight gleamed softly off the strange object nestling in his scarf. He had no doubt that this was what the creature was talking about. "Then it's an egg?" he said.

"My egg," the great pointed mouth said.

With a dreadful feeling of loss and desolation, Cat said, "You want it back?"

"I can't take it," the creature answered sadly. "I'm under a sundering spell. I can only get free at full moon nowadays. We put the egg outside the spell, and I wanted to be sure that my child was in safe hands. It should be buried in warm sand."

There was no difficulty about that. Cat turned toward the gleaming egg and converted his warmth spell into a warm sandy one. "Is that right? What else should I do?"

"Let it live free when it hatches," the creature replied. "Give it food and love and let it grow."

"I'll do that," Cat promised. Even in his dream he wondered how he would do it.

"Thank you," the great beast said. "I will repay you in any way I can." It withdrew its head from the window. There was a slight shuffling overhead. Then a great shadow dropped past the window on enormous outspread wings and wheeled away across the moon as noiselessly as an owl.

Cat staggered sleepily toward the egg, wondering how else he could fulfill the creature's trust. In his dream, he doubled the amount of warm sand, made trebly sure that no one could knock it down or disturb it and, as an afterthought, covered it all over with love and friendship and affection. That should do it, he thought, wriggling down into his bed again.

He was quite surprised in the morning to find the window wide open. As for the egg, he could warm his hands on it from a yard away. It must have been one of those real dreams, Cat thought as he went off for his shower. Chrestomanci had said that they happened to enchanters.

When Cat came back, the redheaded maid, Mary, was in his room, glaring at the egg. "You expect me to dust that thing?" she said angrily.

"No," Cat said. "Don't touch it. It's a dragon's egg."

"Mercy me!" Mary said. "As if I'd go near it!

I've enough to do with the place in this uproar as it is."

"Is Chrestomanci still missing?" Cat asked.

"Not a sign of him," Mary said. "They've all been sitting in the main office doing spells to find him all night. The cups of tea and coffee I've taken in there for them, you wouldn't believe! Lady Chant looks like death this morning."

Cat was sorry that Millie was so upset. In the middle of the morning, when there had been no further news, he went along to the main office to tell Millie that Chrestomanci was all right—or, not *quite* all right, he thought, feeling around in the distance as he went. There was a bit of something wrong, but no danger.

Millie was not in the office when he got there. "She's gone to lie down," they told him. "You mustn't disturb her, dear, not when she's so worried."

"Then could you tell her that Chrestomanci's more or less all right?" Cat said.

He could tell that they did not believe he could possibly know. "Yes, dear," they said, humoring him. "Run along now."

Cat went away, feeling sad, as he always did when this kind of thing happened. As he went, he remembered that "Run along" was exactly what Marianne's two great-uncles had said to her. And he had told Marianne that this was undermining her— Cat stopped short halfway along one of the Castle's

454

long pale green corridors. He realized that he knew how Marianne was being made to feel unsure of herself because exactly the same thing was always happening to him. He wondered if he should go back to the office and *insist* on being allowed to find Chrestomanci for them.

But why should they *allow* him to do something they couldn't do for themselves?

Cat stood and thought. No, if he insisted or even asked, someone would forbid him to try. The obvious thing was to go and *get* Chrestomanci and bring him back, without any fuss or bother or asking. And why not do it straightaway? Cat stood until he had fixed in his mind precisely where in the dim distance Chrestomanci was. Then he launched himself and shot over to the place.

He hit a barrier that was like an old, wobbly fence. The fence swayed and shot him back with a *twang*. The next second, he was back in his own tower room with all the breath knocked out of him.

Cat sat on his carpet and gasped. He was truly indignant. He *knew* he should have gotten to Chrestomanci. And that barrier was so shoddy. It was made of magic, but it was like rusty barbed wire and old chicken netting. It ought to have been a pushover.

All the same, his next thoughts were for the dragon's egg sitting on his chest of drawers. He could have hurt it or cracked it, arriving back with such violence. He got up and anxiously put his hands on it.

It was not cracked. It was warm and peaceful and comfortable, basking in the hot sand spell, enfolded in the spells of affection. Cat could feel the life in it through his fingers. It was almost purring, like Nutcase in Irene's arms. So *that* was all right. Now he had to get to Chrestomanci. He sat on his bed and considered.

The mistake had been to dive straight at the barrier, straight at Chrestomanci, he decided. It must have been designed to throw you off if you did that. Yes, it *was*. It had been made to throw you off and throw you off the scent too. But Cat now knew the barrier was there, and he knew Chrestomanci was somehow behind it. That ought to mean he could sneak up to it and perhaps slip through it sideways. Or it was so shoddy that he could even break it, if that was the only way to get through. And he was fairly sure that being a left-handed enchanter gave him an advantage. That barrier felt as if it had been constructed by right-handed people who had been—rather long ago—very set in their ways. He could take them by surprise if he was clever.

Cat got up and sauntered out of his room and down the spiral stair. Keeping his mind deliberately vague, in case the barrier people expected him to try again, he made his way down through the Castle and out beside the stables. Here he had a wistful moment when he longed to go and talk to Syracuse, but he told himself he would do that afterward, whatever Chrestomanci said, and sauntered on toward the hut where Roger and Joe met to talk machinery. They were in there at that moment. He heard Roger say, "Yes, but if we patent *this*, everyone will try to use it." Cat grinned and sidled in among their "Don't Notice" spells. Now it was not even his own magic that was hiding him. Then he launched himself again.

This time, he went quite gently and left side first. Holding his strong left hand out in front of him, he felt at the barrier as he floated up to it, until he found a weak place. There, quite quietly, he bent a section of what seemed to be chicken wire aside and popped through the space.

He felt a thump as his feet hit a roadway and he opened his eyes.

He was standing on a road that was more of a mossy track than a road. The huge trees of an old wood stood on either side of it, making an archway where the road vanished into distance.

He smelled bacon cooking.

Cat thought of Marianne's bacon spell and grinned as he looked for where the scent was coming from. A few yards on, there was an old man in a squashy felt hat sitting by a small fire on the grass verge, busily frying bacon and eggs in an old black frying pan. Beyond the old man was an ancient, decrepit wooden cart, and beyond that, Cat could just see an old white horse grazing on the bank. All his pleasure and triumph at fooling the barrier vanished. This was not Chrestomanci. What had happened?

"Excuse me, sir," he said politely to the old man.

The old man looked up, revealing a little fringe of gray-white beard, a brown seamy face, and a pair of very wide, shrewd brown eyes. "Good afternoon to you," the old man said pleasantly, and he gave Cat a humorous look because it *was* by now after midday. "What can I do for you?"

"Have you seen an enchanter anywhere around here?" Cat asked him.

"The only one I've seen is you," the old man said. "Care for some lunch?"

It was early for lunch, but Cat found that launching himself at the barrier had made him ravenous, and the smell of that bacon made him even hungrier. "Yes, please," he said. "If you can spare it."

"Surely. I'm just about to put in the mushrooms," the old man said. "You like those? Good. Come and sit down then."

As Cat went over to the fire, the horse beyond the cart raised its head from grazing to look at him. There was something odd about it, but Cat did not properly see what, because he went to sit down then and the old man said, quite sharply, "Not there. There's a thriving clump of milkwort there I'd like to keep alive, if you please. Move here. You can miss the strawberries, and silverleaf and cinquefoil never mind being sat on much."

Cat moved obediently. He watched the old man

fetch out a knife that had been sharpened so much that it was thin as a prong and use it to slice up some very plump-looking mushrooms.

"You have to put them in early enough to catch the taste of bacon, but not so early that they go rubbery," the old man explained, tossing the mushrooms hissing into the pan. "A fine art, cooking. The best mushrooms are sticky buns, the ones the French call cèpes, and best of all are your truffles. It takes a trained dog or a good pig to find truffles. I've never owned either, to my sorrow. Do you know the properties of the milkwort I stopped you sitting on?"

"Not really," Cat said, somewhat surprised. "I know it was supposed to help mothers' milk, but that's not true, is it?"

"With the right spell done, it's perfectly true," the old man said, turning the mushrooms. "Your scientific herbalists nowadays always neglect the magics that go with the properties, and then they think the plants have no virtue. A great waste. Change the spell from womanly to manly, and your milkwort does wonders for men too. Pass me over those two plates there beside you. And what's the special virtue of the small fern beside your foot?"

Cat picked up the two wooden plates and passed over while he inspected the fern. "Invisibility?" he said doubtfully. Now he came to look, the grassy verge was a mass of tiny plants, all different. And the wild strawberries almost underneath him were ripe. He felt as he often did with

Syracuse, as if he was being given a whole new way of looking at the world.

The old man, pushing bacon, eggs, and mushrooms onto the plates with a wooden spatula, said, "Not invisibility so much as a very good 'Don't Notice.' You can be a tree or a passing bird with some of this under your tongue, but you have to tell it what you need it to do. That's mostly how herb magic works. Tuck in and enjoy it."

He passed Cat a full plate, still sizzling, with a bent knife and a wooden fork lying across it. Cat balanced the plate on his knee and ate. It was delicious. While he ate, the old man went on telling him about the plants he was sitting among. Cat learned that one plant made your breath sweet, another cured your cough, and that the small pink one, ragged robin, was very powerful indeed.

"Handled one way, it slides any ill-wishing away from you," the old man said, "but if you pick it roughly, it brings a thunderstorm. It's not good to be rough with any living thing. Handle it the third way, and ask for its help, it can bring strong vengeance down on your enemy. Has the egg hatched yet?"

"No, not yet," Cat said. Somehow it did not surprise him that the old man knew about the egg.

"It will soon, once it's warm and being loved," the old man said. He sighed. "And its poor mother can set her mind at rest at last."

"What—what's it going to be?" Cat asked. He found he was quite nervous about this.

"Ah, it will bring its own name with it," the old man answered. "Something weak and worried and soft, it will be at first, that's certain. It'll need all your help for a while. Finished?" He held out his big brown hand for the plate.

"Yes. It was really good. Thank you," Cat said, passing the plate, knife, and fork over.

"Then you'd better be going after your Big Man," the old man said. Cat, in the middle of standing up, stared at him. The old man looked slightly ashamed. "My fault for distracting you," he said. "I was very desirous of meeting you, you see. Your Big Man's not far away."

Cat could feel Chrestomanci quite near. He thought the old man must be pretty powerful to have distracted him from knowing until now. So he thanked him again and said good-bye, rather respectfully, before he set off along the mossy road.

As he passed the cart, the old white horse once more raised her head to look at him. Cat found himself facing a most unhorselike pair of interested blue eyes with a tumble of white mane almost across them. Sticking out from that swatch of white horsehair was quite a long pointed horn. It was pearly colored, with a spiral groove around it.

He turned to the old man incredulously. "Your horse has got—your horse is a unicorn!" he called out.

"Yes, indeed," the old man called back, busy with his fire.

And the horse said, "My name is Molly. I was interested to meet you too."

"How do you do," Cat said respectfully.

"Not so bad, considering how old I am," the unicorn said. "I'll see you." She went back to grazing again, tearing up mouthfuls of grass and tiny flowers.

Cat stood for a moment, sniffing the smell of her. It was not quite like a horse. She smelled of incense, almost, together with horse smell. Then he said, "See you," and went on his way.

About a hundred yards down the road, he found he needed to turn off and plunge into the wood to the right. He waded through bracken and crunched across thorny undergrowth, until he came to clearer ground under some bigger trees. There he found an open space, knee-deep in old leaves. As Cat waded into the leaves, Chrestomanci came wading out into the space as well from the opposite direction. They stopped and stared at one another.

"Cat!" said Chrestomanci. "What a relief!"

He was wearing clothes Cat had never seen him in before, plus fours with thick knitted socks and big walking shoes, and a sweater on his top half. Cat had never seen Chrestomanci in a sweater before, but as he was also carrying a walking stick, Cat supposed that these were what Chrestomanci thought of as clothes for walking in. He had never seen

Chrestomanci in need of a shave before, either. It all made him look quite human.

"I came to get you," Cat said.

"Thank heavens!" Chrestomanci replied. "There seemed no reason why I should ever get out of this wood."

"How did you get in?" Cat asked him.

"I made a mistake," Chrestomanci admitted wearily. "When I set off, my aim was simply to check up on what you told me about the roads, by walking to Ulverscote Wood if I could. But when I found myself repeatedly walking back to the Castle, whatever direction I took, I got irritated and pushed. I got to the wood with a bit of a fight, but then I couldn't get *out*. I must have been walking in circles for twenty-four hours now."

"This isn't really Ulverscote Wood," Cat told him.

"I believe you," Chrestomanci said. "It's a sad, lost, empty place whatever it is. How do we get home?"

"There's a funny sort of a barrier," Cat told him. "I think they put you behind it if you break their turn-you-back-to-the-Castle spell, but I'm not sure. It's pretty old and rusty. Just start a slow teleport to the Castle and I'll try to get us through."

"I've tried that," Chrestomanci said wryly.

"Try again with me," Cat said.

Chrestomanci shrugged, and they set off. Almost at once, they were up against the barrier. It seemed much more real from this side. It looked almost exactly like chicken wire and old corrugated iron that was grown all over with brambles, goose-grass, and thickly tangled honeysuckle. In among the tangle Cat thought he saw swags of bright red briony berries and the small pink flowers of ragged robin. Aha! he thought, remembering what the old man had told him. A slide-you-off spell. He turned himself left side foremost and scratched about among the creepers to find a join. While he groped, he felt Chrestomanci being slid away backward. Cat had to seize hold of Chrestomanci's walking stick with his other hand and drag him forward to the place where he *thought* he could feel two pieces of corrugated iron overlapping. Luckily, before they were both swept away backward again, Chrestomanci saw the overlap too and helped Cat force the two pieces apart. It took all the strength of both of them.

Then they squeezed through. They arrived, panting and strung with creepers, halfway up the Castle driveway, where Cat found he still had hold of Chrestomanci's walking stick.

"Thank you," Chrestomanci said, taking his stick back. He needed it to walk with. Cat saw he was limping quite badly. "Lord knows what that barrier was really made of. I refuse to believe such strong magic can be simply chicken fencing."

"It was the creepers, I think," Cat said. "They were all for binding and keeping enemies in. Have you hurt your ankle?"

"Just some of the biggest blisters of my life,"

Chrestomanci said, pausing to pull a long strand of clinging goosegrass off his sweater. "I've been walking for a day and a night, in shoes I'm beginning to hate. I shall throw the socks away." He limped on a few steps and started to say something else, in a way that seemed quite heartfelt, but before he could begin, Millie came dashing down the driveway and flung her arms round Chrestomanci.

Millie was followed by Julia, Irene, Jason, Janet, and most of the Castle wizards. Chrestomanci was engulfed in a crowd of people, welcoming, exclaiming, asking where he had been, congratulating Cat, and wanting to know if Chrestomanci was all right.

"No I am *not* all right!" Chrestomanci said, after five minutes of this. "I have worldwide blisters. I need a shave. I'm tired out and I haven't had anything to eat since breakfast yesterday. Would *you* feel all right in my position?"

Saying this, he vanished from the driveway in a cloud of dust.

"Where's he gone?" everyone said.

"To have a bath, I imagine," Millie said. "Wouldn't *you*? Someone go and find him some foot balm while I go and order him something to eat. Cat, come with me and explain how on earth you managed to find him."

An hour later, Chrestomanci summoned Cat to his study. Cat found him sitting on a sofa with his sore feet propped on a leather tuffet, shaved and smooth again and wearing a peach satin dressing gown that put Cat in mind of a quilted sunset. "Are you all right now?" Cat said.

"Perfectly, thank you, thanks to you," Chrestomanci replied. "To continue the conversation we were about to have when the welcoming hordes descended, I can't stop thinking about that barrier. It's a real mystery, Cat. Twenty-odd years ago, when I was around your age, I was dragged off on the longest, wettest walk of my life up to then. Flavian Temple marched me right across Hopton Moor almost to Hopton. I set Hopton Wood on fire. There were no turn-you-round spells then and no kind of barrier. I know. I would have welcomed either of them heartily. Temple and I walked miles in a straight line, and nothing stopped us."

"The barrier looked quite old," Cat said.

"Twenty years can grow a lot of creepers," Chrestomanci said, "and a lot of rust. Let's take it that the barrier is no older than that. The real puzzle is, why is it *there*?"

Cat would have liked to know that too. He could only shake his head.

Chrestomanci said, "It may only apply to Ulverscote Wood, of course. But I see I shall have to investigate the whole thing. The real reason I asked you in here, Cat, is to tell you that I can't, after the way you rescued me, keep you apart from that wretched horse any longer. The stableman tells me its feet are sounder than mine are. So off you go. There's just time for a ride before supper."

Cat hurtled off to the stableyard. And there would have been time for a ride, except that Syracuse saw Cat coming and hurdled the paddock gate, and hurdled Joss with it as Joss tried to open the gate. Syracuse then dashed several times round the yard and jumped back into the paddock, where he spent a joyous hour avoiding the efforts of Joss, Cat, and the stableboy to catch him. After that, there was no time left before supper.

10

❧✦❧

"NO SHE IS *not*!" Gammer shouted, so loudly that the Dell's crowded little living room rang all over with the noise. "Pinhoes is Pinhoes and make sure you look after Nutcase for me, Marianne."

"I don't understand you, Gammer," Marianne said boldly. She thought Cat had been right to say she was downtrodden, and she had decided to be brave from now on.

Gammer chomped her jaws, breathed heavily, and stared stormily at nothing.

Marianne sighed. This behavior of Gammer's would have terrified her a week ago. Now she was being brave, Marianne felt simply impatient. She wanted to go home and get on with her story. Since her meeting with Irene, the story had suddenly turned into "The Adventures of Princess Irene and Her Cats," which was somehow far more interesting than her first idea of it. She could hardly wait to find out what happened in it next. But Aunt Joy had sent Cousin Ned down to Furze Cottage to say that Gammer wanted Marianne *now*, and Mum had said,

"Better see what she wants, love." So Marianne had had to stop writing and hurry round to the Dell. Uselessly, because Gammer was not making any sense.

"You *have* got Nutcase, have you?" Gammer asked anxiously.

"Yes, Gammer." Marianne had left Nutcase sitting on the drainboard, watching Mum chop herby leaves and peel knobby roots. She could only hope that he stayed there.

"But I'm not having it!" Gammer said, switching from anxiety to anger. "It's not true. You're to contradict it whenever you hear it, understand?"

"I would, but I don't know what you're talking about," Marianne said.

At this, Gammer fell into a real rage. "Hocum pocum!" she yelled, beating the floor with her stick. "You're all turned against me! It's insurpery, I tell you! They wouldn't tell me what they'd done with him. Put him down it and pull the chain, I told them, but *would* they do it? They lied. Everyone's *lying* to me!"

Marianne tried to say that no one was lying to Gammer, but Gammer just yelled her down. "I don't *understand* you!" Marianne bawled back. "Talk *sense*, Gammer! You know you can if you try."

"It's an insult to Pinhoes!" Gammer screamed.

The noise brought Aunt Dinah striding cheerfully in. "Now, now, Gammer, dear. You'll only tire yourself out if you shout like that. She'll fall asleep,"

Aunt Dinah said to Marianne, "and when she wakes up she'll have forgotten all about it."

"Yes, but I don't know what she's so angry about," Marianne said.

"Oh, it's nothing, really," Aunt Dinah said, just as if Gammer was not sitting there. "It's only that your Aunt Helen was in here earlier. She likes to have all your aunts drop in, tell her things, cheer her up. You know. And Helen was telling her that the new lady that's just bought Woods House is a Pinhoe born and bred—"

"She is *not*!" Gammer said sulkily. "*I'm* the only Pinhoe around here."

"Are you, dear?" Aunt Dinah said cheerily. "And where does that leave the rest of us?"

This seemed to be the right way to treat Gammer. Gammer looked surprised, ashamed, and amused, all at once, and took to pleating the clean, clean skirt that Aunt Dinah had dressed her in that morning. "These are not my clothes," she said.

"Whose are they, then?" Aunt Dinah said, laughing. She turned to Marianne. "She'd no call to drag you over here for that, Marianne. Next time she tries it, just ignore it. Oh, and could you ask your mum for more of that ointment for her? She gets sore, sitting all the time."

Marianne said she would ask, and walked away among the chickens and the ducks, taking care to latch the gate behind her. Joe was always forgetting to shut the gate properly. Last time Joe forgot, the goats had gotten out into everyone's gardens. The things Aunt Joy had said about Joe! Marianne discovered herself to be missing Joe far more than she had expected. She wondered how he was getting on.

"Mum," Marianne asked, as she came into the herby, savory steam of the kitchen in Furze Cottage. Nutcase, to her relief, was still there, sitting on the table now, among the jars and bottles waiting to be filled with balms and medicines. "Mum, *is* Mrs. Yeldham a Pinhoe born and bred?"

"So your Great-Uncle Lester says," Mum said. Her narrow face was fiery red and dripping in the steam. Wet curls were escaping from the red-and-white checked cloth she had wrapped round her head. "Marianne, I could use your help here."

Marianne knew how this one worked: help Mum, or she would get no further information. She sighed because of her unfinished story and went to find a cloth to wrap her hair in. "Yes?" she said, once she was hard at work beating chopped herbs into warm goose grease. "And?"

"She really is a Pinhoe," Mum said, carefully straining another set of herbs through a square of muslin. "Lester went up to London and checked the records in case he did wrong to sell her the house. You remember those stories about Luke Pinhoe, who went to London to seek his fortune a hundred years ago?"

"The one who turned his Gaffer into a tree first?" Marianne said.

"Only overnight," Mum said, as if that excused

it. "He did it so that he could get away, I think. There must have been quite a row there, what with Luke refusing to be the next Gaffer, and his father crippling both his legs so that he'd have to stay. Anyway, they say that Luke stole his father's old gray mare and rode all night until he came to London, and the mare made her way back here all on her own. And Luke found an enchanter to mend his legs—and that must be true, because Lester found out that Luke set up as an apothecary first, which would have been hard to do as a cripple. He'd have been more likely to have been begging on the streets. But there he was, dealing in potions because he was herb-cunning, like me. But Luke seems to have found out quite soon that he was an enchanter himself. He made himself a mint of money out of it. And his son was an enchanter after him, and *his* son after that, right down to this present day, when William Pinhoe, who died this spring, had only the one daughter. They say he left his daughter all his money and two servants to look after her, and *she's* the Mrs. Yeldham who bought Woods House."

While Mum paused to spoon careful measures of fresh chopped herbs into the strained water, Marianne remembered that Irene had talked about someone called Jane James, who must have been her cook. It did seem to fit. "But why is Gammer so angry about it?"

"Well," Mum said, rather drily, "I *could* say it's because she's lost her wits, but between you and me and the gatepost, Marianne, I'd say it's because Mrs.

Yeldham's more of a Pinhoe than Gammer is. Luke was his Gaffer's eldest son. Gammer's family comes down from the second cousins who went to live in Hopton. See?" She covered her bowl with fresh muslin and went to put it in the cold store to steep.

Marianne started to lick goose grease from her fingers, remembered in time that it was full of herbs you shouldn't eat, and felt rather proud of being a Pinhoe by direct descent—or no! Her family descended from that Gaffer's *second* son, George, who had been by all accounts a meek and rather feeble man, and did just what his father told him. So Irene was more Pinhoe than Marianne— "Oh, what does it *matter*?" she said aloud. "It was all a hundred years ago!" She looked round for Nutcase and was just in time to catch him sneaking through the window Mum had opened to try to get rid of the steam. Marianne grabbed him and shut the window. "No, you mustn't," she told Nutcase as she put him on the floor. "Some of them move into Woods House today. They won't want you."

As everyone in Ulverscote somehow knew— without anyone's precisely being *told*—Irene's two servants arrived that morning. They came in a heavy London van that took two cart horses to pull it, bringing some basic furniture to put into the house. The good furniture was supposed to arrive later, when the Yeldhams moved in. Uncle Simeon and Uncle Charles went up there in the afternoon to see what alterations were going to be required.

They came away chastened.

"Massive job," Uncle Simeon said, in his untalkative way, when the two of them arrived in Furze Cottage to report to Dad and drink restorative tea. "And the new stove and water tank to come from Hopton before we can even start."

"That Jane James!" Uncle Charles said feelingly. "You can't put a foot wrong there. Proper old-time servant. All I did was think the two of them was married and—ooh! And there was he, little trodden-on-looking fellow, but you have to call him *Mister* Adams, *she* says, and show proper respect. So then I call her *Miss* James, showing proper respect like she told me, and she shoots herself up and gathers herself in like an umbrella and 'I'm Jane James, and I'll thank you to remember it!' she says. After that we just crawled away."

"Got to go back, though," Uncle Simeon said. "The Yeldhams come to see what's needed tomorrow, and *she* wants you to start on the whitewash, Charles."

Irene and Jason were indeed due to set off to confer with Pinhoe Construction Limited in Woods House that next day. Irene took a deep breath and invited Janet and Julia to go with them. "Do come," she said. "Whatever Jane James has done to it, I know it's going to look a depressing mess still. I need someone to tell me how to make it livable in."

Janet looked at Julia and Julia looked at Janet. It was more a sliding round of eyes than a proper look. Irene seemed to hold her breath. Cat could see Irene knew the girls did not like her for some reason, and it obviously worried her. At length, Julia said, not altogether politely, "Yes. Please. Thank you, Mrs. Yeldham," and Janet nodded.

It was not friendly, but Irene smiled with relief and turned to Cat.

"Would you like to come too, Cat?"

Cat knew she was hoping he would help make the girls more friendly, but Syracuse was waiting. Cat smiled and shook his head and explained that Joss was taking him for a ride beside the river in half an hour. And Roger was not to be found. Irene looked a little dashed, and only Janet and Julia went with Jason and Irene to Ulverscote.

In the normal way, all Ulverscote would have come out to stare at them. But that day only a few people—who had all had the presence of mind to call on the Reverend Pinhoe in order to stare over the vicarage wall—caught sight of the four of them getting out of Jason's car. They all told one another that the fair-haired girl looked as sour as Aunt Joy, and what a pity, it just showed you what they were like at That Castle, but Mrs. Yeldham did credit to the Pinhoe family. A real lady. She was born a Pinhoe, you know.

The rest of the village was in the grip of a mysterious wave of bad luck. A fox got into the chick pen at the Dell and ate most of the baby chicks that Nutcase had not accounted for. Mice got into the grocer's and into the pantry at the Pinhoe Arms. The wrong bricks were delivered to mend the Post Office wall.

"Bright yellow bricks I am *not* having!" Aunt

Joy screamed at the van men. "This is a Post Office, not a sandcastle on a beach!" And she made the men take the bricks away again.

"Before I could even take a look at them too!" Uncle Simeon complained. He was in Dr. Callow's surgery when the bricks were delivered, with a sprained ankle. He had been forced to send his foreman, Podge Callow, to consult with the Yeldhams in his place. Besides Uncle Simeon, the surgery was crowded with sprains, dislocations, and severe bruises, all to Pinhoes and all of them acquired that morning. Uncle Cedric was there, after falling from his hayloft, and so was Great-Uncle Lester, who had shut his thumb in his car door. Almost all of Marianne's cousins had had similar accidents, and Great-Aunt Sue had tipped boiling water down her leg. Dr. Callow had to agree with her that this spate of injuries was not natural.

Down at Furze Cottage, Mum was trying to deal with further cuts and scrapes and bruises, working under great difficulty, as she said to Marianne. Half of her new infusions had got mildew overnight. Marianne had to sort the bad jars out for her before they infected the rest. Meanwhile, Uncle Richard, carefully carving a rose on the front of a new cabinet, let his gouge slip somehow and plowed a deep bloody furrow in the palm of his other hand. Mum had to leave her storeroom yet again and sort him out with a wad of cobwebs and some lotion charmed to heal.

"I don't think this is natural, Cecily," Uncle

Richard said while Mum was bandaging his hand. "Joy shouldn't have cursed Gammer like that."

"Don't talk nonsense," said Dad, who had come in to make sure his brother was all right. "I stopped Joy before she started. This is something else."

Dad was about the only person who believed this. As the bad luck spread to people who were only distantly related to Pinhoes, and then to people who had no witchcraft at all, most of Ulverscote began to blame Aunt Joy. Aunt Joy's face, as Mum said, would have soured milk from a hundred yards away.

The bad luck extended to Woods House too. There, to Jane James's annoyance, the man installing the new stove dropped it on his foot and then mystified her by limping away into the village saying, "Mother Cecily will fix me up. Don't touch the boiler till I get back."

While Mum was dealing with what she suspected was a broken bone in this man's foot, Marianne discovered—mostly by the severely bad smell—that the whole top shelf of jars in the storeroom had grown fuzzy red mold. And Nutcase disappeared again.

Nutcase reappeared some time later in the hall of Woods House, just in time to trip Uncle Charles up, as Uncle Charles crossed the hall carrying a ladder and a bucket of whitewash. Uncle Charles, in trying to save himself, hit himself on the back of the head with the ladder and dropped the bucket of whitewash over Nutcase.

The clang and the crash fetched Jane James and Irene from the kitchen and Janet, Julia, and Jason from what was going to be the dining room. Everyone exclaimed in sympathy at the sight of the house painter lying under a ladder in a lake of whitewash, while beside him the desperate white head of a cat stuck out from under the upturned whitewash pail.

Uncle Charles stopped swearing at the sight of Jane James's face, but continued telling the world at large just what he would like to do to Nutcase. As he told Marianne later, a bang on the head does that to you. And those two girls *laughed*.

"But are you all right?" Jason asked him.

"I'd be better off if that cat was dead," Uncle Charles replied. "I didn't chance to kill him, did I?"

Janet and Julia, trying—and failing—not to laugh too much, tipped the pail up and rescued Nutcase. Nutcase was scrawny, clawing, and mostly white. Whitewash sprayed over everyone as Nutcase struggled. Janet held him at arm's length, with her face turned sideways, while Irene and Jason dived to help Uncle Charles. "Oh, it's a *black* cat!" Julia exclaimed as the underside of Nutcase became visible. Jason's foot skidded in the white-wash. He tried to save himself by grabbing Irene's arm. The result was that Jason fell flat on his face in the whitewash and Irene sat in it. Janet's opinion of Irene changed completely when Irene simply sat on the floor and laughed.

"All their good clothes ruined," Uncle Charles told Marianne. He arrived, a trifle dizzily, at Furze Cottage with Nutcase clamped under one arm. "It just goes to show that even an enchanter can't avoid a bad-luck spell. That fellow's a full enchanter, or I'm a paid-up Chinaman. Don't tell Gammer he is. She'd take a fit. He had me standing up while his face was still in the matting. Take your cat. Wash him. *Drown* him if you like."

Marianne took Nutcase to the sink and ran both taps on him. Nutcase protested mightily. "It's your own fault. Shut up," Marianne told him. Dad was sitting at the table assembling the flowers and frondy leaves of ragged robin in the careful overlapping pattern of a counter-charm, and Marianne was trying to listen to what he was saying to Uncle Charles about the bad-luck spell.

"It's an ill-chancing. Positive," Uncle Charles was saying. "I knew that as soon as that damn ladder hit my head. But I don't know whose, or—"

Mum interrupted by bawling from the front room, where she was treating a small boy for a sudden severe cough. She wanted to know if Uncle Charles was concussed.

"Just a bit dizzy like," Dad bawled back. "He's fine. Yes," he said to Uncle Charles. "It feels like a nudge job to me. One of those that lies in wait for all the things you *nearly* get wrong, like you *nearly* trip and you *nearly* drop a pail of whitewash, and it gives those a nudge so that you do it *really*. It doesn't have to be strong to have a big effect."

"That doesn't account for the fox," Uncle Charles objected. "Or they're saying a lot of little ones have got the whooping cough. It can't account for that."

"Those could be separate," Dad said. "If they *were* a part of it, then I'd have to say, to be fair, that it's stronger than a nudge—and nobody's dead yet."

Meanwhile, Jason's whitewash-spattered party was leaving Woods House in order to get some clean clothes. Jason looked particularly spectacular, as not only the front of him, but the tip of his nose and the fringe of his hair were white. He was annoyed enough to shout with rage when his car refused to start. He called the car more names than Uncle Charles had called the cat. Janet's theory was that the car eventually started out of pure shame. Julia told her that Jason had used magic, a lot of magic.

When the car was finally chugging, they drove out into the road and out beyond the last small houses of the village. There Jason stopped, with a screech and a violent jerk. He jumped out of the car and stood in the middle of the road, glaring around at the hedges.

"What's he *doing*?" Janet said.

They all looked anxiously at Jason's clownlike figure.

"Magic," Julia said, and got out too.

Janet and Irene followed Julia just as Jason made a dive for a clump of plants growing on the verge. "*And* right in the middle of the artemisia to lend it power!" they heard him say. He hacked into the clump with the heel of his boot. "Come out, you!"

A little black lump with trailing strings came out of the plants. It looked like a dirty lavender bag that someone had not tied up properly. Jason hacked it out of the grass and down the bank to the road. "*Got* you!" he said. Irene took one look at the thing and went back to the car, looking white and ill. Julia felt queasy. Janet wondered what was the matter with them both. It was only a greasy gray bag of herbs. "Keep back," Jason said to her. He kicked the bag into the center of the road and bent over it warily. "Someone's been very nasty here. This is a brute of an ill-wishing—it's probably infecting the whole village by now. Get in the car while I get rid of the thing."

By this time even Janet was feeling something wrong about the bag. She stumbled and nearly fell over as Julia pulled her back to the car. "I think I'm going to be sick," Julia said.

They watched from inside the car while Jason levitated the bag fifteen feet into the air and made it burst into flames. It burned and it burned, with improbably long crimson flames, and gave off a whirl of thick black smoke. Jason kept collecting the smoke and sending it back to the flames to burn again. They all, even Janet, had the feeling that the bag was trying to fall on Jason and burn him too. But Jason made it stay in the air with batting motions of his left hand, the way you make a balloon stay in the air, batting and batting, while his other hand collected smoke and fed it back to the flames, over and over, until at last there was nothing left of it, not even the smallest flake of ash. He was sweating through the whitewash when he came back to the car.

"Phew!" he said. "Someone around here is not nice at all. That thing was designed to get worse by the hour."

All this while, Cat was trotting blissfully on Syracuse along the bank of the river, following Joss on his big brown horse. Syracuse was drawing Cat's attention to the smells of the river valley—the mildly churning river on one side with its rich watery smells, and the damp grassiness from the plants on its banks, and the way the scents from the rest of the valley were those of late summer. Cat sniffed the dry incense smells from the fields and thought he would know it was the end of August even if he suddenly went blind. Syracuse, who was feeling quite as blissful as Cat, helped him sense the myriad squishy things in the river going about their muddy lives, all the hundreds of creatures rustling about on its banks, and the truly teeming life of birds and animals in the meadows above.

Cat set a spell to keep off the midges and horse-flies. They were teeming too. They came pouring out of the bushes in clouds. While he set the spell, he had the feeling that he always had now when he rode out, the same feeling he had first had in Home

Wood, that despite the thronging of living things, there ought to have been *more*. Behind the bustle of creatures, and behind the flitting and soaring of birds, there was surely an emptiness that should have been filled.

Cat was once again trying to track down the emptiness, when everything stopped.

Birds stopped singing. Creatures stopped rustling among the rushes. Even the river lost its voice and seemed to flow milklike and silent. Joss stopped too, so suddenly that Syracuse nearly shot Cat off into the water, going sideways to avoid the rear end of Joss's horse.

Mr. Farleigh stepped into sight beyond a clump of willows, with his long gun under his arm.

"Morning, Mr. Farleigh," Joss said respectfully.

Mr. Farleigh ignored the politeness, just as he ignored Cat too, sitting slantwise across the path behind Joss. His grim eyes fixed accusingly on Joss. "Tell the Pinhoes to stop," he said.

Joss clearly had no more idea than Cat did what this meant. He said, "Sorry?"

"You heard me. Tell them to stop," Mr. Farleigh said, "or they'll be having more than a bit of ill-chancing coming down on them. Tell them I told you."

"Of course," Joss said. "If you say so."

"I do say," Mr. Farleigh said. He shifted a little, so that he was now ignoring Cat more than ever. Pointedly and deliberately ignoring him.

"And you've no business letting Castle people out all over the place," he said. "Keep the Big Man's nose out of things, do you hear me? I had to take steps over that myself the other day. Do your job, man."

In front of Cat, Joss was making helpless movements. Cat could feel Syracuse, underneath him, making movements that suggested it would be a good plan to barge past Mr. Farleigh and tumble him into the river. Cat entirely agreed, but he knew this was not wise. He made movements back at Syracuse to tell him not to.

"My job's not to *stop* things, Mr. Farleigh," Joss said apologetically. "I only report."

"Then report," Mr. Farleigh said, "or I don't know where it will all end. Take some steps, before I have to get rid of the lot of them." He swung round on the heel of his big boot and plodded away down the river path.

When Mr. Farleigh had vanished ahead of them behind the willows, Joss turned to Cat. "Got to go up through the meadows now," he said. "It won't do to shove Mr. Farleigh off the path."

Cat longed to ask Joss what was going on here, but he could tell Joss was hoping that Cat had not understood a word of what had been said. So he said nothing and let Syracuse follow Joss up through the fields at the side of the valley. Around them, birds flew and creatures rustled, and the river behind them went back to churning again.

11

❧•❧

THE EGG STARTED hatching that night.

Cat was not really asleep when it did. He was lying in bed thinking. That night at supper, Julia had told everyone about the greasy gray lavender bag. Chrestomanci had not said anything, but he had looked unusually vague. When Chrestomanci looked vague, it always meant that he was attending particularly closely. Cat was not surprised when Chrestomanci took Jason away to his study afterward to ask him all about it. An ill-chancing was a bad misuse of magic, and it was, after all, Chrestomanci's job to stop such things. The trouble was, Cat knew he should have told Chrestomanci about Mr. Farleigh too, because he was fairly sure that bag was one of the things Mr. Farleigh had been talking about by the river.

He tried to work out why he had said nothing. One good reason was that Joss Callow was obviously some kind of spy, and telling Chrestomanci would give Joss away. Cat liked Joss. He did not want to get Joss into trouble—and it would be very bad trouble, Cat knew. But the real reason was because Mr. Farleigh had said these things while Cat was sitting there on Syracuse, hearing every word. It was as if Mr. Farleigh had no need to worry. If he was powerful enough to lock Chrestomanci himself away behind a barrier of chicken wire, then he had enough sour, gnarled power to get rid of everyone in the Castle if he wanted to. He had more or less said so.

Let's face it, Cat thought. It's because I'm scared stiff of him.

It was then that Cat began to hear a muffled tapping.

At first he thought it was coming from the window again, but when he sat up and listened, he knew the noise was coming from inside his room. He snapped the light on. Sure enough, the big mauve-speckled egg was rocking gently in its nest of winter scarf. The tapping from inside it was getting faster and faster, as if whatever was in there was in a panic to get out. Then it stopped, and there was an exhausted silence.

Oh, help! Cat thought. He jumped out of bed and quickly took off the safety spell and then the warm-sand spell, hoping this would make things easier for the creature. He bent anxiously over the egg. "Oh, don't be dead!" he said to it. *"Please!"* But he knew the thing must have been for years in a cold attic. It was surely at the end of its strength by now.

To his huge relief, the tapping started again, slower now, but quite strong and persistent. Cat could tell that the creature inside was concentrating on one part of the egg in order to make a hole. He wondered whether to help it by making the hole for it, from outside. But he was somehow sure this was a bad idea. He could hurt it, or it could die of shock. The only thing he could do was to hang helplessly over the egg and listen.

Tap, *tap*, TAP, it went.

And a hair-fine crack appeared, near the top of the egg. After that, there was another exhausted silence. "Come *on*!" Cat whispered. "You can do it!"

But it couldn't. The tapping started again, weaker now, but the crack did not grow any bigger. After a while, the tapping was going so fast that it was almost a whirring, but still nothing happened. Cat could feel the creature's growing panic. He began to panic too. He didn't know what to *do*, or what would help.

There was only one person in the Castle that Cat knew could help. He rushed to his door, opened it wide, and then rushed back to the egg. He picked it up, scarf and all, and raced away down his winding stair to find Millie. He could feel the egg vibrating with terror as he ran. "It's all *right*!" he panted to it. "Don't panic! It'll be all right!"

Millie had her own sitting room on the next floor. She and Irene were sitting there, chatting quietly over mugs of cocoa before bed. Millie's big gray cat, Mopsa, was on her knee, filling most of it, and Irene had two more of the Castle cats, Coy and Potts, wedged into her chair on either side. All three cats sprang up and whirled to safe, high places when Cat slammed the door open and rushed in.

"Cat!" Millie exclaimed. "What's wrong?"

"It won't break! It can't get out!" Cat panted. He was almost crying by then.

Millie did not waste time asking questions. "Give it to me, here on the floor. Gently," she said, and kneeled quickly on the furry hearth rug. Cat, shaking, panting and sniffing, passed her egg at once. Millie put it carefully down on the rug and carefully unwrapped the scarf from it. "I see," she said, running her finger lightly along the thin, almost invisible crack. "Poor thing." She put both hands around the egg, as far as they would reach. "It's all right now," she murmured. "We're going to help you."

Cat could feel calmness spreading into the egg, along with hope and strength. He always forgot that Millie, apart from Chrestomanci and himself, was the strongest enchanter in the country. People said she had been a goddess once.

Irene came to kneel on the hearth rug too. "The shell seems awfully thick," she said.

"I don't think that's the problem—quite," Millie murmured. Her hands moved to either side of the crack and began gently, gently trying to spread it wider. Mopsa edged in under Millie's elbow and stared as if she were trying to help. She probably was, Cat realized. All the Castle cats descended from Asheth temple cats and had magic of their own. Coy and Potts, on the mantlepiece, were staring eagerly too. "Ah!" Millie said.

"What?" Cat asked anxiously.

"There's a stasis spell all round the inside of the shell," Millie said. "I suppose whoever put it there was trying to preserve the egg, but it's making things really difficult. Let's see. Cat, you and Irene put your hands where mine are, while I try to get rid of the spell. Hold the split as wide as you can, but very gently, not to crack it further."

They kneeled with their heads touching, Cat and Irene—Irene rather timidly—pulling at the crack, while Millie picked at the tiny space they made. After a moment, Millie made an annoyed noise and grew the nails on her thumb and forefinger an inch longer. Then she picked again with her new long nails, until she succeeded in pulling a tiny whitish piece of something through.

"Ah!" they all said.

Millie went on pulling, slowly, steadily, gently, and the filmy white something came out farther and farther, and finally came out entirely, with a faint whistling sound. As soon as it was free, it vanished. Millie said, "Bother! I'd like to have known whose spell it was. But never mind." She leaned down to the egg. "Now you can get to work, my love."

The creature inside did its best. It tapped and hammered away, but so feebly by then that Cat could scarcely bear to listen.

Irene whispered, "It's very weak. Couldn't we just break the shell for it?"

Millie shook her head, tangling her hair into Irene's and Cat's. "No. Much better to feed it strength. Put your hands on mine, both of you." She took hold of the egg, with her fingernails normal length again. Cat laid his hands over Millie's, and Irene doubtfully did the same. Cat could tell that Irene had no notion of how to give strength to someone else, so he did it for her and pushed Irene's strength inside the egg, along with his own and Millie's.

The creature inside now hammered away with a will. Tap, tap, taptaptap, *taptaptap*, BANG. *CRACK*. And a thing that might have been a beak—anyhow, it was yellowish and blunt—came out through the mauve shell. There it stopped, seeming to gasp. It looked so tender and soft that Cat's nose and mouth felt sore in sympathy. Fancy having to break this thick shell with *that*! he thought. Next second, the beak had been joined by a small, thin paw with long pink nails. Then a second paw struggled out, tiny and weak like the first.

The cats were all on the alert now. Mopsa's nose was almost on the widening dark crack.

"Is it a dragon?" Irene asked.

"I'm—not sure," Millie said.

As she spoke, the weak claws found the edges of the crack, scrabbled, and then shoved. The egg split into two white-lined halves, and the creature rolled loose. It was much bigger than Cat expected, twice the size of Mopsa at least, and it was desperately thin and scrawny and slightly wet, and covered with pale, draggled fluff. It opened two round yellow eyes above its beak and looked at Cat imploringly. "Weep, weep, weep!" it went.

Cat did what it seemed to want and gathered it up into his arms. It snugged down against him with an exhausted sigh, beak and front paws draped over his right arm, and hind claws quite painfully hooked on his left pajama sleeve. It had a tail like a piece of string that hung down on his knee. "Weep," it said.

It was much lighter for its size than Cat thought it should be. He was just about to ask Millie what on earth kind of creature it was, when the door of Millie's sitting room opened and Chrestomanci hurried in, looking anxious, with Jason behind him. "Is there some kind of crisis?" Chrestomanci asked.

"Not exactly," Millie said, pointing to the creature in Cat's arms.

Chrestomanci looked from the two broken eggshell halves on the hearth rug to the creature Cat was holding. He said, "Bless my soul!" and came over to look. He ran a finger down the creature's back, from soft beak to stringy tail, and picked up the tail to look at the tuft on its end. Then he went to the other end of it and examined the long pink front claws. Finally, he spread out one of the two funny little triangular things that grew from the creature's shoulders. "Bless my soul!" he said again. "It really is a griffin. These are its wings. Look."

They did not look much like wings to Cat. They had no feathers and were covered with the same pale fluff as the rest of it, but he supposed that

Chrestomanci knew. "What do they eat?" he asked.

"Blowed if I know," Chrestomanci said, and looked at Jason, who said, "Me neither."

As if it had understood, the baby griffin promptly discovered that it was starving. Its beak opened like a fledgling bird's, all pink and orange inside. *"Weep!"* it said. "Weep, weep, weep, weep! *Weep. WEEP, WEEP, WEEP!"* It struggled about in Cat's arms so painfully that he was forced to put it down on the hearth rug, where it lay spread-eagled and weeping miserably. Mopsa rushed up to it and began washing it. The baby griffin seemed to like that. It hunched itself toward Mopsa, but it did not stop its shrill, miserable "Weep, weep, weep!"

Millie stood up and did some quick conjuring. When she kneeled down again, she was holding a jug of warm milk and a large medicine dropper. "Here," she said. "Most babies like milk, in my experience." She filled the dropper with milk and gently squirted some into the corner of the gaping beak.

The baby griffin choked and most of the milk came out on to the hearth rug. Cat did not think it liked milk. But when he said so, Millie said, "Yes, but it's got to have *something*, or it'll die. Let's get some milk into it for now—it can't do any *harm*—and in the morning we'll rush it down to the vet—Mr. Vastion—and see what he can suggest."

"Weep, weep, weep," went the griffin, and choked again when Millie squeezed some more milk into it.

There followed three hours of hard work, during which they all five tried to feed the baby griffin and only partly succeeded. Irene was best at it. As Jason said, Irene had a knack with animals. Cat was next best, but he thought that by the time his turn came, the baby griffin had gotten the hang of being fed from a dropper. Cat got most of a jugful into it, but that seemed to do very little good. He had barely laid it down looking contented, when it raised its beak and went "Weep, weep, weep!" again. And it was the same for the other four. Eventually, Cat was so exhausted that he only stayed awake because he was so desperately sorry for the baby griffin. It needed a parent.

Chrestomanci yawned until his jaw gave out a sort of *clop*. "Cat, if you don't mind my asking, how did you come by this insatiable beast?"

"It hatched," Cat explained, "from the egg in Jason's attic. A girl called Marianne Pinhoe said I could have it. The house belonged to her father."

"Ah," Chrestomanci said. "Pinhoe. Hmm."

"It was under a stasis spell," Millie said. "It must have been in that house for years."

"But Cat somehow succeeded in hatching it. I see," Chrestomanci said, sighing. It was his turn to feed the baby griffin. He sat on the hearth rug, a very strange sight in a frilly apron that Millie had conjured for him, over his dark crimson velvet evening dress, and aimed the dropper at the griffin's open beak. The griffin choked again and most of the milk dribbled out. Chrestomanci looked resigned. "I think," he said, "that the only way to deal with this poor creature is to cast a four-hour sleep spell over it and get it to the vet as soon as it wakes up."

Everyone wearily agreed. "I'll conjure a dog basket for it," Millie said.

"No," Cat said. "I'll have it in bed with me. It needs a parent."

He set off back to his room with the sleep-bespelled griffin draped on his arms. Millie went with him to make sure they got there safely, and Mopsa followed them. Mopsa seemed to have decided to be the griffin's mother. No bad thing, as Millie said. Cat fell asleep with the baby griffin snuggled against him, snoring slightly, and Mopsa snuggled against the griffin. Between them, they had nearly pushed Cat out of the bed by the morning.

He woke to find that the griffin had wet his bed. That was scarcely surprising after all that milk, Cat supposed. And here the poor thing was, going "Weep, weep" again.

Millie arrived on the third "Weep!" as anxious as Cat was. "At least it's still alive, poor little soul," she said. "I've telephoned Mr. Vastion, and he says he can only see it this morning if we bring it down to his surgery now. He's got to go and see to a very sick cow after that. You get dressed, Cat, and I'll see if it will drink some more milk."

Cat climbed over the griffin and Mopsa and got out of his somewhat smelly pajamas, while Millie once more aimed the dropper at the griffin's desperate beak. It spat the milk out. "Oh, well," Millie said. "They're going to have to change your bedding anyway. I've told Miss Bessemer. It's lucky I thought to bring it a clean blanket. Are you ready yet?"

Cat was just tying his boots. He had dressed all anyhow, in his old suit trousers and the red sweater he wore to ride in. Millie had done much the same. She was in a threadbare tweed skirt and an expensive lace blouse, and too worried about the griffin to notice. She spread out the fluffy white blanket she had brought and Cat tenderly lifted the griffin onto it. It was shivering. And it continued shivering even when it was wrapped in the blanket.

They left Mopsa finishing the milk Millie had brought and hurried down to the main door of the Castle. Millie had not bothered to wake the Castle chauffeur. She had brought the long black car round to the front of the Castle before she came to wake Cat. The griffin was still shivering when Cat got into the passenger seat with it, and it went on shivering while Millie drove the short distance down into Helm St. Mary and along to the vet's surgery on the outskirts of the village.

Cat liked Mr. Vastion at once. He wore glasses like little half-moons well down on his nose and looked humorously at Cat and Millie over them. "Now what have we here?" he said. His voice was a gloomy kind of moan, with a bit of a grunt to it. "Bring it in, bring it in," he told them, waving them through to his consulting room, "and put it down here," he said, pointing with a thick finger at a high, shiny examining table. When Cat carefully dumped the bundle of blanket on the table, Mr. Vastion unwrapped it in a resigned way, moaning, "What a parcel. Is this necessary? What have we in here?"

To Cat's surprise, the griffin seemed to like Mr. Vastion too. It stopped shivering and looked up at him with its great golden eyes. "Weep?"

"And *weep* to you too," Mr. Vastion grunted back at it, unwrapping. "You shouldn't coddle them, you know. Not good for any animal. Now— Oh, yes. You have a fine boy griffin here. Small still, but they grow quite quickly, you know. Does he have a name yet?"

"I don't think so," Cat said.

"Quite right," Mr. Vastion moaned. "They always name themselves. Fact. I read up about griffins before you got here. Just in case this wasn't a complete hoax. Very rare things in this world, griffins. First one I've ever seen, actually. Just a moment."

He paused, holding the griffin down with one expertly spread hand, while, with the other hand, he picked up a frog that had somehow appeared on the table and threw it out of the window.

"Damn nuisance, these frogs," he moaned, while he turned the griffin this way and that, feeling its stomach and its ribs and its legs and examining both sets of claws. "They've got a plague of frogs here," he explained. "Came to me and asked me to get rid of them. I asked them what I was supposed to do—poison the duck pond? Told them to get rid of the things themselves. They're Farleighs. Should know how. But there's no doubt too many frogs are a pest. They get in everywhere. And they strike me as half unreal anyway. Some magician's idea of a joke, I'd say." He held the griffin's beak open and looked down its throat. "Fine voice in there, by the look of it. Now let's have you over, old son."

Mr. Vastion set the griffin on its feet and unfolded the little triangular stubs of its wings. He felt round the bottom of them. "Plenty of good flight muscles here," he grunted. "Just need a bit of growing and fledging. The feathers will come, along with the proper coat at the back end. You'll find this fluff will drop out as he grows. Just what were you worrying about?"

"We don't know what to give him to eat," Cat explained. "He doesn't like milk."

"Well, he wouldn't, would he?" Mr. Vastion moaned. "The front half of him's bird. Look."

He turned the griffin deftly over on its side, where it lay peacefully. Cat could see that it liked this firm handling. Mr. Vastion slid his hand over the creature's beak, and then upward, so that its small tufty ears were flattened.

"Now you've got the contours," he grunted. "Reminds me of nothing so much as an osprey. Or a sea eagle, even more. Magnificent birds. Huge wingspan. Take that as your guide, but chop the food up small or he'll choke. Sea eagles do take fish, but they take rabbits even more. Easier to catch. I expect this fellow will be quite happy with minced beef. But he'll want raw vegetables chopped into it too, to keep him healthy. I'd better show you. Hold him for me a minute, Lady Chant."

Millie put both hands on the peacefully lying griffin. "He's so thin and weak!"

Mr. Vastion gave out a long moan. "Of *course* he is. Just hatched. All newborn creatures are like this. Skinny. Feeble. Bags under their eyes. Excuse me a moment. I'll get him some puppy food." He left the room in the sort of shuffling plod that seemed to be his way of walking.

Another frog landed on the table while they waited. Cat picked it up and, like Mr. Vastion had done, threw it out of the window. A flopping feeling on his feet showed him two more frogs that had somehow landed on his boots. In the dim light down there, parts of them glowed transparent green, with touches of red. Cat saw Mr. Vastion had been quite right. These frogs were only partly real. He bent down and collected both frogs in his left hand, just as Mr. Vastion shuffled back into the room. The baby griffin leaped up from under Millie's hands with its beak wide open, going, "Weep, weep, weep!" in such excitement that it seemed about to leap right off the table. Cat quickly sent all the frogs back to where they came from and dived to catch the griffin.

"That's right," Mr. Vastion grunted. He was holding a large handful of raw mince mixed with shredded carrot. They watched him put the meat into his bunched-up fingers, so that his hand was roughly beak shaped. "Like this, see," he moaned, and popped the handful expertly down the griffin's throat. "Think you can do that?"

The griffin swallowed, clapped its beak, and looked soulfully up at Mr. Vastion. "Weep?"

"In a bit, fellow. Lady Chant will take you home and give you a square meal there," Mr. Vastion moaned. "Bring him back again if you're worried. That will be ten and sixpence, Lady Chant."

They got back into the car again, Cat carrying the griffin without the blanket. Millie tossed the blanket into the backseat, saying, "I think we were worrying too much, Cat. Raw meat! Thank goodness he told us!" She drove off, around the village green and up the long driveway to the Castle, where she did not stop at the main door; she drove on around to the kitchen door and stopped outside that.

Cat was surprised at how many people were crowded into the kitchen to meet them. Mr. Frazier, the butler, opened the kitchen door to them. Mr. Stubbs, the head cook, met them as they came in, surrounded by his apprentices, and asked anxiously just what it was that griffins ate.

"Raw mince," Millie said, "with grated carrots—and chopped parsley, I think, for clean breath."

"I rather thought that might be it," Mr. Stubbs said. "Eddie, fetch out that minced rabbit. Joan and

Laurie, grate us some carrots, and Jimmy, you chop parsley. And you'll be wanting breakfast yourselves while you feed him, I guess. Bert, coffee, toast."

Miss Bessemer the housekeeper was there too, hurrying to spread newspaper on a table for Cat to put the griffin down on. "A basket in your room?" she asked Cat. "I've found you a nice roomy one. And we'll bespell the lining until he's house-trained, dear, if you don't mind."

As the mince arrived, the baby griffin stood up on wobbly legs, whirling its stringlike tail and going "Weep!" again. A crowd surrounded the table to watch. Cat saw Joe the boot boy, Mary, Euphemia and two other maids, several footmen, all the kitchen staff, Mr. Frazier, Miss Bessemer, nearly all the Castle wizards, Roger, Janet, Julia, Irene, Jason, and Mopsa, looking possessive. He even caught a glimpse of Chrestomanci, in a purple dressing gown, at the back of the crowd, watching over people's heads.

"We don't get a griffin every day," Millie said. "You feed him, love. He came to you, after all."

Cat took up a fistful of meat, made his fingers into a beak, and posted the lump down the griffin's expectant throat. "Oh, bless!" someone murmured as the griffin swallowed, looked pleased, and looked up for more. "Weep?" That plateful went in no time. Cat had only time to snatch a piece of toast before there was a further, louder "Weep, *weep*!" and Mr. Stubbs had to fetch more meat. The baby griffin ate all the rabbit there was, followed by a pound of minced steak, and then went "Weep!" for more. Mr. Stubbs produced smoked salmon. It ate that. By this time its scrawny stomach was round, and tight as a drum.

"I think that will do," Millie said. "We don't want him ill. But he obviously needs a lot."

"I sent an order down to the butcher, ma'am," Mr. Stubbs said. "I can see it's going to be quantities. Every four hours, if you ask me, if he's anything like a human baby."

"Oh, help!" Cat said. "Really?"

"Pretty certainly," Mr. Frazier said, suddenly revealing himself as a bird fancier. "Your fledgling bird eats its own weight in food daily, and often more. Better weigh it, Mr. Stubbs. You may need to increase your order."

So the kitchen scales were fetched and the griffin was discovered to weigh over a stone already, sixteen pounds, in fact. It objected to being weighed. It wanted to go to sleep, preferably in Cat's arms. While Cat carried it away upstairs, with its beak contentedly resting on his shoulder and Mopsa following watchfully, Mr. Stubbs did sums on the back of an old bill. The total came to so much that he sent Joe down to the butcher's to double his first order.

Joe stopped to exchange an urgent look with Roger before he left. "I'll wait," Roger said. "Promise."

"Get *going*, Joe Pinhoe!" Mr. Stubbs said. "You lazy layabout, you!"

12

❧❦

OVER IN ULVERSCOTE there was suddenly a plague of frogs.

Nobody had seen the like before. There were thousands of them, and there was a sort of green-redness to them if you saw them in the shade. They got in everywhere. People trod on them when they got out of bed that morning and found them in the teapot when they tried to make tea. About the only inhabitant of the village who enjoyed the plague was Nutcase. He chased frogs all over Furze Cottage. His favorite place to hunt them into was Marianne's bedroom. Then he killed them on Marianne's bedside rug.

Marianne picked up the strange, small black remains. The frogs seemed to shrink when they were dead and die away into something dark and dry with holes in. Not real, she thought. There was a smell coming off them that she knew. Where had she smelled that particular odor before? She knew Joe had been there when she smelled it. Was it when they stole the stuffed ferret? No. It was before that.

It was when Gammer had sent that blast of magic at the Farleighs.

That's it, Marianne thought. These are Gammer's.

She went downstairs and put the dry remains into the waste pail. "I'm going round to see Gammer," she told Mum.

"Does she want you *again*?" Mum said. "Don't be too long. I'm still finding jars with mildew in them. We're going to have to scald the lot out."

Though the wave of bad luck had stopped as suddenly as it had begun, the effects of it were still there, in the mildew, in half-healed cuts, sprained ankles, and—this seemed to be the final thing the spell had done—an outbreak of whooping cough among the smaller children. Dismal coughing came from most of the houses Marianne passed on her way to the Dell. But the right kind of red bricks were just now being delivered at the Post Office as she went by.

Aunt Joy was standing on her lawn above the broken wall, watching the delivery. "I may have my bricks," she grumbled to Marianne, "but that's as far as it goes. Your Uncle Simeon's too busy doing the renovations at Woods House, hobbling around with a stick, if you please! All for that new woman who says she's a Pinhoe. If he can do it on one leg for *her*, why not for *me*? As if my money wasn't as good as hers!"

There was a lot more on these lines, but Marianne only smiled at Aunt Joy and went on. As Dad often said, if you stayed to listen to Aunt Joy, you'd be there a week and she still wouldn't have finished grumbling.

There were frogs in the lane all the way to the Dell, and the pond in front of the cottage was a seething, hopping mass of them. The ducks had given up trying to swim and were sitting grumpily on the grass.

"I don't know what we've done to deserve this," Aunt Dinah said, opening the door for Marianne. "Anyone would think we'd offended Moses or something! Go on in. She's been asking for you."

Marianne marched into Gammer's crowded living room. "Gammer," she said.

Gammer's ruined face turned up to her. "I'm not in my right mind," Gammer said quickly.

"Then you shouldn't do magic," Marianne retorted. "There's frogs all over the village."

Gammer shook her head as if she were saddened by the way people behaved. "What's this world becoming into? Those shouldn't be there."

"Where should they be, then?" Marianne challenged her.

Gammer shook her head again. "No need to take on. Little girls shouldn't worry their heads over such things."

"Where?" Marianne said.

Gammer bent her face down and pleated her freshly starched skirt.

"Where?" Marianne insisted. "You sent those frogs somewhere, didn't you?"

Very reluctantly, Gammer muttered, "Jed Farleigh should have left me alone."

"Helm St. Mary?" Marianne said.

Gammer nodded. "And all over. There's Farleighs in all the villages over there. I forget the names of those places. I don't remember so well these days, Marianne. You have to understand."

"I do," said Marianne. "You sent frogs to Helm St. Mary, right outside Chrestomanci Castle, so that they were almost bound to notice, and you made the Farleighs so angry that they ill-wished us and sent the frogs right back. Aren't you ashamed, Gammer?"

"That's Jed Farleigh all over," Gammer said. "Hides out over there, thinks he's safe from me. And they're spying on me all the time, spying and lurking. It wasn't me, Marianne. It was Edgar and Lester. I didn't tell them to do it."

"You know perfectly well that Edgar and Lester would *never* send anyone frogs!" Marianne said. "I'm disgusted with you, Gammer!"

"I have to defend myself!" Gammer protested.

"No, you don't, not like *this*!" Marianne said, and stormed out among the frogs, down the lane and past the stack of new bricks. Feeling angrier and braver than she had ever been in her life, she stormed on down Furze Lane and into the shed behind Furze Cottage. There, Dad and Uncle Richard were trying to saw wood without cutting frogs in half. "Gammer did these frogs," she told them.

"Oh, come now, Marianne," Dad said. "Gammer wouldn't do a thing like that!"

"Yes, she would. She *did*!" Marianne said. "She

sent them to Helm St. Mary, but the Farleighs sent them back here and did an ill-wishing on us because Gammer made them so angry. Dad, I think we're in the middle of a war with the Farleighs without knowing we are."

Dad laughed. "The Farleighs are not that uncivilized, Marianne. These frogs are just someone's idea of a joke—you can see they're creatures bewitched from the way they glow. Run along and don't worry your head about them."

Whatever Marianne said after that, Dad simply laughed and refused to believe her. She went indoors and tried to tell Mum.

"Oh, *really*, Marianne!" Mum said, holding a kettle with a cloth round the handle, amid clouds of steam. "I grant you Gammer's mad as a coot these days, but the Farleighs are sane people. We *cooperate* with them around the countryside. Just get your hair tied up and give me a hand here and *forget* about the beastly frogs!"

Marianne spent the rest of the day boiling kettles in a sort of angry loneliness. She did not trust Gammer simply to stop at frogs. She knew she had to get someone to believe her before the Farleighs got so angry that they did something terrible, but Dad and Mum seemed to have closed their minds. Some of the time, she was tempted just to keep quiet about Gammer and let bad things happen. But she had started being brave now, and she felt she had to go on. She wondered who else might believe her. Someone who might stop Gammer and explain to the Farleighs. Apart from Uncle Charles, she could think of no one, and Uncle Charles was working up at Woods House with Uncle Simeon. I'll talk to him when he gets off work, she decided. Because I think it really is urgent.

By that afternoon, the frogs had become such a nuisance that Uncle Richard took action. He harnessed Dolly the donkey to the cart and filled the cart with bins and sacks. Then he called in all Marianne's cousins, all ten of them, and the troop of them went round the houses collecting frogs. They were handed frogs by squirming fistfuls everywhere. For those people who were too old or too busy with the whooping cough to collect frogs for themselves, the boys went in and tipped frogs out of tea caddies and scooped frogs out of cupboards, shoes, and toilets, while the rest hunted frogs in the gardens. They came joyfully out again with squirming, croaking sacks and dumped them in the cart. Then they went on to the next house. They caught two hundred frogs in the vicarage and twice that number in the church. The only place with more frogs was the Dell.

"Stands to reason," Uncle Richard said, refusing to believe a word against Gammer. "There's a pond at the Dell."

When, finally, the cart was piled high with bulging sacks and croaking bins and there was hardly a loose frog to be seen, they took Dolly down Furze Lane to the river and tipped all the frogs in. Uncle Richard scratched his head over what happened then. Every frog, as it hit the running water, seemed to dissolve away to nothing. The cousins could not get over it.

"Well, they say running water kills the craft," Uncle Richard told Mum and Marianne, when he came to Furze Cottage for a cup of tea after his labors, "but I'd never believed it until now. Melted away into black like foam, they did. Astonishing."

Here, Marianne looked round and noticed that Nutcase was missing again. "Oh, *bother* him!" she wailed, and hurried to the table to set the knife spinning. It was still whirling round and round when there was a knock at the front door.

"See who that is, Marianne!" Mum called out, busy pouring hot water on the tea.

Marianne opened the door. And stared. A very tall, thin woman stood there, carrying a basket. She had straight hair and a flat chest and she wore the drabbest and most dust-colored dress Marianne had ever seen. Her face was long and severe. She gazed at Marianne, and Marianne was reminded of a teacher about to find fault.

Before Marianne could ask what this stranger wanted, the woman said, "Jane James. From Woods House. Wrong way to make your acquaintance, I know, but did you know your cat walks through walls? He was in my kitchen eating the fish for Mr. Adams's supper. Doors all shut. Only explanation. Don't know how you'll keep him in."

"I don't either," Marianne said. She looked up at the grim face and found it was full of hidden humor. Jane James evidently found the situation highly amusing. "I'm sorry," she said. "I'll come and fetch him back at once."

"No need," said Jane James. She opened the basket she was carrying and turned Nutcase out of it like a pudding onto the doormat. "Pleased to meet you," she said, and went away.

"Well I'll be—!" Uncle Richard said, as Marianne shut the front door. "Quite a touch of the craft in that woman, if you ask me!"

"And no *wonder* we can't keep that cat in!" Mum said, putting the teapot on the table.

Nutcase sat on the doormat and glowered at Marianne. Marianne glowered back. They can believe Jane James that Nutcase walks through walls, but they can't believe *me* about Gammer, she thought. "You," she said to Nutcase, "you're as bad as Gammer! And I can't say worse than that!"

Meanwhile, back at the Castle, Cat was trying to get used to the way he had to feed a baby griffin every four hours—at least, it was usually only about three and half hours before the griffin woke, with its stomach all flat and thin again, and went "Weep, weep, weep!" for more food. He was carrying it to the kitchen yet again—and it felt a good deal heavier than it was when it first hatched—when Julia stopped him on the stairs.

"Can I help you feed him?" she asked. "He's just so sweet! Janet wants to help too."

Cat realized that this was exactly what he

needed. He said quickly, "We can have a feeding rota, then. You can feed him in the day, but I'll have to look after him at night."

In fact, as he soon discovered, a surprising number of people wanted to help feed the griffin. Miss Bessemer wanted to, and so did Mr. Stubbs and Euphemia. Millie wanted to, having, as she said, a personal interest in this griffin. And Irene, when she was not over in Ulverscote seeing to the alterations to her new house, begged to have a turn as well.

At first Cat found himself sitting over the person feeding the griffin as possessively as Mopsa did. He knew it was happier when he was beside it. But when the griffin seemed perfectly used to somebody else putting lumps of meat into its beak, Cat—rather guiltily—sighed with relief and went off to ride Syracuse. Before long, he only had to feed the griffin during the nights.

He went up to his room every night carrying two large covered bowls of meat, each with a stasis spell on it to keep it fresh. By the third night he was—well, *almost*—used to being woken at midnight and again at four in the morning by the griffin's "Weep, weep, weep!" If this did not wake Cat, then Mopsa did, pushing her cold nose urgently into Cat's face and treading heavily on his stomach.

What he never seemed to get used to was how sleepy he was during the day.

On the third night, Mopsa as usual woke him at midnight. "All right. I know, I *know*!" Cat said, rolling out from under Mopsa's nose and feet. "I'm coming." He sat up and switched on the light.

To his surprise, the griffin was still heavily asleep, curled in its basket with its yellow beak propped on the edge, making small whistling snores. But there was something tapping on his big window. It was exactly like that strange dream he had had. I think I know what that is! Cat thought. He got out of bed and opened the window.

An upside-down face stared at him, but it was human.

Cat stared back, finding this hard to believe.

"Can you give us a bit of help?" the face asked, rather desperately. "It's raining."

Because it was upside down, it took Cat a moment or so to recognize that the face belonged to Joe the boot boy. "How did you get *there*?" he said.

"We made this flying machine," Joe explained, "but we didn't get it right. It crashed on your roof. Roger's up here too, wedged like."

Oh, my lord! Cat thought. *That's* what they've been up to in that shed! "All right," he said. "I'd better bring you in here. Let yourself go loose."

By using a spur-of-the-minute mixture of conjuring and levitation, Cat managed to pull Joe off the roof and bend him around through the window and into his room. Unfortunately, this seemed to dislodge the crashed flying machine. As Joe flopped heavily onto Cat's carpet, there was a set of long sliding sounds from above, followed by a cry of horror from Roger. Cat was only just in time to catch Roger as he fell past the window and to levitate him inside too.

"Thanks!" Roger gasped.

Both of them stood by the window, panting, pale, and speckled with rain. Instead of doing as Cat would have expected and crawling away to bed, the two of them went into an anxious conference. Joe said, "Where do you reckon we went wrong, then? Think it was the rain?"

Roger answered, "No. I think we got the wiring wrong on the stuffed eagle."

Joe said, "May have to start again from scratch, then."

"No, no," Roger said. "I'm sure we've got the basics. We just need to refine it some more."

They're mad! Cat thought. He looked past them at the wreckage. It was now hanging down across the window, growing wetter by the second. As far as Cat could see, it was a number of inter-locked pieces of tables and chairs, with a three-legged stool in there somewhere, and dangling upside down in the midst of it a forlorn and drag-gled stuffed golden eagle. The eagle had wires coming out of it, together with a few damp tufts of herbs.

"I belong to Chrestomanci Castle," the eagle remarked sadly. Everything in the Castle was bespelled to say this if it was taken more than a few feet from the castle walls.

"Where did you get the eagle?" Cat asked.

"It was in one of the attics," Roger said. "We

have to insulate the dandelion seeds, for a start."

"We might try using willow herb instead," Joe replied.

The griffin woke up. Instead of screaming for food, it sat up and stared at the two wet boys and the dangling wreckage with interest. Mopsa sat on Cat's bed and stared, too, disapprovingly.

"You can't leave all that stuff hanging there," Cat said.

"We know," said Roger. "Or we could use both kinds of seeds."

"And gear up the bikes a bit," Joe replied.

"It's a real nuisance," Roger said, "having to do things at night in order not to be found out. Cat, we'll go down into the garden. When we whistle, can you levitate the flying machine down to us? Gently, mind, in order not to break it any more."

"I suppose so," Cat said.

Joe went down on one knee to pet the griffin as if it were a dog. "Aren't you *soft*!" he said to it. "All that fluff. Where have I seen one of you before? It'll come down in bits, you know. Part of it got hooked on your turret."

Cat giggled. If he had been Chrestomanci, he knew he would have said, The *griffin* got hooked on the turret? "All right," he said. "I'll send it up first, to unhook it, before I send it down. You two get down to the garden before someone notices it."

The two aviators hurried off, both limping slightly. The griffin opened its beak.

"All right," Cat said. "Don't say it!"

He had time to feed the griffin a square meal before a soft whistle came from the garden below. Cat put the bowl away and leaned out of the window to levitate the wreckage.

"I belong to Chrestomanci Castle," the stuffed eagle said piteously.

"I know," said Cat. "But this is difficult."

The remains of the flying machine were wedged onto the turret. Cat had to spread the various bits of it apart and send them downward piece by piece. He had no idea what most of the bits were. He simply floated them away from his roof and down to the ground. Another soft whistle and a faint chorus of voices singing "I belong to Chrestomanci Castle!" told him when all the parts had landed safely under the cedar trees. Wooden clatterings and the occasional soft *clang* showed that the two aviators were now hauling the stuff away, protesting that it belonged to the Castle.

"They're *mad*!" Cat told Mopsa and the griffin. "Quite mad." He went back to bed.

The griffin did not wake him again that night. In the morning, it climbed out of its basket and woke Cat by nudging him with its beak. Cat opened his eyes to find two yellow griffin eyes staring into his, interested and friendly. "Oh, I do like you!" Cat said, before he had had time to think. Then he felt guilty, because Syracuse was bound to be jealous.

Still, there was nothing to be done about Syracuse just then. Cat got dressed, while the griffin staggered around the room investigating everything

Cat owned. There was no doubt that it had grown again in the night. The dark beginnings of feathers were showing on its neck and on its absurd, stubby wings.

"Isn't it growing too quickly?" Cat asked Millie anxiously, when he had gotten it down to the kitchen. The griffin was now far too heavy for Cat to carry. The two of them came downstairs in a mixture of staggering and levitating—and some flopping—and the griffin looked very pleased with himself for getting there.

Millie pursed up her mouth and studied the griffin. "You have to remember," she said, "that griffins are strongly magical creatures, and this one must have spent years inside that stasis spell in the egg. I think it's making up for lost time. I wonder how big it's going to be."

Only about the size of Syracuse, Cat hoped. Any bigger would be really awkward. He was about to say so, when Millie added, "Cat, I'm worried about Roger. He seems so tired today."

"Um," Cat said. "He could have been up all night reading."

"He must have been," Millie agreed. "He had six books by his bed when I went in, all from other worlds. They were all about flying. I do hope he's not going to do anything silly."

"He won't," Cat said, because he knew Roger already had.

He left Millie shoving mince into the griffin and went to muck out Syracuse, soon done by enchanter's methods. While Cat was grooming Syracuse, wishing that there was some magical method to do this too, Joss Callow came in.

"It's my day off today," Joss said. "If you want a ride, you'd better make it now before breakfast."

"Yes, please," Cat said.

He had Syracuse out in the yard and saddled up, and Syracuse was bouncing, tugging, and dancing as usual, too glad to be ridden to let Cat get up and ride him, when Syracuse abruptly stopped dead and flung his head up. Cat looked round to see the griffin staggering enthusiastically toward them. Cat could only stare at it. He could not think what to do.

Syracuse stared, too, down his upheld nose. It was hard to blame him. The griffin was such a plump, scrawny, unfinished-looking creature. It still had not gotten the hang of walking. It rolled from side to side, scratching the stones of the yard with its long pink claws, and whirling its stringy tail behind it. Cat could see it was terribly proud at having found him.

"It's only a baby," he said pleadingly to Syracuse.

As the griffin staggered near, Syracuse swayed backward on all four feet, snorting. The griffin stopped. It stared upward at Syracuse. Its beak fell open with what seemed to be admiration. It made a whirring noise and stretched its face up. And Syracuse, to Cat's relief and astonishment, lowered his own shapely head and nosed the griffin's beak. At this, the griffin's little wings worked with excitement. It cooed, and Cat could have sworn that a grin grew at the sides of its beak. But he had to stop it when it put out a clumsy front paw that was obviously meant to be friendly but threatened to scratch Syracuse's nose.

"That'll do. So you like one another. That's good," Cat said. "How did you get out here anyway?"

Millie came dashing across the yard. "Oh, I only turned my back for a minute when Miss Bessemer came to ask about towels! And off he went. Come on, come back with Millie, little griffin. Oh, I wish he had a name, Cat!"

"Klartch," said the griffin.

"*That's* a new noise," said Millie. "Whatever it means, you've got to come in, griffin."

"No—wait," Cat said. "I think it's his name. *Is* your name Klartch, griffin?"

The griffin turned its face up to him. It was definitely smiling. "Klartch," it said happily.

"Mr. Vastion *said* they named themselves," Millie said, "but I didn't realize that meant they *talked*. Well, Klartch, that goes two ways. If you can talk, you can understand too. Come indoors with me at *once* and finish your breakfast. Now."

The griffin made a small noise like "Yup" and followed Millie obediently back to the kitchen. Well, well! Cat thought.

Joss, who had been standing looking utterly dumbfounded, said, "That creature—where did it come from?"

"A girl called Marianne gave me his egg," Cat said.

"*Marianne* did?" Joss said. "Marianne *Pinhoe*?" Cat nodded. Joss said dubiously, "Well, I suppose in a way she had a right to. But you'd better not let Mr. Farleigh get a sight of the thing. He'd go spare."

Cat could not really see why the sight of a baby griffin should annoy Mr. Farleigh, but he was sure Joss knew. *Everything* seemed to annoy Mr. Farleigh anyway.

13

❧•❧

MARIANNE DID CATCH Uncle Charles on his way home from Woods House, but he refused to believe that Gammer could do any wrong. He laughed and said, "You have to be older to understand, my chuck. None of us Pinhoes would do a thing like that. We *work* with the Farleighs."

Though this seemed to show that no one was going to believe her, Marianne went on trying to make *someone* understand about Gammer. Almost everyone she spoke to over the next few days said, "Gammer wouldn't do a thing like that!" and refused to talk about it anymore. Uncle Arthur gave Marianne a pat on the head and a bag of scrittlings for Nutcase. "She was a good mother to me and a good Gammer to all of us," he said. "You never knew her in her prime."

Marianne wondered about this. She supposed that a mother with seven sons had to be a good one, but she went and asked Mum about it all the same.

"Good mother!" Mum said. "What gave you that idea? When I was your age, my mother and her friends were always looking out cast-off clothes for your dad and his brothers, or they'd have been running round in rags. She said those boys were too scared of Gammer to tell her when they'd grown out of their things."

"But didn't Gammer notice their clothes?" Marianne said.

"Not that I ever saw," Mum said. "She left the younger ones to Dad to look after."

But Mum had never liked Gammer, Marianne thought, trying to be fair. Uncle Arthur truly believed what he had said. In many ways Uncle Arthur was very like Dad, though, always believing the best of everyone. Mum snorted whenever Dad said kind and respectful things about Gammer, and called it "rewriting history." So where did the real truth lie? Somewhere in the middle? Marianne sighed. The facts seemed to be that no one, even Mum, was going to believe that Gammer had sent the Farleighs a plague of frogs or— Marianne stopped on her way upstairs to go on with her story of Princess Irene.

Oh, heavens! she thought. Suppose it wasn't *only* frogs!

She turned and went downstairs again. "Just going down to the Dell!" she called to Mum, and went straight there to talk to Aunt Dinah.

As she passed the Post Office, she was glad to see that some of Uncle Simeon's people were now working on the ruined wall. They were working in that deceptively slow way that witchcraftly workmen did such things, and the wall was nearly waist high already. That must mean that the alterations up at Woods House were almost finished, with the same deceptive, witchcraftly speed.

And here was an example of the way no one would believe any ill of Gammer, Marianne thought. Gammer had broken that Post Office wall. But everyone was treating it as an accident, or an act of God.

She had half a mind to go into the Post Office. Aunt Joy would believe her. But Aunt Joy always believed the worst of everyone. And, more importantly, no one believed Aunt Joy. Marianne went on down the lane toward the Dell. There were still a few of the charmed frogs jumping about in the hedges there. It had been impossible to catch every single one.

Aunt Dinah had surprise all over her square blond face, when Marianne said she wanted to talk to *her* and not Gammer. But she led the way into her little, dark kitchen, where there were fresh-cooked queen cakes on wire trays all over the table. Aunt Dinah pushed them aside, telling Marianne to eat as many as she wanted, and made them both a cup of coffee. "Now, dear. What is it?"

Marianne had decided to approach this very carefully. Sniffing the lovely smell of new cake, she said, "Does Gammer do any magic at all these days?"

Aunt Dinah looked perplexed, and a little worried. "Why do you want to know, dear?"

"Well," Marianne said. "It looks as if I might have to be the next Gammer, doesn't it? And I don't really know enough." This was perfectly true, but the next bit wasn't. She said, in a bit of a rush, "I wondered if she was up to giving me some lessons, seeing her mind isn't quite right these days. Does she do any workings? Does she get them wrong at all?"

"You have a point," Aunt Dinah agreed. "But I don't see how she *can*, dear. You'd be better off asking your dad to teach you. Gammer just sits these days. Of course she mutters a bit."

"Don't tell me," Marianne said artificially, "that she's still going on about the Farleighs!"

"Well, you've heard her," said Aunt Dinah. "I admit she can sound quite abusive at times, but it doesn't mean a thing, bless her!"

"Does she do anything else at all?" Marianne asked, trying to sound disappointed.

Aunt Dinah smiled and shook her head. "Nothing. She just sits and plays with things like a child. The other day she'd got hold of a rose hip and a bit of sneezewort, and she was taking them apart and twiddling them for hours." (Oh dear! That's itches and rashes and colds in the head! Marianne thought.) "Lately," Aunt Dinah said, "she's been asking for water all the time. I've watched her pour it from one glass to another and smile—" (What's *that* for? Marianne wondered. It *has* to be another spell, if she smiled!) "And she mixed soot with some of it," Aunt Dinah went on, "and made it so dirty I had to take it away from her." (So some of it's a filth spell, Marianne thought.) "Oh, and the other day," Aunt Dinah admitted, lowering her voice because this was disgraceful, "she caught a *flea*. I was *so* ashamed. I don't mind her catching ants, the way she does, but a *flea*! I try to keep her clean as clean, but there she was, holding it and saying, 'Look, Dinah, here's a flea!' I offered to kill it for her, but she did it herself."

So now she's done a plague of ants and a plague of fleas! Marianne thought. Right under Aunt Dinah's nose, too! Those poor Farleighs! No wonder they ill-chanced us! Nerving herself up to say such a thing to a grown-up aunt, Marianne asked, "But don't all those things seem to be spells of some kind, Aunt Dinah?" Particularly the water, Marianne thought. If she's poisoned their water, that's wicked!

"Oh, no, dear," Aunt Dinah said kindly. "She's just amusing herself, bless her. She's left the craft behind her now."

Marianne drew in a deep, cake-scented breath and said boldly, "I don't think she has."

Aunt Dinah laughed. "And I know she has. Don't worry your head, Marianne, and get your dad to teach you. You can trust Isaac and I to look after Gammer for you."

So here was another person who would only believe the best of Gammer, Marianne thought sadly as she got up to go. It was almost as if they were under a spell. "I'll let myself out. Thanks for the coffee," she told Aunt Dinah.

She strode straight through the hall and ignored Gammer's voice, raised from behind the door of the front room. "Is that you, Marianne?" Gammer always seemed to know when Marianne was in the Dell.

"No, it *isn't*!" she muttered with her teeth clenched.

As she marched off down the lane between the rustling, croaking hedges, Marianne considered Gammer's spells and wished she knew how to cancel them. They would be strong. If she had any doubts about *how* strong, she only had to remember the blast of magic Gammer had sent at the Farleighs. That wasn't just a plain blast, either. It was meant to send the Farleighs away, certainly, but it was also intended to make them believe that Gammer was upright and innocent and in her right mind. Gammer was an expert at interwoven spells.

"Oh!" Marianne said out loud, and almost stopped walking.

Of *course* Gammer had laid a spell on everyone. She didn't want anyone to stop her getting her revenge on the Farleighs and she didn't want to be blamed when the Farleighs fought back. So she had bespelled every single Pinhoe in the village to think only the best of her. The thing that had confused Marianne was the way she herself seemed to be immune to the spell.

Or not quite immune. Marianne walked slowly on, remembering the day they had moved Gammer out of Woods House. It had been perfectly reasonable to her then—if annoying—that Gammer should have rooted herself to her bed, and not at all unreasonable that Gammer should have chased Dolly with the kitchen table and knocked the Post Office wall down. Now she looked back on it, she saw that it was *dreadful* behavior. Gammer must have been pouring on the ensorcellment that day.

But she had probably started setting the spell before that, probably while she was poltergeisting those poor nurses. None of the aunts and uncles had blamed Gammer for that—but then they almost never did blame Gammer for anything she did—

Marianne's eyes went wide as she realized that Gammer might have been setting this spell all of Marianne's own life. No one *ever* blamed Gammer. She had only to look at the Farleighs to realize how unlikely that was. The Farleighs certainly obeyed old Mr. Farleigh, because he was their Gaffer, but they grumbled that he was set in his ways and very few of them *liked* him. But the Pinhoes treated Gammer as if she was something natural and precious, like rain in April that was good for the crops—and people grumbled about rain, but never about Gammer.

It puzzled Marianne why she herself seemed to be mostly immune to Gammer's spell. She thought it must be that Mum was always saying sour things about Gammer—even though Mum was not immune to the spell herself. Mum was not going to help Marianne deal with Gammer. Marianne wondered, rather desperately, if anyone could. Then it occurred to her that the spell almost certainly only applied to people who actually lived in Ulverscote. There were Pinhoes who lived in other places, outside the village. Who could she ask?

The nearest and most obvious person was Great-Uncle Edgar. He and his wife, Great-Aunt Sue, lived a couple of miles out, along the Helm St. Mary road. It was no good expecting Great-Uncle Edgar to believe anything bad about Gammer. He was her brother, after all. But, when she thought about it, Marianne had hopes of Great-Aunt Sue. Aunt Sue had come from a wealthy family on the other side of Hopton, according to Mum, and might be expected to take a more outside view of things—and she surely couldn't see Gammer as blameless after nearly getting squashed to death between Gammer's bed and the doorpost. Mum had been taking Aunt Sue jars of her special balm for her bruises ever since.

"Shall I take Aunt Sue another jar of your balm?" Marianne asked Mum as soon as she got back to Furze Cottage.

"Oh, *would* you!" Mum said. "I'm so busy making up tinctures to help whooping cough, you wouldn't believe! They say little Nicola's really poorly with it. She could hardly fetch her breath last night, poor little mite!"

Marianne took off her pinafore and went to fetch her bike from the shed. The first thing she saw there was Mum's new broomstick. Marianne eyed it, wondering whether to borrow that instead. The stick was white and fresh and the bristles thick and stiff and pinkish. She could see it would fly splendidly. But Mum might object, and Aunt Sue was more likely to look kindly on Marianne if she arrived on an ordinary bicycle. She sighed and wheeled out her bike instead.

It felt strange to be doing this. Last time Marianne had ridden her bike, she had been on her way to school, with Joe pedaling beside her. Joe always made sure Marianne got safely to the girls' school, although Marianne was not sure that he always went on to the boys' school after that. Joe was not fond of school.

Joe would have believed me about Gammer! Marianne thought. He said worse things about Gammer than Mum did. And he was surely outside the spell, ten miles away at the Castle. Now *there* was a thought! But try Aunt Sue first.

As Mum came to the front door with the jar of balm, the bicycle obviously put her in mind of school too. "Remind me to beg us a lift to Hopton from your Uncle Lester," she said, putting the jar of balm into Marianne's bike basket. "We have to get there for your school uniform sometime this week. School starts again the week after this, doesn't it? Goodness *knows* how I'm to get Joe *his* new uniform, with him away working. He'll have grown a foot, I know."

This gave Marianne a sad feeling of urgency as she rode away up the hill. There would be no time for anything once she went back to school. She would have to get someone to believe her about Gammer *soon*, she thought, standing on her pedals to get up the steep part of the road by the church.

She saw the Reverend Pinhoe out of the corner of her eye as she puffed upward. He was in the churchyard by one of the graves, talking to someone very tall and gentlemanly. A stranger, which was odd. Pinhoes didn't exactly welcome strangers in the village. But Marianne was distracted then, by two furniture vans up ahead of her, each labeled PICKFORD & PALLEBRAS. Each van was pulled by two dray horses, and both drivers were cracking whips and shouting as they made the difficult turn in through the gates of Woods House. It looked as if the Yeldhams were moving in already.

Marianne put one foot on the ground when she came level with the gates—saying to herself it was not curiosity: she had to stop to get her breath—and watched men in green baize aprons spring down and unlatch the backs of the vans. The van she could see into best had some very nice Londonish furniture stacked inside it. She saw chairs with round backs and buttons, covered in moss green velvet, and a sideboard that Dad would have put his head on one side to admire greatly. Good old work—she could almost hear Dad saying it—beautiful marquetry.

She inherited that from Luke Pinhoe, Marianne thought. It somehow brought home to her that Irene really was a Pinhoe. And she's coming back home to live! Marianne thought, getting back on her bike. That's good.

She pedaled past the last few houses and came between the hedges, where the road bent. And there, coming toward her, were six other cyclists, all girls. As soon as they saw Marianne, they stopped and swung their cycles sideways in a herringbone pattern, blocking the road. Marianne recognized the one in front as Margot Farleigh and the next one as Margot's cousin Norma. She didn't know the names of the others, but she knew they were all Farleighs too, and probably best friends with one another because they all had the same hairstyle, very smooth and scraped back, with one little thin dangling plait down one cheek. Oh dear! she thought. She could smell, or feel—or whatever—that each girl had a spell of some kind in the basket on the front of her bike.

"Well, look who's here!" Margot Farleigh said jeeringly. "It's Gammer Pinhoe's little servant!"

"Off to Helm to put another ill-chancing on us, are you?" Norma asked.

"No, I'm not," Marianne said. "I never put a single ill-chance on anyone."

This caused a chorus of jeering laughs from all six girls. "Oh, didn't you?" Margot said, pretending to be surprised. "My mistake. You didn't bring us frogs, then, or fleas, or nits?"

"Or the rashes, or the flu and the whooping cough, I suppose?" Norma added.

At this, the rest began calling out, "Nor you didn't put ants in our cupboards, did you?" and "What about all the mud in our washing?" and "What made Gammer Norah swell up, then?" and "So you didn't make Dorothea fall in the pond—like hell you didn't!"

Marianne sagged against her bicycle, thinking, Oh lord! Gammer *has* been busy! "No, honestly," she said. "You see, Gammer's not right in her head, and—"

"Oh? Really?" Margot drawled.

"Excuses, excuses," said Norma.

"She's right enough in her head to flood all Farleigh houses knee deep in water!" Margot said. "*All* our houses, from Uphelm to Bowbridge. Not anyone else's, mark you. Our Gammer Norah's in a raving rage about it, let me tell you."

"She's not sent us the stomachache so far," Norma said. "Is that what you're bringing us now?"

Marianne knew they had a right to be angry. She began to say, "Look, I'm sorry—"

That was a mistake. But then anything she said would have been, Marianne knew. Margot said, "*Get* her, everyone!" and all the girls threw down their bicycles and went for Marianne.

She was kicked and punched and had her hair pulled, agonizingly. She tried to defend herself by making a bull-like rush at Margot, and went floundering among bicycles, tripping, crashing and being hit and pinched and scratched by any girl who could lay hands on her. Spell bags fell out of bicycle baskets and got trodden on. The air from hedge to hedge filled with strong white powder. Everyone was sneezing in it, but too angry to notice. Marianne threw punches in all directions, some of them magical, some with her fists, but this only made the Farleigh girls angrier than ever. She ended up crouching half underneath her own bicycle, while Margot jumped on it.

"That's *right*!" screamed the others. "Squash her! *Kill* her!"

"Here, here, *here*!" Joss Callow said loudly, riding up behind the fight. "Stop that at *once*, you girls! You hear me?"

Everyone turned round guiltily and stared at Joss Callow parking his bike meaningly against the hedge. Marianne stood up from under her bent bike. Her hair was all over her face and she could feel her lips swelling.

"Now what was this all about?" Joss said. "Eh?"

"*She* started it!" Margot said, pointing at Marianne. "The hateful little *slime*!"

"Yes, look what she did to me!" Norma said, holding out a torn sleeve.

"And she's *ruined* my bike!" said another girl. "She's *disgusting*!"

They all knew Joss because his mother lived in Helm St. Mary. He knew them too. He was not impressed. "Funny thing," he said. "I never see you girls except you're making trouble. Six to one is cowards' work in my book. Ride away home now."

"But we've got an errand to run—" Norma began, and stopped in dismay, looking at the burst spell bag under her feet. "Just look what she did to this!"

"I don't care what you think you're doing here," Joss said. "Go home."

"Who are you to tell us that?" Margot asked rudely.

"I mean what I say," Joss said. He nodded to each girl in turn and, as he nodded, each girl's hairstyle writhed on her head and stood itself straight up in the air. Hairgrips and rubber bands pinged off into the road. In instants, the hairstyles had become long, upright bundles on the top of heads, with the little pigtails waving off to one side like feelers.

All the girls clutched their heads. Several of them screamed. "I can't go home like *this*!" Norma wailed.

"People'll laugh!" Margot screeched. She took a double handful of her bushy Farleigh hair and tried to pull it down. It sprang upright again through her fingers.

"Yes," Joss said. "Everyone who sees you will laugh like a drain. And serve you right. It'll go down when you go into your own house, and not before. Now get going."

Sullenly, the girls picked up their bicycles and mounted them, snarling and complaining to one another when most of the mudguards proved to be loose. Norma said, among the clanking and clattering, "Why has he left *her* hair alone?"

As they rode off, looking long headed and decidedly peculiar, Margot answered loudly, "He's a mongrel half-Pinhoe, that's why."

She meant Joss to hear, and he did. He was not pleased. When Marianne said, "Joss, they were angry because Gammer's been putting spells on the Farleighs," he simply scowled at her.

"I'm not standing here to listen to accusations, Marianne," he said. "I don't care what it was about. I'll straighten your bike for you, but that's your lot."

He picked up Marianne's bicycle and, with a few expert twists and bangs and the same number of well-directed stabs of witchcraft, he straightened the bent frame and twisted pedals and made the wheels round again. Tears in Marianne's eyes distorted the sight of him putting the chain back on. Gammer has been *so* thorough! she thought. *No one* believes a word I say!

"There," Joss said, handing her the restored bike. "Now get wherever you were going, get your face seen to, and don't try insulting any Farleighs again." He picked up his own bike, swung his leg swiftly across the saddle, and rode away into the village before Marianne could think of what to say.

She stood in the road for a moment, softly weeping in a way she thoroughly despised. Then she pulled herself together and took a look at the little burst bags and the white powder from them lying in a trail across the road and dusting the hedges on either side. Those girls had been bringing some fierce stuff to wish on the Pinhoes. From the sore feeling down her back, Marianne was sure it was another illness of some kind. Luckily, it was so fierce that whoever sent it had made it so that it did not work until someone said the right word, but, even so, Marianne knew she ought not to leave it here. Someone could say the right word accidentally at any time.

Sighing, she laid her bike down and wondered how to deal with it. This was something Mum would have been better at than she was.

There was one thing she could do that might work. Marianne had not tried it very often because Mum had been so alarmed when she discovered Marianne could do it.

Marianne took a deep breath and, very carefully and gently, summoned fire. She summoned it to just the surface of the road and very tops of the leaves in the hedges. And in case that was not enough, she instructed it to burn every scrap of the powder wherever it was.

Little blue flames answered her, flickering an inch high over road, grassy banks, and hedges. Almost at once, the flames filled with tiny white sparks, hissing and fizzing. Then the powder underneath caught fire and burned with a most satisfactory snarling sound, like a bad-tempered dog. The six little bags went up with six soft powdery *whoomp*s and made clumps of flame that were more green than blue and sent up showers of the white sparks. Like a fireworks display, Marianne thought, except for the strong smell of dragon's blood. When she called the flames back, every scrap of the powder was gone and there was no sign of the bags.

"Good," Marianne said, and rode onward.

She must have been an alarming sight when she arrived at Great-Uncle Edgar's house, what with her swollen mouth, scratched face, and wild, pulled hair. Her knees were scraped too, and one of her arms. Great-Aunt Sue exclaimed when she opened the door.

"Good gracious, dear! Did you fall off your bicycle?"

Aunt Sue was so crisp and starched and orderly and looked so sympathetic that Marianne found she was crying again. She held out the jar of balm and gulped, "I'm afraid it got cracked."

"Never mind, never mind. I haven't finished the last one yet," Aunt Sue said. "Come on in and let me see to your scrapes." She led Marianne through to her neat and orderly kitchen, surrounded by Great-Uncle Edgar's five assorted dogs, all of them noisily glad to see Marianne, where she made Marianne sit on a stool and bathed her face and knees with some of Mum's herbal antiseptic. "What a mess!" she said. "Surely a big girl like you knows enough charms by now not to fall off a bike!"

"I didn't fall off." Marianne gulped. "There were some Farleigh girls—"

"Oh, come now, dear. You just told me you fell

off," Aunt Sue said. And before Marianne could explain, Aunt Sue hurried to fetch her a glass of milk and a plate of macaroons.

Aunt Sue's macaroons were always lovely, pale brown and crusty outside and softly white and luscious inside. Biting into the first one, Marianne discovered that one of her teeth was loose. She had to concentrate hard for nearly a minute to get it fixed back in again. By then she had completely lost her chance to point out to Aunt Sue that she had *not* said she had fallen off her bike, and that Aunt Sue had just assumed she had.

Nothing could make it clearer that Aunt Sue was not going to listen to her properly. But Marianne tried. "I met six Farleigh girls," she said carefully, when the tooth was firm again. "And they told me that Gammer has been sending them ill-chance spells. They've had frogs and nits and ants in their cupboards, and now they've got whooping cough too."

Great-Aunt Sue looked disgusted. She passed both hands down her crisply flounced skirt and said, "There's no believing how superstitious some of these country girls can be! It's amazed me ever since I came to live in Ulverscote. Anything that's caused by their own dirty habits—and the Farleighs are not a clean clan, dear—they try to blame on somebody's use of the craft. As if anyone would *stoop*—and certainly not your poor grandmother! She can barely walk these days, so Dinah tells me."

Marianne knew it was no good then, but she said, "Gammer sits there and does spells, Aunt Sue. Little cunning things that Aunt Dinah doesn't notice. The latest one was water."

"And what does she do with that? Cause a flood?" Aunt Sue asked, brightly and disbelievingly.

"Yes," Marianne said. "In all their houses. And mud in their washing."

Aunt Sue laughed. "Really, dear, you're as credulous as the Farleighs. Anyway, this whooping cough is simply a natural epidemic. It's all over the county now. Edgar tells me they have cases from Bowbridge to Hopton."

Spread by the widening rings of an ill-chance spell, before someone put a stop to the spell, Marianne thought. But she did not say so. There was no point, and she felt tired and sore and shaken. She sat quietly and politely on the stool and listened to Aunt Sue talking about all the things Aunt Sue always talked about.

Aunt Sue's two sons first, Damion and Raphael. Aunt Sue was very proud of them. They were both in Bowbridge, doing very well. Damion was an accountant and Raphael was an auctioneer. It was a pity they were both going bald so young, but baldness was in Aunt Sue's family and it always came from the female, didn't it?

Then the dogs. Mr. Vastion said they were all too fat and needed more exercise. But, said Aunt

Sue, how were they to get walked properly with Edgar so busy and the boys not at home anymore? Aunt Sue had enough to do in the house.

Then the house. Aunt Sue wanted new wallpaper. It was a lovely house, and Aunt Sue had never stopped being grateful to Gammer for giving it to them when Gaffer died. Gammer was so generous. She had given Uncle Arthur the Pinhoe Arms, Uncle Cedric the farm, and let Isaac have the smallholding. But truly, Marianne, this place was almost as run-down as Woods House.

Marianne looked round the bright, empty, efficient kitchen and wondered how Aunt Sue could think that. And for the first time, she wondered if all this property had been Gammer's to give away. If Dad was the one the property came to, shouldn't it have been *Dad* who gave it away? She thought she must ask Mum.

Aunt Sue said that she had booked Uncle Charles, over and over, to redecorate the house, but Uncle Charles always seemed to have something more urgent to do. And Aunt Sue was not going to employ anyone else, because Uncle Charles used the craft in his work, which made him quicker and neater than anyone in the county. But now he had gone to redecorate Woods House. Why should a newcomer, even if she was a Pinhoe born, have the right to take up Uncle Charles's time?

By this time, Marianne had had enough. She did not want to hear either Uncle Charles or the lovely Princess Irene being gently criticized by Aunt Sue. She stood up, thanked Aunt Sue politely, and said she had to be going now.

Meanwhile, Joss Callow arrived at the Pinhoe Arms, ready to report to Marianne's father. As he was parking his bike in the yard, little blue flames broke out all over the front of him, hissing and fizzing and sending out small white sparks. They squirted from under his boots and even sizzled for a moment on the front wheel of his bicycle. Joss beat at them, but they were gone by then.

"Have to do better than that, girls," he said, naturally thinking it was a revenge from Margot Farleigh and her friends.

Then he forgot about it and went into the Snug, where Harry Pinhoe was waiting for him and Arthur Pinhoe leaning through the hatch. "Search me what the Big Man's up to just now," he said, when he was comfortably settled with beer and pickled eggs. "He's very busy with something, but I don't know what. They've got all the old maps and documents out in their library and you can feel the magic they're using on them, but that's all I can tell you."

"Can't Joe tell you?" asked Joe's father, puffing at the pipe he allowed himself at these times.

"That Joe," said Joss, "is bloody useless, excuse my French. He's never *there*. I don't know what he does with his time, but I'm not the only one to complain. Mr. Frazier was about ready to blow his top yesterday when Joe went missing. And Mr. Stubbs was fit to kill, because he wanted an order taken to the butcher and Joe had vanished off the face of the earth."

Harry Pinhoe and Joe's uncle Arthur exchanged sad shrugs. Joe was always going to be a disappointment.

"Oh, that reminds me," Joss said. "Young Cat Chant—Eric, the nine-lifer, you know—has hatched an abomination somehow. Griffin, I think. I saw it this morning. I hardly knew what it was at first. It was all fluff and big feet, but it's got wings and a beak, so that's what it must be."

Uncle Arthur shook his head. "Bad. That's bad. We don't want one of those out."

"Not much we can do, if it's living in the Castle," Harry Pinhoe observed, puffing placidly. "We'd have to wait to catch it in the open."

"And when I asked him, this young Eric said your Marianne gave him the egg," Joss added.

"What?!" Harry Pinhoe was disturbed enough to let his pipe drop on the floor. Groping for it, red in the face, he said, "That egg was stored safe in the attic. It should have been safe there till Kingdom Come. I put the workings on it myself. I don't know what's got into Marianne lately. First she goes round telling everyone that poor Gammer's setting spells on the Farleighs, and now she does *this*!"

"She said that about Gammer to me too," said Joss. "She was in a hen fight with some Farleigh girls about it, out on the Helm road just now."

"Let her just wait!" Harry said. His face was still bright red. "I'll give her what for!"

All unknowing, Marianne free-wheeled down past the Pinhoe Arms, more or less at that moment. At the bottom of the hill, she braked, put one foot down, and stared. The expensive taxi from Uphelm was standing throbbing outside the house where Nicola lived. As Marianne stopped, Nicola's dad, who ought to have been working on the Post Office wall, hurried out of the house carrying Nicola wrapped in a mass of blankets and got into the taxi with her. Marianne could hear the wretched, whooping, choking breathing of Nicola from where she stood.

"Taking her to the hospital in Hopton," old Miss Callow said, standing watching. "Doctor says she'll die if they don't."

Nicola's mother, looking desperately anxious, hurried out of the house in her best hat, calling instructions over her shoulder to Nicola's eldest sister as she left. She climbed into the taxi too, and it drove away at once, faster than Marianne had ever seen it go.

Marianne rode on to Furze Cottage, almost crying again. It might have been the Farleighs who sent the whooping cough, but it was Gammer who had provoked them. As she wheeled her bike into the shed, she decided she would *have* to have another talk with Mum.

But that all went out of her mind when Dad—

red faced and furious—burst in through the front door as Marianne came through the back and began shouting at her at once. He began with, "What do you mean, giving away that egg?" and went on to say that Marianne was a worse disappointment than Joe was and, having torn her personality to shreds, accused her of spreading evil talk about Gammer. Finally he sent her to her room in disgrace.

Marianne sat there with Nutcase, doing her best to stop the tears trickling off her face onto Nutcase. "I was only trying to be brave and truthful," she said to Nutcase. "Does this happen to everyone who tries to do the right thing? Why does no one believe me?" She knew she would have to talk to Joe. He seemed to be the only person in the world who might listen to her.

14

❧✦❧

THE GRIFFIN BECAME very lively that day. He was also growing an odd small tuft of feathers on his head, like an untidy topknot.

"I think that is going to be his crest," Chrestomanci said when Janet asked. "I believe all griffins have one." Chrestomanci seemed to be taking as much interest in Klartch as everyone else. He came into the playroom—in a more than usually embroidered dressing gown—while Janet, Julia, and Cat were finishing breakfast, and kneeled down to inspect Klartch all over. "Accelerated growth," he said to Klartch. "You have a lot of magic, don't you? You've been held up in your egg for years, and you're trying to make up for lost time, I imagine. Don't overdo it, old fellow. By the way, where is Roger?"

Cat knew Roger was in that shed with Joe by now. Roger had snatched a piece of toast and raced away eating it, to get on with rebuilding the flying machine. But he had not *said* that was what he was going to do. Cat held his tongue and let Julia and Janet tell Chrestomanci that they had no idea where

Roger had gone. Luckily Chrestomanci seemed satisfied with this.

As soon as Chrestomanci had sailed away again, Klartch invited everyone for a romp. Cat was not sure how Klartch did this, but it was not long before all four of them were rolling about on the floor and leaping from the sofa to the chairs in a mad game of chase. This was when they discovered that griffins could laugh. Klartch laughed in small, chuckling giggles when Julia caught him, rolled him over, and tickled him, and he laughed in long hoots when Cat and Janet chased him round the sofa. Then Janet jumped on him and Klartch dodged. His long front claws caught in the carpet and tore three large strips out of it.

"Oh—oh!" they all said, Klartch included.

"And just look what that creature's done!" Mary the maid said, coming in to clear away the breakfast. "That's what comes of having a wild beast indoors."

Cat guiltily put the carpet back together. They collected three balls and a rubber ring from the cupboards and took Klartch out into the gardens instead. As soon as they came out onto the great smooth lawn, gardeners appeared from all directions and hurried toward them.

"Oh, they're not going to let us play!" Janet said.

But it was not so. They all wanted to see Klartch. "We heard no end about him," they explained. "Odd-looking beast, isn't he? Does he play?"

When Julia explained that playing was what they had come out to do, a gardener's boy ran and fetched a football.

Klartch pounced on it. All six of his front claws sank into it. The football gave out a sad hiss and went flat. Klartch and the gardener's boy both looked so miserable about it that Cat picked up the football and, after thinking hard, managed to mend it, blow it up again, and make it griffin-proof in future.

Then everyone, even the head gardener, joined in a game that Janet called Klartchball. The rules were a little vague and mostly involved everyone running about, while Klartch galloped and rolled and tripped other players up. It was such fun that Roger and Joe emerged from their shed and joined in for a while. The game only stopped when Klartch suddenly stood still, hunched himself, and rolled over on his side in the middle of the lawn.

"He's dead!" Julia said, appalled. "Daddy *told* him not to overdo things!"

They all raced over to Klartch, fearing Julia was right. But when they reached him, Klartch was breathing steadily and his eyes were shut. "He's asleep!" Cat said, hugely relieved.

"We forgot how young he really is," Janet said.

The gardeners put Klartch in a wheelbarrow and trundled him to the kitchen door. Klartch did not stir the entire time. They trundled him indoors and parked him in a pantry, where he slept until Mr. Stubbs had his lunch ready. Then he woke up eagerly and, instead of opening his beak and going "Weep!" he said, "Me!" and tried to eat the mince by himself.

"You *are* coming on well," Millie said to him admiringly. "Cat, at this rate, he won't be needing you to feed him in the night for much longer."

Cat did hope so. He was so sleepy most of the time that he was sure he would never manage to stay awake during lessons, when lessons started again.

The holidays were indeed almost over. The children's tutor, Michael Saunders, arrived back in the Castle that evening, keen and talkative as ever. He talked so much over supper that even Jason could hardly get a word in, let alone anyone else. Jason wanted to tell everyone about the changes they were making to Woods House, but Michael Saunders had been to the worlds in Series Eight to take the young dragon he had been rearing back into the wild, and he had a longer tale to tell.

"I had to take the wretched creature to Eight G in the end," he said. "We tried Eight B, where he came from, and all he would do was shiver and say the cold would kill him. Eight A's colder, so we went to C, D, and E, and C was too wet for him, D was too empty, and it was snowing when we got to E. I skipped F. There are more people there, and I could see he was itching for the chance to eat a few. So we went on to G, and he didn't like it there either. It began to dawn on me that the wretch was so pampered that nothing less than tropical was going to suit him. But G has equatorial forests, and I took him down there. He liked the climate all right, but he refused to catch his own food. All he would say was 'You do it.' I thought about it a bit, and then I trapped him one of the large beasts they call lumpen in that Series, and as soon as he was eating it, I left him to it and came away. If he wants to eat again, he'll have to hunt now—"

Here Michael Saunders noticed the way Roger, Janet, Julia, and Cat were all looking at him. He laughed. "Never fear," he said. "I don't intend to start giving you lessons until next Monday. I need a rest first. Nursemaiding a teenage dragon has worn me ragged."

In Cat's opinion, nursemaiding a baby griffin was quite as bad. He gave Klartch a large meal before he went to bed that night and fell asleep seriously hoping that Klartch would not wake up until the morning. It seemed a reasonable hope. When Cat put the light out, Klartch was lying on his back in his basket, with his tight, round stomach upward, snoring like a hive of bees.

But no. Around one o'clock in the morning, Mopsa's dabbing nose and treading paws woke Cat up. When he groaned and put the light on, there was Klartch, thin as a rake again, standing on his hind legs to look into Cat's face. "Food," he told Cat mournfully.

"All right." Cat sighed and got up.

It was a very messy business. Klartch insisted on feeding himself. Cat's main job seemed to be to scoop up dropped dinner and dump it back into Klartch's bowl for Klartch to spill again. Cat was sleepily scraping meat up from the carpet for the thirtieth time, when he heard a sharp tapping on the window. This was followed by a thump.

What have Roger and Joe done with their flying machine *this* time? he thought. Mad. They are quite *mad*! He went and opened the window.

A broomstick swooped inside with Marianne riding sidesaddle on it. Cat dodged it and stared at her. Seeing Cat, Marianne gave a cry of dismay, slipped off the broom, and sat down hard on the carpet. "Oh, I'm *sorry*!" she said. "I thought this was the attic!"

Cat caught the broomstick as it tried to fly away through the window again. "It's a tower room, really," he said as he shut the window to stop the broom escaping.

"But your light was on, and I thought it was bound to be Joe in here!" Marianne protested. "Which is Joe's attic, then? He's my brother, and I need to talk to him."

"Joe has one of the little rooms down by the kitchen," Cat told her.

"What—downstairs?" Marianne asked. Cat nodded. "I thought they always put servants in the attics," Marianne said. "*All* the way down?"

Cat nodded again. By this time he was awake

enough to be quite shocked at how pale and miserable Marianne looked. One side of her face was bruised and she had a big, sore-looking scrape across her mouth, as if someone had beaten her up recently.

"So I'd have to go down past all your wizards and enchanters to get to Joe?" she said dismally.

"I'm afraid so," Cat said.

"And I'm not sure I *dare*," Marianne said. "Oh, dear, why do I keep doing everything *wrong* just lately?"

Cat thought she was going to cry then. He could see her trying not to, and he had no idea what to say. Fortunately Klartch finished his meal just then—all of it that was in the bowl anyway—and came bumbling across the room to see why this new human was sitting dejectedly on the floor. Marianne stared, and stared more when Klartch caught one of his front talons on the carpet and fell on his beak beside her knees.

"Oh, I thought you were a dog! But you're *not*, are you?" Marianne put her hands under Klartch's face and helped him struggle to his feet. Then she helped him unhook his claw from the carpet. "You've got a beak," she said, "and I think you're growing wings."

"He's a griffin," Cat told her, glad of the interruption. "He's called Klartch. He hatched from that egg you gave me."

"Then it really *was* an egg!" Marianne was distracted from her troubles enough to kneel up and stroke Klartch's soft fluffy coat. "I wonder if they had that egg because we've got a griffin on the Pinhoe Arms. And a unicorn. My Uncle Charles painted both of them on the inn sign when he was young. Mind you," she told Klartch, "you've got a long way to go before you look like *our* griffin. You need some feathers, for a start."

"Growing some," Klartch said, rather offended.

At this Marianne said, just like Millie, "I didn't know they *talked*!"

"Learning," said Klartch.

"So perhaps it was worth it, giving the egg away," Marianne said sadly. "I don't think you were going to hatch where you were." She looked up at Cat, and a tear leaked its way down the swollen side of her face. "I got into terrible trouble for giving you his egg," she said. "And for trying to do what you said and tell the truth. Be confident, you know, how you said to me. No one in Ulverscote is speaking to me now."

Cat began to feel a slow, guilty responsibility. "I was saying it to myself too," he confessed. "What did I make you do?"

Marianne put her face up and pressed her scratched lips together, trying not to cry again. Then she burst into tears anyway. "Oh, drat it!" she sobbed. "I hate crying! It wasn't my fault, or yours. It was Gammer. But no one will believe me when I say it was her. Gammer's lost her mind, you see, and she keeps sending the Farleighs frogs and nits and things, and dirtying their washing and flooding their houses. So the Farleighs are furious. And *they* sent *us* bad luck and whooping cough. My distant cousin Nicola's been taken to hospital with it and they think she'll *die*! But Gammer's cast this spell on everyone so that no one will blame *her* for any of it."

Marianne was sobbing in such earnest now that Cat conjured her a pile of his handkerchiefs.

"Oh, *thanks*!" Marianne wept, pressing at least three of them to her wet face. She went on to describe the fight with the Farleigh girls and the way she had gotten rid of the white powder. "And that was silly of me," she sobbed, "but it was really *strong* and I had to do something about it. But Joss Callow had told Dad about the fight, and Dad shouted at me for insulting the Farleighs, and I *didn't*! I told Dad about the powder they were bringing, and he went up there this evening to see it and of course there wasn't any, because I'd burned it all, and he came back and shouted at me again for trying to stir up trouble—"

"What *was* the powder?" Cat asked.

"A bad disease with spots and sores," Marianne said, sniffing. "I think it may have been smallpox."

Ouch! Cat thought. He did not know much about diseases, but he knew *that* one. If it didn't kill you, it disfigured you for life. Those Farleigh girls had not been joking. "But wouldn't they have caught it too?"

"They must have made some immunity spells, I suppose," Marianne said. "But those wouldn't have stopped it spreading all over the county to people who haven't done a thing to the Farleighs. Oh, I don't know what to *do*! I want to ask Joe if he can think of a way to stop Gammer, or at least take off the spell she's got on everyone. I want *someone* to believe me!"

Cat thought about Joe, who had rather impressed him on the whole. Joe had brains. Marianne was probably right to think Joe would know what to do, except—there was this mad flying machine. Joe's head was, at the moment, literally in the clouds. "Joe's pretty busy just now," he said. "But I believe you. My sister was a witch who got out of hand like your Gammer. If you like, I could go and tell Chrestomanci."

Marianne looked up at him in horror. Klartch yelped as her hand closed on a fistful of his fluff. "Sorry," Marianne said, letting go of Klartch. "No! No, you can't tell the Big Man! Please! They'd all go *spare*! Pinhoes, Farleighs, Callows, everyone! You don't understand—we all keep hidden from him so he won't boss us about!"

"Oh," said Cat. "I didn't know." It seemed a bit silly to him. This was the kind of problem Chrestomanci could solve by more or less simply snapping his fingers. "He doesn't boss people unless they misuse witchcraft."

"Well, we *are* doing," Marianne said. "Or Gammer is. Think of something else."

Cat thought. He was so tired, that was the problem. And the more he cudgeled his sleepy brain, the more responsible he felt. There was no doubt that he had said just the one thing to Marianne likely to start her getting into the mess she was now in. He ought to help her, even though what he said had really been to tell himself something instead. But how was he to stop a witch war among people he didn't even know? Walk up to this Gammer person and put her in a stasis spell? Suppose he got the wrong old lady? He wanted to tell Marianne that it was hopeless, except that she was so upset that she had come miles at night on a broomstick. She must have sneaked off from her angry father to do it too. No, he had to think of something.

"All right," he said. "I'll think. But not now. I'm too sleepy. Klartch keeps needing to be fed in the night, you see. I'll have a real, serious think in the morning. Is there anywhere I can meet you to tell you any ideas I get?"

"Tomorrow?" Marianne said. "All right, as long as it's secret. I don't want Dad to know I talked to you—you're as bad as the Big Man to him. He says you're a nine-lifed enchanter too. I didn't know. I thought you were Irene's son. Can you get Irene to bring you to Woods House again? People from the Castle have to be with a Pinhoe to get there, you see. Otherwise they stop you and send you back here."

"I think so," said Cat. "She goes there most days with Jason. And I tell you what—I'll try to get Joe to come too if he's free. Meet me around midday. I have to think first, and exercise Syracuse."

Marianne looked puzzled. "I thought his name was Klartch."

"Syracuse," Cat explained, "is a horse. Klartch is this griffin. The cat sitting on my bed staring at you is Mopsa."

"Oh," said Marianne. She almost grinned. "You do seem to be surrounded in creatures. That's a dwimmer-thing, I think. I can tell you have quite strong dwimmer. See you tomorrow at midday, then." Looking much more cheerful, she scrambled up and stared round for her broomstick.

Cat plucked the broomstick away from the window and handed it politely to Marianne. "Will you be all right?" he asked, trying not to yawn. "It's pretty dark."

"As long as the owls miss me," Marianne said. "They never look where they're going. But if you had any idea how uncomfortable it is riding a broomstick, you wouldn't ask. I suppose one more set of bruises won't notice. See you." She sat herself sideways on the hovering broomstick. "Ouch," she said. "This is Mum's broom. It doesn't like me riding it."

Cat opened the window for her and Marianne swooped out through it, away into the night.

Cat stumbled back to bed. He had not a clue how to solve Marianne's problems. He simply hoped, as he pushed Mopsa out of the way, that a good idea came into his head while he was asleep. He was asleep the next second. He forgot to turn out the light. He did not see the offended way Mopsa jumped down and joined Klartch in his basket.

He woke—much too soon, it seemed—when Janet barged cheerfully into his room, saying, "Breakfast, Klartch. Come on down to the kitchen. I'm going to start house-training him today," she told the yawning Cat. "It *should* be all right if we can get downstairs fast enough."

When Janet and Klartch had crashed out of the room, Cat sat up, searching his sleepy brain for any ideas that might have landed in it during the night. There was one, but it struck him as very poor and stupid indeed, one only to be used if nothing else occurred to him. He got up and went along to have a shower, hoping that might liven his brain up a little. The water in the Castle was bespelled, and Cat had hopes of it.

But nothing happened. With only the poor, thin idea in his head, Cat got dressed and went downstairs. He met a strong disinfectant spell on the next flight down. This was followed by the angry clattering of a bucket and Janet's raised voice. "Purple nadgers, Euphemia! He's only a baby! And he's terribly ashamed. Just look at him!" It sounded as if Klartch had not gotten downstairs quite fast enough after all.

Cat grinned and galloped down the other set of stairs that led to the stable door. They came out past the cubbyhole where Joe was supposed to clean shoes. Rather to Cat's surprise, Joe was actually there, busily blacking a large boot.

Cat leaned into the little room. "Your sister was

here last night, trying to find you," he said. "She's got troubles. She says your Gammer is secretly putting spells on the Farleighs."

"Our Gammer?" Joe said, calmly rubbing away at the boot. "You must know she is. You saw me on my way to set the first spell for her, didn't you?"

"The tadpoles?" Cat said.

"Frogs," said Joe.

"Oh," Cat said. "Um. *Those* frogs. In Helm St. Mary?"

"That's right," Joe said. "Gammer said if I could get the one spell out for her, then she could follow the thread with a load of others, and if she did, it would work her free of the containment my dad had put on her. By-product, she called it. She pointed her stick at me to make me do it. And I didn't want to have rode all the way to Ulverscote for nothing and I knew Gaffer Farleigh did put an addle spell on her—Marianne swears he did, and she knows—so I took the jar to Helm St. Mary and tipped it into their duck pond there for her."

Cat was hugely relieved. He had no need to use his poor, thin idea. Joe could solve Marianne's problems with a word. "Then do you think you could come to Ulverscote with me this morning and tell your father? Marianne says Gammer's set a spell on everyone so that they don't believe her and the Farleighs are sending them plagues in revenge."

Joe's head went sulkily down as he pondered. He shrugged. "If Gammer's done that, then they won't believe me neither, not if they don't believe

Marianne. She's strong in the craft, Gammer is, and I'm no one. Besides, Mr. Frazier says he'll have me up before the Big Man if I don't stay here where I'm paid to be. *And* just when we've got our machine near perfect! No. Sorry. Can't oblige you."

And, to prove that Joe was not just making excuses, Mr. Frazier came along the kitchen corridor just then, saying, "Joe Pinhoe, are you working? Master Cat, I'll trouble you not to interrupt Joe in his work. We're privileged today. Master Pinhoe has actually cleaned a boot."

"Just going," Cat told Mr. Frazier. He leaned farther into the cubbyhole and asked, "Is Mr. Farleigh the gamekeeper any relation to the Farleighs who got the frogs?"

"Jed Farleigh," said Joe. "He's their Gaffer." Hearing Mr. Frazier treading closer, he picked up two more boots and tried to look as if he was cleaning all three at once.

Cat said "Thanks" to him and hurried toward the stables, thinking. If he understood rightly, these Gammers and Gaffers were the heads of these tribes of witchy people, and if Mr. Farleigh the gamekeeper was one, the whole thing was much more frightening than Cat had realized. No wonder Marianne had been so upset. And here was he, Cat, with only one poor, second-rate idea to put against it all. Joe was no help. Cat hurried out into the yard, feeling small and weak and heartily wishing he had not agreed to help Marianne.

As Cat crossed the yard, Jason came out of his

herb shed with a stack of flat wooden boxes. Cat went over to him. Jason, by the time Cat reached him, was standing on one leg, holding the boxes on one knee while he locked the shed. He spared Cat a harried smile. "What can I do for you, young nine-lifer?" The smells of many kinds of herbs, faint and sweet or rich and spicy, swam round the pair of them.

"Can you give me a lift to Woods House today?" Cat asked.

"Well, I *could*," Jason said, "but you'd have to find your own way back. We're moving in there for good today. Irene's busy packing."

Cat had not realized that things had moved on so quickly. He was quite taken aback. But he supposed that when an enchanter did things, he did them more swiftly than other people. And he was going to miss Irene. "Not to worry, then," he said. "Thanks."

He stood aside and watched Jason carry the boxes away across the yard. That did it, then. He was let off. But somehow that did not make him terribly happy. Marianne would be expecting him. He would have let her down. No, he would have to find a way to get to Ulverscote on his own. It was a pity that he had such a poor, thin idea to take there.

He could teleport, he thought, there and back. That ought to been easy, but for the misdirection spell—and then there was that barrier. If he tried it without one of the Pinhoes, he could end up caught behind the barrier like Chrestomanci. Better think of some other way. Cat walked slowly over to Syracuse's stall to tell it to muck itself out, considering.

Joss Callow met him as he got there. "When you're ready, we'll ride out over the heath," he told Cat. "Half an hour?"

Cat's mind had this way of making plans without Cat knowing it was. "Can you make it later than that?" he asked, without having to think. "Jason and Irene are leaving today and I'll need to say good-bye."

"Suits me," Joss said. "I've plenty to do here. Eleven o'clock, then?"

"Fine," Cat said gratefully. While he cleaned the stall and gave Syracuse his morning peppermint, he found out what he meant to do. His mind had it all neatly worked out. He was going to ride to Ulverscote on Syracuse, and the way to make sure he got there was to follow the river. He was fairly sure the same river ran past the Castle and through Ulverscote. And, surely, even the most secretive of Pinhoes and the angriest of Farleighs could not change the way a river ran. They might deceive him into *thinking* it ran the other way, but Cat was fairly sure he could guard against that if he kept his witch sight firmly on the way it was *really* flowing.

Cat gave Syracuse a pat and a strong promise to ride him later and went indoors. Before he went upstairs to the playroom for breakfast, he dodged into the library where, much to the surprise of old Miss Rosalie, the Castle librarian, he asked for a map of the country between the Castle and Ulverscote.

"I don't understand this," Miss Rosalie grumbled, spreading the map out on a table for him. "*Everyone* seems to want this map at the moment. Jason, Tom, Bernard, Chrestomanci, Millie, Roger. Now you."

Miss Rosalie always grumbled. She thought all books and maps should be on shelves. Cat paid no attention to her. He leaned over the map and carefully followed the wavy blue line of the river as it snaked through its steep valley beside the Castle. Sure enough, the valley, and the river with it, curved its way on, around the hill with Ulverscote Wood on it, and ran along the bottom of the slope where Ulverscote village was. By that stage, the valley was a simple dip, but it was the same river. Cat's brain had gotten it right. He thanked Miss Rosalie and raced away.

In the schoolroom, Klartch was sitting on the sofa trying very seriously to eat a banana. "He's in disgrace," Euphemia snapped, banging toast and coffee down in front of Cat. "Don't you go and be nice to him."

While Janet was loudly protesting that Klartch was only a baby and that the way to teach babies was to be nice to them, Julia said to Cat, "Jason and Irene are moving out today, did you know? Are you coming down to the hall to say good-bye to them?"

Cat nodded. His mind was busy with the problem of how to get rid of Joss without making Joss suspicious. He thought he had it.

Julia said, "Roger?"

Roger just grunted. He was busy making diagrams on scraps of paper. He had been doing this at every meal for weeks now. Julia looked at the ceiling. "Boys! Honestly!"

Here Chrestomanci sailed in, wearing a kingly red dressing gown with ermine down the front. He took a long stride and got the banana skin away from Klartch just as Klartch tried to eat it. "I think not," he said. "We don't want any more accidents on the stairs."

"Good morning, Daddy," Julia said. "Why does everyone always have their minds on something *else*?"

"A good question," Chrestomanci said, tossing the banana skin into the air. It disappeared. "I suppose it must be because we all have a lot to think about. Roger." Roger looked up guiltily. The scraps of paper had somehow disappeared, like the banana skin. "Roger, I need to talk to you," Chrestomanci said, "on a matter of some urgency. Can you come with me to my study, please."

Roger got up, looking pale and apprehensive. Chrestomanci politely ushered him out of the schoolroom ahead of himself and gently closed the door behind them both. The other three looked at one another, glanced at Euphemia, and decided to say nothing.

Roger had still not come back when everyone gathered in the hall to say good-bye to Irene and Jason. He and Chrestomanci were almost the only people missing.

"Never mind," Jason said, shaking hands with Millie. "We'll see him when we give our house-warming party."

"I'll make sure he's there," Millie said. "Jason, it's been a pleasure having you."

Jason went round shaking hands with everyone. Irene followed, hugging people. Cat stood a little back from the throng. He was engaged in the most delicate piece of long-distance magic he had ever done, trying to make Joss's big brown horse lose a shoe in a way that looked completely natural, without hurting the horse. He took its off hind foot up in imaginary hands and gently prized at the long iron nails that held the shoe on, going round them each several times, easing them out a bit at a time, until the horseshoe was hanging away from the hoof. Then he gave the horseshoe a sharp sideways push. It flew off. At least Cat thought it did. He certainly felt the horse give a jump of surprise. He let its foot carefully down. Then he picked the shoe up in imaginary hands and looked at it with imaginary eyes. Good. All the nails were most satisfactorily bent, as if the horse itself had twisted the horseshoe off. He tossed the shoe into a corner of the stall so that the horse was less likely to tread on it and injure itself.

He came back to himself to find Irene hugging him. "You're very quiet, Cat. Is something wrong?" she asked. There were scents around Cat of spice and flowers. Irene always smelled lovely.

"I shall miss you," Cat said truthfully. "May I

come and visit you later today, or will you be too busy?"

"Oh, what a nice idea!" Irene said. "Be our first visitor, Cat. I'm longing to show off what we've done to the house. But make it after midday so that we can unpack a little first."

Cat grinned a trifle anxiously as he shook hands with Jason. How soon would Joss notice that missing horseshoe? He hadn't yet. Perhaps the shoe hadn't really come off. It was often quite hard to tell if magic had worked or not.

He came to the door with everyone else and watched as Jason and Irene climbed into the small blue car. They could not have fitted Cat into it anyway. There was luggage strapped all over it and more piled into the backseat, with Jason's herb boxes on top of that. They drove off in a waft of blue smoke, herb scent, and Irene scent, waving joyously as they vanished down the drive.

"I think they'll be very happy," Millie said. "And I'm longing to see their house. I think I shall drive over there as soon as they're settled in."

She won't get there, Cat thought, without a Pinhoe to take her. I wonder what will happen then. He was edging away as he thought, wondering more about that horseshoe than about Millie. As soon as no one was looking at him, he turned and ran for the stables. It was nowhere near eleven yet, but he had to know.

He got there just as Joss was leading the big brown horse out through the stableyard gate. "Cast a shoe," Joss called over his shoulder to Cat. "I have to get him down to the blacksmith before we can ride out. So don't hold your breath. We could be gone hours if the forge is busy. I'll send someone to tell you when I'm back. All right?"

"All right," Cat said, trying not to look as relieved and joyful as he felt.

❧⋆❧

15

Marianne was having even more difficulty getting away than Cat was. She was in such disgrace at home that Mum was making her do all sorts of chores in order to keep Marianne under her eye.

"I'm not having you going round spreading any more tales," Mum said. "If you've cleaned your room, you can come and sort these herbs and worts for me now. Throw out any leaves and berries that look manky. Then put worts in this bowl and just the fresh tips of the leaves in that one. And I want it done right, Marianne."

As if I was four years old again! Marianne thought. I *know* how to sort herbs, Mum! It looked as if she was *never* going to get out of the house today. The only good thing about today was that, thanks to Mum's lotions, Marianne's bruises and scrapes had almost disappeared in the night. But what was the good of that when she was a prisoner? Marianne sighed as she spread the fresh green bundles of plants apart on the table. Nutcase jumped up beside her and rubbed sympathetically against her arm. Marianne looked at him. Now *there* was an idea. If she could persuade Nutcase to wander off again . . .

"Go and visit Woods House, Nutcase," she whispered to him. "Why don't you? You *like* going there. Go on. As a favor to me? Please?"

Nutcase moved his ears and twitched his tail and stayed sitting on the table. But I live *here* now, he seemed to be saying.

"Oh, I *know* you do, but pay a visit to Woods House anyway," Marianne said. She opened the side window and put Nutcase out through it.

Two minutes later, Nutcase came in through the back door with Mum when she brought in an armful of plants and unloaded them in the sink to be cleaned. He jumped onto the drainboard and gave Marianne a smug look.

As soon as Mum had gone out into the garden again, Marianne picked Nutcase up and carried him through the house to the front door. She opened the door and dumped him on the path outside. "Go to Woods House!" she whispered fiercely to him.

Nutcase's reply was to sit in the middle of the tiny front lawn, stick a leg up, and wash. Marianne shut the front door, hoping he would leave when he was ready.

Five minutes later, Nutcase came in through the back door again, with Mum and another bundle of herbs.

This is *hopeless*! Marianne thought, while Mum ran water in the sink. I shall just have to walk off without an excuse and get into worse trouble than ever. Wasn't there *any* way she could tempt Nutcase to Woods House? Could she do something like the bacon spell she had tempted him with, the time she gave Cat the egg? But I can't do that from *here*, she thought, right at the other end of the village. Or could she? When she looked at Woods House in a special, witchy way, she could feel that the bacon spell was still there. It only needed reactivating. But could she manage to start it up again from here, strongly enough to tempt Nutcase all the way from Furze Cottage? No, I'm not strong enough, she thought.

But Cat had said she *was*. He had said she had nearly enchanter-strength magic but just didn't trust herself. He had made her bold enough to get into this trouble. Surely she could be bold enough to get herself out of it.

All right, she said to herself. I'll try.

Marianne nipped the last fresh leaf tips into the bowl and concentrated. And concentrated. And trusted herself and concentrated some more. It was odd. She felt as if each new push she gave herself spread her mind out, wider, and then wider still, until she almost seemed to be hovering beside the faded remains of the bacon spell in the hall of Woods House. She gave it a flip and brought it to life again, and then a further flip to make it stronger—or she hoped she did. It was so hard to tell for sure.

But look at Nutcase!

Nutcase's head went up and then went up farther, until he was nose upward, sniffing. Marianne watched him, hardly daring to breathe. Nutcase gave himself a shake and got up and stretched, front legs first, then back legs. Then, to Marianne's acute amazement, Nutcase really did walk through the kitchen wall. He trod toward the wall, steadily and deliberately, but when his head touched the whitewashed bricks, he didn't stop. He didn't even slow down. He walked on. His head disappeared into the wall, then his shoulder ruff, then most of his body, until he was just a pair of black, walking hind legs and a tail. The legs walked out of sight and left only the bushy, waving tail. Then there was only the tip of the tail, which vanished with a jerk, as if Nutcase had given a pull to fetch it through. Marianne was left staring at the bricks of the wall. There was no sign of the place where Nutcase had gone through. Well, well! she thought.

She gave Nutcase ten minutes to get on his way. Then, when Mum came in from the garden again, she said, "Mum, have you got Nutcase?" She was surprised how natural she sounded.

Mum said, "No. I thought he was with you. Oh—*bother*!"

They searched the house as they always did, then Dolly's stall, because Dolly and Nutcase seemed to have struck up a friendship, and then they went to Dad's work shed and asked if Nutcase was there. Of course Nutcase was in none of these places. Mum said, "Better go after him quick, Marianne. If he gets down to the Dell again and your Uncle Isaac finds him, there'll be hell to pay. Hurry. Get a wiggle on, girl!"

Marianne shot out of Furze Cottage, delighted.

At the top of Furze Lane, the men building the Post Office wall all pointed uphill with their thumbs, grinning. "Off again. Went that way."

It was a relief that Nutcase had not suddenly decided to visit the Dell instead. Marianne turned uphill. There was no Nicola to shout to her where Nutcase had gone, but Nicola's mum was standing in her doorway. She pointed uphill and nodded to Marianne.

Marianne hovered backward on one foot for a second. "How's Nicola?"

Nicola's mother put one hand out and made swaying motions with it. "We're hoping."

"Me too!" Marianne said, and went on, past the grocer, past the Pinhoe Arms and then the church.

The big gates to Woods House, when she came to them, seemed really strange, newly mended, newly painted, and shut. Marianne had never known those gates to be shut since Gaffer died. It felt odd to have to open one half of the gates and slip round it into the driveway. The overgrown bushes there seemed to have been cut back a bit. They gave Marianne a sight of the front door long before she was used to seeing it. A small, battered blue car was parked outside.

Oh, they're here! Marianne thought. She suddenly felt a total trespasser. This was not one of the family houses anymore. She had had no business arranging to meet Cat here. And she would have to knock at the front door—which was now painted a smooth olive green—and ask for Nutcase.

Marianne found she could not face doing this. She sheered away round the house into the garden, hoping Nutcase had gone to sun himself there. She could always say, quite truthfully, that she was looking for Gammer's cat if anyone asked, and it was always possible that Cat would see her out of one of the windows—always supposing Cat was here, of course.

The garden was transformed.

Marianne stood for a moment in amazement, looking from the smoothly trimmed square shape of the beech hedge to the lawn that was almost a lawn again. Someone had scythed and then mowed the long grass. It still had a stubbly gray look, but green was pushing through in emerald lines and ovals, showing where there had once been flower beds. Marianne went along the trim hedge, pretending to look into it for Nutcase, and marveling. The gooseberry bushes at the end, where the wood began, had been cleared and pruned, along with the old lilac trees behind them. No sign of Nutcase there. But there had been currant bushes there all these years, and Marianne had never known, and a stand of raspberry canes that still had raspberries on them. When she turned alongside the canes—keeping to the edges just like a cat might—she saw that the long flower bed against the wall that hid the vegetable garden actually had flowers in it now: long holly-hocks, asters, dahlias, and montbretia mostly at this time of year, but enough to make it look like a flower bed again.

She slipped guiltily round the end of the wall and found that the vegetable garden was most transformed of all. It was like Uncle Isaac's professional market garden. Everything was in neat rows in moist black earth, pale lettuces, frilly carrots, spiky onions. A lot of the beds were plain black earth with string stretched along, where seeds had not yet come up. And—Marianne stared around—she had not known that the walls had roses trained along them. They had always seemed a mass of green creeper. But this had been pared away and the roses tied back, and they were just now coming into bloom, red and peach colored and yellow and white, as if it were June, not nearly September.

Marianne crunched her way timidly down a newly cindered path toward the house. I'm looking for my cat when somebody asks. When she reached the archway beside the conservatory, she peered cautiously through.

The little man energetically digging in Old Gaffer's herb patch drove his spade to a standstill beside the tall mugwort and smiled at her. "Made a bit of a change here," he remarked to her. "How do you like it?"

Marianne could not help staring at him, even while she was smiling back. He was so small, so bandy, and so brown. His hair grew in tufts round his bald head and his wrinkly face had two tufts of beard on it, just under his large ears. If there were such things as gnomes, Marianne thought, she would be sure he was one. But his smile was beaming, friendly, and full of pride in his gardening. Her own smile enlarged to beaming in reply. "You've done so *much*! In no time at all!"

"It was the dream of my life," he said, "to work in a country garden. Mistress Irene, bless her, promised me that I should, and she kept her promise as you see. I've hardly started yet. August's not the best time to dig and sow, but I reckon that if I can get it all in good heart by the autumn, then when spring comes, I can *really* begin. They call me Mr. Adams, by the way. And you are?"

"Marianne Pinhoe," said Marianne.

"Oh," said Mr. Adams, "then you're quite a personage around here, as I read it."

Marianne made a face. "Not so's you'd notice. I—er—came looking for my cat."

"Nutcase," said Mr. Adams. "In the house. He went past me into the conservatory five minutes ago. Before you go in, come and look how your grandfather's herb bed's coming along. It went against the grain with me to leave it till last, when it's so near the house, but I had to wait for Mr. Yeldham to come and tell me which were the weeds. Awful lot of strange plants here."

He beckoned to Marianne so imperiously that she came nervously out from the archway, to find the big plot looking almost as she remembered it from Gaffer's time: low cushions of plants round the edges, tall gangly ones near the middle, and medium-sized ones in between, each one carefully placed in sun or shade as it needed, and growing in different-colored earths that were right for them. The spicy whiffs of scent made her throat ache, remembering her Old Gaffer.

She smiled down at Mr. Adams. She was a lot taller than he was. "You've made this almost how it should be, Mr. Adams. It's wonderful."

"For my pleasure," he said. "And to be worthy of Princess Irene."

Thoroughly surprised, Marianne said, "I call her that too!"

Cat rode quite slowly along the river path, so that Syracuse waltzed and bounced, wanting to go faster. Even after galloping round the paddock before they set out, Syracuse was still bored by walking.

They were going the same way that the river flowed, and Cat kept firmly remembering this. The water had already tried to deceive him twice by seeming to flow the other way. Last spring, when Mr. Saunders had been teaching him how you used witch sight, Cat had been rather bored. It had seemed so obvious. Now he was glad of those lessons. The lessons had not been so much about how you saw things truthfully when they were bespelled—Cat could do that standing on his head—but about how to *keep* seeing them when other spells were trying to distract you. Mr.

Saunders, being the keen, fierce kind of teacher he was, had invented a dozen fiendish ways to take Cat's mind off what he was seeing. Cat had hated it. But now it was paying off.

Cat kept that river firmly under his witch sight and did not allow it to get away once. He did not look at the surrounding valley at all. Now he was warned, he could feel it swirling about, trying to suggest he was going the wrong way.

Thanks to Syracuse, he could attend to the valley by smelling it instead of looking. The scents of water, rushes, willows, and the tall meadows had changed quite a lot in the short time since he had last come this way with Joss. The spiciness was damper, sadder, and smokier and smelled of summer giving way to autumn. Cat surprised himself by thinking that a year was really a short time. Things changed so *fast*. Which was silly, he thought, almost getting distracted, because you could do so much in a year.

Mr. Farleigh was suddenly standing in front of them in the path.

He was there so abruptly and unexpectedly—and so solidly—that Syracuse was startled into trying to rear. There was a difficult few seconds when Cat nearly fell off and Syracuse's back hooves walked off the path and squelched among the rushes. Cat managed to keep himself in the saddle and Syracuse right way up, but only with a frenzy of magic and of spells he had no idea he knew. Mr. Farleigh watched his struggles sarcastically.

"I told you not to come here," he said, as soon as

Syracuse's front hooves were on the ground again.

Cat was quite angry by then. It was an unusual experience for him. Up to now, when things happened that would have made most people angry, Cat had just felt bewildered. But now, he faced Mr. Farleigh's pale-eyed glare and was surprised to find himself filled with real fury. The man could have hurt Syracuse. "This is a public bridle way," he said. "You've no right to tell me not to use it."

"Then use it to go home on," Mr. Farleigh said, "and I'll not turn you back."

"But I don't want to turn back," Cat said with his teeth clenched. "How do you think you can stop me going on?"

"With the weight of this whole county," Mr. Farleigh said. "I carry it with me, boy."

He did, too, in some odd way, Cat realized. Though Syracuse was trampling and sidling, highly disturbed by the magic Cat had used, Cat managed a small push of power toward Mr. Farleigh. He met a resistance that felt as old as granite, and as gnarled and nonhuman as a tree that was petrified and turned to stone. The stony roots of Mr. Farleigh seemed to have twined and clamped themselves into the earth for miles around.

Cat sat back in his saddle wondering what to do. He was *not* going to go tamely back to the Castle, just because a bullying witchmaster with a gun told him to.

"*Why* don't you want me to ride this way?" he asked.

Mr. Farleigh's strange pale eyes glowered at him from under his bushy brows. "Because you mess up my arrangements," he said. "You have no true belief. You trespass and you trample and you unveil that which should be hidden. You try to release what should be safely imprisoned."

It sounded religious to Cat. He bent forward to pat Syracuse's tossing head and wondered how to say that he had not done any of these things. As to Mr. Farleigh's arrangements, he should just make them some other way! People should be allowed to ride where they wanted.

He was just deciding that there was no way to say this politely, and he had opened his mouth to be rude, when he was interrupted by a most unusual set of sounds coming from somewhere behind his right shoulder. There were voices, chattering, singing, and murmuring, as if quite a large crowd of people were walking along the top of the meadows. This noise was mixed with a strange, shrill whispering, which was combined with creakings and clatterings and a wooden thumping. Cat's head swiveled to see what on earth it was.

It was the flying machine. It was coming slowly across the top of the meadow about a hundred yards away and about twenty feet in the air. And it was the most peculiar object Cat had seen in his life. To either side of it, a jointed set of broken tables slowly flapped. Something that looked like a three-legged stool whirled furiously on its nose. The rest of it looked like a tangle of broken chairs all loosely hooked together, with each bit of it working and waving and making little flaps of wood go in and out. It had a long feather duster for a tail. In the midst of it, Cat could just see the dismantled frames of two bicycles and two people on them, pedaling madly. And every bit of this strange contraption was calling out as it came, "I belong to Chrestomanci Castle, I belong to Chrestomanci Castle!" high, low, shrill, and steady.

Mr. Farleigh said, in a voice that was almost a groan, "The very air is not safe from them!" Cat's head whipped back to find Mr. Farleigh staring up at the machine in horror. As Cat looked, Mr. Farleigh pulled something on his gun and raised it.

The gun barrel moved to track the flying machine and, before Cat could do more than put one hand out and shout, *"No!,"* Mr. Farleigh fired.

Cat thought there was a yell from the machine. But the *crack-bang!* of the shot sent Syracuse into a panic. He squealed and reared in earnest. Cat found himself clinging to a vertical horse and fighting to keep Syracuse's trampling back hooves from going into the river. He saw everything in snatches, among flying horsehair and clods of mud and grass splashing into the water, but he saw Mr. Farleigh slam another cartridge into his gun and he saw, uphill, the flying machine tipping to one side so that one set of flapping tables almost brushed the grass.

Then Syracuse came down, quivering with terror. Cat saw the flying machine right itself with a clap and a clatter. Then it was off, with astonishing speed, tables flapping, feather duster wagging, boys' feet flashing round and round. It had slipped over the top of the hill and vanished from sight before Mr. Farleigh could raise his gun again.

While Mr. Farleigh lowered his gun, looking grim and frustrated, Cat patted Syracuse and pulled his ear to quiet him. He said to Mr. Farleigh, "That would have been murder." He was surprised that his voice came out firm and angry and hardly frightened at all.

Mr. Farleigh gave him a contemptuous look. "It was an abomination," he said.

"No, it was a flying machine," Cat said. "There were two people in it."

Mr. Farleigh paid no attention. He looked beyond Cat and seemed horrified again. "Here is another abomination!" he said. He lowered his gun farther and aimed at the path behind Cat.

Cat snatched a look behind him. To his terror, he found that Klartch had followed them. Klartch was standing in the path with his beak open and his small triangular wings raised, obviously paralyzed with fear. Without having to think, Cat put out his left hand and rolled the barrel of Mr. Farleigh's gun up like a party whistle or a Swiss roll.

"If you fire now, it'll blow your face off!" he said. He was truly angry by then.

Mr. Farleigh looked grimly down at his rolled-up gun. He looked up at Cat with his bushy eyebrows raised and gave him a sarcastic stare. The gun, slowly, started to unroll again.

Behind Cat, Klartch went "Weep, weep, weep!" Syracuse shook all over.

What shall I do? Cat thought. He knew, as clearly as if Mr. Farleigh had just said so, that after he had shot Klartch, Mr. Farleigh would shoot Syracuse and then Cat, because Cat was a witness and Syracuse was in the way. He had to do something.

He pushed at Mr. Farleigh with his left hand out and came up against flinty, knotty power, like an oak tree turned to stone. Cat could not move it. And the gun steadily unrolled. Mr. Farleigh stared at Cat across it, immovable and contemptuous. He seemed to be saying, *You can do nothing.*

Yes, I *can!* Cat thought. I must, I *will!* Or Klartch and Syracuse will be dead. At least I've still got three lives left.

The thought of those three lives steadied him. When Mr. Farleigh shot him, Cat would still be alive, on his eighth life, just like Chrestomanci was, and he could do something then. All the things he had been taught by Chrestomanci surged about in his head. There must be *something* Chrestomanci had said— Yes, there was! After Cat had sent Joe to the ceiling, Chrestomanci had said, "Even the strongest enchanter can be defeated by using his own strength against him." So instead of pushing *against* Mr. Farleigh's heavy, stony power, suppose Cat pushed *with* it? And quick, because the gun was nearly unrolled.

Then it was not difficult at all. Cat pushed out

hard with his left hand and made Mr. Farleigh into a petrified oak tree.

It was a weird thing. It stood nine feet high, made of bent and twisted gray rock, and it had huge and knotty roots that had somehow delved and gouged their way into the earth of the path where it stood. It had a broken-looking hump at the top, which had probably been Mr. Farleigh's head, and three lumpy, writhen branches. One branch must have been the gun, because the other two had stone oak leaves clinging to them, each leaf with a glitter of mica to it.

Syracuse hated it. His front feet danced this way and that, trying to take him away from it. Klartch gave out another frightened "Weep, weep!"

"It's all right," Cat said to both of them. "It won't hurt you now. Honestly." He got down from Syracuse and found he was shaking as badly as the horse was. Klartch crept up to him, shaking too. "I *wish* you hadn't followed me," Cat said to him. "You nearly got killed."

"Need to come too," Klartch said.

Cat had half a mind to take them all back home to the Castle. But he had promised to meet Marianne and they were well over halfway by now. And he could tell, by the sound of the river and the feel of the meadow, that Mr. Farleigh had been the center that held the misdirection spells together. They were so weak now that they were almost gone. It would be easy to get to Woods House, except for— Cat looked up at the ugly stone oak, looming above them. There would be no getting Syracuse past that thing, he knew. Besides, it was right in the path and a terrible nuisance to anyone trying to go this way.

Cat steadied his trembling knees and sent the stone oak away somewhere else, somewhere it fitted in better, he had no idea where. It went with a soft rumble like thunder far off, followed by a small breeze full of dust from the path, river smell, and bird noises. The willows rattled their leaves in it. For a moment, there were deep trenches in the path where the stone roots had been, but they began filling in almost at once. Sand and earth poured into the holes like water, and then hardened.

Cat waited until the path was back to the way it had been and then levitated Klartch up into Syracuse's saddle. Klartch flopped across it with a gasp of surprise. One pair of legs hung down on each side, helplessly. Syracuse craned his head round and stared.

"It's the best I can do," Cat said to them. "Come on. Let's go."

16

❦

MARIANNE LOOKED UP gladly as Cat came across the stubbly lawn, leading Syracuse. She was sad to see that Joe was not with him, but at least Cat was here. She had begun to think he was not coming.

"Friend of yours?" asked talkative Mr. Adams. "That's a fine piece of horseflesh he's got there. Arab ancestry, I shouldn't wonder. What's he got on the saddle?"

Marianne wondered too, until Cat came near. She saw that Cat stared at Mr. Adams much as she had done herself. "Oh, you've brought Klartch!" she said.

"He followed me. I had to bring him," Cat said. He did not feel like explaining how lethal that had nearly been.

"I love your horse," Marianne said. "He's beautiful." She went boldly up to rub Syracuse's face. Cat watched a little anxiously, knowing what Syracuse could be like. But Syracuse graciously allowed Marianne to rub his nose and then pat his neck, and Marianne said, "Ah, you like peppermints, do you? I'm afraid I—"

"Here you are," Mr. Adams said, producing a paper bag from an earthy pocket. "These are extra strong—he'll like these. They call me Mr. Adams," he added to Cat. "Been in Princess Irene's family for years."

"How do you do?" Cat said politely, wondering how he would get a private word with Marianne with Mr. Adams there. While Marianne fed Syracuse peppermints, he hauled Klartch off the saddle and dropped him in the grass—with a grunt from both of them: Klartch was heavy and landed heavily. Mr. Adams stared at Klartch in some perplexity.

"I give up," he said. "Is it a flying bird-dog, or what?"

"He's a baby griffin," Cat explained. He tried to smile at Mr. Adams, but the word *flying* made him terribly anxious suddenly about Roger and Joe, and the smile was more of a grimace. He didn't think that Mr. Farleigh's bullet had hit either of them, but it had certainly hit the flying machine somewhere, and one of them had yelled. Still, there was nothing he could do.

"Shall I look after the horse for you while you go indoors?" Mr. Adams offered. "Second to gardening, I love tending to horses. He'll be safe with me."

Cat and Marianne exchanged relieved looks. Marianne had been wondering how they were going to talk in private too.

"I'll look after this griffin fellow too, if you like," Mr. Adams offered.

"Thanks. I'll take Klartch with me," Cat said. He did not feel like letting Klartch out of his sight just then. He handed Syracuse over to Mr. Adams and managed to thank him, although he was nervous again, knowing what Syracuse could be like. But Syracuse bent his head to Mr. Adams and seemed prepared to make a fuss of him, while Mr. Adams murmured and made little cheeping whistles in reply.

It seemed to be all right. Marianne and Cat went to the open door of the conservatory, with Klartch lolloping after them. "Is something the matter?" Marianne said as they went. "You look pale. And you only talk in little jerks."

Cat would have liked to tell Marianne all about his encounter with Mr. Farleigh. He was almost longing to. But that strange thing happened in his head that made him so bad at telling people things, and all he could manage to say was, "I had a—a turn up with Gaffer Farleigh on the way." And as soon as Marianne was nodding in perfect understanding, Cat was forced to change the subject. He leaned toward her and whispered, "Is Mr. Adams a *gnome*?"

Marianne choked on a giggle. "I don't *know*!" she whispered back.

Cat was feeling much better and they were both trying not to laugh as they entered the conservatory. It was transformed. When Cat had last been here, the glass of the roof and walls had been too dirty to see through, and the floor had been coconut matting with dead plants standing about on it. Marianne could hardly remember it any other way. Now the glass sparkled and there were big green frondy plants, some of them with huge lilylike flowers, white and cream and yellow, which Jason must have brought here from his store. The floor that the plants stood on was a marvel of white, green, and blue tiles, in a gentle eye-resting pattern. There were new cane chairs. Best of all, a small fountain—that must have been covered up by the old matting—was now playing, making a quiet chuckling and misting the fronds of the plants. The smell this brought out from the flowers reminded them both of Irene's scent.

Marianne said wonderingly, "This must all have been underneath! How *could* Gammer have kept it all covered up?"

Thoroughly curious to know what the rest of the house was like now, they went on into the hall. The same tiles were here, blue, white, and green, making the hall twice as light. To Marianne's surprise, the tiles went on up the walls, to about the height of her shoulders, where she had only known dingy, knobbly cream paint before. Above the tiles, Uncle Charles had painted the walls a paler shade of the blue in the tiles. Marianne wondered if Uncle Charles had chosen it, or Irene. Irene, certainly. There were plants here too, one of them a whole tree. The stairs had been polished so that they gleamed, with a rich, moss-colored strip of carpet down the middle.

Klartch had difficulty walking on the tiles. His front talons clattered and slid. His back feet, which were more like paws, skidded. Cat turned and waited for him.

Marianne, watching Klartch, said, "I suppose Gammer covered the tiles with matting because they were slippery. Or was it in case they got spoiled? What was your idea for helping me?"

Cat turned back to her, wishing it was a bigger, better idea. "Well," he began.

But Jason came out of one of the rooms just then. "Oh, hello!" he said. "I didn't hear you arrive. Welcome to the dez rez, both of you!"

And Irene came racing down the moss-carpeted stairs, crying out in delight. She seized Marianne and kissed her, hugged Cat, and then kneeled down to lift Klartch up by his feathery front legs so that she could rub her face on his beak. Klartch made little crooning noises at her in reply. "This is splendid!" Irene said. "Not many people can say that their very first visitor was a griffin!" She lowered Klartch down and looked anxiously up at Marianne. "I hope you don't mind what we've done to the house."

"Mind?" Marianne said. "It's wonderful! Were these tiles always up the walls like this?" She went over and rubbed her hand across them. "Smooth," she said. "Lovely."

"They were painted over," Irene said. "When I discovered them under the paint, I just had to have it scraped off. I'm afraid the painting Mr. Pinhoe wasn't very pleased about the extra work. But I cleaned the tiles myself."

Uncle Charles was an idiot then, Marianne thought. "It was worth it. They glow!"

"Ah, that's Irene's doing," Jason said, with a proud, loving look toward his wife. "She's inherited the dwimmer gift. Dwimmer," he explained to Cat, "means that a person is in touch with the life in everything. They can bring it out even when it's hidden. When Irene cleaned those tiles, she didn't just take the paint and dirt of ages off them. She released the art that went to making them."

A slight noise made Marianne look up at the stairs. Uncle Charles was standing near the top of them, in his paint-blotched overalls, looking outraged. None of the adult Pinhoes liked to hear the craft openly spoken of like this. Not even Uncle Charles, Marianne thought sadly. Uncle Charles was becoming more of a standard Pinhoe and less of a disappointment every day. Oh, I *wish* they'd let him go and study to be an artist, like he wanted to after he painted our inn sign! she thought.

Uncle Charles coughed slightly and came loudly down the wooden part of the stairs. Marianne knew that, although it looked as if Uncle Charles was trying to keep paint off the mossy carpet, what he was really doing was making a noise in order to stop Jason talking about dwimmer. "I've finished the undercoat in the small bathroom,

587

madam," he said to Irene. "I'll be off to my lunch while it dries and come back to do the gloss this afternoon."

"Thank you, Mr. Pinhoe," Irene said to him.

Jason said, trying to be friendly, "I don't know how you do it, Mr. Pinhoe. I've never known paint to dry as quickly as yours does."

Uncle Charles just gave him a fixed and disapproving look and clumped across the tiles to the front door. The look, and Uncle Charles's head with it, jerked a little when he saw Klartch. For a fraction of an instant, delight and curiosity jumped across his face. Then the disapproving looked settled back, stronger than ever, and Uncle Charles marched on, and away outside.

He left a slightly awkward silence behind him.

"Well," Jason said at length, a bit too heartily, "I think we should show you all over the house."

"I only came to find my cat, really," Marianne said.

"Jane James has got him," Irene said. "He's quite safe. *Do* come and see what we've done here!"

It was impossible to say no. Jason and Irene were both so proud of the place. They swept Cat and Marianne through into the front room, where the moss green chairs, new white walls, and some of Irene's design paintings on it in frames, made it look like a different room from the one where Gammer had shouted at the Farleighs. Then Cat and Marianne were swept to Jason's den, full of books and leather, and Irene's workroom, all polished wood and a sloping table under the window, with an antique stand for paints and pencils that Marianne knew Dad would have admired: it was so cleverly designed.

After this they were whirled through the dining room and then on upstairs, into a moss green corridor with bedrooms and bathrooms opening off it. Irene had had some of the walls moved, so that now there were bedrooms, sunny and elegant, which had not been there when Marianne last saw the house. The trickling cistern cabinet had become a white warm cupboard that was full of towels and made no noise at all. Uncle Simeon, Marianne thought, had done wonders up here, sprained ankle and all.

"We're still thinking what to do with the attics," Irene said, "but they need a lot of sorting out first."

"I want to check all those herbs for seeds. Some of them are quite rare and may well grow, given the right spells," Jason explained as he swept everyone downstairs again.

Marianne sent Cat an urgent look on the way down. Cat pretended to be waiting for Klartch in order to look reassuringly back. They had to let Jason and Irene finish showing them the house. It was no good trying to talk before then.

Down the passage from the hall, which turned out to be lined with the same blue, green, and white tiles, Jason flung open the door to the kitchen. More of those tiles over the sink, Marianne saw, and in a line round the room; but mostly the impression was of largeness, brightness, and comfort. There was a rusty red floor, which the place had always needed, in Marianne's opinion, and of course the famous table, now scrubbed white, white, white.

Nutcase leered smugly at her from Jane James's bony knees. Jane James was sitting in a chair close to the stove, stirring a saucepan with one hand and reading a magazine she held in the other.

"I've taken the scullery for my distillery," Jason said. "Let me show—"

"Lunch in half an hour," Jane James replied.

"I'll tell Mr. Adams," Irene said.

Jane James stood up and put the magazine on the table and Nutcase on the magazine. Nutcase sat there demurely until Klartch shuffled and clacked his way round the door. Then Nutcase stood up in an arch and spat.

"Don't be a silly cat," Jane James said, as if she saw creatures like Klartch every day. "It's only a baby griffin. Will he eat biscuits?" she asked Cat. She seemed to know at once that he was responsible for Klartch.

"*I'll* eat biscuits," Jason said. "She makes the best biscuits in this world," he told Marianne.

"Yes, but not for you. You'll spoil your lunch," Jane James said. "You and Irene go and get cleaned up ready."

Cat was not surprised that Jason and Irene meekly scurried out of the kitchen. Nor was he surprised when Jane James gave a secret smile as she watched them go. He thought she was quite certainly a sorceress. She reminded him a lot of Miss Bessemer, who was.

Her biscuits were delicious, big and buttery. Klartch liked them as much as Cat and Marianne did and kept putting his beak up for more. Nutcase looked down from the table at him, disgustedly.

After about her tenth biscuit, Marianne found herself searching Jane James's face for the humor she was sure was hidden there. "That time you brought Nutcase home in a basket," she said curiously, "you weren't cross about him, really, were you?"

"Not at all," Jane James said. "He likes me and I like him. I'd gladly keep him here if he's too much trouble for you. But I kept seeing you chasing around, worrying about him. Did you get *any* holiday to yourself this year?"

Marianne's face crumpled a little as she thought of her story of "Princess Irene and her Cats," still barely started. But she said bravely, "Our family likes to keep children busy."

"You're no child. You're a full-grown enchantress," Jane James retorted. "Don't they *notice*? And I don't see any of your cousins very busy. Riding their bikes up and down and yelling seems to me how busy *they* are." She stood up and planted Nutcase into Marianne's arms. "There you are. Tell Mr. Adams to come for his lunch on your way out."

You had to go when Jane James did that, Cat

thought. She was quite a tartar. They thanked her for the biscuits and went out into the passage again. As they turned left toward the hall, they nearly collided with a person who appeared to come out of the tiled wall.

"Ooops-a-la!" that person said.

They stared at him. Both of them had a moment when they thought they were looking at Mr. Adams and that Mr. Adams had shrunk. He had the same tufts of hair and the same wrinkled brown face with the big ears. But Mr. Adams had not been wearing bright green, blue, and white checkered trousers and a moss green waistcoat. And Mr. Adams was about the same height as Cat, who was small for his age, where this person only came up to Cat's waist.

Klartch clacked forward with great interest.

The little man fended him off with a hand that appeared to be all long, thin fingers. "Now, now, now, Klartch. I'm not food for griffins. I'm only a skinny old househob."

"A *househob*!" Marianne said. "When did you move in here?"

"About two thousand years ago, when your first Gaffer's hall was built in this place," the little man replied. "You might say I've always been here."

"How come I've never seen you before, then?" Marianne asked.

The little man looked up at her. His eyes were big and shiny and full of green sadness. "Ah," he said, "but I've seen *you*, Miss Marianne. I've seen most things while I've been sealed inside these walls these many long years, until the dwimmer-lady, Princess Irene, let me out."

"You mean—under the cream paint?" Marianne said. "Did Gammer seal you in?"

"Not she. It was more than paint and longer ago than that," the househob said. "It was in those days after the devout folk came. After that, the folks in charge here named me and all my kind wicked and ungodly, and they set spells to imprison us—all of us, in houses, fields, and woods—and told everyone we were gone for good. Though, mind you, I never could see why these devout folk could believe on the one hand that God made all, and on the other hand call us ungodly—but there you go. It was done." He spread both huge hands and brought his pointed shoulders up in a shrug. Then he bowed to Marianne and turned and bowed to Cat. "Now, if you'll forgive me, dwimmer-folk both, I believe Jane James has my lunch ready. And she doesn't hold with me coming in through her kitchen wall. I have to use the door."

Amazed and bemused, Cat and Marianne stepped back out of the househob's way. He set off at a crablike trot toward the kitchen. Then turned back anxiously. "You didn't eat all the biscuits, did you?"

"No, there's a big tinful," Cat told him.

"Ah. Good." The househob turned toward the kitchen door. He did not open it. They watched him walk through it, much as Marianne had watched

Nutcase walk through the wall in Furze Cottage. Nutcase, at the sight, squirmed indignantly in Marianne's arms. He seemed to think he was the only one who should be able to do that sort of thing.

Cat and Marianne looked at each other, but could think of nothing to say.

It was not until they were halfway across the hall that Marianne said, "You think you have an idea for what I can do about Gammer?"

"Yes—I hope," Cat said, wishing it was a better idea. "At least, I think I know someone you could ask. I met a man in your wood here who I think could help. He was awfully wise."

Marianne felt truly let down. "A man," she said disbelievingly. "In the wood."

"*Really* wise," Cat said rather desperately. "Dwimmer wise. And he had a unicorn."

Marianne supposed Cat was speaking the truth. If he *was*, then a unicorn did make a difference. If householhobs were real, then might not unicorns be real too? A unicorn was part of the Pinhoe coat of arms and could—surely?—be expected to be on her side. And they were in such a mess, she and the Pinhoes and the Farleighs, that anything was worth a try.

"All right," she said. "How do I find them?"

"I'll have to take you," Cat said. "There was a queer barrier in the way. Do you want to come now?"

"Yes, please," Marianne said.

17

OUTSIDE, BEYOND THE conservatory, Mr. Adams was leaning against Syracuse with his arms round Syracuse's neck, amid a strong smell of peppermint. Positively canoodling, Cat thought, rather jealously. But then, Cat thought, looking at Mr. Adams closely, besides seeming as if he had gnome in his ancestry—or was it househob?—Mr. Adams had more than a little of this strange thing called dwimmer. He was bound to get on with Syracuse, because Syracuse had it too.

Mr. Adams, however much he was enjoying Syracuse, was only too ready to hand Syracuse over and go in for his lunch. "There's no doubt," he said, in his talkative way, "that working a garden gives you an appetite. I've never *been* so hungry as I am since I moved here."

He went on talking. He talked all the time he was helping Cat heave Klartch up across Syracuse's saddle. He talked while he checked the girths. He talked while he carefully cleaned his spade. But eventually he talked his way through the archway in the wall and round to the kitchen door. They could hear him begin talking to Jane James as he opened it. As soon as the door shut, Marianne put Nutcase secretly down in the beech hedge. "You go on home to Furze Cottage," she told him. "You know the way."

"Not happy," Klartch said plaintively from the saddle.

Cat could see Klartch was uncomfortable, but he said, "It's your own fault. You *would* follow me. You can't walk fast enough to keep up, so stay up there and I'll let you down when we find the road."

He and Marianne set off, Cat leading Syracuse, across the stubbly lawn to the row of lilacs at the back. There they found the small rickety gate Cat had come in by. It was green with mildew and almost falling apart with age, and they had to shove it hard to get it open again.

"I'd forgotten this was here," Marianne said, as they went through into the empty, rustling wood. "Gaffer used to call it his secret escape route. Which way do we go?"

"Keep straight on, I think," Cat said.

There was no path, but Cat set his mind on the whereabouts of that barrier and led the way, over shoals of fallen leaves, past brambles and through hazel thickets, deeper and deeper among the trees. Some of the time he was dragged through bushes by Syracuse, who was getting very excited by the wood and wanted to throw Klartch off and run. Poor Klartch was jogged and jigged and bounced and was less happy than ever. "Down!" he said.

"Soon," Cat told him.

They came to the barrier quite unexpectedly on the other side of a holly bush. It stretched as far as either of them could see in both directions, rusting, ramshackle, and overgrown. Marianne looked at it in astonishment.

"What's this? I never saw *this* before!"

"You didn't know to look for it, I expect," Cat said.

"It's a *mess*!" Marianne said. "Creepers and nettles and rusty wire. Who put it up?"

"I don't know," Cat said. "But it's made of magic, really. Do you think you could help me take it down? We won't get Syracuse past it the way I got in last time."

"I can *try*, I suppose," Marianne said. "How do you suggest?"

Cat thought about it for a moment and then conjured the nearest clothesline from Ulverscote. It came with a row of someone's underpants pegged on it, which made them both struggle not to give shrieks of laughter. Each of them had the feeling that loud laughter might fetch the person who had made the barrier here. From then on, they spoke in low voices, to be on the safe side.

While Marianne carefully unpegged the pants and put them in a pile by the nearest tree, Cat fastened each end of the rope to the back of the saddle on Syracuse, using a thick blob of magic to fix it there. Klartch reared up and watched with interest as Cat took the rest of the clothesline and stretched high to loop it along the ragged top of the barrier. Klartch was an actual help here. Because Klartch was attending to the barrier, Cat somehow knew that it was mostly unreal. It had been made out of two small pieces of chicken wire and one length of corrugated iron, plus a charm to make the weeds grow over it, and then stretched by magic to become the long, impenetrable thing it was now. This meant that the clothesline was going to slide straight through it and come loose, if Cat was not careful.

"Thanks, Klartch," Cat said. As soon as the rope was jammed in along the ragged spikes of rusty iron, he fixed it there with a truly enormous slab of magic. He jerked it to test it. It was quite solid. "You take one side and pull hard when I say," Cat murmured to Marianne, and took hold of the rope on the other side.

"What charm do I use when I pull?" Marianne asked.

"Nothing particularly," Cat said, surprised that she should ask. Ulverscote witchcraft must be very different from enchanter's magic. "Just think hard of the barrier coming down."

Marianne's eyebrows went up, but she obediently took hold of the rope on her side. She was terribly obedient, Cat thought. He remembered Janet once telling him that *he* was too obedient, and he knew that had been the result of the way his sister always despised him. He was suddenly, firmly, decided that, however much Marianne protested, he was going to tell Chrestomanci about her.

"Right," Cat said to Syracuse in a low voice. "Work, Syracuse. Walk on."

Syracuse turned his head and stared at Cat. Me, *work?* said every line of him. And he simply planted himself and stood there, whatever Cat said.

"You can have another peppermint," Cat said. "Just walk. We need your strength."

Syracuse put his ears back and simply stood.

"Oh, lord!" Marianne said. "He's as bad as Nutcase. You go and lead him, and I'll pull on both halves of the rope." She collected Cat's side of the rope and stood in the middle, holding both lengths of clothesline.

If Syracuse decided to kick out, he could hurt Marianne there. Cat hurried round to Syracuse's head and took hold of his bridle. He found a slightly furry peppermint in one of his pockets and held it out at arm's length in front of Syracuse's nose, before he dared pull on the bridle. "Now come *on*, Syracuse! Peppermint!"

Syracuse's ears came up and he rolled an eye at Cat, to say he knew exactly what Cat was up to.

"Yes," Cat said to him. "It's because we really need you."

Syracuse snorted. Then, when Cat was ready to give up, and to his huge relief, Syracuse started to trudge forward, stirring up clouds of broken dead leaves that got into Cat's eyes and his mouth and down his boots and even somehow down his neck. Cat blinked and blew and urged Syracuse and encouraged him and willed at the barrier. He could feel Marianne behind them, willing too with surprising power, as she pulled on the clothesline like someone in two tug-of-wars at once.

The barrier rustled, grated, groaned, and keeled slowly over in front of Marianne. When Cat turned to tell Syracuse he was a good horse and to feed him the peppermint, he could see the long line of metal and creepers in both directions, slowly falling flat, piece by piece, rather like a wave breaking on a beach. He could hear metal screaming and branches snapping, off into the distance both ways. Cat was rather surprised. He had not expected to bring the whole thing down. But he supposed it must be because the barrier had been made out of just the one small piece, really.

"Hooray!" Marianne said quietly, letting go of the rope.

Though the barrier now looked like a pile of nettles, brambles, and broken creepers, there was still jagged metal underneath. Cat flicked the rope loose from it and undid the fastenings from Syracuse and, while Marianne busily pegged the pants back onto the rope, he tried growing a mat of ivy over the barrier, to make it safer for Syracuse to walk on. Chrestomanci was always telling him that he should never waste magic, so Cat fed the slab of magic that had fastened the rope back into the fallen creepers.

This was quite as startling as the way the whole barrier had come down. Ivy surged and spread and gnarled and tangled, a mature and glossy dark green, in a whispering rush, that put out yellowish flowers and then black fruits in seconds, not just in one place as Cat had intended, but off along the fallen barrier in both directions. By the time Marianne had turned round with the pants pegged back on the clothesline, the barrier was a long mound of ivy as far as she could see both ways. It looked as if it had been growing there for years.

"My!" she said. "You do have dwimmer, don't you!"

"It may be the magic in this wood," Cat said. He sent the clothesline back where it had come from, then he turned Syracuse round and led him carefully over the ivy bank and down into the mossy road beyond. While Marianne crunched her way across after them, Cat stopped and got Klartch down. Klartch immediately became hugely happy. He gave out whistling squeaks and went lolloping off toward the nearest bend in the road. The mossy surface seemed perfect for his clawed feet. Syracuse felt it was perfect for hooves too. He bounded and waltzed and tried to take off after Klartch so determinedly that Cat was dragged along in great hopping bounds, with Marianne pelting after them.

They whirled round the bend in the road with Klartch in the lead. The old cart was there, parked in a new place on the verge, with the seeming old white mare grazing beside it. Beyond that, the old man looked up in amazement from his panful of mushrooms and bacon. He just managed to let the pan go and brace himself, before Marianne rushed up and hurled herself on him.

"Gaffer!" she screamed. "Oh, Gaffer, you're not

dead after all!" She pushed her face into the old man's tattered jacket and burst into tears.

Syracuse stopped dead when he saw the old unicorn. She raised her head from the grass and looked at him inquiringly. A ray of sun, slanting between the trees, caught her horn and lit it into pearly creams and greens and blues. Or was that blue and green and white, like the tiles in Woods House, Cat wondered. Syracuse tiptoed respectfully toward her and put out his nose. Graciously, the old unicorn touched her nose to his.

"He's got unicorn blood in him somewhere," she remarked softly to Cat. "I wonder how that happened."

Beyond her, Klartch was creeping toward the pan of mushrooms and bacon with his beak out. Cat thought he ought to go and drag him away. But Marianne was kneeling in the old man's arms, sobbing out what seemed to be private things, and Cat was embarrassed about interrupting. However, while Cat hesitated, the old man swiveled himself around and spared an arm from Marianne in order to tap Klartch firmly on the beak. "Wait," Cat heard him say. "You shall have some presently." And he went back to listening attentively to Marianne.

"Do you understand a little more about dwimmer now?" the unicorn said conversationally to Cat.

"I—think so," Cat said. "Irene has it. Marianne keeps saying I've got it too. Have I?"

"You have. Even more strongly than my old

Gaffer," the unicorn told him. "Didn't you just grow several miles of ivy?"

Nearly a year ago now, Cat had been forced to accept that he was a nine-lifed enchanter. That had been hard to do, but he supposed it made it easier to accept having dwimmer too. He grinned, thinking of himself stuffed full of every kind of magic—except, he thought, Joe Pinhoe's kind. But then, when he thought about it, he knew that Joe had been using dwimmer to animate that stuffed ferret of his. How muddling. "Yes," he said. "Can you tell me what I ought to be doing with it?"

"We all hoped you might ask me that," said the unicorn. "You can do many thousands of folk the same favor that Irene did for her househob, if you want."

"Oh," said Cat. "Where are these people?"

Syracuse nudged up to the unicorn and snorted impatiently.

"I'll have a long talk with you in a moment," she said to him. "Why don't you graze on this tasty bank for a while?"

Syracuse looked at her questioningly. She stumped forward a step or so and flicked her horn affectionately along his mane. All his tack vanished, saddle, bit, reins, everything, leaving him without so much as a halter. He looked much better like that to Cat's eyes. Syracuse twitched all over with relief, before he bent his head and started tearing up mouthfuls of grass and little fragrant plants.

"If you can taste it through all the peppermint you've eaten," the unicorn remarked drily. She said to Cat, "I'll put it all back later. The folks are here. Hidden behind. Imprisoned for no fault that I can see, except that they scare humans. Can't you feel this?"

Cat examined the wood with his thoughts. It was quiet, too quiet, and the silence was not peace. It was the same emptiness that he had felt whenever he rode out with Syracuse, by the river and on the heath, and behind the emptiness was misery, and longing. It was the same thing that he had felt in Home Wood when he first encountered Mr. Farleigh. As for this wood, he remembered Chrestomanci saying, rather irritably, what a dreary, empty place it was. But here there seemed to be no rack of dead animals to act as a gate between the emptiness and the misery in the distance behind.

"I don't know what to do about it," he told the unicorn. He had not managed to do anything in Home Wood, even with a gate. What did you do here, against complete blankness? "You can't clean a wood the way Irene cleaned those tiles."

"You can make an opening, though," the unicorn suggested quietly. "Make a road between the background and the foreground. That's how roads usually go."

"I'll try." Cat stood and thought. If he thought of it as like stage scenery, he supposed he could make the empty wood seem like a solid sort of curtain that had been drawn across the real scenery, the blue distance behind, and then tightly fixed. "Draw it like a curtain?" he asked the unicorn.

"If you want," she answered.

The trouble was, it was only the *one* curtain. There was no opening, the way there was with window curtains, where you take hold of the two sides and pull them apart. Cat could not see himself tearing trees and grass and bushes in two. Even if he *could*, it would kill everything. No. The only thing to do seemed to be to find the edge of the curtain, wherever that was, and pull it from there.

He looked for the edge. There was *miles* of this curtain. Like a sheet of rubbery gauze, it stretched and stretched, out across the country, out across the continent, over the oceans, right to the edges of the world. He had to stretch and stretch himself to get near it, and the rubbery edge kept slipping away from his imaginary clutching fingers. Cat clenched his teeth and stretched himself more, just that little bit further. And at last his reaching left hand closed on the thin, slippery edge of it. He put both hands to it and hauled. It would hardly budge. Someone had pegged it down really firmly. Even when the unicorn came and rested her horn gently on Cat's shoulder, Cat could only move the thing an inch or so.

"Try asking the prisoners to help," the unicorn murmured.

"Good idea," Cat panted. Still hanging on to the distant end of the curtain, he pushed his mind into the empty blue distance behind it, and it was not empty. The ones inside were all swarming, drifting, and anxiously clustering toward the other side of the curtain. "Pull, pull!" he whispered to them. "Help me *pull*!" It was so like making Syracuse pull down the barrier that he almost offered them peppermint.

But they needed no bribery. They were frantic to get out now. They swooped on the place where Cat's imaginary hands were clutched, in a storm of small, fierce strangenesses, and fastened on beside Cat and heaved. Beside Cat, the unicorn put her horn down and heaved too.

The curtain tore. First it came away in a long strip across the middle, making Cat stagger back into the unicorn. Then it tore downward, then diagonally, as more and more eager creatures inside clawed and hauled and pulled at it. Finally it began flopping down in wobbly dead heaps, which folded in on themselves and melted. Cat could actually smell it as it melted. The smell was remarkably like the disinfectant spell Euphemia had used on the stairs. But this smell was overwhelmed almost at once by a sweet, wild scent from the myriad beings who came whirring out past Cat's face and fled away into the landscape. Cat thought it was, just a little, like the incense smell from the meadows by the river.

"Done it, I think!" he gasped at the unicorn. He slid down her hairy side and sat on the bank with a bump. He was weak with effort. But he was glad to see that the trees of the wood were still there. It would have been a mistake to have tried to tear the wood in half.

"You have," the unicorn said. "Thank you." Her horn gently touched Cat's forehead. It smelled like the meadows too.

When Cat recovered and sat up properly, he saw that the old man was still talking earnestly with Marianne. But he knew what had been going on. His bright brown eyes kept turning appreciatively to the woods, although he now had the pan on his knees and was feeding a soothing mushroom to Marianne and then some bacon to Klartch, as if there was no difference between them.

"But, Gaffer," Cat heard Marianne say, "if you've been trapped here all these years, where do you get your bacon from?"

"Your Uncle Cedric puts it through the barrier for me," Gaffer said. "And eggs. They all know I'm here, you know, but Cedric's the only one who thinks I might need feeding."

While they talked, the wood was making a great rustling and heaving. Like a sail filling with wind, it seemed to be filling with life around them. Cat looked down and saw, almost between his knees, a multitude of tiny green beings milling and welling out of the ground. Other, bigger ones flitted at the corners of his eyes. When he looked across the road, he could see strange gawky creatures stalking among the trees and small airborne ones darting from bush to bush. There seemed to be a tall green woman walking dreamily through a distant patch of sunlight. Someone came up behind Cat—all he could see of him or her was a very thin brown leg—and bent over to whisper, "Thank you. None of us are going to forget." He or she was gone when Cat turned his head.

Hooves sounded on the mossy road. The unicorn, who was now standing head to tail with Syracuse, presumably having the talk she had promised, looked up at the sound. "Ah," she said. "Here comes my daughter, free at last. Thank you, Cat."

Cat and Marianne both found themselves standing up as a splendid young unicorn dashed along the road and stopped beside the old man's cart. She was small and lissome and silvery, with quantities of white mane and tail. Cat could see she was very young because her horn was the merest creamy stub on her forehead. Syracuse, at the sight of her, began to prance and sidle and make himself look magnificent.

"Ah, no," the old unicorn said. "She's still only a yearling, Syracuse. She's been a yearling for more than a thousand years. Give her a chance to grow up now."

The small unicorn ignored Syracuse anyway and trotted lovingly up to her mother.

"Beautiful!" Gaffer said admiringly. He put the food down on the grass for Klartch and leaned over to concentrate on the young unicorn.

Klartch, to Cat's surprise, turned away from the food and went shambling and stumbling across the road, making squeaks and hoots and long quavering whistles. The sounds were answered from inside the wood by a deeper whistling, like a trill on an oboe. A blot of darkness that Cat had taken for a holly brake stirred and stretched and moved out into the road, where she lifted great gray wings and put her enormous horn-colored beak down to meet Klartch. Cat knew it was the creature that had landed on his tower before Klartch was hatched. She was surprisingly graceful for something that huge, gray and white from her sleek feathered head to her lionlike furry body and swinging tufted tail. She lifted a feathered foot with six-inch talons on the end and gently, very gently, pulled Klartch in under one of her enormous wings.

She was Klartch's mother, of course. For the first time in his life, Cat knew what it was like to be truly and wretchedly miserable. Before, when he had been miserable, Cat had mostly felt lost and peevish. But now, when he was going to lose Klartch, he felt a blinding heartache that not only devastated his mind but gave him a real, actual pain somewhere in the center of his chest. It was the hardest thing he had ever done, when he heaved up a difficult breath and said, "Klartch ought to go with you now."

The mother griffin drew her beak back from Klartch squirming and squeaking under her wing and turned her enormous yellow eyes on Cat. Cat could see she was as sad as he was. "Oh, no," she said in her deep, trilling voice. "You hatched him. I'd prefer you to bring him up. He needs a proper education. Griffins are meant to be as learned and wise as they are magical. He ought to have teaching that I never had."

Gaffer said, rather reproachfully, "I did my best to teach you."

"Yes, you did," the mother griffin replied. She smiled at Gaffer with the ends of her beak. "But you could only teach me when I got out at full moon, Gaffer man. I hope you can teach me all the time now, but I'd like Klartch to have an enchanter's upbringing."

"So be it," Gaffer said. He said to Cat, "Can you do that for her?"

"Yes," Cat said, and then added bravely, "It depends what Klartch wants, though."

Klartch seemed surprised that anyone should question what he wanted. He dived out from under the griffin's big wing and scuttled over to Cat, where he leaned heavily against Cat's legs and wiped his beak against Cat's riding boots. "Mine," he said. "Cat mine."

The pain lifted from Cat's chest like magic. He smiled—because he couldn't help it—across at Klartch's mother. "I really will look after him," he promised.

"That's settled, then," Gaffer said, warm and approving. "Marianne, my pet, would you do me the favor of running down to the village and telling your dad I'll be along shortly to sort things out? He won't be too pleased, I'm afraid, so tell him I insisted. I'll follow you when I've tidied up here."

18

❧❦

NOW THAT MARIANNE was leaving, Cat realized that he ought to be going too. Joss Callow would have complained to Chrestomanci by this time. He went up to the big griffin and held his hand out politely. She rubbed it with her great beak. "May I visit Klartch from time to time?" she asked.

"Yes, of course," Cat said. "Any time." He hoped Chrestomanci wouldn't mind too much—he hoped Chrestomanci wouldn't mind too much about all of it. He would have to confess what he had done to Mr. Farleigh sometime soon. He decided not to think about that yet.

When he turned round, Syracuse was stamping irritably because his saddle and bridle were back. Marianne was staring at the two unicorns.

"Gaffer," she said, "when did old Molly turn into a unicorn?"

Gaffer looked up from cleaning out his pan. "She always was one, pet. She chose not to let people see it."

"Oh," Marianne said. She was very quiet,

thinking about this, as she walked along the mossy road with Cat and Syracuse. The old gray mare who took Luke Pinhoe to London and then came back on her own—had that been Molly too? Unicorns lived for hundreds of years, they said. Marianne wished she knew.

Cat was letting Klartch bumble along behind them since the surface suited his feet so well. Around them, the woods were full of green distances that had not been there before and alive with rushings, rustlings, and small half-heard voices. There was laughter too, some of it plain joyful, some of it mean and mocking.

Marianne said to Cat, "You've let all the hidden folk out, haven't you?"

Cat nodded. He was not going to apologize, even to Chrestomanci, about that.

Marianne said, "My family are going to be furious with you. They fuss all the time that it's their sacred task to keep them in."

A particularly mocking and malevolent laugh rang out among the trees as Marianne said this. "Some of them don't sound very nice," she added, looking that way uneasily.

"Some humans aren't very nice either," Cat said.

Marianne thought of Great-Uncle Edgar and Aunt Joy and said, "True."

The road ran out into strong daylight a moment later. They found themselves on a rocky headland, looking down on Ulverscote across a long green meadow. They were above the church tower here and could see down into the main street over the roof of the Pinhoe Arms. It was quiet and empty because everyone was indoors having lunch.

This rocky bit, Cat thought, was the part of Ulverscote Wood that he and Roger had kept seeing when they tried to get to it before. While they waited for Klartch to catch up, he looked out the other way, across the wide countryside, over humping hills, hedges, and the white winding road, wondering if he could see the Castle from here.

He saw a most peculiar bristling black cloud coming across the nearest hill. It spread across a stubble field on one side and a pasture on the other, and it appeared to be trickling and wobbling along the road too. It was rushing toward them almost as fast as a car could go. An angry buzzing sort of sound came with it.

"What on earth is that?" he said to Marianne. "A swarm of huge wasps?"

Marianne looked, and went pale. "Oh, my lord!" she said. "It's the Farleighs. On broomsticks and bicycles."

Cat could see it was people now: angry, determined women of all ages whizzing along on broomsticks and equally angry men and boys pedaling furiously along the road.

Marianne said, "I must go down and warn everyone!" and set off at a run down the meadow.

But it was too late. Before Marianne had gone three steps, the horde of Farleighs had swept down into Ulverscote and the place was black with them. Yelling with fury and triumph, the broomstick riders sprang off onto their feet, lofted their brooms, and began smashing windows with the butt ends. The cyclists arrived, braking and howling, and threw powdered spells in through the smashed windows. Inside the houses, Pinhoes screamed.

At the screams, a whole crowd of Pinhoe men, who must have been having lunch in the inn, came swarming out of the Pinhoe Arms, carrying stools and chairs and small tables. Marianne saw Uncle Charles there, brandishing a chair leg, and Uncle Arthur charging in front with a coatrack. They all fell on the cyclists, whacking mightily. More Pinhoes poured into the street from the houses, and others leaned out of upstairs windows and threw things and tipped things upon the Farleighs.

Round the smashed windows of the grocer's and the chemist's, there were instant battles. Feet crunched in broken glass there, cheeses and big bottles were hurled. Broomsticks walloped. In almost no time, the main street was a fighting tangle of bent bicycles and shouting, screaming people. Marianne could see Gammer Norah Farleigh at the back of the fight, yelling her troops on and cracking an enormous horsewhip.

Down the hill at the other end, Aunt Joy raced out of the Post Office carrying a long bar of scaffolding like a lance and screaming curses. Uncle Isaac and Uncle Richard were pelting up behind her. Marianne saw her parents running behind them. Mum was carrying her new broom, and Dad seemed to be waving a saw. Nicola's mother came out of her house dressed in her best, on her way to visit Nicola, screamed, went in and slammed her door. Up the hill at the other end, Great-Uncle Lester, who was coming in his car to give Nicola's mother a lift to the hospital, bared his teeth and drove straight at the back of Gammer Norah. She saw him coming in time and levitated to the roof of his car, where she rode screaming, cracking her whip and trying to break his windscreen with her broomstick. Uncle Lester drove slowly on regardless, trying to run over Farleighs, but mostly running over bicycles instead.

Behind the car, Great-Uncle Edgar and Great-Aunt Sue, who must have been out exercising their dogs, were arriving at a tired trot. They were surrounded by exhausted dogs, who were mostly too fat and tired to bite Farleighs, although Great-Aunt Sue shrieked at them to "Bite, bite, bite!" They settled for barking instead.

The Reverend Pinhoe appeared on the churchyard wall, waving a censer of smoking incense on a chain and making prayerful gestures. When that made no difference to the struggling mayhem in the street below him, he swung the censer at any Farleigh head he could reach. There were clangs and terrible cries. And down near the Post Office, Marianne's parents had entered the fray, Mum batting with her broom and Dad swinging the flat of the saw at any Farleigh near. Even above the noise of the rest, Marianne could hear the dreadful *ker-blatt SWAT* from Dad's saw. And she and Cat both winced at what Aunt Joy was doing with her scaffolding pole.

They both turned their eyes away to the upper end of the village again. There, behind the row of yelping dogs, the long black car from the Castle edged cautiously out of the gates of Woods House and crawled to a halt at the back of the battle, as if Millie, who was driving it, was at a loss to know what to do. Nearly a thousand fighting witches seemed a bit much even for an enchantress as strong as Millie.

"Do something! *Do* something!" Marianne implored Cat.

Nearly a thousand fighting witches were a bit much for Cat too. And he was not going to take Syracuse and Klartch in among that lot. But someone was going to be killed soon if he didn't do *something*. That man with the saw down the hill was starting to hit people with the edge of it. There was blood down that end of the street. A giant stasis might stop it, Cat thought. But what happened when he took the stasis *off*?

All the same, Cat drew in his power, as he had been taught, in order to cast the stasis. He almost had enough when, with a violent clattering and screams of "I belong to Chrestomanci Castle!" the flying machine swept in from above the Post Office. The faces of the fighters turned upward in alarm as it clapped and flapped and shouted its swift way over their heads.

A giant voice, magically amplified and accompanied by a steady chant of "I belong to Chrestomanci Castle!" shouted, "OUT OF THE WAY! We're CRASHING!"

Everyone dived to the sides of the street. The machine did not so much crash as simply keep on in a straight line. It seemed to get lower with every flap of the jointed tables, but in fact it was the street that got steeper and the flying machine just flew into it. It landed with a great clatter and a tremendous crunching of bicycles underneath, exactly opposite the Pinhoe Arms. The chanting from the broken furniture faded to a murmur. Joe and Roger sat back gasping. Joe was without his shirt, and both were covered with sweat. Roger's hair was so dark with perspiration that, for a moment, he looked quite strikingly like his father.

Every person there was able to make that comparison quite easily. Chrestomanci stood up among the tangle of chairs at the back of the machine. Chrestomanci's left arm was in a bloodstained sling that seemed to have been Joe's shirt, and his smooth gray jacket was torn. He looked very unwell, but no one had any doubt who he was. Pinhoes and Farleighs, panting, with hair hanging over their faces and, in some cases, blood running down among the hair, stopped fighting and said to one another, "It's the Big Man! That's torn it!"

Cat sighed and sent his gathered magic off as a goodwill spell. "Mr. Farleigh shot him!" he said to Marianne.

Marianne merely nodded and went running off

down the meadow, making for the alleyway beside the Pinhoe Arms. As she ran, she could hear tinny bongings as Gammer Norah trampled up and down the roof of Great-Uncle Lester's car, shouting, "Don't you dare interfere! We don't need you from the Castle! These Pinhoes turned our Gaffer into a stone tree! So keep out of it!"

"I believe you have made a serious error there, ma'am," Chrestomanci replied.

When Marianne hurtled out of the other end of the alley into the street, Gammer Norah was still shouting. Her hair had come down from its bun into a sort of wad on one shoulder. What with that, and her long eyes narrowed with rage, she looked as menacingly witchy as a person could. But Chrestomanci was just standing there, waiting for her to stop. The moment Gammer Norah had to pause to take a breath, he said, "I suggest you join me in the Pinhoe Arms to discuss the matter."

Gammer Norah drew herself up to her full squat height. "I will not! I have never been inside a public house in my life!"

"In the inn yard, then," Chrestomanci said. He climbed out of the flying machine, which seemed to settle and spread once he was out of it. As Marianne rushed up to it, she could hear all the chairs, stools, tables, and even the feather duster at the tail, still whispering that they belonged to Chrestomanci Castle.

"Are you all right?" she asked Joe. He looked almost as pale as Chrestomanci.

Joe stared up at her as if she was a nightmare. "He *shot* him!" he said hoarsely. "Gaffer Farleigh shot the Big Man! We had to land on Crowhelm Top and do first aid. He was bleeding in *spurts*, Marianne. I'd never done a real healing before. I thought he was going to die. I was *scared*."

Marianne said soothingly, "But he's got nine lives, Joe."

Roger looked up at her. "No, he hasn't. He's only got two left, and he could have been down to just the one. I was scared too."

Meanwhile, all around them, Farleighs were sullenly separating from Pinhoes, picking up bicycles and broomsticks and kicking them into working order. Two particularly hefty Farleigh men came and stood beside the flying machine. "You're on top of our bikes," one of them said, in a way that suggested trouble.

At this Chrestomanci came and put his hand on Joe's shoulder. He gave Marianne a long, vague look as he said, "You two get yourselves back to the Castle now." Joe and Roger both groaned at the thought of further effort. "Well, you *are* blocking the main road," Chrestomanci said, "and these gentlemen need their bicycles."

"Who are you calling gentlemen?" the Farleigh man demanded.

"Not you, obviously," Chrestomanci said. "Roger, tell Miss Bessemer to give you both hot, sweet tea and then lunch, and ask her to send Tom and Miss Rosalie here to me at once. Miss Rosalie is to bring the folder from my study, the blue one." His bright dark eyes met Marianne's, making her jump. "Young lady, would you mind very much giving them a strong boost to get them airborne? I see you have the power. And you," he added to the Farleigh men, "please stand clear."

Marianne nodded, highly surprised. As the Farleigh men grudgingly moved back, Joe and Roger exchanged a look of misery and Joe said, "Right. One, two, three." The two of them began pedaling. The three-legged stool revolved on the front and the machine trembled all over.

Help! Marianne thought. How do you boost? There was no charm for this any more than there was for pulling the barrier down. She supposed she had better do it the way Cat had told her, by willing.

She willed, hard and ignorantly. The flying machine went straight upward, with a mighty clattering and a scream of "I belong to Chrestomanci Castle!" It tipped left wing downward, and the bent bicycle that had been caught in the woodwork clanged out of it, almost on top of the Farleigh it belonged to.

"Straighten her out!" Joe shrieked.

Marianne did her best, Roger did *his* best, and Joe swayed himself madly to the right. Marianne realized what to do and gave them another boost, forward this time. The pieces of table began to flap at last and the machine sailed forward up the hill, forcing Gammer Norah to slide quickly off Uncle Lester's car or be smacked on the head. The machine then swayed sideways the other way, to only just miss the Castle car as it crept downhill toward the Pinhoe Arms, and then pitched the other way to skim across the heads of Uncle Cedric and Aunt Polly, who were arriving too late, both perched on the same cart horse. After that it straightened out and went majestically flapping, creaking, and whispering over the chimneys of Woods House. Most of Aunt Sue's dogs decided it was the real enemy and went off up the road after it, yapping fit to burst.

"Oh, I wish it hadn't gone!" one of Marianne's smaller cousins wailed. "I wanted a go in it!"

Marianne shuddered. The thing looked even chancier than riding Mum's broomstick at night. She watched the Castle car stop by the Pinhoe Arms. It had all four tires thickly coated in spells against the broken pieces of glass in the road. Clever, she thought. Uncle Lester's car had three flat tires and several bicycles sticking out from underneath it. Millie got out from the driver's seat and hurried toward Chrestomanci, horrified at the state he was in. Jason sprang out from the other side. The back door opened to let out Joss Callow, to Marianne's surprise. Joss turned to help out Irene, who was holding Nutcase in her arms.

I think Nutcase really is going back to Woods House to live, Marianne thought, not sure whether she was sad or relieved. And really, some of my uncles are so *slow*! she added to herself, as Uncle Cedric and Aunt Polly clopped massively downhill and Uncle Simeon came thundering uphill in his builder's van, both of them far too late to do any good.

There was almost a quiet moment after this, while Chrestomanci conferred quickly with Jason and Millie and Millie seemed to be trying to patch Chrestomanci up. Marianne looked up at the sign on the Pinhoe Arms that Uncle Charles had painted the year she was born. The unicorn was definitely Molly, and the griffin facing her was, equally definitely, Klartch's mother. Uncle Charles had *known*. Then why had he always pretended that things like unicorns and griffins didn't exist?

And where was Gaffer? Marianne wondered anxiously. He said he would come.

Chrestomanci looked round, checking up on everybody. "I need all the principals in this matter in the inn yard with me now," he said.

The words caught Cat as he was halfway down the meadow. Chrestomanci was using Performative Speech, the enchanters' magic Cat had been wrestling with after he put Joe on the ceiling. He recognized it as he arrived with a jolt in the inn yard with Syracuse. Klartch, draped across the saddle, was shot off backward as Syracuse made his usual objections to people using magic on him. Cat was carried off his feet for a moment, and it was Marianne who rescued Klartch with a quick levitation spell, and lowered him gently to the cobbles.

"Thanks!" Cat gasped, and then had to turn the

other way as, to his dismay, Joss Callow dodged up and grabbed Syracuse from the other side.

"I'll walk him back home for you if you like," Joss said breathlessly, searching in his pocket for a peppermint.

Joss was not angry with him, Cat realized. Joss was extremely anxious to get away from here. Cat did not blame him. The people Joss spied *for* and the people Joss spied *on* were all here in the yard, and most of them were strong magic users.

"Thanks. Would you?" he said, and gave Syracuse over to Joss gladly, wishing he had the same excuse to leave. But Chrestomanci's eye was now on Cat, bright and vague. Cat looked back, appalled at all the blood on Chrestomanci and at how unwell Chrestomanci looked. He knew he should have stopped Mr. Farleigh firing that gun at all.

19

CHRESTOMANCI TURNED TO have a word with Uncle Arthur, who had a black eye again. "Yes," he said. "Find her something as much like a throne as you can. That may calm her down. And drinks all round on the Castle, if you please." Cat could see Chrestomanci was feeling dreadful, but holding himself together by magic.

As Joss led Syracuse out of the inn yard, things settled down into a sort of open-air conference. Gammer Norah was given a mighty carved wooden chair from the Snug—where she sat and glared round aggressively—and sour Dorothea was given a smaller chair next to her. Various Farleigh cousins sat on barrels around them, trying to look dignified. Cat and Marianne sat on crates with Klartch between them. Everyone else pulled around the weather-beaten benches and settles from beside the inn walls to sit in a rough circle, while Uncle Arthur hurried out again with a cushioned chair from the saloon bar for Chrestomanci. Chrestomanci sank into it gratefully.

Drinks began arriving then. Chris Pinhoe and Clare Callow came out with trays of mugs, followed by Aunt Helen and most of her boys with trays of glasses. But they were not the only ones giving out drinks. Cat saw a thin green nonhuman hand reach round Gammer Norah's chair to present her with a foaming mug.

"Not for me. I never drink anything but water," Gammer Norah said, loftily pushing the mug aside.

The hand drew back so that it was out of Gammer Norah's sight, and the mug it held changed to a straight glass full of transparent liquid, which it held out to Gammer Norah again. A very quiet titter of laughter came from behind the chair as Gammer Norah seized the glass and took a hearty swig from it.

Cat was wondering what it really was in that glass, when two brownish purple hands pushed themselves between himself and Marianne, invitingly holding out glasses of something pink. Cat was going to take one, but Millie caught his eye and shook her head vigorously. "No, thank you," Cat said politely.

Marianne looked at him and said, "No, thank you," too. The hands drew back in a disappointed way. "Look what you did!" Marianne whispered to Cat. "They're *everywhere*!"

They were too, Cat realized, as he gratefully took a glass of real ginger beer from the tray Marianne's cousin John held out to him. The brownish purple hands were now offering what looked like beer to Uncle Charles and Marianne's dad. Marianne could not help giggling while she sipped her lemonade, when both men took the not-beer. Sour Dorothea was swigging from an enormous glass of not-water. At the gate of the yard, where a crowd of Pinhoes and Farleighs stood looking on, small half-seen shapes were flitting among legs and peering round skirts, and hands of strange colors were passing people glasses and mugs. Things that were almost like squirrels skipped along the walls of the yard. Up on the inn roof someone invisible was playing a faint skirling tune behind one of the chimneys.

"Oh, well," Cat said.

"I can't think what this Big Man thinks he's got to say to us," Gammer Norah said to Dorothea, loudly and rudely. "*We* did nothing wrong. It was all those Pinhoes' fault." She held out her empty glass. "More, please." The green hand obligingly filled it with not-water again.

Chrestomanci watched it rather quizzically. "I am not," he said, "in a very forgiving state of mind, Mrs.—er—Forelock. Your Gaffer did his best to shoot me this morning, when all I was doing was testing from the air the extent of your quite unwarranted misdirection spells. Let me make this clear to all of you: those spells are a misuse of magic that I am not prepared to treat lightly. It makes it worse that the fellow who shot at me—I presume to prevent me investigating—appears to be my own employee. My gamekeeper." He turned to Millie in a bewildered way. "Why do we need a gamekeeper, do you know? Nobody at the Castle shoots birds."

"Of course not," Millie said, quickly taking up her cue. "According to the records, the last people to go shooting were wizards on the staff of Benjamin Allworthy, nearly two hundred years ago. But the records show that, when the next Chrestomanci took over, everyone quite unaccountably forgot to dismiss Mr. Farleigh."

Jason leaned forward. "More than that," he said. "They increased his salary. You must be quite a wealthy lady these days, Mrs. Farleigh."

Gammer Norah tossed her head, causing her bun to unroll even further. "How should I know? I'm only his wife, and his third wife at that, I'd have you know." She pounded her broomstick on the cobbles of the yard. "None of that alters the fact that the poor man's turned into a stone tree! I want justice! From these Pinhoes here!" Her long eyes narrowed, and she glared along the row of Marianne's uncles and aunts.

All of them glared back. Uncle Arthur said, "We. Did. Not. Do. It. Got that, Gammer Norah?"

"We wouldn't know how," Dad added in his pacific way. "We're peaceful in our craft." He looked down and noticed the saw he was still carrying and became very embarrassed. He bent the saw about, boing *dwang*. "We always cooperated," he said. "We've lent Gaffer Farleigh our strength for the misdirections for eight years now. We lent him strength for one thing or another as long as I've been alive."

"Yes, and what did your Gaffer *do* with it?

That's what *I* want to know!" Marianne's mother asked, leaning forward fiercely. "If you ask me, he had the whole countryside under his thumb, doing what *he* wanted. And now I hear he's been at it for nearly two hundred years! Using *our* craft to lengthen his days, wasn't he?"

"Go it, Cecily!" Uncle Charles murmured.

"Never mind that!" Gammer Norah shouted, pounding with her broom again. "He's still unlawfully turned to stone! If you didn't do it, who *did*? Was it *you*?" she demanded, turning her long-eyed glare on Chrestomanci.

"I wonder what you mean by 'unlawfully,' Mrs. Farlook," Chrestomanci told her. "The man tried to kill me. But it was not my doing. When one has just been shot, it is very hard to do anything, let alone create statues." He gazed around the inn yard in his vaguest way. "If the person who did it is here, perhaps he would stand up."

Cat felt Chrestomanci using Performative Speech again and found himself standing up. His stomach felt as if it was dropping out of his body, ginger beer and all. "It was me, Mrs. Farleigh," he said. His mouth was so dry he could hardly speak. "I—I was riding by the river." The frightening thing was not so much that they were all witches here. It was the way they were all people he didn't know, gazing at him in accusing amazement. But behind Gammer Norah's chair, green and purple-brown hands were punching the air in joy. The ones like squirrels were bounding about on the walls.

And behind the inn chimneys, the music changed to loud, glad, and triumphant. This helped Cat a great deal. He swallowed and went on, "I wasn't quick enough to stop him firing at the flying machine— I'm sorry. But after that he was going to shoot Klartch, then Syracuse, then me. It was the only way I could manage to stop him."

"*You?*" said Gammer Norah, leaning incredulously on her broom. "A little skinny child like *you*? Are you lying to me?"

"Deep in evil," Dorothea said. "They're all like that."

"I was born with nine lives," Cat explained.

"Oh, you're *that* one, are you?" Gammer Norah said venomously. She was going to hurl a spell at him, Cat knew she was. But Millie made a small, quick gesture and Gammer Norah's attention somehow switched back to the Pinhoes. "I don't see any of *you* looking very sorry!" she yelled at them.

This was true. Grins were spreading across most of the Pinhoe faces. Cat sat down again, hugely relieved, and gave Klartch's head a comforting rub.

Gammer Norah screamed, "And what about the rest of it? Eh? What about the rest?"

"What rest is this?" Chrestomanci asked politely.

"The frogs, the ill-wishing, the fleas, the nits, the ants in all our cupboards!" Gammer Norah yelled, pounding with her broomstick. "Deny all that *if* you can! Every time we sent a plague back on you, you did another. We sent you whooping cough, we sent you smallpox, but you still didn't stop!"

"Bosh. We never sent you anything," Uncle Richard said.

"It was *you* sent *us* frogs," Uncle Charles added. "Or is *your* mind going now?"

Cat felt his face grow bright and hot as he remembered sending those frogs away from Mr. Vastion's surgery. He was wondering whether to stand up and confess again, when Marianne spoke up, loudly and clearly. "I'm afraid it was Gammer Pinhoe sending all those things on her own, Mrs. Farleigh."

Cat realized she was a lot braver than he was. She was the instant target of every Pinhoe there. The aunts glared at her, even more fiercely than they had glared at Gammer Norah. The uncles looked either contemptuous or reproachful. Dad said warningly, "I *told* you not to spread stories, Marianne!"

Mum added, "How *could* you, Marianne? You *know* how poorly Gammer is."

And from the back, Great-Uncle Edgar boomed, "Now that's enough of that, child!"

Marianne went pale, but she managed to say, "It is true."

"Yes," Chrestomanci agreed. "It *is* true. We at the Castle have been checking up on all of you rather seriously for the last few weeks. Ever since young Eric here pointed out to me the misdirection spells, in fact, we have had you under observation.

We noted that an old lady called Edith Pinhoe was sending hostile magics to Helm St. Mary, Uphelm, and various other villages nearby, and we were preparing to take steps."

"Though we did wonder why none of you tried to stop her," Millie put in. "But it's fairly clear to me now that she must have bespelled all of you as well." She smiled kindly at Marianne. "Except you, my dear."

While the Pinhoes were turning to one another, doubtful and horrified, Gammer Norah kept beating with her broomstick. "I want justice!" she bellowed. "Plagues and stone trees! I want justice for both! I want—" She broke off with a gurgle as a green hand clapped itself over her mouth. A purple-brown hand firmly took away her broomstick.

Cat thought that most people there decided that Chrestomanci had shut her up. He was fairly sure only a few of them could see the hidden folks. But Chrestomanci could.

Chrestomanci swallowed a slight grin and said, "Presently, Mrs. Farago, although you may not like the justice when you have it. There are a few serious questions I have to ask first. The most important of these concerns the *other* Gaffer in the case, the Mr. Ezekiel Pinhoe who was said to be dead eight years ago. Now a short while ago, I visited Ulverscote—"

"But you couldn't!" quite a number of Pinhoes protested. "You're not a Pinhoe."

"I took the precaution of getting a lift with Mr. and Mrs. Yeldham here," Chrestomanci said. "As

you may know, Mrs. Yeldham was born a Pinhoe."
Beside him, Irene colored up and bent over Nutcase
on her knee, as if she were not sure that being a
Pinhoe was altogether a good thing. Chrestomanci
looked over to where the Reverend Pinhoe was quietly sipping lemonade over by the inn door. "I called
on your vicar— Perhaps you could explain,
Reverend."

Oh, it was *him*! Marianne thought. The day I
met the Farleigh girls. He was in the churchyard.

The Reverend Pinhoe looked utterly flustered
and extremely unhappy. "Well, yes. It is a most terrible thing," he said, "but most impressive magic, I
must admit. But appalling, quite appalling all the
same." He took an agitated gulp of lemonade.
"Chrestomanci asked me to show him Elijah
Pinhoe's grave, you see. I saw no harm in that, of
course, and conducted him to the corner of the
church where the grave was—is, I mean.
Chrestomanci then most politely asked my permission to work a little magic there. As I saw no harm
in that, I naturally agreed. And—" The vicar took
another agitated gulp from his glass. "You can judge
my astonishment," he said, "when Chrestomanci
caused the coffin to emerge from the grave—
without, I hasten to say, disturbing a blade of grass
or any of the flowers you Pinhoe ladies so regularly
place there—and then, to my further surprise,
caused the coffin to open, without disturbing so
much as a screw."

The Reverend Pinhoe tried to take another

gulp from his glass and discovered it was empty. "Oh, please—" he said. A blue-green hand emerged from behind the rain barrel beside him and passed him a full glass. The Reverend Pinhoe surveyed it dubiously, then took a sip and nodded.

"I thank you," he said. "I think. Anyway, I regret to have to inform you that the coffin contained nothing but a large wooden post and three bags of extremely moldy chaff. Gaffer Pinhoe was not inside it." He took another sip from his new glass and turned a little pink. "It was a great shock to me," he said.

It was a great shock to some of the aunts too. Aunt Helen and Great-Aunt Sue turned to each other and gaped. Aunt Joy said, "You mean someone *stole* him? After all we spent on flowers!"

Chrestomanci was looking vaguely around the yard. Cat knew he was checking to see who was surprised by the news and who was not. The Farleighs looked a little puzzled but not at all surprised. Most of the Pinhoe cousins were as surprised as Aunt Joy was and frowned at one another, mystified. But to Marianne's dismay, none of her uncles turned a hair, though Uncle Isaac tutted and tried to pretend he was upset. Dad took it calmest of all. Oh, dear! she thought sadly.

"A very strange thing," Chrestomanci said. Cat could feel him using Performative Speech again. "Now who can explain this odd occurrence?"

Great-Uncle Edgar cleared his throat and

looked uneasily at Great-Uncle Lester. Great-Uncle Lester went gray and seemed to get very shaky. "*You* tell them, Edgar," he quavered. "I—I'm not up to it after all this time."

"The fact is," Great-Uncle Edgar said, looking pompously around the inn yard, "Gaffer Pinhoe is not—er—actually dead."

"What's this?" Gammer Norah cried out, catching up rather late. "What's this? Not *dead*?" She's drunk! Marianne thought. She's going to start singing soon. "What do you mean, not dead? I *told* you to kill him. Gaffer Farleigh *ordered* you to kill him. Your own Gammer, his *wife*, said you had to kill him. Why didn't you?"

"We felt that was a little extreme," Great-Uncle Lester said apologetically. "Edgar and I simply used that spell that was used on Luke Pinhoe." He nodded at Irene. "Your ancestor, Mrs. Yeldham. We disabled both his legs. Then we put him in that old cart he loved so much and drove him into the woods."

Irene looked aghast.

"It had been our intention," Uncle Edgar explained, "to stow him beyond and behind with the hidden folks. But, upon experiment, we found we couldn't open the confining spell. So we made another confining spell by building a barrier and left him behind that."

"Please understand, Gammer Norah," Great-Uncle Lester pleaded. "Gaffer Farleigh knew all about it, and he didn't object. It—it seemed so much *kinder* that way."

Chrestomanci said, so softly and gently that both great-uncles shuddered, "It seems to *me* exceedingly cruel. Who else knew about this *kind* plot of yours?"

"Gammer knew, of course—" Great-Uncle Edgar began.

But Chrestomanci was still using Performative Speech. Dad spoke up. "They told all of us," he said, bending his saw about. "All his sons. They needed to, because of dividing out his property. We weren't surprised. We'd all seen it coming. We arranged for Cedric and Isaac to leave him eggs and bread and stuff behind the barrier." He looked earnestly up at Chrestomanci. "He must be still alive. The food goes."

Here, Great-Aunt Sue, who had been sitting holding the collar of the one fat dog that had come back from chasing the flying machine, quite suddenly stood up and slapped her hands down her crisp skirt. "Alive in the woods," she said. "For eight years. Without the use of his legs. And all of you lying about it. *Nine* grown men. I'm ashamed to belong to this family. Edgar, that does it. I'm leaving. I'm going to my sister outside Hopton. Now. And don't expect to hear from me again. Come on, Towser," she said, and went striding briskly out of the yard, with the dog panting after her.

Great-Uncle Edgar sprang up despairingly. "Susannah! Please! It's just—we just didn't want to upset anyone!"

He started after Great-Aunt Sue. But

Chrestomanci shook his head and pointed to the bench where Great-Uncle Edgar had been sitting. Great-Uncle Edgar sank back onto it, purple faced and wretched.

"I must say I'm glad Clarice isn't here to hear this," Great-Uncle Lester murmured.

I wish *I* wasn't here to hear it! Marianne thought. Tears were pushing to come out of her eyes, and she knew she would never feel the same about any of her uncles.

Aunt Joy, who seemed to have waited for this to be over, stood up too, and folded her arms ominously. "Eight years," she said. "Eight years I've been living a lie." She loosed one arm in order to point accusingly at Uncle Charles. "Charles," she said, "don't you expect to come home tonight, because I'm not having you! You spineless layabout. They do away with your own father, and you don't even mention the matter, let alone object. I've had enough of you, and that's final!"

Uncle Charles looked sideways at Aunt Joy, under her pointing finger, with his head down, rather like Joe. Marianne did not think he looked enormously unhappy.

Aunt Joy swung her pointing finger round toward the rest of the aunts. "And I don't know how you women can sit there, *knowing* what they've all done and lied about. I'm ashamed of you all, that's all I have to say!" She swung herself round then and stalked out of the yard as well. The invisible person on the roof played a march in time to Aunt Joy's banging shoes.

Marianne looked at her other aunts. Aunt Polly had not turned a hair. Uncle Cedric had obviously told her everything years ago. They were very close. Aunt Helen was staring trustingly at Uncle Arthur, sure that he had good reasons for not telling her; but Aunt Prue was looking at Uncle Simeon very strangely. Her own mother looked more unhappy than Marianne had ever seen her. Marianne could tell Dad had never said a word to her. She looked at Uncle Isaac's grave face and wondered what— if anything—he had told Aunt Dinah.

"I hope no one else wishes to leave," Chrestomanci said. "Good." He turned his eyes to Dad. Though his face was pale and pulled with pain, his eyes were still bright and dark. Dad jumped as he met those eyes. "Mr. Pinhoe," Chrestomanci said, "perhaps you would be good enough to explain just *what* you had seen coming and *why* everyone felt it was necessary to—er—do away with your father."

Dad laid the saw carefully down by his feet. The brownish purple hand at once obligingly offered him another tankard of drink. Harry Pinhoe took it with a nod of thanks, too bothered by what he was going to say to notice where the drink had come from. "It was that egg," he said slowly. "The egg was the last straw. Anyone had only to look at it to know Gaffer had fetched it from behind the confinement spell. Everything else led up to that, really."

"In what way?" Chrestomanci asked.

Harry Pinhoe sighed. "You might say," he

answered, "that Old Gaffer suffered from too much dwimmer. He was always off in the woods gathering weird herbs and poking into things best left alone. And he kept on at Gammer that the hidden folk were unhappy in confinement and ought to be let free. Gammer wouldn't hear of it, of course. Nor wouldn't Jed Farleigh. They had rows about it almost every week, Gammer saying it has always been our *job* to keep them in, and Gaffer shouting his nonsense about it was high time to let them out. Well, then——"

Harry Pinhoe took a long encouraging pull at his strange drink and made a puzzled face at the taste of it before he went on.

"Well, then, the crisis came when Gaffer came out of the woods with this huge, like, egg. He gave it to Gammer and told her to keep it warm and let it hatch. Gammer said why should she do any such thing? Gaffer wouldn't tell her, not until she put a truth spell on him. *Then* he told her it was his scheme to let the hidden folks out. He said that when this egg hatched, he would be there to watch the bindings on the hidden folks undone." Harry Pinhoe looked unhappily over at Chrestomanci. "That did it, see. Gaffer said it like a prophecy, and Gammer couldn't have that. *Gammer's* the only one that's allowed to prophesy, we all know that. So she told her brothers Gaffer was quite out of hand and ordered them to kill him."

Marianne shivered. Cat found he had one hand protectively on Klartch, gripping the warm fluff on his back. Klartch, luckily, seemed to be asleep. Chrestomanci smiled slightly and seemed entirely bewildered. "But I don't understand," he said. "*Why* is it necessary to keep these unfortunate beings confined?"

Dad was puzzled that he should ask. "Because we always have," he said.

Gammer Norah came abreast of the talk again. "We always have," she proclaimed. "Because they're abominations. Wicked, ungodly things. Sly, mischievous, wild, and *beastly*!"

Dorothea looked up from her enormous glass. "Dangerous," she said. "Evil. Vermin. I'd destroy every one of them if I could."

She said it with such venom that a desperate, terrified shiver ran round all the half-seen and invisible beings in the yard. Cat and Marianne found themselves clutched by unseen, shaking hands. One half-seen person climbed into Marianne's lap. A hard head with whiskers—or possibly antennae—butted pleadingly at Cat's face and, he was fairly sure, another person ran up him and sat on his head for safety. He looked at Chrestomanci for help.

Chrestomanci, however, looked at Dorothea and then, sternly, at Harry Pinhoe. "I regret to have to tell you," he said, "that Gaffer Pinhoe was quite right and the rest of you are quite, quite wrong."

Dad jerked backward on his bench. There was an outcry of shocked denial from Pinhoes and

Farleighs alike. Dad's face turned red. "How come?" he said.

Millie glanced at Chrestomanci and took over. "We've been finding out all about you," she said. "We've traced Pinhoes, Farleighs, and Cleeves right back almost to the dawn of history now."

There was another shocked muttering at this, as everyone realized at last that their secrecy was truly at an end. But they all listened attentively as Millie went on.

"You've always lived here," she said. "You must be some of the oldest witch families we know about. We found you first almost like clans, most of you living in tiny houses round the chief's great hall, and the rest of you living *in* the hall as followers of the chief. Woods House is certainly built on the exact spot where the Pinhoe hall was—and that was built a surprisingly long time ago too. Before the church, in fact. The Farleigh hall seems to have been destroyed in the trouble that came, but the Cleeves still have theirs, although it's the Cleeve Arms now, over in Crowhelm."

This caused some interest. Pinhoes and Farleighs turned to one another and murmured, "I never knew that. Cleeve Arms *is* old, though."

Heads turned back to Millie as she continued. "Now there are at least three important things you should know about those early days. The first is that your chief, who was known as Gaffer from quite early on, was chosen from among the old chief's family, and he was always chosen for having the most dwimmer. And he wasn't just chief, he was a prophet and a foreteller too. Your Old Gaffer was behaving just as he should, in fact. *He* was the one who chose the Gammer—and she wasn't always his wife, either. She was the woman with the most dwimmer. And the pair of them not only governed the rest, they worked in *partnership* with the hidden folks. These folks were cherished and loved and guarded. You shared magics with them, and they repaid you with healings and—"

This was too much for everyone. Millie was drowned out with cries of "That *can't* be!" and "I never *heard* such twaddle!"

Millie smiled slightly, and her voice suddenly came out over and above the objections, clear as a bell and, seemingly, not very loud. But everyone heard when she said, "Then comes the awful gap, with all sorts of horror in it." Everyone hushed to hear what this horror was.

"A new religion came to this country," Millie said, "full of zeal and righteousness—the kind of religion where, if other people didn't believe in it, the righteous ones killed and tortured them until they did. This religion hated witches and hated the hidden folk even more. They saw all witches and invisible folks as demons, monsters, and devils, and their priests devised ways of killing them and destroying their magic that really worked.

"All three Gaffers at this time prophesied, as far as we can tell, and all of you, Pinhoes, Farleighs, and Cleeves, at once made sure that no one knew you were witches. What craft you used, you used in utmost secrecy, and because the hidden folk were even more at risk than you were, you all combined to keep them safe by locking them away behind the back of the distance. It was only intended to be a temporary measure. The Gaffers were all quite clear that the bloodthirsty righteous ones would go away in time. And so they did. But before they did, their priests became even more skillful and learned to conceal their plans even from the Gaffers. Even so, the Gaffer Farleigh of the time started to prophesy disaster. But that was the night the bloodthirsty ones attacked.

"They came with fire and swords and powerful magics, and they killed everyone they could." Millie looked round the yard and at the people clustering at the gate. "When they had finished," she said, "the only people left were children, all of them younger than any of the children here. We think the bloodthirsty ones took all the children they could catch and educated them in their own religious ways, and some children escaped to the woods. The gap lasts about fifteen years, so those children had time to grow up. Then, thank goodness, the bloodthirsty ones were conquered themselves, probably by the Romans, and you all came together again, those from the woods and those who had been captured, and started to rebuild your lives."

Chrestomanci took a deep breath as Millie finished and steadied himself on the arms of his chair. He was looking awfully ill, Cat thought anxiously.

"But you see what that means," Chrestomanci said. "These children had been too young to understand properly. They only knew what their anxious parents had impressed on them before the slaughter. They thought they had to keep their craft secret. They believed it was their duty to keep the hidden folks confined—and they had a vague notion that danger would come if they didn't. And they all knew that if a Gaffer prophesied, horrible things would happen—so they chose Gaffers that were good at giving orders, rather than those with dwimmer or the gift of foresight. And," Chrestomanci said ruefully, "I am afraid to say that the bloodthirsty doctrines of the religious ones had rubbed off on quite a lot of them, and they saw it as their religious duty to do things this way."

A long, thoughtful silence followed this. While it lasted, Cat watched a spidery hand, a new one that was a silvery white color, reach from behind Chrestomanci's chair to pass Chrestomanci a small glass of greenish liquid. Chrestomanci took it, looking rather startled. Cat watched him sniff it, hold it up to the light, and then cautiously dip a finger into it. His finger came out sparking green and gold like a firework. Chrestomanci examined it for a moment. Then he murmured, "Thank you very much," and drank the glassful off. He made the most dreadful face and clapped his hand to his stomach for a moment. But after that he looked a good deal better.

Everyone stirred then, except for Gammer

Norah and Dorothea, who seemed to be asleep. Dad looked up and said, "Well, it makes a good story."

"It's more than a story," Chrestomanci said. He turned to a piece of the air beside him and asked, "Have you got a record of all this, Tom?"

Chrestomanci's secretary, Tom, was unexpectedly standing there, holding a notepad. Beside him stood old Miss Rosalie, the Castle librarian. She had her glasses down her nose and her nose almost inside the large blue folder she held, which she seemed to be reading avidly.

Tom said, "Every word, sir, right from the start."

Miss Rosalie looked up from the folder and, in her usual tactless, downright way, declared, "I've never met such flagrant misuse of magic, not *ever*. Not to speak of conspiracy to misuse. You can prosecute the lot of them."

Chrestomanci and Millie looked as if they had rather Miss Rosalie had kept her mouth shut. There was an outcry of anger and dismay from all round the yard. The Pinhoe uncles stood up threateningly and so did most of the Farleigh cousins. Gammer Norah woke up with a jump, glaring.

Unfortunately, that was the moment when Klartch woke up too, and staggered inquiringly out across the cobbles.

20

❧✦❧

CAT WAS SURE that either Chrestomanci or Millie—
or possibly both of them—had caused Klartch to
wake up. It was otherwise hard to understand
how Klartch slipped so easily between Cat's clutching fingers, or how Marianne missed her grab for
his tail.

Dad said, "What the hell is *that*?"

"It's what came out of the egg," Uncle Charles
told him. "Didn't I mention it to you? I know I told
Arthur."

Their voices were almost drowned in
Dorothea's screams. "It's an abomination! Kill it,
Mother! Oh, the folks are loose! We're all dead
meat! *Kill* it!"

Gammer Norah sprang to her feet and pointed
at Klartch, who turned his head toward her inquiringly. "Death," Gammer Norah intoned. "*Die*, you
misbegotten creature of night."

To Marianne's embarrassment and Cat's heartfelt relief, nothing happened. Klartch just blinked
and looked wondering. Dorothea pointed a finger

at him and shrieked, "*Melt! Die! Begone!*" Klartch stared at her, while a crowd of hard-to-see beings rushed to him and hovered round him protectively. Quite a number of people could see these. Everyone began shouting, "The folks are loose! The folks are loose!" Some of those gathered by the gate screamed as loudly as Dorothea.

Rather shakily, Chrestomanci stood up. "Do be quiet, all of you," he said wearily. "It's only a baby griffin."

The noise died down, except for Gammer Norah, who said angrily, "Why didn't I kill it? Why is it not dead?"

"Because, Mrs. Furlong," Chrestomanci said, "while we were talking, my colleague Jason Yeldham here has been busy removing your magic."

Gammer Norah gaped at him. *"What?"*

Dad said, "That *has* to be nonsense. Magic's an inborn part of you. And, Marianne, you had no business at all giving that blasted boy that egg. You've betrayed our sacred trust and I'm very angry with you."

Chrestomanci sighed. "You didn't listen to a word we said, did you, Mr. Pinhoe? There *is* no sacred trust and the hidden folks were only confined as a temporary measure for their own safety. And magic may be inborn, but so are your appendix and your tonsils. They can be removed too. Better show them, Jason."

Jason nodded and made a gentle pushing

motion. A huge ball, made up of half-transparent green-blue strands, all wound up like a vast ball of knitting wool, rolled away from beside Jason's knees. In a light, drifting way it rolled to the middle of the yard and came to a stop there. "There," Jason said. "That's all the Farleigh magic. Every bit of it."

Gammer Norah, Dorothea, and the Farleigh cousins stared at it. One cousin said, "You'd no right to do that to us."

"I not only have the right," Chrestomanci said, "but as a government employee it's my duty to do this. People who use their magic to give a whole village a dangerous disease like smallpox are not to be trusted with it."

"That was just Marianne telling stories," said Dad.

Chrestomanci nodded at Tom, who flipped back pages in his notebook and read out, "'We sent you whooping cough, we sent you smallpox, but you still didn't stop!' Those are Mrs. Farleigh's exact words, Mr. Pinhoe."

Dad said nothing. He picked up his saw again and bent it about, meaningly.

Irene nudged Jason and whispered to him. Jason grinned and said, "Yes!" He turned to Chrestomanci. "Irene thinks the wood folks ought to have this magic as compensation for wrongful imprisonment."

"A very good idea," Chrestomanci said.

Irene stood up to make happy beckoning movements to the walls, forgetting that Nutcase was asleep on her knee. Nutcase thumped to the ground, looked irritably around, and saw all the half-seen creatures leaving Klartch in order to dive delightedly upon the ball of magic. He was off like a black streak. He got to the ball of magic first and plunged into it, straight through and out the other side. Trailing long strings of blue-green, with a crowd of angry beings after him, he raced up across Dorothea, up the pile of barrels behind her, and from there to the top of the wall.

There will be no holding Nutcase now, Marianne thought, watching Nutcase jump off the wall into the alley and Dorothea resentfully licking scratches on her arm. She was depressed and worried. Dad was never going to understand and never going to forgive her. And Gaffer had still not turned up. On top of that, school started on Monday week. Though look on the bright side, she thought. It'll keep me away from my family, during the daytime at least.

Meanwhile, the hard-to-see people were helping themselves enthusiastically to the rest of the ball of magic. The ball shrank, and tattered, and seemed to dissolve away like smoke in a wind. There were a lot more of the folks than Cat or Marianne had realized. Some of them must have been completely invisible.

Cat conjured a sausage roll from somewhere inside the Pinhoe Arms and set out to coax Klartch away from the middle of the yard. He did not like the way Gammer Norah and some of the Pinhoes were looking at Klartch. He found himself, with the sausage roll held out in front of Klartch's beak, backing away past a row of Marianne's aunts.

"Strange-looking creature, isn't he?" said one.

"You can see it's a baby from the fluff. Rather sweet in a yicky way," said a second.

The third one said, "What are you doing with one of my sausage rolls, boy?"

And the one who Cat was sure was Marianne's mother said, thinking about it, "You know, it's going to look just like Charles's painting on the inn sign when it's grown. And it's going to be vast. Look at the size of the feet on it."

Before Cat could think of anything to say in reply, the Farleighs were leaving, trudging sullenly out of the yard, muttering murderously about having to walk home now they had no magic.

"It isn't exactly like tonsils," Chrestomanci remarked as they tramped past him. "It can grow back in time if you're careful." He was standing with Tom on one side of him and Miss Rosalie on the other, and it is doubtful if any of the Farleighs heard him, because Miss Rosalie was saying brightly at the same time, "I make that forty-two charges of misuse of magic, sir, in Ulverscote alone. Shall I read them out?"

"No need," Chrestomanci said. "Yet." He said to all the Pinhoes, "You all understand, do you, that

I can take your magic too, or have nearly all of you arrested? Instead of doing that, I am going to ask for your cooperation. You have a whole new set of magics here, and one of my duties is to study unknown magic. I would particularly like to know more about the kind you call dwimmer." His eyes flicked to Cat for a moment. "I think I need to know more of dwimmer as soon as possible. We would like as many of you as feel able to visit the Castle and explain your working methods to us."

He got eight outraged glowers from Marianne's uncles and great-uncles for this. Dad twanged his saw disgustedly. Millie bustled happily up to the aunts, who all turned their backs on her, except for Marianne's mother, who folded her arms and stared, rather in Aunt Joy's manner.

"You're the famous herb mistress, aren't you, Mrs. Pinhoe?" Millie said. "I really would be grateful if you'd come and give me a lesson or so—"

"What, give away all my secrets?" Mum said. "You've got a hope."

"But, my dear, why ever do you need to keep things secret?" Millie asked. "Suppose you'd been killed in the fight just now."

"I've tried to bring Marianne up to know herbs," Mum said. She gave Marianne an irritated look. "Not that it seems to have taken very well."

"Well, of course it wouldn't," Millie said, smiling at Marianne. "Your daughter's an enchantress, not a witch. She'll have quite a different way of doing things."

While Mum was staring at Marianne as if Marianne had suddenly grown antlers and a trunk, Millie sighed and whirled away to Chrestomanci, saying, "Get in the car, love. You look wiped."

"I need to have a word with Gammer Pinhoe first," Chrestomanci said.

"I'll drive you down to the Dell, then," Millie said.

This caused Cat to have to tempt Klartch all the way back across the yard to the car. They went rather slowly because both Cat and Klartch were constantly turning to watch strings of blue-green magic fluttering along the walls, or being dragged into barrels, or flying in tatters from chimneys, as the half-seen folk carried it away. Millie waited for them, and Jason held the rear door open and helped Cat heave Klartch in beside Irene. Klartch instantly ramped upright to look out of the window. There were loud popping sounds as his talons went into the expensive leather upholstery.

By that time, the Pinhoes had gathered that Chrestomanci was going down to the Dell. They were not going to let him loose on Gammer on her own. Cat found himself between Marianne and Miss Rosalie, inside a crowd of Pinhoes, all of them trotting, jogging, and crunching broken glass behind the car as it glided down the hill.

"Gaffer must be *somewhere*," Marianne said miserably as they passed Great-Uncle Lester's ruined car.

Dad answered her by giving vent to his feelings.

"Look what you brought us to, Marianne! This is all your fault for thinking you know better than the rest of us. The good old ways are not good enough for you. No. You had to get us noticed by the Castle. And see where we are now, at the mercy of these jumped-up, jazzy know-it-alls in good suits, who'll have us arrested if we don't do—"

He was interrupted for a second here by Nicola's mother, swooping uphill past them on her broomstick. "I can't wait, Lester!" she called out. "I'll miss visiting hours."

As Great-Uncle Lester gave her a dismal wave, Dad took up his diatribe again. "Them and their threats! How can they say we've misused magic and then want to know what it is we do? It makes no sense. But they think they have the right to give us a going-over with their new-fangled stuck-up ways and their stupid stories about slaughter in history and children misunderstanding—I don't believe a word of it. We're just ordinary folk, doing what we've always done, and they come along—"

Miss Rosalie, who had been looking increasingly annoyed, snapped, "Oh, shut *up*, man! Of *course* you can go back to your good old ways. We want to *study* them."

This simply set Dad off again. "Poking and prying. Going on about craft things nobody should talk about. Letting out the hidden folk. That's just what I'm complaining about, woman! What are we, a flaming *fish tank*?"

"I refuse to argue with you!" Miss Rosalie panted haughtily.

"Good!" said Dad, and went on with his diatribe in an increasingly breathless mutter as the car gathered speed down the hill. He did not stop, even when the car was turning the corner at the bottom of the hill, where they encountered Aunt Joy standing on her half-built wall.

"I meant what I said!" Aunt Joy shouted, and hurled a suitcase at Uncle Charles. "You're not coming back, and here's your things, wedding suit and all. I jumped on it."

Uncle Charles did not try to answer. He simply picked up the battered suitcase and trotted on, smiling sheepishly at Uncle Richard. "Staring at us," went Dad. "Thinking they're so clever. Fish tank. All Marianne's fault."

At the Dell, they found Gammer outside the front door, surrounded by hard-to-see flying folk. They did not appear to love Gammer. They darted in, pulled her hair, tweaked and scratched at her, and darted back away. Gammer beat at them with a rolled-up newspaper. "Shoo!" she shouted. "Gerroff! Shoo!"

Aunt Dinah, who could not seem to see the flying ones at all, was dodging helplessly in and out, ducking under the newspaper and saying, "That's enough now, Gammer dear. Come inside now, dear."

"Fish tank," said Dad, and ran down in a kind of moaning sound as he saw how easily Gammer had managed to walk out through his careful containment spells.

Gammer stared at Chrestomanci as he climbed stiffly and shakily out of the car. She seemed to know at once who he was. "Don't you dare!" she shouted at him as he walked toward her round the duck pond. "You've only come to interferret me. I didn't do it. It was Edgar and Lester."

The half-seen ones knew who Chrestomanci was too. They flew up from Gammer in a body and roosted on the cottage roof to watch.

"I know about Edgar and Lester, ma'am," Chrestomanci said. "I want to know why you were persecuting the Farleighs."

"Jedded my head," Gammer said. "My mouth is porpoised."

"Means her lips are sealed," Uncle Charles translated from among the crowd.

"Utterly dolphined," Gammer agreed.

"And possibly whaled as well," Chrestomanci murmured. "I think you had better unwalrus them, ma'am, and—"

The gate from the back way, through Uncle Isaac's vegetable acres, clicked quietly open to let Molly and Gaffer through.

Not everyone saw them straightaway, because the corner of the cottage was in the way. But Marianne saw. And she knew why Gaffer had been so long on the way. His legs were bent and bowed and his feet twisted so that it was all but impossible

654

for him to walk. He had both arms across the unicorn's back. She was walking one careful step at a time, and then stopping so that Gaffer could swing himself along beside her. Each time his legs had to take his weight, Marianne saw him shudder with pain.

She turned and screamed at her great-uncles. She was so angry that both of them recoiled from her, almost into the hedge at the back. "That is the cruelest thing I ever saw! Uncle Edgar, I shall never speak to you again! Uncle Lester, I shall never go *near* you!" She raced toward Gaffer and tore the ensorcellment off him. It was a bit like clearing weeds and creepers off a struggling overgrown tree in Mum's garden. Marianne clawed and pulled and dragged, and the spell fought back like thorns and nettles, but she finally hauled it all away, panting, with stinging hands and tears in her eyes, and threw it to the hard-to-see folk to get rid of. They swooped on it and took it away gladly.

Gaffer slowly and creakily stood to his proper height, the same height as Chrestomanci. He smiled at her. "Why, thank you, pet," he said.

Molly turned her head to say sadly, "I can heal wounds of the flesh, but that was magic." She added to Gaffer, "Keep your arm over me. You won't walk easily straightaway."

They moved on, around the corner of the cottage. Chrestomanci, now leaning beside Cat on the long black bonnet of the car, could see them perfectly, but Gammer, with Aunt Dinah dodging around her, was too busy screaming insults at Chrestomanci to notice.

"Inkbubble chest of drawers!" she yelled. "Unstuck bog!"

Cat thought that both the unicorn and the tall old man had a curious, unreal, silvery look as they came round into the sunlight at the front of the cottage.

There was a long murmur from the Pinhoes. "It's old Gaffer!" and "Isn't that his old mare, Molly?" they said.

This alerted Gammer. She swung around, with dismay all over her ruined face. "You!" she said. "I told them to kill you!"

"There were times when I wished they had," Gaffer answered. "What have you been up to, Edith? Let's have the truth now."

Gammer shrugged a little. "Frogs," she said. "Ants, nits, fleas. Itching powder." She giggled. "They thought the itching was more fleas and washed till they were raw."

"Who did?" Gaffer asked. He took his arm off Molly and stood looking down at her on his own. The unicorn backed herself round and stepped across to Chrestomanci. There she stretched her neck out and gave Chrestomanci's ragged, bleeding arm the merest flick with her horn.

Chrestomanci jerked and gasped. Cat could feel the warm rush of health from the horn, even though it was not aimed at him. "Thank you,"

Chrestomanci said gratefully, looking into the unicorn's wise blue eyes. "Very much indeed." He was a better color already and, although the blood was still there, all over Joe's shirt, Cat was fairly sure that there was now no bullet wound in Chrestomanci's arm.

"My pleasure," replied the unicorn. She winked a blue eye at Cat and stepped around again toward Gaffer.

"*Who* did?" Gaffer was repeating. "Who have you been tormenting now?"

Gammer looked mulishly down at the grass. "Those Farleighs," she said. "I hate the lot of them. That Dorothea of theirs met a griffin by the Castle gates and they said I let it out."

"The griffin was only looking for her egg, poor creature," Gaffer said. "She thought it might have arrived at the Castle by then. What had you done with it?"

Gammer scrubbed at the grass with one toe. She giggled a little. "It wouldn't break," she said, "not even when I threw it downstairs. I made Harry stick it in the attic with a binding on it and hoped it would die. Nasty thing."

Gaffer pressed his lips together and looked down at her with great pity. "You've gone like a wicked small child, haven't you?" he said. "No thought for others at all. But your spells on them are stronger than ever, and they still all do your bidding."

The unicorn softly approached.

Gammer looked up and saw the long, whorled horn coming toward her. "No!" she said. "It wasn't me! It was Edgar and Lester."

Gaffer shook his head, floppy old hat and all. "No, it was *you*, Edith. Let go now. You've gone your length."

He stood aside and let Molly gently touch the tip of her horn to Gammer's forehead. Cat felt the warm blast of this too, but this time it seemed to be blowing the other way. Gammer gave out a small noise that was horribly like Klartch's "Weep!" and crumpled slowly down on the grass, where she lay curled up like a baby.

Aunt Dinah charged forward. "What has that monster done?"

Gaffer looked at her with tears running on his withered cheeks and into his beard. "You wouldn't wish to be forced to obey madness for the next ten years, would you?" he said. His pleasant voice was all hoarse. He coughed. "She'll last three days now," he said. "You'll have time to choose your new Gammer before she dies."

Aunt Dinah looked helplessly at the other Pinhoes crowded around the car and the pond. "But there's only Marianne," she said. Marianne's heart sank.

"Ah no," Gaffer said. "Marianne has her own way to go and her own race to run, bless her. You mustn't lumber anyone with this who hasn't found her own way in life first." He looked toward the rear door of the car, where Irene and Jason were trying to shove Klartch back inside. Klartch wanted to get out and examine the ducks. "My friend Jason's lady has more dwimmer than I've known for many years," Gaffer said. "Think about it."

Irene looked up into the massed stares of the Pinhoes and turned bright, warm red. "Oh, my goodness!" she said.

21

✦✦

UNCLE RICHARD AND Uncle Isaac walked carefully around the edge of the pond, and the Reverend Pinhoe followed them. Warily, giving the unicorn a very wide berth, the two uncles picked Gammer up and carried her away indoors. Aunt Dinah rushed in after them. Dad watched them with a scowl. "I wouldn't have Marianne anyway," he said. "She's not suitable."

"No indeed," Chrestomanci agreed. "She can override any of your spells any time she pleases. Awkward for you. Tell me, Marianne, how do you feel about being educated at the Castle? As a weekly boarder, say, coming home every weekend? I've just made the same arrangement with your brother Joe. Would you like to join him?"

Marianne could hardly think, let alone speak, for huge, nervous delight. She felt her face stretching into a great smile. Looking up at Gaffer, she saw his eyes twinkling encouragement to her, even though he was busy mopping his cheeks on his ragged sleeve.

Before either of them could say anything, Dad burst out, "*Joe*, did you say? What do you want with *him*? He's even more of a disappointment than Marianne is!"

"On the contrary," Chrestomanci said. "Joe has immense and unusual talent. He has already invented three new ways of combining magic with machinery. A couple of wizards from the Royal Society are coming down to interview him tomorrow. They're very excited about him. So what do you say, Marianne?"

"I see!" Dad burst out, again before Marianne could speak. "I see. You're going to take them off and make them think they're too good for the rest of their family!"

"Only if you make it that way," Chrestomanci replied. "The surest way to make them think they're too good for you is to keep telling yourself that and then telling them that they are."

Dad looked a trifle dazed. "I can't get my head around this," he said.

"Then you have a problem, Mr. Pinhoe," Chrestomanci said, and then turned away to Gaffer. "Are you going to be taking your former place again as Gaffer, sir?" he asked.

Gaffer slowly shook his head. "Molly and I are not really with this world anymore," he said. The twinkle with which he was looking at Marianne began to glow. "I was always one for walking the woods," he said. "Now I can walk again, I'll be going far and wide with Molly, bringing young

Jason more odd herbs than he's seen in his life, I reckon. Besides," he added, and the glow blazed into humor now, "if you're wanting them all to go on the way they always did, then Harry will do you a fine stout job at that. Let him carry on." He bent and kissed Marianne, a soft, tickly brushing with his beard. "Bye, pet. You go and find who you really are, and don't let anyone stop you."

He and Molly turned to go. Chrestomanci went striding back to the car, where Tom was standing with Miss Rosalie. "Tom, take Miss Rosalie back with you," Cat heard him say. "Make a list of her forty-two misuses of magic and send a copy to each of the Pinhoe brothers and both their uncles. I want them all to know what trouble they could be in if they don't cooperate with us." Tom nodded and took hold of Miss Rosalie's skinny arm. Both of them vanished. Chrestomanci turned to tell Cat to get into the car.

But there was a frantic, pattering, yelling disturbance at the back of the crowd. Marianne's uncles and aunts scattered this way and that, and the Reverend Pinhoe, who was still only halfway round the pond, was dislodged into the water with a splash. He stood up to his knees in green weeds, staring as Dolly the donkey came racing past. She was somehow not Dolly as Marianne had always known her. She was taller and slenderer, and her ears were not so big. Her usual yellowish color was now silvery, almost silver gilt. And a small, elegant spire of horn grew from her forehead.

"My other daughter!" Molly said, and turned

round to lay her head across Dolly's back.

"I thought I'd missed you!" Dolly panted. "It's been such years. I had to break the door down."

Uncle Richard, who was just coming out through the cottage door, stood astonished. "Dolly!" he said. "Why did I never know—how didn't I know?"

"You never looked," Dolly said, rubbing herself against Molly's shaggy side.

Chrestomanci said impatiently to Cat, "Get in. Let's go."

But Klartch had decided he wanted to meet Dolly. Jason had to grab him around his wriggling body and dump him in the backseat of the car, where he somehow covered Irene in green pond weed. And now Millie was climbing out of the driver's seat to help the Reverend Pinhoe out of the pond and offer him a lift back up the hill. More pond weed arrived in the car. Chrestomanci looked exasperated. He went back to Marianne. "The car will come for you at eight thirty on Monday," he said to her. "I hope it will be cleaner by then. Pack for five days."

I see how Dad feels, Marianne thought. He *does* expect everyone to do what he says. And she thought, I'll miss school. Suppose they throw me out of the Castle after a week? Will school have me back? But I'll learn all sorts of new magic. Do I want to? She gave Chrestomanci a nervous and slightly indefinite nod.

"Good." Chrestomanci strode back to the car.

Cat was now packed in beside everyone else, with Klartch across their knees. Nothing would possess Klartch to get down on the floor. He wanted to look out of the window. "Thank *goodness*!" Chrestomanci said, throwing himself in beside Millie. "I really *must* have a word with Gaffer Farleigh before all the other Farleighs get back!"

The Pinhoes stood aside and watched unlovingly while Millie turned the car and drove out of the Dell. She drove along the lane, where a few enchanted frogs still croaked in the hedges, and then on up the hill, past groups of mournful people sweeping up broken glass, past Great-Uncle Lester's stranded car, and stopped by the vicarage to let the Reverend Pinhoe squelch away, along with Irene and Jason, all of them covered in green weed. After that, Cat and Klartch expanded in the backseat and Millie put on speed.

It was not long before they began passing Farleighs. Gammer Norah and Dorothea first, since they had been the last to leave, shot the car poisonous looks as it purred past them. After that came a whole line of Farleighs, trudging along the side of the road pushing bent bicycles or carrying useless broomsticks. Some of them made rude gestures, but most of them dejectedly ignored the car as it whispered by. When they had passed the last Farleigh, still only about halfway home, Chrestomanci seemed to relax. "How come you turned up so providentially?" he asked Millie.

"Oh, I only went down to the village to post a

letter," Millie said, "and the first thing I saw was a really *peculiar* statue of a tree, standing in the middle of the green. Norah Farleigh was stamping about beside it, haranguing people. As I walked past, I heard her say something like 'and we'll do for those Pinhoes!' and I saw there was going to be trouble. Then while I was posting the letter and wondering what to do, I recognized one of our horses outside the smithy. So I hurried over there and found Joss Callow. I said, 'Leave the horse and come with me at *once*. We may be in time to stop a witches' war in Ulverscote.' I knew I had to have a Pinhoe with me, you see, or their spells would stop me getting there. And Joss was only too glad to come with me. He was afraid someone was going to get killed—he kept saying so. But we hadn't reckoned on the Farleighs being so *quick*. By the time we'd gone back to the Castle and I'd gotten the car out, they were already on the way. The road was blocked by bicycles and the air was thick with broomsticks. We had to crawl behind them the whole way. So I went to Woods House and picked up the Yeldhams, in case they got hurt—I knew I could keep them safe in the car—but when we came out into the village they were fighting there like mad things and none of us could think of how to stop them. I don't know what would have happened if you hadn't come along in that flying machine."

"I was *not* happy to be there," Chrestomanci said. "I'd only persuaded Roger to take me in order to get an overview of the misdirection spells."

"I'm glad the boys survived it," Millie said. "I *must* remind Roger that he has only one life."

They purred on for another couple of miles. They were almost in Helm St. Mary when they saw a man in the distance wrestling with a horse. The man was being bounced and dangled and dragged all over the road.

Cat said, "It looks as if Joss has run out of peppermints."

"I'll handle it," said Chrestomanci.

Millie crept up behind Joss and whispered to a stop far enough away not to outrage Syracuse any further. Chrestomanci rolled down his window and held out a paper bag of peppermints. More of Julia's, probably, Cat thought.

"*Thank* you, sir!" Joss said gratefully.

Cat said sternly, "Syracuse, *behave!*"

Chrestomanci said, "By the way Mr.—er—Carroway—"

"Callow," Joss managed to say. He was hanging on to the reins with both hands, with the paper bag between his teeth.

"Callow," Chrestomanci agreed. "I do hope you are not considering giving in your notice at all, Mr. Carlow. You are by far and away the best stableman we have ever had."

Joss flushed all over his wide brown face. "Thank you, sir. I—well—" He spat the bag into his hand and waved it enticingly under Syracuse's nose. "It's a job I'd be glad to keep," he said. "My mother lives in Helm St. Mary, see."

"She was born a Pinhoe, I take it," Chrestomanci said.

Joss flushed redder still and nodded. Chrestomanci did not need to say he knew that Joss had been planted in the Castle as a spy. He gave Joss a gracious wave as Millie drove on.

Very soon after this, the car was scudding round the village green of Helm St. Mary, just below the Castle. There, slap in the middle of the green, stood the stone oak tree, looking like a twisty, granite, three-armed memorial of some kind. Hard for Gammer Norah to miss it there, Cat thought guiltily. He'd had no idea he had sent it here.

"Dear me," Chrestomanci murmured as the car crunched to a halt beside the green. "What a very ugly object." He climbed out. "Come on, Cat."

Cat scrambled out and persuaded Klartch to stay inside the car. He was not looking forward to this, he thought, as he followed Chrestomanci over to the stone tree.

"Uglier than ever, close to," Chrestomanci said, looking up at the thing. "Now, Cat, if you could turn at least his head back, I'd be glad of a word with him. You can leave the gun as granite, I think."

Cat was somehow very much aware of Klartch watching anxiously through the car window as he put his hands on the cold, rough granite. And because Klartch was watching, Cat knew there was also a ring of half-seen beings watching quite as anxiously from behind every tuft of grass on the green. In fact, Klartch made him see that they were everywhere, swinging on the inn sign, sitting on the roofs, peering out of hedges, and perched on chimneys. Cat saw that he had let them all out, all over the country. They would always be everywhere now.

"Turn back into Mr. Farleigh," he said to the stone oak.

Nothing happened.

Cat tried again with his left hand alone, and still nothing happened. He tried putting both hands on the rough, knobby place that must have been Mr. Farleigh's face, and then pushing both hands apart to clear the stone away. Still nothing happened. Chrestomanci moved Cat aside and tried himself. Cat knew that this was unlikely to work. Chrestomanci almost never could turn anything back once Cat had changed it: their magic seemed to be entirely different. And he was right. Chrestomanci gave up, looking exasperated.

"Let's try together," he said.

So they both tried, and still nothing happened. Mr. Farleigh remained a gray, faintly glistening, obdurate oak made of stone.

"It comes to something," Chrestomanci said, "when two nine-lifed enchanters together can make no difference whatsoever to this thing. What did you *do*, Cat?"

"I told you," Cat said. "I made him like he really was."

"Hmm," said Chrestomanci. "I really must learn more about dwimmer. It seems to be your great strength, Cat. But it's very frustrating. I wanted to tell him what I thought of him—not to speak of asking him how he managed to be a game-keeper we didn't need for all those years." He turned discontentedly away to the car.

A flitting half-seen being drew Cat's attention to Joss's bored horse, still hitched up outside the smithy. "I'd better bring Joss his horse back," Cat said. "You go on."

Chrestomanci shrugged and got into the car.

Cat ran over to the horse. It had all four shoes again. "All right if I take him?" he called to the blacksmith, deep inside his coaly cave of a shed.

The blacksmith looked up from hammering and called back, "About time. I'll send the bill up to the Castle."

Cat mounted the horse from the block of stone beside the smithy. It was much taller than Syracuse. Otherwise, it had no character at all. He got no feel-ings from it, not even a wish to go home. This felt very strange after Syracuse. But at least its dull mind left Cat free with his own thoughts. As he clopped round the green in the early evening light, Cat won-dered if he had left Mr. Farleigh as a stone tree because he *wanted* him that way. Mr. Farleigh had scared him. He had scared the half-seen beings even more. As Cat turned up through the Castle gates, the beings skipped and skittered among the trees lining the driveway, laughing in their delight that Mr. Farleigh was no longer a threat. Cat wondered if they had helped him leave Mr. Farleigh as he now was.

He had had no lunch, and he was starving. Klartch would be hungry too. Cat made the lumpish horse go faster and—because it was now thinking dimly of home and food—he took it the short way he was not supposed to go, along the gravel in front of the newer part of the Castle. The flying machine was spread out on the lawn there, in front of four deep brown skidmarks in the grass. It looked as if Roger and Joe had had a rough landing.

Janet and Julia were cautiously inspecting the machine. Janet called out, "Cat, I can't find Klartch anywhere!"

Julia called out, "What have you been up to without *us*? It isn't fair!"

"You wouldn't have enjoyed it," Cat called back. "Millie's got Klartch."

"I don't care," Julia shouted. "It still isn't fair!"

Marianne arrived very apprehensively the next Monday. She found she was in for ordinary lessons at first with Joe, Roger, Cat, Janet, and Julia, taught by a tall, keen man called Michael Saunders. She was impressed by Mr. Saunders. No one else had ever made Joe do any schoolwork at all. But Joe had been promised a big new work shed where he and Roger could experiment with all their new ideas, provided he pleased Mr. Saunders. So Joe sat at a desk and worked, and very soon proved to be quite extraordinarily good with figures.

Marianne began to enjoy herself. She made friends instantly with both the other girls, and she liked Cat anyway, although she was shy of Roger. Roger *would* talk about machinery or money.

Most afternoons, Marianne and Cat had a lesson with Chrestomanci. At first, Marianne could hardly speak for nerves. Enchanter's magic was all so strange, and Cat knew so much more than she did. But she discovered on the second afternoon that Cat was slow with Magic Theory, whereas Marianne found it so easy that she almost felt she knew most of it already. Anyway, the next half of the lesson was always more like a conversation, with Cat and Chrestomanci asking her interested questions about the craft and dwimmer and herb lore. After the first terrifying afternoon, Marianne felt entirely at ease and talked and talked.

She had brought her story with her, of "Princess Irene and Her Cats," but she never got very far with it, because she was always being roped in for games with the girls or with Klartch and half the people in the Castle, and these were all so much fun that she never seemed to have time for anything else.

By the end of the week, she was enjoying herself so much that it was a real wrench when she and Joe had to go home to Ulverscote. They found they had missed Gammer's funeral. But at least they arrived in time to welcome Nicola home from hospital, pale and skinny but no longer seriously ill. As they walked back from the welcome party, Joe and

Marianne talked all the time about Chrestomanci Castle. In fact, they talked of nothing else all weekend. Dad was morose about it, but Mum listened, doubtfully but intently. When the car came and fetched Joe and Marianne away again the next Monday, their mother went thoughtfully along to Woods House to talk to Irene.

Irene had never been officially named as the next Gammer, but people were always going to talk to her as if she was. Irene would lay her pencil down across her latest delicate design work and listen seriously with Nutcase on her knee. Nutcase was now able to get into any cupboard or at any food he fancied, and only Jane James could control him. Mum told Marianne it was a blessing that Irene liked that cat so much.

Irene's advice was always considered to be excellent—though Irene told Marianne that all she did was to tell people what they were really trying to say to her. One of the first people to consult her was Uncle Charles. He put on his badly crumpled wedding suit and went up to Woods House as an official visitor, where he told Irene many things. Shortly after that, he enrolled as an advanced student at the Bowbridge College of Art. Mum told Marianne that Uncle Charles was intending to go to London to seek his fortune in a year or so.

"There's another who's above his own family now," Dad said.

Mum's own visit to Irene resulted in her sharing the car that came for Joe and Marianne on the third Monday and arriving at Chrestomanci Castle too. Millie welcomed her with delight. Mum spent a most enjoyable morning talking to Millie over coffee and biscuits—good, but not as good as Jane James's, Mum said, but then whose were?—talking about everything under the sun, including the deep mysteries of herbs. After a bit, she agreed to let Chrestomanci's secretary, Tom, come in and take notes, because, as Millie said, she was saying things that even Jason had never heard of. Marianne's mum enjoyed this visit so much—including the chance to have lunch with both her children—that she went back to the Castle many times. It annoyed Dad, but, Mum said, there you go, that's Dad.

After this, the car going to the Castle on a Monday was often quite crowded with Pinhoe ladies—and their broomsticks for the return journey—visiting various people in the Castle. Mr. Stubbs and Miss Bessemer were busy learning from the craft too. Amazing new chutneys and tangy pickles made their way into the Castle, along with certain magical embroideries for sheets, clothes, and cushions. The Castle gave them spells in return, but most Pinhoe ladies were agreed that Castle spells were not a patch on the spells of the craft. It made them feel pleasantly useful and superior.

The men mostly went over by bicycle. They were even more superior, particularly Uncle Richard and Uncle Isaac, when they found themselves giving lessons in woodworking and the craft of growing things to a ring of earnest gardeners and footmen.

"Bah!" said Dad. "Letting them pick your brains!"

By this time, it was all round the country, beyond Bowbridge in one direction and Hopton the other way, that Edgar and Lester Pinhoe had done away with Gaffer Pinhoe. Both of them lost clients. In the end, neither of them could stand the gossip anymore. They moved away to Brighton, where they lived together in a bachelor flat. Great-Aunt Clarice moved in with Great-Aunt Sue, where they lived in the house just outside Ulverscote among more fat, lazy dogs than anyone could count. Dad called the house The Fleapit from then on.

Gammer Norah and her daughter Dorothea naturally bore a grudge. They were the ones who spread the gossip about Edgar and Lester. When Marianne's two great-uncles left, Gammer Norah and Dorothea took to standing on the green of Helm St. Mary, where they scowled so at any Pinhoes visiting the Castle that, as Mum said, it made you nervous in case they still had the evil eye. But that stopped when Gammer Norah won a lottery ticket for two to go to Timbuktu, and both Norah and Dorothea went. "We can't have them festering away on our doorstep," Millie said, with a wink at Mum. "They had to go before their magic grew back."

"Typical interference," Dad said.

Klartch continued to grow. By Christmas he

was developed enough to join the others in the now crowded schoolroom and learn to read and write. Even Janet began to realize that Klartch was a friend and not a pet. Games of Klartchball still got played on the lawn, but the rules changed with Klartch's size. Klartch was a team on his own by the New Year.

Often, usually around dusk, the Castle staff got used to seeing a huge female griffin come ghosting down to the lawn. This was sometimes confusing, because Joe's latest flying machine was also liable to arrive home at dusk, whereupon it usually crashed. The way to tell the difference, Mr. Frazier explained, was that if it was the griffin, you got knocked down in the corridor by Klartch rushing out to see his mother. If Klartch did not appear, then *you* rushed out with healing spells and mending crafts the Pinhoes had taught you.

And sometimes, sometimes, when Cat rode out on Syracuse into the more distant woods, they would see a tall old man striding along in the distance with his hand on the back of a glimmering white unicorn.